★ "In the city-state of Radezha—a towering metropolis constructed vertically to reach the five slumbering gods in the heavens—discontent is stirring. Devoted to the mecha god, patron of the city's warriors and keeper of the law, Zemolai has spent 26 years rising in the ranks of her sect until she receives the ultimate sign of devotion: mechanized wings attached to ports along her back. One fateful evening, returning home from a brutal, month-long mission patrolling Radezha's borders, Winged Zemolai performs a single act of mercy that results in the destruction of everything she has ever known. Zemolai is shunned by her god, and the wings are ripped from her back, leaving her permanently disfigured. With no one to turn to but the rebels that she unknowingly saved, the Once-Winged Zemolai's disillusionment continues to grow as her eyes are opened to the increasingly fascist state she has spent her life defending. *The Wings Upon Her Back* is a triumphant debut novel. The complex narrative examines the intricacies of blind devotion, self-image, and the hidden motivations behind martial control. For fans of C. L. Clark's *The Unbroken* looking for a timely perspective on the human cost of destructive nationalism."
—*Booklist*, starred review

★ "Mills juxtaposes Zemolai's adult regrets and childhood hopes to devastating effect. Much like the winged warriors it follows, the story begins on the ground and takes flight as the characters attempt higher stakes battles and plans, eventually achieving a complete aerial view of Zemolai's life and the full history of Radezhda. This cathartic adventure will stay with readers long after the final page."
—*Publishers Weekly*, starred review

"Samantha Mills has crafted a truly innovative world filled with deeply flawed, compelling characters. A thought-provoking and achingly beautiful story of faith, doubt, regret, and redemption."
—Amy Avery, author of *The Longest Autumn*

"An intense, astute, and moving tale of redemption, by turns relentlessly grim and courageously hopeful."
—Kate Elliott, author of *Servant Mage*

"I've been hoping for a novel from Samantha Mills for years, ever since first stumbling upon her short story 'Strange Waters.' *The Wings Upon Her Back* didn't disappoint, giving us a thoughtful, wrenching, and beautifully crafted story of disappointment, failure, and redemption."
—C. L. Clark, author of *The Unbroken*

"*The Wings Upon Her Back* is a masterful fantasy novel in which a powerful woman confronts the threats of fascism, zealous faith, and disillusionment."
—*Foreword*

"A frightening look at the cost of war and unquestioning loyalty against the backdrop of a gorgeous secondary world. Mills perfectly blends real-world horrors with the fantastic in this wonderful novel."
—A. C. Wise, author of *Wendy, Darling*

"The prose in Samantha Mills' *The Wings Upon Her Back* is truly incredible. Every sentence beautifully written, her worldbuilding is both refreshing and captivating. Readers will appreciate an older main character and the extensive cast around her."
—Charlie N. Holmberg, author of *Spellbreaker*

"Mills weaves a deft and jagged narrative of choices and consequences, raw and real and heartbreaking."
—K. Eason, author of the *Thorne Chronicles*

"*The Wings Upon Her Back* is a gripping, gorgeous exploration of the perils of worshipping gods and humans alike."
—Emet North, author of *In Universes*

"A fierce, aching battle cry of a book, both cinematically epic and painfully intimate. Mills has crafted a striking world of sleeping gods, disillusioned revolutionaries, and metal wings—and from it, she wrenches equal amounts of love and pain."
—Julie Leong, author of *The Teller of Small Fortunes*

SAMANTHA MILLS

THE WINGS
UPON HER BACK

TACHYON - SAN FRANCISCO

The Wings Upon Her Back
© 2024 by Samantha Mills

Interior and cover design by Elizabeth Story
Author photo © 2023 by Samantha Mills

Tachyon Publications LLC
1459 18th Street #139
San Francisco, CA 94107
415.285.5615
www.tachyonpublications.com
tachyon@tachyonpublications.com

Series editor: Jacob Weisman
Editor: Jaymee Goh

Print ISBN: 978-1-61696-414-6
Digital ISBN: 978-1-61696-415-3

Printed in the United States by Versa Press, Inc.

First Edition: 2024
9 8 7 6 5 4 3 2

For Boo. I wish you could see this.

CHAPTER ONE

In the beginning, there was a city of stone and sod, a people of humble means, a home in a valley of no consequence.

And then the gods came.

—Saint Lemain, *A History, v.1*

O N THE NIGHT that Winged Zemolai fell from grace, a cold wind was blowing from the east. She would remember that wind later—the wind of her last flight—and in her memory she would ascribe an extra chill to the air, animalistic and biting.

At the time it was a downslope breeze like any other, and she didn't spare it another thought. Zemolai was flying back to Radezhda after a month patrolling the eastern border. Her back was hot, aching beneath the press and pull of her mechanical wings. Her thoughts were occupied by a long catalog of physical complaints: knees, bad; hips, very bad.

She was too tired to thank the wind.

Ahead, faint glimmers of light peeked through the midnight cloud cover. She saw orange, red, gold—flame colors without the fire. No other city in the world could boast that sight. No other city was blessed the way that Radezhda was blessed.

Those fireless flames were portals. Gateways to another realm. And on the other side of their strange and slippery light, there were five gods, fast asleep.

Zemolai loved the fifth of their number: the mecha god, patron of the city's warriors and keeper of the law. In order to serve her god and keep her city safe, Zemolai had to leave both behind and spend long shifts in the mountains, flying the border till her wings were practically hot enough to melt the implants in her back. She was tired of it. She was tired.

It was in this state that Zemolai arrived—exhausted and smelling of hot metal—at tower Kemyana, the heart of the warrior sect. Twenty-five stories of brick, wood, and metal reaching all the way up to the mecha god's portal; a marvel within a city of marvels.

Zemolai checked in at the twenty-third floor watch balcony, as expected.

She had an argument there, less expected.

And then she stormed down to the workers' quarters on level three, where she launched a surprise inspection. The substance of her argument did not really matter (it mattered a great deal). The inspection was simply overdue and somebody had to do it (it did not have to be her; she was looking for a fight).

It was there that she ruined her life.

The workers' quarters were empty when Zemolai arrived. Five rows of cots and trunks stretched across the room, every sheet tucked and every handle latched. The ceiling thrummed with distant music—a party, two floors up. It was Saint Orlusky's festival day. The trainees would be raising toasts to his name all night, taking advantage of the extra day off.

The absurdity of the situation hit her all at once. Half of the district was celebrating, but here she was, sweaty and aching and in dire need of sleep, and instead of celebrating *or* sleeping, she'd let her temper drive her to this lonely bunk room, picking through strangers' things. And such things: repeatedly patched clothing; books, both religious and recreational in nature; bags of sweets. *Well done, Zemolai, this was definitely worth your time.*

She was about to leave when she found an idol.

It was wrapped in a shirt, an attempt at concealment likely made in haste when the bells rang for an unscheduled kitchen shift. She dug deeper, and discovered a false panel at the bottom of the trunk, something that should have been found earlier if anyone took the job seriously.

Zemolai sighed and pressed a call button over the cot.

A harried voice came through, made tinny by the speaker: "Kitchens."

She glanced at the nameplate on the trunk. "I need Chae Savro at his bunk."

"On his way."

Had there been a note of hesitation there, or was that a trick of the static? It didn't matter. In a minute or three the worker would arrive, and fall on his belly, and deny everything, and kick a terrible fuss on his way out the door—but for the minute or three until that happened, Zemolai held the idol.

It was a beautiful thing, finely wrought of copper and lovingly maintained, molded in the shape of a sleeping figure with its arms crossed over its chest. There was a hint of a face—soft hollows where eyes might be and the barest lump of a nose—and feet tapering down to a single point, like a writing utensil.

The scholar god.

The door slid open, quiet as a sigh, and Chae Savro entered the room. He was an older man, a *tired* man, his skin faintly blue from decades of cheap enhancements. He didn't protest when he walked in, though he surely knew why he'd been summoned. He only sank to his knees in front of Zemolai and waited, letting slip a single soft, "*please*," under his breath like he didn't even notice it escape. A prayer not meant for her ears.

And Zemolai hesitated.

She wasn't uncertain about procedure—the law was perfectly clear. And she didn't pity the man kneeling at her feet—she was accustomed to being implored.

But there was a quiet dignity to his resignation, a bone-deep weariness that she felt more and more each day, and she found herself wavering, for the first time in a very long time.

"How long have you worked in the kitchens?" she asked.

His voice was gravelly and low. "Fifteen years."

"And how many years have you pretended to serve the worker god?"

"Twenty."

She appreciated that he didn't lie. There were no time-consuming pro-tests about his true allegiances, his loyalty, some error in her inspection, *please Winged Zemolai there has been some mistake this isn't even my bed—!*

Zemolai turned the idol in her hands, running her fingers over the silky-smooth impressions where other fingers had repeatedly done the same. The law was clear. No private worship. No falsified allegiance. Chae Savro was an undocumented disciple of the scholar sect—*unacceptable*. Those few scholars who remained were isolated in their tower, tending their archives and writing down history. It was the safest place for them. (It was safest for everyone else.)

Chae Savro had disguised himself as a worker to access the mecha god's own temple, the very heart of administration tower Kemyana. It was devi-ous. Abominable.

But . . .

But she was thinking of that argument again (the one that had led her here; the one that didn't matter).

Zemolai didn't know how many people she had detained over the years, and she didn't care to add it up. Her memory was a blur of rainbow-tinted hair, cheap mechanical limbs, enhanced eyes flashing with anger and grief and defiance, roughened voices asking *what*, asking *how*, asking *why, why, why.*

She only knew that she was tired, and she was angry, and she hadn't seen the scholar god in a very long time.

"Get rid of it," Zemolai said roughly, and she thrust the idol into his hands.

Chae Savro gaped at her. He glanced at the far door, no doubt looking for the warrior trainees who would drag him away to his conviction. Chae Savro had worked in this tower far too long to believe the mecha god's judgment ever fell in favor of the accused.

"The hall is going to empty soon," Zemolai said. "I won't tell you twice."

He sprang to his feet, the idol clutched to his chest. Zemolai watched him go, and her stomach lurched. She told herself it was her liquid dinner to blame: painkillers washed down with a mug of nerve-deadening sludge.

The dose grew larger every year, and she was beginning to suspect her guts would give out before her implants did.

She felt giddy. She felt sick. For one fleeting moment she felt more than a machine, more than the mechanical wings on her back—but also far less. Wings meant nothing if they were not in service to the mecha god.

A hairline crack ran through Zemolai's devotion; had, perhaps, been there for decades. She'd expected to break years ago. She'd expected to die screaming in battle or berserk in a cage—a fate taken out of her hands, a violent mercy. She hadn't expected the end to come like this. Quietly. Gently. Without fanfare.

One small hesitation had opened a window of fresh air in a place that had not breathed clean in ages.

Zemolai was waking up.

But she didn't know it yet.

Zemolai took an interior elevator to the fifteenth floor, too weary to exit the tower again and fly up to her balcony (an opportunity missed).

Her room was sparse and dusty. A bed, a writing desk, a trunk of belongings. It was little different than the workers' quarters, except that it was private and lockable, and there were wing hooks mounted on the wall opposite the bed.

She backed up to the wall and hit the disengage lock on her spine. Threaded cylinders spun counterclockwise in her ports—whirring louder than she liked, they needed oiling—and then the hooks abruptly took the weight off her back.

Zemolai groaned with relief and stepped out from beneath her wings. Cool air flowed over the open ends of her ports, making her flinch. The thick-grooved cylinders were anchored deep into a layer of callus on her back, their mechanical nerve endings wired directly to her spine. She felt exposed. *Raw.* She wanted nothing more than to collapse in bed and forget this entire day, this entire year.

A month, she'd been on patrol this time. A *month*.

A month of three-day shifts, scouring the horizon by light of day, withstanding the chill winds at night, alighting only briefly to relieve herself and fill the bandoliers of food and water crisscrossing her chest. And then a night's rest on a rocky outpost while a traveler took her spot, before another three days in the air.

Zemolai was fucking exhausted.

But her wings were filthy, and that couldn't stand.

She stretched them open. These days the smithies were beating out metals in all the colors of the sky, but Zemolai had never desired anything more than gleaming copper. Old-fashioned, maybe, but the sight still brought a faint smile to her face.

Please, whispered the memory of Chae Savro, and Zemolai's smile vanished.

What she'd done tonight was foolish. She'd been angry (she didn't want to think about it), because (*she didn't want to think about it*)—

Zemolai clamped down hard on her thoughts. In that direction lay panic, because in that direction lay Mecha Vodaya. Vodaya—the leader of their sect, and by extension the city-state of Radezhda—was a permanent fixture in Zemolai's thoughts, warning her away from sedition, demanding more, demanding better.

Vodaya was not the mecha god, but she may as well have been.

Zemolai focused on wiping down hundreds of individual feathers. They were thin and flexible and expertly wired to a hollow frame—not actual copper, but a more conductive compound developed by the creator god's finest engineers.

Zemolai didn't pray anymore, but in this way she showed her devotion. She bottled up her worries, her fears, her anger and despair, and she spent that energy on every joint, every wire, every gear. She buffed out scratches and smoothed out dents. She lost herself in the work.

A body was a machine and a machine was an extension of the body. The mecha god crafted them, and in return they crafted themselves.

Zemolai had not come so far by thinking past that.

But as her usual cocktail of stabilizers and stimulants leached from her system, doubt took their place. The sour feeling in her stomach intensi-fied, and her body grew numb.

She finished, at last, and crawled into bed without bothering to wash. A familiar weight held her flat, her ports bare to the cool sheets, and she braced herself against the crush of oncoming sleep. She wanted it, desper-ately, but she also dreaded it, because in a blink the night would end, and she would wake, and she would begin this routine all over again.

Eventually, she slept.

They came for her in the dark hours before morning, and it shouldn't have been a surprise, but it was. Two pairs of hands, Winged Chava and Winged Teskodoy hauling her up like she was a trainee late to breakfast. She swayed in their grip, still drowning in fatigue, but she had the presence of mind to ask, "For how long?"

Winged Chava glowered. "Till Mecha Vodaya returns."

They stepped onto the balcony. Zemolai looked down at the city, spread out like a ring of doll houses below. Her heart sank. It had taken her twen-ty-six years to move up fifteen floors. How far would this error knock her back?

The Winged gathered themselves to launch, hands clamped tight around Zemolai's arms, an awkward means of transporting a prisoner, meant to embarrass her.

But then her thoughts cleared, and she nearly laughed. That's all this was meant to be: an embarrassment. A reprimand. Chae Savro had been caught, and he'd given up her name in self-defense. She only needed to explain herself to clear all of this up.

They never made the jump.

An explosion rocked the tower, shocking and loud. Wood cracked. Glass shattered. A fireball blossomed up from one of the granaries, tickling their feet with heat and their nostrils with burning grasses, and Winged Chava shoved Zemolai to the deck, screaming at her to stay still, *stay still*, and Winged Teskodoy launched into flight, his radio in one hand, his bolt-gun in the other, and a dozen more Winged leapt from their balconies, the chaos below matched by chaos above—

And Zemolai was in far worse trouble than she'd thought.

13

CHAPTER TWO

Consider the paradox of heresy: these are beliefs contrary to commonly accepted doctrine; beliefs which must be suppressed, so as not to become commonly accepted themselves; and so these heresies are perpetuated—kept heretical—by the very fact of their suppression.

—Scholar Vikenzy, *On Heresy*
(as quoted in *Saint Lemain, On Heretic Scholar Vikenzy*;
original text lost)

CHAE SAVRO was picked up in the fifth-floor furnace room and detained indefinitely, pending interrogation and judgment.

Witness accounts were compiled throughout the night.

The dishwasher Savro, purportedly of Chae District, fifteen-year kitchen worker in central administration tower Kemyana, was completing his duties near the end of the festival-day feast when there was a direct call to the kitchen, summoning him back to staff quarters. A separate account confirmed that Winged Zemolai was conducting an inspection at that time. They were alone together for no more than fifteen minutes.

After leaving staff quarters, Chae Savro was spotted on several floors of the tower. On the third floor, he turned a potted plant ninety degrees counterclockwise. On the fourth floor, he drew an X on the bottom right corner of an east-facing window with a grease pen. And on the fifth floor, he entered the furnace room without authorization, and remained there for approximately twenty minutes before a floor guard, Yeven, entered the room to investigate.

Yeven immediately took Savro to a holding cell, where the kitchen worker was compelled to explain his actions. The idol. Winged Zemolai's mercy. The coded messages left via potted plant and grease pen (which, unfortunately, witnesses did not report until after their intended recipients had time to see them).

When Yeven described Savro's detention, he admitted some uneasiness over the incident. Twenty minutes should have been more than enough time for Chae Savro to melt the idol and return to the kitchen, but when Yeven entered the room, he found the man sitting in front of an open furnace with sweat pouring down his face.

Savro was turning the copper idol over in his hands, over and over and over, and even when Yeven shouted his name, he made no move to destroy it.

To understand the city of Radezhda, one must understand the nature of a people who built their way to the heavens.

Consider tower Kemyana:

The first two levels were made of stone: enormous blocks chipped laboriously from a distant quarry. The following five levels were brick. Some were wood and plaster; others were metal and glass. There was an earnestness to the tower's creation, a determination to continue regardless of budget, scarcity of resources, or labor. If one method failed, they pivoted and kept going—technology always evolved, and purpose was more important than aesthetics.

All five of Radezhda's towers had been built in this way: level by level, generation by generation, an entire city yearning upward toward those tantalizing shimmers in the sky—through which they found their missing gods, fast asleep.

These were not the actions of a people who took their worship lightly.

And so Zemolai found herself imprisoned beneath the tower, not merely cast down to ground level but below it, and she remained in that underground cell for two days, wingless and coming down hard from the drugs that had kept her aloft during her long patrol.

The cell contained no food, no water, no furniture of any kind. Zemolai chose the far corner and sat with her back to the red brick wall. She marked the passage of hours internally, but lost time when she dozed. Once, she relieved herself in the opposite corner. Soon she was dehydrated enough not to worry about that.

Sometimes she slept. More often she didn't. She ran over the events of that evening repeatedly. The idol. Chae Savro. Why had she let him go? He hadn't even begged! Begging, she could ignore. She had seen them cry. She had seen them reach for their children, their partners, their family, their friends, and she had dragged them away regardless.

That was the problem, she decided. She could harden herself against tears. She could cling to self-righteousness in the face of expletives and violence. But it was exhaustion in an old dishwasher's face that had finally cracked her.

Zemolai had grown into a sentimental old fool. Wings were for the young.

By the time Teskodoy returned, Zemolai was flush and jittery. Her hips ached like an old dog's, and she couldn't have launched herself at him if she tried.

Teskodoy's wings were locked high and back, forcing him to duck through the doorway. He filled the small chamber, forcing her to cower. Wings were useless underground.

Down here, they were an intimidation tactic.

Zemolai knew this game. As much as it pained her, she rolled forward onto her bad knees and placed her palms flat on her thighs. They trembled but held steady. She knew Teskodoy would take any opportunity to correct her form during the interview, and she wasn't intending to give him the pleasure.

"How long have you known Chae Savro?" Teskodoy asked. He was soft, warm. A blade in the forge.

"We met only once."

"What transpired at this meeting?"

Summarizing the incident made her burn with humiliation, but it was far better to make a clean case of it now than to be caught out in a lie.

Even the short speech winded her, and she fought to keep her shaking hands flat.

If her admission upset him, Teskodoy didn't show it. They had known one another for decades, and Zemolai still couldn't read his face. "When did you begin to suspect Chae Savro's sedition?" he asked.

"I didn't. I thought the idol was a . . . a nostalgic fancy. An old worship, difficult to dispose of."

"You know the law," he said. "There's no point in reciting it."

"No," she agreed.

"Then why did you let him go?"

"Because . . ."

Because every time she flew patrol, Zemolai's body ached a little more. And every time she came back, she had to dodge the pity on the surgeon's face when she requested an uptick in her medications.

Because Zemolai wanted to come *home*. Not for a few days between assignments, a week here or there to sleep off the grime and isolation of the mountains Kelior before being sent out again—but forever, for good, for whatever years remained before her joints went out.

Because she had gone straight to the watchhouse, and she had demanded to see Mecha Vodaya, intent upon asking her—begging her—for city patrol, and the watchman had said, "No. The Voice has not asked for you." And Zemolai had argued, oh she had argued, because there was a time when she'd never left Vodaya's side and now she couldn't get an audience?

Because she had been angry. So angry.

"It was poor judgment," Zemolai said instead, wrestling the memory down.

"Did Chae Savro show you heretical materials?"

"No!"

Teskodoy's questions continued. How did Savro plead his case? What did he promise her? How long had she been breaking the edicts? To how many others did she grant clemency? Who else? Who else? Who else?

Zemolai was sweating terribly, dizzy with hunger and thirst and withdrawal, but she was adamant: it was the first time, the only time. He didn't believe that. She wouldn't have believed it either. But another thread of desperation wove through her, pulling tighter the longer Teskodoy questioned her: a Winged should not have been interrogating another Winged. Only one person ranked highly enough to question Zemolai.

"When is Mecha Vodaya returning?" she finally asked.

It was the first real emotion she had prompted in him: scorn. "She's already here," Teskodoy said. "Now tell me again. How did Chae Savro react when you let him go?"

Real fear seized her then. Vodaya was in the tower, but she had still delegated Zemolai's detention to Winged Teskodoy, like she wasn't even a warrior. Like she was an ordinary citizen. If there had been anything but acid in Zemolai's stomach, it would have landed in her lap.

"Answer the question," Teskodoy said.

She shook her head, dazed. "When is Vodaya coming?"

It wasn't the right answer. Teskodoy shoved her down. He said, "You do not drop the Voice's title! You do not ignore a Winged's question!"

Zemolai gasped, "I have to speak to her. You have to let me speak to her."

Teskodoy made his feelings about that request clear. If Zemolai prayed, it was with a single thought: Vodaya will fix this.

Another day passed, or an hour that felt like a day, or a week. The lighting never changed, and Zemolai's internal clock unwound. Heat gathered in the flesh of her back, concentrated in the rings of keloid scar surrounding her wing ports. The pain went bone-deep, a familiar song playing on her vertebrae like drumbeats. In the absence of her regular dose of mechalin, her body was rejecting the artificial nerve connections.

Without intervention, Zemolai's body would soon begin to cannibalize her implants.

A waft of cool air brought her out of a feverish doze. The door had opened, and she knew the person standing there.

Finally, finally, finally.

Mecha Vodaya, Winged for more than forty years, Voice of the mecha god and enforcer of her edicts, stood over Zemolai with an expression of grave disappointment. Her leathers were embellished with silver and brass, as befit the Voice, but it wasn't the uniform that filled the room, stretching floor to ceiling and swallowing all residual light. It was the *woman*. Vodaya had always been handsome and forbidding, but years of travel in the gods' realm leant her skin a subtle glow. She brimmed with power, from the silver of her hair to the dust on her boots.

Vodaya was always dusty. She didn't believe in sitting idly while others did her work.

Zemolai hadn't seen her in more than a month, and the sight made her dry mouth go thick as desert sand. She rolled onto her knees and placed her palms flat on her thighs.

"Explain yourself," Vodaya said softly, and each word was a thread in a noose.

"He was only an old man," Zemolai said. Her voice was hoarse; her lips cracked. "A kitchen worker clinging to the idol of his youth. There was no sign of sedition . . ."

"That *was* your sign." Vodaya's voice reverberated with all the weight and finality of a funeral toll. She didn't step forward, but her energy advanced, pinning Zemolai where she knelt. "There is no passing worship of the scholar god, just as there are no passing engineers. He was an old man, and therefore even more set in his ways. You should have recognized this, Zemolai."

The disappointment in her voice was more damning than any verbal abuse. Zemolai shrank beneath that wave of dissatisfaction. Vodaya was right.

She was always right.

Vodaya said, "After a long interrogation, Chae Savro gave up the name of his conspirators. An entire insurrectionist cell was embedded in our tower. Thanks to your *compassion*," and here her voice dripped acid, "he had time to warn them before he was captured. All four vanished from their posts. Escaped, and no telling what information they obtained while here. No telling what they had planned, or what plans might already be set in motion. As a parting gift, they set off a bomb and burned our secondary storehouse to the ground."

Zemolai couldn't look Vodaya in the face, so instead she stared at the buttons of her vest: each one a small silver fist.

Zemolai said, "My motives were pure."

It was a lie, and her realization that it was a lie shook her to her core. She hadn't known if Chae Savro was harmless, and she hadn't cared. She didn't arrest him, because she didn't want to. She had *wanted* to say no. She had wanted to savor one tiny autonomous moment of making a decision at odds with orders.

It was only a shame that she'd picked her moment so poorly.

Vodaya could see it in her face. Of course she could. She always knew what Zemolai was thinking, and what to say to bring her back into the fold.

And for a moment, Vodaya's expression softened. It was a familiar blend of sympathy and regret, the look she got after she pushed too hard.

Hope kindled in Zemolai's chest. In the next breath, Vodaya would offer her an assignment—something brutal, something that was both punishment and validation, and when Zemolai proved her loyalty again, she would return to the sky and put this humiliating interlude behind her. It was a familiar dance.

But Vodaya offered no penance. She said, "I'm sorry, Zemolai, there is nothing I can do for you this time. Your motives will be tested in the traditional way."

And Zemolai broke. "I've served you faithfully for twenty-six years," she cried.

Vodaya drew up, indignant, one hand to her fist-buttoned chest. "Me?" she said. "You have served *me*?" She bent forward, so that her wingtips brushed the dangling light and caused it to chime, so that Zemolai had no choice but to look up into the unforgiving obsidian of her eyes. She said, "That was your mistake, then. You were sworn to serve the mecha god, and she did not ask for twenty-six years.

"She asked for a lifetime."

Zemolai fought the entire way. A pair of well-rested, well-fed, well-muscled guards walked on either side of her. It was pointless to try, and it only caused her more pain when they pulled her shoulders back and marched her onward, but she thrashed and raged and kicked nonetheless.

Zemolai fought, because she didn't know how to do anything else.

They dragged her into a lift and rode up the interior of the tower, bobbing and swaying with the efforts of aging hydraulics. It was an old elevator without a gate, and if they hadn't secured her, she might have jumped through, to escape or to death crushed between floors—same ending, different route.

She glared at twenty-five empty hallways. Everyone was already waiting on the roof.

The ceiling opened like a blooming flower and they rose through petals made of steel. Zemolai looked out and immediately wished she hadn't.

A hundred people were arranged in rings around the circular rooftop. Bricks stretched under their feet and up around the edges of the tower in fanciful dips and waves, painted blue and red and pink to reflect the colors of the sky. Some of the people assembled there had wings. Most did not.

At the center of this somber audience, Mecha Vodaya waited beneath the god-tree.

The tree was somewhat like an oak, if the oak was fed tar instead of water and if three competing suns had drawn its branches in three competing directions. There were no leaves on the god-tree, only scorched arms extending into scorched fingertips, a black and gnarled monster raising her hands to the sky in supplication.

The tree's highest branches stopped just below a shimmer in the sky; a strange thing, pale orange against the morning's reddish haze and only fully visible from one direction. Turn left or right, and it narrowed to a nearly invisible slit.

There were five gods sleeping above Radezhda. Five gods in five distant beds, and five sects on the ground debating how best to worship them. These days, it was the mecha god's methods that reigned supreme, and she did not take disappointment lightly.

Zemolai dug her feet in, dignity be damned, and forced the guards to drag her bodily past line after line of witnesses.

Only one person would meet her eye: Winged Mitrios, a fresh-faced warrior airborne for scarcely three years. His wings were a two-toned riot of green and yellow feathers that looked garish to Zemolai but were increasingly popular with the younger set. He'd been a member of Zemolai's border five-unit for his very first assignment, until Vodaya broke up their shift patterns. She'd summoned the young man back to the city, his tour done in the blink of an eye, but for Zemolai the summons had never come.

Mitrios stepped forward as Zemolai approached, and with awful earnestness he said, "Do not succumb to fear! Zemolai, it is a mistake, I am sure of it. The mecha god will see your true heart, and all will be well."

Oh, such youthful devotion. But there was no uncertainty about today's outcome. Zemolai gave him a weak nod—what else could she do? He'd see soon enough.

She stared up at the shimmer as they pulled her to the tree. They pressed her chest against its flaking bark and wrapped her arms around the trunk. They stretched ropes across her shoulders, her back, her knees, her thighs.

Winged Teskodoy appeared in her peripheral vision, carrying a large bundle. Winged Chava helped him wrestle it open, and the contents shone brilliant and copper in the morning light.

Zemolai's wings.

Teskodoy and Chava lifted them up, and it was a relief to feel the familiar weight lock into place, even if the gesture was ceremonial. She flexed one shoulder and confirmed: the main nerve lines had been clamped. She wasn't going anywhere.

"We are here to entreat the mecha god," Vodaya said. She walked a slow circle around the tree, along the line where dirt met brick. "We are here to seek wisdom and judgment." She passed out of Zemolai's sight, then back into it. "We are here to obey her edicts, to *enforce* her edicts, to protect the people of her city-state by any means necessary."

The shimmer above the god-tree brightened and darkened in tune with Vodaya's words. "Winged Zemolai, formerly Pava Zemolai, formerly Milar Zemolai, is accused of breaking the seventh edict. She discovered a dissident in private worship, a man exhibiting false allegiance, and she conspired to conceal his crime. In doing this, she failed to protect her tower."

The shimmer swelled and stretched, swelled and stretched, a portal easing open, with clear white light slipping through from the other side. The light poured down over the scorched branches, down the trunk, down Zemolai's body.

She panicked then. This was god-light, the clarity of heaven, through which no wrong could be concealed. She felt it like electricity in her wing ports. It vibrated through the implants in her eyes and in her joints and rattled the very breath in her lungs.

Vodaya's voice was drowned out by the roar in Zemolai's ears, but she knew the ceremony by rote. Words of accusation and summoning and power. Vodaya shouted to wake the mecha god, and the mecha god stirred. They all felt it when the portal cracked wide, though the light was too bright for any of them to see what lurked on the other side.

Vodaya lifted her arms and spoke the final word to summon retribution: the name of the mecha god. A name that was a scream, a name that buffeted their ears like a million birds taking flight, a name that tore the barrier between worlds and roused the goddess from her eternal slumber, if only for a moment.

No other city in the world bore such a direct connection to the heavens. Nowhere else could a person of faith ask their god a question, and have the answer delivered in detailed schematics. Nowhere else was the rule of law delivered with such clarity and conviction.

But a window looked both ways.

An enormous hand emerged from the portal, encased in light so bright that it scorched the outline of fingers against the back of Zemolai's eyelids. She heard the blackened bark of the tree squeal and smolder afresh.

The tip of one finger touched Zemolai's head, and her thoughts disintegrated. There was only heat, and fear, and an intensifying vibration that knocked her bones together. Zemolai clutched the god-tree and screamed. She could not see her own body, or what the god-light was revealing to everyone who watched. Was she shining clear, or was her heart riddled with strands of doubt?

There was a moment when she glimpsed Vodaya beyond the base of the tree, her expression full of benign affection. Hope struck Zemolai in a lightning flash of certainty: the mecha god would forgive her, because this had only been a mistake, a fleeting impulse, quickly passed. Zemolai's motives had always been pure. She had always done exactly as she was told.

And just as swiftly that flash of hope was gone, because the hand of the goddess wrapped around her wings.

The metal vibrated, rattling harder and harder until Zemolai thought she would be ground to death against the tree, until she *wanted* to be ground to death against the tree, if only to make the rattling stop—

And then, with a horrifying screech, her wings came loose. The rattling ceased. The mecha god clenched her fist, and the torturous sound of metal grinding against metal nearly stopped Zemolai's heart.

The great shadow hand opened, revealing a broken, tangled snarl. The wing-snarl plummeted to the rooftop, cracking the bricks with its weight.

And Zemolai was no longer Winged.

It almost didn't matter when the god-hand plucked her from the tree, snapping the ropes like tissue. Zemolai's body was engulfed by that painful, rattling energy again, as immobile as a mouse in the grip of a hawk. The god-hand lifted her into the air, presenting her face-up to the blinding god-light. Zemolai expected to be crushed, and she didn't care.

But the mecha god didn't kill her. She devised a worse punishment.

At first the agony in Zemolai's shoulders was indistinguishable from the agony of the rest of her body. But it *burned*, and the burn crept deeper, snaking into her ports, heating the metal rings within her back. The wires turned molten, malleable.

The mecha god was disfiguring her ports beyond repair.

By the time Zemolai fell to the rooftop, she was delirious with pain. She crumpled in a heap beside the remains of her wings and lay there, her cheek pressed against sky-colored bricks, staring at the once-delicate arc of a broken feather.

Vaguely, she was aware of the god-hand retreating and the portal shrinking back into a harmless shimmer. Mecha Vodaya faded away, and the other guards crowded close. She glimpsed Mitrios briefly, his face a rictus of shock.

There was no need to execute her. There was no reason to imprison her. Once-Winged Zemolai would be exiled to the ground, and there she would die, right where she began.

CHAPTER THREE

He was a madman, running room to room with a lit torch,
crying. He's been subdued now, but the damage to the archives
is extensive.

There are calls to reconstruct what we can, while our memories are still fresh. Though I cannot help but worry—what if
he is right?

What if it *is* better to forget?

—Scholar Parush, letter to a colleague

LONG BEFORE THE SKY was cut by the fearsome warrior Winged Zemolai, there was only the student Milar Zemolai, known to her loved ones
as Zenya.

Zenya was a precocious child (her parents would have accepted nothing less). She was also prone to mischief, and shortly after her eighth
birthday, she jumped from the Ario-Zavet bridge with nothing but a bit
of wood and paper on her back.

It was the greatest moment of her young life.

The night before the bridge incident, Zenya sat on a rug in her mother's
study with her younger brother, Niklaus. The siblings were only one year
apart, dark-haired and round-faced, a matched pair—inseparable. Their
parents were always busy with research projects of their own, but if the
children were very quiet and very good, and there was time remaining
before they were sent to bed, they'd be told a story.

Niklaus was working his way through a dog-eared history book while
Zenya pretended to do math. A thin thread of tension stretched between

them, strengthened by furtive glances at the clock that ticked so ominously on the opposite wall. They both longed for attention, and they both knew how easily a plea for more could backfire in stern lectures about learning to entertain oneself.

When their mother cleared her throat, they snapped their books shut and spun to face her, and Natulia laughed at their enthusiasm. "I'm sorry, children, it's been another long evening, hasn't it?" she said. "Why don't you come here and I'll tell you what I'm working on."

Zenya darted behind the enormous desk first, peering at the familiar swirl of her mother's handwriting on three tidy stacks of cream-colored paper. "A new book?" she asked.

Natulia smiled. "A supplement to a volume of Lemain. I'm up to the last stand of Saint Radezhda."

"The giant bird!" Niklaus exclaimed, poking his head around Zenya's arm.

"Yes," Natulia said dryly. "The giant bird." She stood up, wafting the scents of ink and forgotten tea, and pointed to the mural painted on the wall behind her desk. It was Radezhda in cartographic caricature: there the mountains Kelior in thick strokes of ocher, and here the city safely nestled in their shadow, sketched in all the colors the land could produce.

Natulia picked up a sheet of paper and read, "The five gods have slumbered for many years, each in their own heaven, but they were awake once, and in their wakefulness they bestowed remarkable technologies on humankind. Each of them whispered secrets to their chosen representatives, for they know that the greatest sign of our humanity is our constant struggle for perfection . . ."

Zenya ran her fingertips over a tiny figure standing atop the tallest mountain in the mural, a slash of red and silver with its arms upraised to the sky.

"Our ancestors understood the magnitude of these blessings," Natulia continued. "They strove to keep them secret from the warmongering nations beyond the mountains, but knowledge exists to be spread and so it did. The people of Rava State were fiercely jealous, and descended upon the infant settlement. It was Saint Radezhda who brought everyone together—the fighters and farmers, the engineers and scholars, the workers—to defend this grand experiment: a city built to reach the heavens."

Above the scarlet blur of a soon-to-be-saint was a winged beast in brown and gray: an enormous ruk—the last of the mountain birds and their enemy's greatest hope of breaking the city's defenses. It snatched up Saint Radezhda during an impassioned speech to her army just before the Battle of Three Gates. She killed the beast mid-flight, then fell to her death.

The war was won, the saint lost, and Radezhda the city-state officially born.

"It is our duty to protect this city," Natulia concluded. "Our joint mission to guard the knowledge that has been entrusted to us, to better ourselves both physically and intellectually in pursuit of our ideals."

Niklaus was enraptured, as always, by the little group of scholars with their arms full of books, standing next to a partially built tower Zhelan. But Zenya wasn't interested in taking robes. She was staring at the top of the mural, at the figures she had studied so many times on these long, lonely evenings while she kept quiet and did not interrupt her mother's work: the Winged, flying fierce and true over the border, sketched in sparkling copper paint.

And just like that, Zenya had a fantastic idea.

She enlisted Niklaus the next day, under cover of a joint expedition to study the sod-covered roofs of Zavet District for a botany project.

"I'm not sure about these numbers," little Niklaus said, squinting at the diagrams Zenya had circled in her math book.

"It's all about ratios!" Zenya insisted. "We scale it up."

"This is a kite," he said doubtfully.

"Why do you think I'm making two?"

This bit of brilliance could not be argued with, and they spent the next hour measuring and cutting a pile of wooden rods that Zenya had smuggled out from their father's garden shed. A great deal of string, glue, and waxed paper later, Zenya had her first set of wings.

Niklaus's concern returned when it came time to tie Zenya's arms into place, but he offered his own solution: "You had better try from higher up, or the wind won't catch."

They crept onto the Ario-Zavet bridge after the lunch hour, when all nearby adults were safely confined to their factories or offices. Zenya climbed onto the railing, awkward in her poorly thought-out personal engineering design, while Niklaus stood ready with a pocket watch to time the gentle descent they felt certain was about to occur.

Zenya jumped.

There was a brief moment when the air hit her face and the world went still, and she was weightless, unstoppable. The cobblestones were far below, and her eyes were filled with clouds.

She crashed, of course. One broken leg, and lucky it wasn't anything worse.

A hectic scene followed, fueled by her own pain and her little brother's panic. She ripped off her crumpled wings and ordered Niklaus to shove them into the trash beneath the bridge, and then she swore him to secrecy before he ran for help, a pact he gladly took to forsake his part in the whole mess—

But that came after. For one moment before the crash, she'd had the sky, and her fate was sealed.

One day, Zenya was going to fly.

CHAPTER FOUR

They were loud and terrible, and for many days we hid in our
. . . [missing]

When they returned, they knew our language. They said:
we can help you, you know. We can help you be better.

—Fragments 12a, 12b, *the Dierka Mountain Scrolls*

THERE WAS OVERWHELMING HEAT. There was unbearable cold. There
was a slab of wood beneath her cheek. There was a sound like bees
and there was vomit and there was pain.

Zemolai was deep in mechalin withdrawal. Without drugs to hold her
immune system at bay, her body was rejecting the artificial nerve endings
buried in her back. The mecha god had only melted the machinery; she
hadn't cauterized the implants.

After the judgment, two Winged carried Zemolai from the rooftop.
They deposited her near a worker's hospital, continuing the illusion that
she was being sentenced to the ground and not to her death—as though
the worker sect had the drugs necessary to manage their own implants.

If they did, they wouldn't have much use for mecha surgeons, would
they?

Zemolai refused to die in a hospital bed. When the Winged left, she
stumbled away. Eventually, she fell.

Night came, or seemed to come. She waited for death.

She barely felt the hands that scooped her up, barely registered as they
placed her on the back of a cart. In between long, nauseating blinks, a

worried face blurred close to her own, and then a blanket covered her eyes. She vomited again in the darkness. Frantic hands rolled her over. Frantic voices argued speed versus discretion. The cart rolled faster, rattled harder, shook her head like a liquid explosive.

Zemolai passed out.

Zemolai awoke. A different sort of darkness. An indoor darkness. She was lucid for nearly a minute, long enough to realize she was in a containment cage. Somebody had placed her in a containment cage. A containment cage.

Her thoughts were stuttering. She wasn't dead yet. She wasn't dead yet. She was alive enough to realize her thoughts were stuttering, and that meant the next phase of withdrawal. Somebody had placed her in a cage.

The berserker phase took her without remorse—the rage without the strength. She rose up, energized, her limbs on marionette strings, angry, angry, angry. The cage smelled of rust. It was old. It might be weak. Zemolai threw herself against the bars, bashed herself like a ship against the rocks. The bright blooms of pain only infuriated her further, invigorated her, sent a riot of decaying chemicals through her blood.

Dark figures appeared in the red haze of her vision. Real? Unreal? She screamed at them. She thrust her arms through the bars and clawed at them. They were out of reach, patient, solemn, silent. Waiting for her to give up.

There were hands on her arms, pinning her down. She thrashed, and every time her inflamed back hit the concrete floor, she howled. A body weighed down her legs. She almost bucked it loose. A hand turned her face. She bit it.

"Bloody Vitalia!"

"I said hold her still."

"She bit me!"

The hand came down again, this time with more strength, and pressed her face to the floor. A needle plunged into her neck. A burning solution. It was worse, oh worse than anything. It was running fire down her throat, it was igniting the pins near her heart, it was pooling lava in her shoulder blades, in her spine, in her thighs knees feet elbows arms fingers.

She was drunk on it, disoriented, caught halfway between meltdown and sedation.

Eventually she succumbed to sedation. She slumped against the back of the cage and plunged into a woozy half-sleep; a sea creature with one eye open for the next predator.

At some point in the long darkness, she felt the ghost of a hand trailing across her back, cool where she was hot, faint pressure where she was scarred.

"This is where the nerves connect," somebody murmured. "She'll need caps on top of her ports."

Another voice, uneasy. "How could they *do* this to themselves?"

A protesting sound. "That's unfair. You've done your eyes. I've done—"

"Look at this! It's nothing alike."

"*Quiet*. You'll wake her."

A long pause. Then: "Well. Is there anything there?"

A long sigh, disappointed. "Plenty. But not what I'm looking for."

Later, when she was semi-lucid again, Zemolai attempted to document her surroundings. A containment cage, yes, old and rusty but standard construction. Bars on all sides. Overhead: a door like a dungeon hatch. At the bottom: a small gap for food trays. But beyond that, beyond the bars: a small, bare room. One door. Stone walls. Cool air. Underground?

The door swung open, letting in a dim triangle of light. Even the hint of illumination burned. Zemolai squinted through the pain, old habits pressing her to catalog everything even when it didn't matter.

A young person crept into the room, food tray in hand. Gender unknown. Age indeterminate in the shadows. Short, rounded edges mostly concealed by a dark cloak, and braided hair reflecting blue. They hesitated an arm's length from the cage, staring intently, and then shoved the tray through the gap and darted back. A bunny rabbit, heart aflutter.

The bunny rabbit didn't immediately flee. They stood in the doorway, watching. No. *Observing.* Their gaze followed Zemolai's hitching crawl across bare concrete, followed the trembling arc of Zemolai's hand toward the first food she'd seen since before her imprisonment.

"My name is Chae Galiana," the bunny rabbit whispered, using the feminine possessive for *my.* There: one piece of tangible information. A bunny rabbit woman.

There were no utensils on the tray. Zemolai scooped up a handful of warm, graying porridge and flung it through the bars the old-fashioned way.

The woman squealed and ran out, a thin dribble of porridge down her cloak. Zemolai sank back, thoroughly exhausted again. She wiped her slimy hand half-heartedly against her pants, emitting a delirious chuckle that petered away as quickly as it had started.

She was weakening. Whatever drug had brought her down to earth was wearing away against the relentless pulse of her heart. She was conscious enough to know when the blood madness returned, even more ruthless for having been suppressed.

Luckily her first wild kick knocked the food tray out of the cage. Otherwise she might have done real damage with it.

Three more times they went through the dance. Three more wrestling matches. Three more needles. Three more periods of semi-lucidity and three more trays of food. She cursed at them. She wailed and punched and kicked and flailed at them. She spat and threw her tray.

Her mind desired to stand on principle (*fuck you and fuck your gruel*), but her body wanted to live. On the third and fourth attempts, she ate the food.

Each time, the same woman returned to observe—the girl, hardly old enough to call a woman—though she stayed right next to the door, the quicker to flee when Zemolai lost control. As though Zemolai could do anything from behind bars. *Girl! That is why they built these cages!*

It was a prolonged agony. Torture. Better to let her die with some dignity intact.

But Zemolai didn't die. After each burning injection, her calm lasted longer and her meltdown came on more grudgingly. She didn't know how, but her captors were staving off the final stages of mechalin withdrawal.

Her senses returned to her, painfully sharp after the long dullness. She heard people whispering outside her door. These were small quarters, then. It was possible they assumed she was insensate. More likely they had no space to spread out. A worker's burrow?

Except workers didn't have spare rooms in which to build containment cages. Zemolai was back to the possibility of an abandoned temple corridor. Or perhaps—

She halted, almost gasping with fury. Fury that her mind was coming back to her. Fury that her body was healing. She was hungry. *Starving.* Like a person expecting to live.

Her anger dissolved into grief. They should have left her in that alley rather than put her through this humiliation.

Imagine. Once-Winged Zemolai, wasting away in a rusty cage.

Chae Galiana returned. She advanced almost to the cage itself. Behind her the door remained ajar, and somewhere out in that dim light an argument was underway. Heated voices, up and down, overlapping like waves.

Zemolai had been awake for some time, wrung out but aware. There was pain, but it was dull. She no longer felt the fever of infection or the bone-rattling rage of mechalin withdrawal.

She waited, silently, for the young woman to speak.

"I think you know what we are doing here," Galiana said softly. "And I think you understand why."

She'd have been easy to dismiss on the street. Another short, stocky, multicolored working woman with blue-green hair in three big braids against her head and old scars on the backs of her hands. She was trembling, but what Zemolai had initially taken for fear was *excitement.* And there was only one thing in the room to be excited about.

Galiana said, "We've healed you."

Zemolai rolled one shoulder. Shifted on aching hips. Tipped one hand over her knee, as though to scoff, *This is healing?*

"You're no longer reliant on mechalin," Galiana clarified. "Your handlers will think you're dead by now."

A little frisson of alarm went through Zemolai at that. Nobody but the mecha god's high command administered the drug cocktail that kept their warriors sane and healthy. It was one of the consequences of taking wings. Once the ports were installed, the wearer was committed to a lifelong dependence on their supervisor's medicine box.

"You understand what this means," Galiana prompted.

Zemolai carried a great deal of privileged information in her head. If Mecha Vodaya had even suspected such a drug existed outside of her control, she would have killed Zemolai outright. And it wasn't only warriors who took mechalin to maintain their enhancements. It was every injured worker, every upgraded engineer, every citizen of Radezhda who strove for godlike perfection.

The rebellion had acquired something more powerful than any weapon.

They had medical independence.

"Galiana, wait for us." Additional young worker-types hurried into the room, full of worry. And so young! She'd been kidnapped by a nursery school gang.

There were four of them total, in assorted states of modification. Zemolai glimpsed longlegs, optics, mechanical fingers—grafted on, not prosthetics. (She was doing it again: cataloging, documenting, noting pressure points and pins.)

"You shouldn't come in alone," one of them whispered. A clear rebuke.

Galiana replied through her teeth, "One is better than four."

It would have been funny, if Zemolai had been in the mood for a laugh.

"I'm Galiana," Galiana repeated, covering her nerves with chatter. She gestured to each of the others in turn. "She's Chae Eleny."

The rebuker. Eleny had a stocky, motherly build and a faint purple sheen to her dark hair. She was older than the others, which could have meant anywhere in her thirties—Zemolai was finding it harder to estimate as time went on.

"He's Zavet Timyan." He was slight and bookish, clutching a leather-bound notebook to his narrow chest. Big, augmented eyes flashed silver in a worried face. He was named for a worker district, but his small frame and high-end optical implants screamed library. Zemolai didn't buy it.

"And they're Chae Rustaya." The last rebel was more what Zemolai had expected. Their body mods were cheap, cobbled together over time. Ugly, practical patches were evidence of factory-funded repairs: skeletal legs, two fleshless fingers. Rustaya was tense, distrustful, with broad shoulders and sharp, dark eyebrows. Their body spoke a brooding history of violence that would have been a hit at mecha parties.

Angry, nervous babies, the lot of them.

Whatever the nursery gang had expected of her, it wasn't silence. They fidgeted, exchanged glances, filled the air between them with old arguments and fresh worries. Zemolai imagined a great deal of time, expense, and risk had gone into her—what to call it?—*rehabilitation*. And there was only one reason for them to heal her; one reason for them to extend all of this information like a hostage to show trust.

They wanted her help.

Galiana said, "I'm sure you've realized who we are. Chae Savro had time to warn us before he was taken. If you hadn't given him that time . . ."

They'd all be dead, and Zemolai's life would be intact. (There was a moment, here, when her breath came in sharp and her chest went thick, but she would not do this here, she would *not* break down in front of these children, she would focus on getting out and not look past that singular goal.)

When Zemolai finally spoke, her voice was ragged, hoarse with dehydration and days of howling. She said, "I'm hungry."

She had disappointed them again. But the motherly one, Eleny, said, "Of course you are. Give me a moment."

Eleny pulled in a camping stove from the next room (poor angle; Zemolai couldn't see the layout). Only canned meat and root vegetables by the look of it, but thank the Five, it was something other than porridge, and it was going to be served hot. Galiana held a cup of water through the bars. Zemolai chugged it down and immediately handed it back for a refill.

"This is a waste of time," snapped Rustaya. Zemolai squinted at them. Right. The longlegs with years of factory injuries.

"Rustaya," Timyan said softly.

"Look at her," Rustaya insisted. "She's a wreck. The drugs burnt her out."

Eleny slammed her pan down harder than necessary, and Rustaya pressed their lips together, temporarily cowed. Yes, Eleny was the one to watch. Even in the midst of her disdain, Zemolai could respect a woman who got her way without speaking a word. Eleny gave Zemolai an apologetic smile as she dumped two slabs of meat and a pile of yellowish veggie cubes onto a plate.

Zemolai's traitorous stomach went wild at the smell, but she still had the dignity to ask, "Do I get utensils? Or do I have to eat like an animal?"

Galiana fetched a fork and a rather dull-looking knife, immediately setting off another argument. Rustaya thought Zemolai was murderous, or maybe suicidal, though they didn't say so in quite those words. Eleny and Timyan commenced furious whispering on the side, weighing the risks—perhaps only the fork?

This morbid comedy ended with Galiana shouting, "I'll cut it myself!" She sawed the meat into cubes, muttering that dictators had one thing going for them and it was centralized decision-making.

Zemolai sat on the ground to eat. It was torturous at first, the food like lead in her stomach. The tension in the room eased the longer she went without killing herself or flinging the fork through the bars.

Eleny nudged Timyan's elbow and he startled, but stepped forward. Next one up.

He hovered for a moment, glancing at his notebook (he'd written *notes*!). "It took us years to work our way into tower Kemyana. During those years, we studied every one of you. You had scholar parents, right?" He was so earnest, Zemolai could hardly stand it. "I've been using the name Zavet, but I was born in Milar too. My parents placed me in a public training school, but at home they taught me philosophy—and about Radezhda before the war."

Before the war. Like it was ancient history. To these bolt-babies, born in the turbulent years directly following the last major skirmishes, Zemolai was a crone. She chewed more slowly. She'd been right, that this one came from fancier stuff than Zavet.

"You joined willingly," he said. "Maybe you thought it was right, at the time. The big cause! Protect the city! Brawling on the border! But you've seen what your government has become. We aren't asking for anything radical. We aren't trying to replace your tyranny with our own. The only justice is in reestablishing the Council of Five. Let the Five convene and decide what's best."

Zemolai remembered those days herself and didn't need a bunch of kids giving her the glowing, watered-down version they'd heard from their parents. The council representing the five gods of Radezhda had operated like any other committee: a lot more talking than doing.

"Our assignment ended when Chae Savro gave up our names," Timyan said. "We're known faces now. Fugitives. What we're proposing is . . . well, you've been stationed out of tower Kemyana for many years . . ."

Zemolai swallowed her final bite. She set down her fork with a small, satisfied sigh. A full stomach was a blessing you didn't much think about until you lost it. "You want me to turn," she said calmly. "You want me to share my knowledge of Kemyana architecture and security protocols so you can sabotage the center of the mecha god administration."

"Well . . . I mean . . ." She'd flustered him. Timyan turned to the others for help, but how could they possibly word it to sound better? He rallied for another effort. "Galiana believes—"

Eleny cleared her throat, sharp and forbidding. A small battle of wills broke out, fought in eyebrows and pursed lips, exasperation and dissent. Zemolai turned her attention to the person in question. Galiana, not so rabbity after all, was staring at Zemolai with such intensity that Zemolai abruptly remembered a conversation half-heard when she was barely conscious:

Is there anything there?

Plenty. But not what I'm looking for.

She met the young woman's gaze and could not read the conclusion being drawn there. Whatever it was, Zemolai had not been plucked from the gutter for pity's sake alone.

Zemolai decided to test the group's fault lines. She cleared her throat and pointed at Galiana. "She's already told me about your new drug."

Galiana's eyes widened. A firestorm broke out around her—what was she thinking, they agreed not to mention that yet, this is why nobody came in alone—

And then Rustaya blurted out the only thing that mattered: "You need a dose of our suppressant twice a day or you'll die."

Eleny sighed and shut her eyes. Timyan and Rustaya looked defiant; Galiana merely sad.

And Zemolai—oh. She did have an ounce of feeling left in her and it was white-hot, it was lava, it was broken kneecaps and black bags and a long fall from a tall cliff.

"All this talk?" she demanded. *"All this talk* and you're telling me I've only traded one addiction for another? You've changed *nothing*!"

"Our formula will be made available to the public," Timyan said. "Nobody has to live or die by the will of mecha command."

"So where can I get it?"

Guilty silence. None of them would meet her eyes, and she thought she'd choke on her own bile. She could hardly blame them, even if she hated them for it. She was an unknown quantity, privy to dangerous information, and they wanted something from her. Of course they had leverage.

And then Galiana looked her straight in the face and said, with absolutely zero shame: "We're going to break into the Pava training grounds. We want you to give us the code to the armory."

For the length of a caught breath, Zemolai could only stare at her, simultaneously outraged and impressed at the sheer ballsiness of escaping one mecha stronghold only to willingly enter another. But it was fury that overrode both—the implication beneath the ask: *help us or get back to dying.*

A stream of vitriol tore loose from her then, as unstoppable as a thunderstorm. They were cowards, idiots, monstrous infants with no idea what they were getting themselves into, and when she got out of this rusty fucking cage—! She threw her plate against the bars, then followed it with a full-booted kick, making dust shake from the ceiling screws.

"All right, all right!" Eleny abruptly began grabbing elbows and shoving people toward the door, and the nursery gang retreated to discuss the situation in private.

It took Zemolai a good half hour to calm down, but by the time she did, she'd formed the seed of an escape plan, and, more importantly: a way to return home.

CHAPTER FIVE

We saw in them a wisdom far beyond ours. We pined for their guidance; we set upon our knees to beg it from them, and they were happy to oblige.

They said: you need not beg. They said: we desire your attention as strongly as you desire our speech.

—Fragment 18, *the Dierka Mountain Scrolls*

WHEN ZENYA WAS SCARCELY ELEVEN, and her brother about to turn ten, their mother traveled to the border for historic site research and never returned.

It was a shocking and sudden absence ("an accident," said the security detail; "a raid, covered up," whispered her colleagues—in either case, a quick cremation far away, and a lifetime of plans gone up in smoke).

If Zenya and Niklaus had been accustomed to quiet self-reliance before, they experienced all new depths of loneliness now. Tomel retreated into his work and expected his children to do the same. Niklaus took his father's example to heart: he became obsessed with Natulia's unfinished manuscript, convinced that one day he would complete it on her behalf. A little scholar already and barely out of kiddie classes.

But Zenya's grief transformed along different lines. She daydreamed of what she might have done, had she been on the mountain that day. She sketched herself in wings (hastily burning the drawings before Tomel could find them), and she grew fixated on the Pava trainee test: the first step toward entering the mecha sect as an intended warrior.

There were two years to prepare, a small lifetime before she turned thirteen. Zenya borrowed every book with even a passing reference to the mecha sect, and attended every festival and religious service where Winged might appear. She charted the succession of Voices as far back as she could find public information, and memorized the names and battle honors of every warrior stationed in the city.

She didn't realize, at first, that she was hiding her plan from her father. Natulia and Tomel had made it clear, in their affectionate yet matter-of-fact manner, that they'd deliberately conceived their children close together, the quicker to move past the demanding baby years and return to work—Tomel in the archives and Natulia in research and publication.

It never occurred to them that one of their children might want another life. Changing sects wasn't unheard of—to the contrary, there were some natural overlaps in interest between, say, the scholars and the engineers. If her parents had thought about the mecha sect at all, they would have imagined the situation in reverse: all those young ruffians yearning toward higher education and a gentler life in Milar. Every farm-born student who pursued robes was a validation; every worker family who kept sending their children past basic reading and arithmetic, an inspiration. Why would it be any different for the warriors?

Privacy had already been the default state of Zenya's life, not something she pursued in earnest. When she began to hide pilfered library books beneath her bed, no one noticed. When she skipped her athletics course to take a boxing class in another district, she thought surely this would do it, her father would ask what was going on—but not a word.

She did *want* to say something. But every time she considered broaching the topic, Zenya imagined the depths of her father's disappointment, and the words dried right up. Natulia and Tomel had been born-and-raised scholars. They'd built a personal library and hired private tutors for their children, even when it meant side work at a printmaker's shop. He could not possibly understand.

She saw Niklaus brilliantly and enthusiastically following in their mother's footsteps, and she saw the way Tomel lit up at his every accomplishment, and she thought: not yet.

Soon, but not yet.

It wasn't certain, after all. If she failed, she would go into higher education like her father wanted, and he would never need to know it was her second choice.

Slowly and then swiftly, two years passed.

On the morning of the final Pava trainee test, Zenya found herself trapped in a reading room in tower Zhelan with her brother while their father finished a research project on the next floor—a project he'd insisted would be finished an hour earlier.

She had already slipped away for the written portion of the exam a week prior, claiming a bout of food poisoning. Now all that was left was the physical, and she desperately wanted time to warm up beforehand.

Niklaus had a mountain of papers spread out in front of him (something to do with political messaging in folk stories; Zenya had only half-listened to his cheerful explanation). Zenya stared at a book without reading it, considering how to skip their lunch plans without raising suspicion.

"Stop tapping your foot," Niklaus murmured.

"I'm not."

Zenya wondered if she could get away with another sudden-onset stomachache, or if she'd used that excuse too many times already. It wasn't inaccurate . . .

"Stop tapping your foot."

"I'm not."

It was bizarre enough that Tomel had asked them to visit him in the tower today. How often did they even eat together—did it have to be *today*?

Niklaus had fallen silent, and that should have been a clue. After a long pause, he said, "I know you're testing for Pava."

Zenya froze. Of all the disaster scenarios she had brainstormed, this had not been one of them.

She cycled through a dozen protests, and could only blurt, "*How?*"

Niklaus rolled his eyes. "Because you're obvious."

43

Zenya's face went hot. "You went through my things."

"No."

"You saw me sneak out."

"I really didn't."

"I'm not that transparent!"

"You really are."

"I swear, if you've been snooping—"

He flicked her in the side of the neck. "Meathead. Remember that time you put Veckle in a headlock for stealing my shoes? Or when you made paper wings and jumped off the Ario-Zavet bridge? Or all those games of Mad Garulian where you never once let me play defense? Or—"

"You can't tell anyone," Zenya said. *"Have you told anyone?"*

He turned away, expression shuttered. "Were you just going to walk out one day?"

"Of course not! I just . . ." Zenya trailed off.

"Just *what*?"

She stared at her brother, grown so much from the round-faced boy who had helped her build that first pair of wings, but still young and, regardless of her intentions, still hurt.

How could she distill five years of yearning into something that wasn't defensive, accusatory? "You're right," she said. "I waited too long. I was afraid of what Tomel would say and I didn't know if I could keep going if he said it. Every night, I dream of flying. Of *fighting*. Of joining the mecha god's warriors and protecting the city. I want to soar with wings of gleaming copper. I want leathers and bandoliers. I want to worship at the base of the god-tree. How do I tell him that I love him, but I don't want to *be* him?"

She saw the guilty truth in his face before he said a word. "Well, now you're making me feel bad . . ."

Zenya groaned. "Oh, Nushki, no."

Too late. There came a brief, authoritative knock at the door, and there was Tomel with his face as grim as a graveside service, and he'd brought along Zenya's childhood tutor, the esteemed Scholar Pyetka, to support his case.

There were tears. Impassioned arguments. Recriminations. By turning her back on the scholar god, Zenya was giving up dialogue for obedience, complexity for duality, moral ambiguity for judgment.

"I am offering you *knowledge*," Tomel said. "And you want to enforce edicts!"

Zenya struggled to present her defense the way her father preferred: with logic. "The oversight of the mecha warriors makes scholarly study possible," she said. "If I join them, I'll be protecting the entire sect! Your work isn't possible without safe borders."

Tomel said, "We stayed in Milar because it's closer to the scholar god's portal. You have every opportunity here. If you go to them, you would become an instrument. You would give up choice!"

"But this *is* my choice," Zenya cried. "How is it more of a choice if you choose for me?"

Niklaus tried to step in at that point, brotherly solidarity at last overcoming his hurt feelings. "She's not wrong . . ."

Tomel cut him off with a curt gesture, and then he launched the argument Zenya had feared most of all: "What would your mother have said?"

All through this humiliating ordeal, Scholar Pyetka had been sitting patiently by. He was new to his robes, a middle-aged man recently initiated to the scholar god's inner circle. During his years teaching the younger students—Zenya and Niklaus included—he'd been candid about his aspirations. Pyetka wanted to study in the god's domain and share greater wisdom with the city. Every moment in his life was a step in a single direction.

Now, he raised one hand and said, "I'd like to speak to Zenya."

A long silence ensued, Tomel waiting expectantly, before Pyetka added, "Alone."

"Oh!" Tomel was taken aback, clearly having expected a roundtable dressing-down to do the trick, but he stood without protest. Niklaus followed after him, throwing Zenya one last look of apology before the door clicked shut.

The room was terribly silent in their absence, the air too hot and the walls too close. Zenya scrubbed at her eyes, angry and humiliated and convinced of her own selfishness. Scholar Pyetka sat down at the table beside her and idly flipped through Niklaus's work.

"He's a passionate student," Pyetka murmured.

Zenya gave a teary sniff. "I'm aware."

"But you're not."

Zenya didn't answer. He'd never liked obvious answers in the classroom. Why start now?

"Do you understand why your father came to me?" he prodded.

"Because he thought you'd make a strong case, and he never attempts anything without corroborating sources?"

That drew a soft laugh out of him.

"Do you feel the way he does?" Zenya asked. Uncertainty clawed its way past her defenses. She'd grown used to disagreeing with her father, even if only in her thoughts. But Pyetka had always treated her as a whole and separate person. His opinion had the weight of neutrality.

He hesitated. "Your parents made a particular plan for their life together, and your father is determined to carry it on in your mother's absence. He has now spent so long following it that he's finding his expectations difficult to let go. You have that in common, I think."

Zenya turned this comment over. "That isn't an answer."

Pyetka spread his hands, beseeching. "Do you want me to say I approve of a life spent serving the mecha god? Of course I do, in the abstract. She's divine, an equal member of the Five, and like all the Five, her teachings contribute to the good of the whole. In the *particular*?" He shrugged. "I think you are meant for better things. The scholar sect is small, select. It isn't an honor to give up lightly."

The honor was the problem. It settled, as always, like a weight on her back: something unwanted, which she was expected to be grateful for.

Her hands twisted together in her lap. "I've wanted this for so long . . . I don't know how to let it go."

Pyetka considered for a solemn moment, and then brightened. "Ah! I believe I have a text for you."

Zenya slumped. "I don't think—"

But Pyetka was full of cheer, certain that he'd found the answer (and that it was, as always, in a book of saints). "It is an essay of Lemain's, about the nature of the self. Is the person who wakes up the same as the one who fell asleep the night before? Scholar Parush famously posited that we are ever-evolving, an entirely new person from one moment to the next, unique iterations of a loosely connected core memory set. But Lemain believed that you are every person you have ever been—not born anew, but continual and simultaneous."

Zenya frowned. "I'm not sure I follow."

Pyetka leaned forward and placed his hands over her tangled fists. His touch was warm, his eyes warmer. "It means that nothing is ever truly lost, and the time you've spent on this pursuit is not wasted, even if your life takes a different turn."

For the first time all day—in years, really—the bubble and churn of Zenya's thoughts went still. Quietly, she asked, "Nothing changes?"

"Nothing is gone," Pyetka corrected. Then he smiled. "You would make an excellent scholar of mecha history. So you see? Nothing wasted."

He was a kind man, and Zenya did not want to disappoint him. She said, "I would like to read that essay, thank you, Scholar Pyetka," and he clapped his hands, satisfied that his intervention had been suitably received.

She sat in freshly resolved silence while he welcomed her family back in, and whispered reassurances to Tomel, and strode off to go search the stacks of the upper-level archives for an essay on the nature of the self.

Zenya's greatest fear had been a simple what-if. What if she changed her mind? What if she diverted from her current path and then regretted it? Pyetka, in his own way, had reassured her of the truth.

She would always be the girl who wanted the sky.

As soon as Tomel had finished his awkward commiseration and gone on with his day, Zenya turned to Niklaus and said, "I'm going."

He sighed. "I know."

"I'll write," she promised, suddenly struck by the reality of her intention to leave him.

"You'd better!" Niklaus said. "I wouldn't want you to forget how, like the rest of those meatsacks."

That startled a laugh out of her. But she sobered just as quickly, whispering, "I might not pass."

Niklaus was sad but certain. "Yes, you will."

Zenya was a born and trained scholar. She'd spent two years preparing.

Of course she passed.

It wasn't the exam itself that was significant (thirteen-year-old Zenya would have protested this fact, but thirteen-year-old Zenya did not yet have the gift of hindsight). It was the event immediately following that would shape the next years of her life.

Zenya was bathed in sweat, legs trembling, standing in a line with dozens of other hopefuls. They'd spent two hours demonstrating their physical fitness: archery and knife-throwing, foot races and ladders. They had grappled one another in wrestling matches, scaled brick walls, crawled through tunnels till their knees bled.

All the while there had been four Winged on the school rooftop, watching from above while older trainees ran drills, making their decisions out of earshot. Any time Zenya had risked a glance in their direction, she'd been blinded by the glare of their wings.

Now one of them peeled away from the rest. She stepped off the edge of that rooftop as though she were taking the next step on a cobblestoned path, weightless, unconcerned, her wings cupping the air like parachutes. Her boots hit the ground, and Zenya's head spun, her brain stuttering over the sight before her: those *wings*, silver and impossibly bright, that dark hair, those eyes, that casual strength—

The woman smiled broadly, and even her teeth glinted. "My name is Winged Vodaya. You all performed admirably today—but alas, we only have so many positions open. Are you ready for your assignments?"

They snapped to attention, and Vodaya walked down the line, confirming their names and then declaring their fates: "Winged Pilivar's unit.

Winged Chava's unit. Back to intermediary until next year. Better luck next time."

The rest of the line kept a frantic tally of remaining spots, their prospects dwindling as she moved through their ranks. Seven positions left, then six.

At last she reached Zenya, who blurted "Milar Zemolai!" like she'd nearly forgotten her own name. A barely suppressed snort of laughter sounded next to her—she ignored it.

"Yes, the girl from Milar." Vodaya leaned in. She was only two inches taller than Zenya, but her presence was overwhelming, everything about her muscled and deeply sky-kissed. She stood too close, just inside the bounds of courtesy, with her wings spread behind her like glittering sails. Zenya could feel herself being appraised, a clinical catalog all the way from her snarled hair to the blood dripping thickly toward her feet.

"You scored very highly on the written exam," Vodaya said finally. "The highest in your test group, in fact. Exactly what we should expect from a scholar."

Zenya flushed with pleasure, but Vodaya was not smiling. "Your background did you well on the page, but there is significantly more conflict in the sky than in a library."

And Zenya's flush turned to pallor.

Vodaya said, with the familiar cadence of recitation: "A warrior must have speed. A warrior must have agility. A warrior expects the unexpected."

She paused, leaving room for Zenya to reply.

Those were the words of Winged Zorska, long-gone warrior and author of *The Battle Arts*. Zenya stared at this woman, waiting so expectantly— and calm settled over her. She knew the next line: "A warrior is our only line of defense against the enemies at our gates."

Vodaya said, "And so a warrior is relentless. A warrior is heartless." She gave a nod of encouragement so slight that Zenya might have imagined it.

The words were already waiting on her tongue. They were a promise, a commitment—a sworn oath. She met Vodaya's eyes as she delivered them. "A warrior is an instrument through which the mecha god applies her will—and so a warrior wins."

And Vodaya smiled, mischievous and bright. She said, "Keep your conviction, and you will go far, Milar Zemolai. There is one spot open in my five-unit. The others have been studying with me for a year already. You will have to work very hard to catch up."

It took half a second for Zenya's brain to register the implication, and then all of her enthusiasm spilled forth in a wild rush. "Oh, thank you! I will study day and night! I will do anything—"

"Anything?" the Winged woman teased.

"Anything!"

Vodaya laughed, long and delighted, and by the time she was done, Zenya had flushed all the way to the roots of her hair. The rest of the yard faded away, trainees and hopefuls and impatiently waiting Winged alike. She forgot about her brother, about what she'd say to her father. Right now, the world consisted of one other person, gleaming silver.

And oh, it was inevitable, this moment of white-hot infatuation. There was Zenya, so recently de-mothered; Zenya, who had scarcely ever gotten more attention than an interesting footnote in an old book. And here was a warrior with wings like the moon and a smile like the sun, and she said, "Be careful what you promise me, girl of Milar."

Then she turned to the next girl in the line and said, "Back to intermediary for you. Better luck next time."

For years afterward, Zenya would reflect on the whims of fortune. She had begun to doubt herself—had nearly missed all that came next, the glorious and the terrible alike—and it was a last-minute conversation with Scholar Pyetka that had set her right.

INTERLUDE

THERE IS A QUESTION that has preoccupied me for many years: What is Radezhda?

I can already hear your complaints. *Why, it is a city, of course!* In that case, I ask you: what is a city?

Creator Stasia wrote that a city is a related network of roads. But this cannot be true. Some of our roads extend clear through the mountains, and we do not claim all the land alongside them there, nor the municipalities where they continue on the other side. This is clearly the musing of an engineer—I built it, therefore it is mine.

Is a city a cluster of homes, then? This answer seems satisfactory when considering an isolated community such as ours, but there are many more cities in the world that neatly abut one another. We find ourselves in the same situation as we were with the roads—where to call an end to it? We include the farmers in our cityhood, and they do not even reside within the city walls.

Borders, then! That is the purpose of borders. To mutually decide upon a limit, and inscribe it upon a map. To you, the homes in the foothills; to you, everything west of the river. . . . Except those borders did not spring from nothing! This is a warrior's answer, a fixation on protecting what is already there without asking how it came to be.

A city, according to the workers within it, is a designation of where one's taxes go and from where one's benefits derive. Industry and government. Centralized economy. This is, by far, the most practical answer. But much like borders, homes, and roads—it only describes a single moment in time. Tomorrow, entire neighborhoods may be traded, abandoned, absorbed.

When I ask, "What is Radezhda?" I do not mean which is the last property beholden to the Council of Five in this year in particular. I am asking: what unites us? What defines us? What is our *purpose*?

A city is ever-changing, a timeline of expansions and contractions, technological advances and social evolution—and so I have no choice but to conclude that a city *is* its history.

Just as generations of family remain linked long after their forebears are dead, a city is united by a sense of community, culture, the acknowledgment that our current existence is the result of ten thousand decisions made before us. For newcomers it is a self-identification—an active choice to join the lineage of a new family.

A city is a place that knows the truth of itself. A city is a story.

And the story of Radezhda is a strange one.

CHAPTER SIX

Divide and attack! That is the preferred way. A series of small victories, cumulative in nature, leave the enemy scattered and confused. A frontal assault—however satisfying it may feel—is not always the path to success.

—Winged Zorska, *The Battle Arts*

AFTER ZEMOLAI'S MELTDOWN in the containment cage, the bolt-babies came to her in pairs, and they came bearing gifts. A refuse bucket (not worth wondering how they'd managed while she was berserk), a sleeping mat (her hips didn't mind), moderately improved gruel (*moderately*). They weren't particularly *good* gifts, but they were peace offerings all the same.

They had recommitted to Eleny's rule—*nobody goes in alone*—but this served Zemolai's purpose just fine. She had already set her sights on Galiana, and how was the young woman supposed to know Zemolai was favoring her if she had nothing to compare the attention to?

Zemolai was going to get out of here soon, and she was going to earn her way back into tower Kemyana by offering up the insurrectionist cell that had bombed their storehouse. (She wasn't under any grand delusions—she knew her best-case scenario was to return in a support role. This was reasonable. Achievable. One thread of hope where she had previously been hopeless. She needed this.)

The next day brought Timyan and Rustaya to her cell—the former with his little notebook of persuasion plans, and the latter with their arms crossed, preemptively defensive.

Timyan clutched that book like an anchor and tried to convince Zemolai to turn on her chosen people.

"We know we're asking a lot of you," he said earnestly. He had no *idea* what he was asking of her. "You've been working with them for years." Her entire adult life. "Which is why you don't have to answer right away." Translation: they were short on time, please do answer, actually. "I'm only asking that you keep an open mind, and really listen to us."

Rustaya's tactic was more aggressive, but no more effective. "They cast you out for letting Chae Savro keep an idol," they taunted. "What kind of a law is that? A citizen of Radezhda can't worship one of the Five?"

Zemolai asked, with dismissive calm, "Were the Winged incorrect? Was Chae Savro *not* part of a conspiracy to infiltrate and damage administration tower Kemyana?"

Timyan's hand flew to Rustaya's arm, beseeching, but Rustaya shook him off. "You decimated his sect!" they said. "You made them become workers or starve, then threatened punishment if they didn't take their new role to heart! I guarantee you—I fucking guarantee you—the more you try to push us down, the more you'll stir us up."

"*Stop*," Timyan whispered.

"Savro didn't rebel because he was a scholar!" Rustaya bellowed. "You gave him no *choice* but to rebel because he was a scholar!"

The door flew open. Timyan and Rustaya were pulled out. That was two down for the day.

Next came Eleny and Galiana. The tension between them was palpable.

Eleny made most of their arguments—none of which Zemolai was inclined to answer during Operation: Isolate the Weak Point—and Zemolai kept her attention on Galiana, watching sidelong for the young woman's reactions. Eleny made a point about mecha factory control, and Galiana was focused. Eleny turned the subject to immigration, and Galiana looked away, bored.

Occasionally Galiana would try to come at a topic sideways herself, blatantly unrelated to anything Eleny was talking about. "How long did you wear wings, by the way? Were you there, at the battle over tower Kemyana?"

But inevitably, Eleny would cut in with a quelling look and turn the subject back to all the reasons the mecha sect was corrupt and Zemolai should therefore turn on her god, commanders, and fellow Winged. It was easy to maintain a sullen silence, waiting for the right moment to give the other woman some bait.

And then Galiana said, "You've already seen the effects of the mecha god's edicts. You relented. For your mercy, you were cast out to die. What kind of a system is that?"

This was too close to Zemolai's own midnight thoughts, and she didn't have to fake a flinch. She reminded herself of her plan: encourage, engage, but give nothing of real value.

After a moment's consideration, she said, "The mecha god's judgment is absolute. She's selfless. She protects the other Four. Every judgment she makes is to achieve that end. She isn't . . . she isn't some sort of dictator, funneling workers into factories for her own glory. She doesn't forbid other forms of worship."

There—a touch of vulnerability, an invitation to pry harder.

But it was Eleny who leaned toward the bars next, her eyes bright. "Why then?" she prompted. "*Why* does the mecha god allow your leader to make these edicts in her name? Because you're right, she doesn't forbid worship of the creator or the scholar. Instead she adjusts the application for rations, or reconfigures the funding for housing, or changes the tariffs on her preferred goods, and their bases dwindle of their own accord. She makes it impossible to live outside her system and then considers her hands clean when citizens voluntarily convert."

This wasn't a question about the mecha god anymore, but her earthly representative, Mecha Vodaya. Mecha Vodaya, who spent so much time in communion with the slumbering god that she was turning silver. Mecha Vodaya, who was the first one scrutinized whenever the god roused enough to shine a light of judgment.

Why did the god allow all of this in her name, unless she approved? The mecha god didn't often wake, but when she did, she passed a gentle hand over her Voice. What other conclusion, than that she truly believed they were doing their best for the city-state?

Zemolai had always believed that Radezhda thrived through the balance of the Five. Citizens chose the service of a single god, but all of their actions contributed to the good of the whole. Civilization was birthed in the division of labor, and in the division of labor, citizens found their individual purpose. That was the word.

What Eleny described—purpose subverted in favor of bald economics—wasn't only offensive, it was blasphemous.

But it also sounded a good deal like Vodaya.

Zemolai let her expression shutter. She turned bodily away, ending the day's amateur attempt at conversion, but not before she saw the look that blossomed on Galiana's face: a dawning suspicion, a contemplative chewing of her lower lip. And Zemolai felt a grim thrill at the tiny victory.

Yes, girl, consider this: the prisoner will only talk to you.

Round and round they went: Timyan stuttering through his notes and Rustaya losing their temper, Galiana with her sideways questions—not nearly as subtle as she imagined herself—and Eleny acting the supervisor, halting conversations whenever they drifted too far into sensitive territory.

Zemolai could see the frustration on Galiana's face each time Eleny cut her off. She understood the desire to shout out a right answer; the willpower it took to restrain one's tongue on a favorite topic. Galiana had an obsession, and she believed Zemolai held information relevant to the cause. Zemolai only needed to chisel Eleny from her side to find out what it was.

They went through days of this, showing up with meals and Zemolai's dose of suppressant—in pill form now, far preferable to another shot in the neck. She tried to calculate how long it had been since her fall from grace. A week? Longer? Nobody would say how many days she had spent raging before the drugs kicked in, and there was no window to mark the days since she had come back to her senses. Nobody mentioned the training grounds again, but the demand hung in the air over every conversation, waiting for the next opening.

They brought a pair of chairs to sit on (more at her level). They kept the chairs just out of reach of the bars (she tried).

There were moments when Zemolai was struck by the absurdity of the situation, and she nearly burst into laughter. But then she'd grow angry again, because she shouldn't find *any* part of this funny, and it was their fault she'd even come close.

They tried calm: "Look at the last year of legislation," Eleny said. "Immigrants pressured to make religious declarations . . . Correspondence monitored in and out of the city . . ."

They tried passion: "Parents are registering their children to a sect before their children are old enough to know the difference!" Galiana exclaimed. "They're conducting worship under supervision! It has to be scheduled! That's not protection. That's *control*."

"Every new edict is made from the top of tower Kemyana," Eleny concluded, "and no hand of judgment comes through that portal. Why does the mecha god allow this in her name?"

Zemolai couldn't answer. Didn't care to answer. Oh, there were justifications she could cite. The pressure to hold neighboring city-states at bay. Previous violent incidents by people disguising themselves as members of other sects. This little rebel cell was perfect evidence of the danger at hand! But that only explained why mecha leadership would desire greater control. What did the god *herself* care about rationing or immigration paperwork?

The time in between these visits was excruciating for Zemolai—an awful blend of boredom and thought spirals with no escape. She tormented herself with visions of her return to Kemyana, bolt-babies in tow. Would it be enough? Would the mecha god accept such penance? Would Vodaya? Her nights were long and terrible, filled with doubt.

But she could see Galiana's impatience rising every time that Eleny spoke and Zemolai shut down. She could see the little wheels turning, now that Galiana had concluded what she wanted her to conclude: *perhaps Zemolai would let her guard down, if . . .*

And then it happened: Galiana began slipping in to see her, alone.

Galiana's first unsupervised visit happened at night, an estimate Zemolai could only make because she'd already received her second drug dose, and the lights were turned off in the adjoining room when Galiana crept through.

"I thought you might appreciate better food," the young woman whispered, one eyebrow raised mischievously, like they were girls sharing sweets after lights out and not prisoner and prison guard.

She'd brought a hot plate—a dish of noodles and mixed meats, popular among late-night socializers, heaped with onions to unite the taste of disparate leftovers. It smelled delicious.

Zemolai did not have to pretend to perk up at the sight.

Galiana used the spare chair as her prep table, cutting the larger bites of meat down before sliding the dish into the cage, and then Zemolai descended upon what was possibly the best hot plate she had eaten in her entire life.

"I didn't mean for things to go like this," Galiana said softly.

Zemolai swallowed her bite. "You didn't mean to imprison a once-Winged warrior and pry out her secrets?"

Galiana winced. "Not exactly, no. If I'm being honest, you sort of fell in our laps."

Zemolai grunted. What could she say? She would have taken the same opportunity in their place.

"How's the hot plate?" Galiana asked.

"Hot."

Galiana laughed, and then clapped a hand over her mouth, glancing worriedly toward the door. "Well. I thought you'd be tired of canned potato by now."

Zemolai made short work of her meal, and they danced through some small talk—a front on both their parts, a tentative testing-of-waters. Galiana tried to draw her out with small personal details (personally she preferred breakfast plates; wasn't it odd that she'd been stationed in the tower all those years, and they'd never crossed paths?) and Zemolai kept her responses vague. Just enough to keep the conversation going, nothing tangible, nothing usable.

And it was working as intended. She could see the flush of excitement on the other woman's face, Galiana's growing conviction that all of this useless small talk was a victory, a successful warming-up, a dam cracked and waiting to spill.

"You were trained by Mecha Vodaya, weren't you?" asked Galiana.

And Zemolai shut her down. "I'm tired," she said stiffly. "I'd like to sleep."

Look at that dismay! Oh, Galiana was kicking herself. She'd over-stepped and now Zemolai was withdrawing, what a mess. Galiana was going to spend the rest of the night poring over every word they'd said.

It was strange to be sitting on this side of a set of bars—in days' old clothing, on a pathetically thin sleep mat, with a plate of precut food and no utensil—and yet to feel entirely in control of the situation.

(It was uncomfortable, to be honest, mimicking the tactics she knew so well from the other side. Give a girl some extra attention—then take it away, leave her wanting more. When had she become this self-aware? It would have been far less embarrassing to carry on, oblivious, rather than to see her insecurities reflected so starkly in this girl's face.)

Galiana made her apologies and slipped away, and Zemolai (a liar) lay awake for several hours after she'd gone.

Galiana visited three more times after that. She always brought food, and she always said more than she intended. Zemolai pretended to want the company (Zemolai pretended to herself that she was only pretending to want the company).

"Did you have anyone?" Galiana asked with a suggestive chin tilt. "Any-one that you . . . left behind?"

"No."

Galiana chewed her lip a moment before declaring, in her tireless quest to elicit information by oversharing her own: "I'm with Timyan and Rustaya."

Zemolai arched an eyebrow. "How lovely."

Galiana flushed. "It matters," she said. "All of you mecha, you—you settle for nothing and no one. But we're a *family*. We're fighting for our friends and loved ones. Your peers fight for themselves, for power. Don't you see what you're missing?"

Zemolai was certain the ringleaders of the rebellion loved it this way. Rope in whole families at a time! How could they betray one another? But this gave her an opening to pry.

"You talk like a farmer," Zemolai said, and was gratified to see the other woman's entire face go hot.

"You—you shouldn't disparage farmers," Galiana stuttered. "Without farmers, the city would starve. No fighting, no building, no working. Farmers are the real foundation of freedom. We—they—" She fumbled, stopped. Rubbed nervously at the thin scars over the tendons on the back of her hands. She turned back to the evening's bribe (a dense nut bread, delicious) and cut another slice. The knife clattered too hard when she set it down.

Zemolai took the bread, but wouldn't be diverted. "I know you're not from Chae." The hands, the eyes. How had any of them remained hidden for so long?

Galiana opened her mouth. Shut it. Finally admitted, "I was born on a farm. I had five parents and eight siblings shared between them when I left."

It was a common arrangement among the earth god's people. Zemolai could almost appreciate it; they concentrated resources in fewer households, with multiple adults sharing the workload and family duties. There was also something to be said for romance, she supposed, but it had never been worth thinking about, for her.

Galiana had the grace to look chagrined at the next part. "I loved them, but I also wanted more for them, and I thought I could *do* more for them if I could bring them better technologies to complete their work. So I enrolled myself in engineering school."

"They must have loved that," Zemolai murmured.

Galiana said, "I was volunteering on a breadline when I met Eleny. Bitter, because engineering wasn't what I'd expected it to be. I wanted to do more than design ballistics, but I couldn't see a way out, not without renouncing the work entirely. And I was so *good* at the work, I couldn't stop. Eleny convinced me to put my training to better use. So now I'm a farmer turned engineer, hiding behind a worker's name."

When Zemolai was young, they'd called people like Galiana sect-hoppers. Always looking to another path, never settling down. She wondered if they even knew the phrase these days, now that registration was so strict.

"You understand me," Galiana said. "You're playing the skeptic, but you know what it's like to leave everything behind in pursuit of a different god. The scholars don't overlap with the mecha god's people the way they sometimes do with the creator's. You must have been extremely passionate to leave them."

The face of Zemolai's father surfaced unwanted in her memory. He'd been angry—but more disappointed than angry. Wounded by her rejection of his faith. By her rejection of everything important to him and to her mother.

For one wobbly, ill-advised moment, Zemolai faltered. She looked at this young woman—*really* looked at her, Galiana-as-she-was and not Galiana-the-playing-piece—and she saw a kindred spirit. Somebody who had left her family behind out of love for them; out of a desire to return, triumphant, full of value; somebody who had failed that goal, and was in desperate need of another.

Softly, Galiana asked, "Would they have taken you back, you think?" Meaning the scholars. Meaning her family. Meaning Milar.

And Zemolai, off guard, let a piece of the truth slip out. "No," she said. "I did something unforgiveable."

"What was it?"

The world shrank down to the two of them, kneeling face-to-face as though they were sharing a prayer nook in an overcrowded shrine. There were no offering dishes here; no icons on the walls; no benches upon which to kneel. There was only a dented plate of cold food, a hushed

61

absence of sanctity, and the cold ground.

Zemolai felt dizzy, her ears buzzing with the rush of her own blood, and for a moment she was back there again, feeling the heat on her face and the realization that some things could never be undone.

She shook her head, banishing the memory once more. She wouldn't speak it—wouldn't even think of it—but her hesitation had opened a doorway.

"What we're doing here," Galiana said, trying to wedge a foot in that doorway, "is simple. We all want the right to pursue the ideals of our god, whether we serve alone or with our families. The others don't really understand what drove you to the mecha god, but *I do*. When you're given a gift . . ." She flexed her hands, displaying the evidence of her old engineering enhancements, scarred and faded. ". . . it would be a greater sacrilege to deny it."

The food in Zemolai's stomach had compressed to stone. She said to Galiana, *willing* her to understand this one point, "The mecha god's first directive is to protect. Whatever else you think of her."

Galiana leaned forward. "Yes. And the creator god's first directive is to create. And the scholar god's first directive is to study the past. You only need to get out of the way and *let us do it*."

Zemolai shut her eyes, imagining a future where that was possible. "It's a nice fantasy," she concluded, with no small trace of bitterness. "But it doesn't matter. The scholar god hasn't spoken in years. Whichever of his disciples still remain barricaded in that tower . . ." She shook her head. "There aren't enough of them left. The scholar sect is all but dead, and if their god has anything to say about it, he's kept it to himself."

Zemolai remembered the end of the scholar god's open services. She remembered the look on Scholar Pyetka's face right before the bag went over his head. The Winged had eradicated heresy from their ranks, and there had hardly been enough scholars left to tend the rooftop shrine.

Galiana shot to her feet, nearly knocking her chair over. There was a new light in her eyes, something halfway between fear and determination. It took Zemolai a moment to realize that she was clutching a key in one hand.

"I want to show you something," Galiana said. "And I think you're ready to see it. Can I trust you?"

The key glinted silver, tauntingly close.

It had worked. Zemolai had lost the thread of her own plan, let herself be caught up by old regrets, but it had worked anyway. Reality crashed back into place, and Zemolai nearly choked on it. She wanted to rage at this woman—for her idealism, her optimism, her belief that she could change anything. *Look* at her, thinking herself the victor, thinking they could speak heart-to-heart through a set of bars and Zemolai's entire life would be turned around—offering that key like it meant nothing and they were about to walk out of here as friends.

Zemolai cleared her throat and said, "I don't have anywhere else to go, do I?"

The key turned in the lock. Galiana took one step back, a too-late concern blooming, but Zemolai kept her movements slow and steady. After the week (plus?) that she'd had, slow and steady was about all she could manage.

Galiana laughed, nervous. "Well. I suppose this is the part where I remind you about the pills. Also, I'm carrying a bolt-gun."

"Of course," Zemolai said.

Galiana backed out of the room, past the visitors' chairs and the half-eaten loaf of nut bread—and the dinner knife she'd so considerately brought each day to cut up Zemolai's food.

Zemolai slowed, letting Galiana get three steps past the doorjamb, and palmed the knife.

In the early days of the war, Zemolai had been tasked with routing resisters out of underground hiding places. At one point, she'd discovered a complex network of tunnels between basements, like a miniature city beneath the city. Some had been connected by original design, while others were hastily dug, reinforced by nothing other than creaking wooden poles and prayer. Rabbit warrens, she'd called them. (And what did that make her, a fox? A snake?)

They had filled as many as they could; detonated the rest. An ugly job.

Now, as Galiana led her through one hallway after another, up one set of stairs and then down, Zemolai was reminded of those warrens again. This tunnel network was more stable, thank the Five, with sturdier struts and safety lights at regular intervals, but she was unlikely to find her way out on her own.

Galiana moved quickly, keeping just out of reach. One hand hovered at her side, but Zemolai was unconcerned. She'd never be able to draw that bolt-gun in the half-second it would take Zemolai to grab her arm.

But Zemolai hesitated. It was the tunnel situation, she told herself (it wasn't the tunnel situation). There was no point in taking the woman hostage prematurely if she was lost underground (Zemolai had persevered through worse before).

"Where are you taking me?" Zemolai asked.

"We might already be too late," came the apologetic nonanswer.

This did not dispel her uneasiness.

The safety lights flickered—a brief interruption in power—and Galiana slowed as they reached the end of the passageway, where tamped earth gave way to tiles and a single door remained. A discreet keypad was embedded on the wall, and Galiana quickly tapped out the code, using her body to block Zemolai's line of sight. They stepped through, into a dark, claustrophobically small space lit only by the glow beneath the doorjamb.

The deadbolt reengaged with a decisive thud. They were alone. Behind them: a locked door. In front: a set of thick, red curtains blocking the next space.

Galiana held up one hand in warning, barely visible in the gloom.

Zemolai stood a hair's breadth behind her. The dinner knife pressed against the curve of her belly, rolled beneath the waist of her pants. Her hand trembled, remembering the feel of the hilt.

Galiana peeked through the curtains. The delicate curve of her neck lay bare.

Now, Zemolai thought. *Now*, while Galiana's guard was down. *Now*, before they stepped into the unknown, before Galiana turned around, before Zemolai lost her nerve, *now*.

"We made it in time!" Galiana turned and smiled, oblivious to the sweat creeping down Zemolai's back, stinging the raw flesh around her mangled ports. "I need you to stay at the back, all right? I don't want anyone getting . . . upset."

She ducked through without further explanation, taking Zemolai's best chance with her.

Zemolai shut her eyes, breathing hard against the vise that had attached itself around her chest. The whole group was about to come back (a number she could have handled easily in her prime, but not here, not in this state) and she'd backed herself into a corner, a literal corner.

But.

She had another option.

It was a lesser option—it would be better to bring the criminals in herself, returning triumphant with intel on the manufacture of mechalin alternatives—but it was an option nonetheless, and she had to go through with it before her shattered nerves betrayed her again.

Zemolai pulled the knife from her waistband. She licked it clean, then wiped each side against the dark, unsoiled fabric of her pants. Dark was good. Dark wouldn't show too badly. She rubbed her thumb against the top of her right thigh, searching, searching . . .

She plunged the knife into her leg.

It took effort not to cry out (because *shit* this hurt a lot worse without drugs) but Zemolai dug past a thin layer of muscle graft without so much as a swear. A light sheen of sweat sprang up on her forehead—for half a second her vision darkened around the edges—and then she plucked out something smooth and warm and wet with blood.

It was a resonance chip; her last remaining link to mecha high command. It emitted a signal that was synced to a companion piece at tower Kemyana. When Zemolai let the chip cool, an alarm would sound back at the tower—*Winged down*—and a ground team would head out to fetch her body. At which point they would realize she was nowhere near the worker's hospital, and they would track the signal here instead.

There. If she held her own against the bolt-babies, she could stick to her original plan and round them up herself. But if her strength or her nerves failed again—well, she wouldn't need either one if an armed five-unit was on its way.

Zemolai ripped out one of her pockets and stuffed the extra fabric into the hole in her pants. A very temporary stopgap, but she only needed to slow the bleeding. Then she stepped through the curtains, the chip held tight in one fist to keep warm until she'd assessed the situation.

She froze at what she saw.

It was a broad, round, low-ceilinged chamber, lit around the edges by orange lanterns. Tile floor. Metal struts reflecting oddly in the dim light. A small crowd milled about, maybe fifty or sixty people total. There were blueskins and longlegs, capheads and fringers and bolt-babies galore, all of them sporting permanent mods.

A figure stood before them. An old man, bowed of back and bald of pate. Under one arm he carried a mirror, and under the other arm he carried a bulging satchel. He set both of them down, his movements quiet, practical, less like those of a criminal mastermind and more like those of an elderly shopkeeper setting out his wares.

When he looked up, his eyes glowed silver as the moon, and the grandfatherly illusion fell away. This was a true disciple of the scholar god.

Zemolai knew exactly where she was. They were in a prayer chamber, deep below temple tower Zhelan in the heart of Milar.

And that was Scholar Pyetka, back from the dead.

CHAPTER SEVEN

It is our sacred duty to create order from chaos; to provide clarity and banish doubt. Nowhere is this imperative more perfectly fulfilled than in the chain of command.

As the mecha god tells the Voice, so the Voice tells the commanders, so the commanders tell the warriors, and so the warriors become the hand on the blade.

—*The Book of the Mecha God*

HERE IS WHAT ZENYA wrote home on her first night in Pava, age thirteen and brimming with victory:

This place is amazing! The entire compound is shaped like an enormous gear . . . the wall is fifteen feet high, with little square buildings spaced out around the perimeter. That's where I'm living—in one of the cogs.

Everything here is done in five-units: four limbs and a head. I'm living with Romil, Lijo, and Dolynne, with Winged Vodaya our head. I was nervous, but they were excited to meet me.

And tower Kemyana is RIGHT THERE . . . Do you think they'll let me in yet? Is it forward if I ask? I should wait before I ask. Should I ask?

It's really happening!!

To which Niklaus replied:

I'm glad you can still spell, but your punctuation has already taken a hit.

And then, in standard Niklaus fashion, he launched into a meandering description of his next research assignment for Scholar Pyetka.

When Zenya moved into the great gear of the training grounds, she found dedication like she'd never before experienced: an exhilarating surety of purpose. Radezhda was already a small world of its own, but Pava was an even smaller world nestled into the heart of Radezhda. It was the only district entirely walled off from the rest; an isolated community nestled against the mountains Kelior with all eyes and hearts aimed at the border.

When she stepped through the gates of Pava, Zenya left everything else behind.

Here is what Zenya did *not* write home, on her first night in Pava:

She stood outside her new apartment that morning for ten straight minutes, frozen with fear. The other students in Vodaya's unit had worked together, lived together, trained and bled and fought together, for more than a year already. Would she fit in, or would she flunk out?

Within seconds of her knock, the door tore inward, revealing three eager faces.

"So you're the one from Milar!" the first one exclaimed.

They laughed and pulled her forward, shamelessly grabbing her bag so they could dig through the contents and praise or condemn each of her books. They introduced themselves too quickly, and Zenya had to make them repeat it (Romil, Lijo, Dolynne; Romil, Lijo, Dolynne).

They were all of the same type: lanky and athletic, eyes bright, hair tied back. They talked with their hands and had no concept of personal space. They were comfortably confident, self-assured but not cocky.

They were everything Zenya wanted to be.

She asked the only question that mattered: "What is it like working with Winged Vodaya?" And they were thrilled to answer.

"She's one of the greatest warriors of our age!" Dolynne declared.

They all chimed in with praise. Winged Vodaya was dedicated, determined, rigorous. Her trainees were *always* early to graduate. She was thoughtful, supportive, a *brilliant* tactician, loyal, well-respected, with numerous accolades in battle and administration. Zenya was lucky to have been taken under her wing. She didn't *know* how lucky!

Nothing broke the stream of chatter until Zenya asked, "Have you been a four-unit long?"

It was a clumsy question. A clumsy way of asking, *Who am I replacing? Were they injured? Did they wash out? What shoes do you expect me to fill?*

Three cheery faces immediately folded into glowers.

Pava Lijo heaved a breath. He said, "You may as well know. Our fourth was Pava Genkolai. Completely unsuitable. Couldn't handle the pace. Three months ago, he crept out in the night, too cowardly to tell us, and took an empty room in Winged Raksa's unit. He isn't worth your time."

Dolynne stood up, their face pinched in disapproval. "So stop wasting it. Let's go."

Zenya hurried after them, furiously castigating herself for bringing down the mood. But all of her embarrassment evaporated when they reached the training yard.

The yard stretched a dizzying two hundred feet in diameter, and everywhere there were clusters of athletic competition underway. Archers and slingshots, runners and tunnelers, knife throwers and boxers. There were slender youths with enormous tool belts racing up ladders and others with net-guns trying to capture the unlucky trainees playing invaders.

Zenya reveled in the details: the colors chalked onto the brick wall, the patterns raked into the sandy ground, the faces filing out by rank and unit (her instructors, her competition, her peers!).

Dolynne took charge of Zenya's orientation, whispering names and gossip. There was Raksa's unit across the yard. There was the traitor Genkolai, his left hand nothing but a metal skeleton. There was Winged Raksa himself, a somber-looking warrior, stocky and muscled where most Winged were lean; a man built like a rock. Wings of gorgeous brass arced over his head, glittering like sunshine on dew.

"He graduated early, at seventeen," Dolynne whispered. "I heard he switched instructors midway to get ahead."

Winged Raksa had patrolled for five years on the eastern border, where he single-handedly held Gente Pass for three days against an invading party from Rava State. Now, at only thirty-three years old, he was rumored to be pursuing quadrant leader, and there were few other Winged willing to get in his way.

"Except Vodaya," Dolynne continued with relish. Vodaya was the only living warrior who had advanced more quickly, emerging in the same class as Raksa, but nearly a year younger. Their training bouts had been the stuff of legend, and their competition had never ceased. But it was Vodaya who was the Voice's favorite, Vodaya who was called up to the inner circle whenever the leader of their sect consulted the mecha god.

Zenya stared at Genkolai, wondering what could have convinced him to leave such a high-profile unit—and even more baffling, to choose his instructor's most heated rival instead.

Then Lijo pointed to the sky. "There she is!"

Winged Vodaya came in fast, her silver wings catching and reflecting the light like a holiday decoration. She circled the yard once and dropped down, her sandals cutting twin furrows across the carefully sculpted rings in the sand.

She looked right at Zenya, and Zenya beamed.

"Good morning, Pava," Winged Vodaya said. "I trust you've all introduced yourselves. For the next few days, I expect you to lead Zemolai through our routine, and after that it will be her responsibility to keep up. Your training will proceed at its current pace, and I will provide her with additional training during free hours to close the gap. Zemolai has a strong aptitude and a fearless nature. It won't take long."

Zenya swelled at the praise—but it came with more than its share of pressure, didn't it? Several days to conquer their routine. A vague but short period to master tactics.

She would do it. She would work around the clock if necessary, but she would do it.

Vodaya led them all in a morning prayer. *In word and in deed, become the protector. Judge the wicked, reward the penitent, uphold the laws of city and state, be the shelter under which they thrive.*

Be the shelter.

The trainees broke into a jog, and Zenya's heart soared. For years, she had run alone in the dim hours before school, with no other soul in the world to urge her on. The citizen gyms had focused only on maintaining health. A sound body for a sound mind.

But now she ran in a pack. This was about self-improvement. Using one's body for a purpose. Not maintenance, but *ability*. And in the mecha sect, Zenya would never be obliged to downplay her ability.

How could she possibly explain any of this to her brother? How could she say *"I was alone"* to the person she had left behind?

But she had been. And now she wasn't.

Here is what life was like in Pava, in those early days before the world changed:

Every morning Zenya awoke at dawn, jostled into line for the washroom, and then hurried to the courtyard. First came prayer, then exercise, then a quiet, pink-haired kitchen worker passed them breakfast through a service window, and they ate on the way to lessons.

Under Vodaya's tutelage, they continued their academics—memorizing books of saints, reciting rules of dress and hygiene, charting out military campaigns—but it was the afternoons they really looked forward to, because the afternoons were reserved for combat training.

They learned it all: slings, bows, throwing knives, net-guns, darts. But their excitement was reserved for *real* fighting: one-on-one, face-to-face. Blades. Fists. *Combat.* The other trainees took turns fighting Zenya, eager to knock her out, and for the next few weeks Zenya spent more time on the ground than on her feet.

Every bruise was a mark of pride.

There were surprises as well, the biggest of which was a biweekly engineering class with an honest-to-goodness engineer from Faiyan District.

"Faiyan Sanador has outfitted our warriors for twenty-two years," Vodaya explained. "Over the course of your training, you must learn to maintain your equipment, to repair wings, to troubleshoot in the field. He'll teach you everything you need to know. Any questions?"

A thousand! And Sanador was happy to answer them, this man who had dedicated his life to the fabrication of wings and weaponry. He was every bit the resident engineer, with bronze caliper pins on his lapels, an overloaded tool belt, and hair so white not even a chemical enhancement could color it.

"Milar!" he exclaimed, when Zenya introduced herself. He looked at her wonderingly. "My, my, I never thought I'd see the day. Well, I won't have to worry about you at test time, will I?"

She flushed at the compliment—then flushed harder at the unfriendly or outright disdainful looks of the other students in her class cohort. Zenya was quick to learn: the mecha sect relied on the engineers for the technologies that kept them aloft, but not happily.

(Faiyan Sanador was correct, however; he didn't have to worry about her at test time.)

Zenya would have liked to spend more time with her team in the evenings, but when everyone else finished for the day, she stayed behind with Vodaya for her catch-up lessons. The loss didn't bother her, not when she had so much to learn.

She was a glass and Vodaya the pitcher.

"Book knowledge is not enough," Vodaya liked to declare. "Scrabbling in a gym is not enough. You can't hesitate in a real fight. You can't shake off your attacker and think things over and try again. If you do not become the weapon, you become the target."

Vodaya removed her wings during the early lessons. The sight was jarring. *Intimate.* But Vodaya conducted every lesson with brisk, business-like efficiency. She demonstrated each sequence of maneuvers, and then Zenya mimicked, over and over, until she had it right.

Zenya crawled back to her apartment each evening, ate the plate of cold dinner left out by her roommates, and crashed into dreamless sleep. Was she catching up? She couldn't say. The work was endless, and Vodaya would not say how much remained.

Months passed in this way, a perpetual cycle of challenge and mastery and further challenge. Zenya could feel and then see the changes in her body.

She was leaner than ever, but her muscles were taut, her body flexible and responsive. Slowly, she began to win bouts against her teammates. Barely at first, more by surprise than by skill, but with enough force to push them, to make them try harder, to make it a real fight.

Some days Vodaya heaped lavish praise on her. "You are a natural, Zemolai! Don't let anyone tell you otherwise."

On other days Zenya could do nothing right. "Stop wasting my time," Vodaya might snap. "You get mired in thinking ahead. Are you a warrior or a researcher? Start over!"

Those days left Zenya trembling with anxiety, convinced that she would be dismissed by dawn. She couldn't eat, couldn't sleep. When dawn came, the transgression inevitably seemed forgotten, but Zenya doubled her efforts in a vain attempt to avoid another rebuke.

Her mood fluctuated wildly—elated when Vodaya was pleased, devastated when Vodaya was disappointed. Zenya heard her husky voice day and night. Her future was in this woman's hands, and she had no idea where she stood.

(*She sounds like an asshole,* Niklaus wrote, age twelve and rapidly expanding his vocabulary.

She wants us to do our best, Zenya replied. *She wants us to work as hard as she does. It's my own fault for overthinking everything . . .*

Still sounds like an asshole, Niklaus wrote.

She stopped telling him about bad days after that.)

After a particularly terrible lesson, Zenya cried herself to sleep, bone-weary and fatalistic. None of her roommates mentioned it the next day, but Vodaya was calmer that afternoon and only led Zenya through a few exercises she had mastered weeks earlier.

"All victorious warriors share these common principles: belief and commitment." Vodaya stood so close that Zenya could feel her breath. "Belief in their god. Commitment to their commander. Belief in moral authority. Commitment to discipline."

She shifted closer. She nudged Zenya's elbow slightly left and tipped Zenya's chin a hair's breadth higher. "I see you, Zemolai," she said softly. "I see how hard you work every day—don't think that I haven't noticed. I say what I have to within the fight ring, but please, never mistake what I say for how I feel. You're doing fine."

Zenya calmed, and the next day she performed flawlessly.

(This was something she could not explain later: the way that Vodaya could read every mood and solve every problem. It didn't work in reverse—Vodaya's moods shifted rapidly, and trying to anticipate them was an exercise in futility. But the woman had a knack for understanding the needs of her students. She *saw* them.

Zenya would cling to these moments later. She would repeat them like catechisms when her nights were plagued by poor sleep. *Why did she say that? Because I needed to hear it. Why did she yell? Because I was wrong.*

Vodaya wasn't her mother, but she was becoming something very close.)

"All warfare is deception," Vodaya said one evening, while Zenya was breathing hard and tangled into the fetal position by a well-cast net. "Bait the enemy. Lull the enemy into false security. *Understand* the enemy, and thereby understand how to undo him. Strike when he is overcome with confidence. Appear where he does not expect." She dropped into a crouch, craning her head down to meet Zenya's eyes. "And *dodge the net-gun.*"

They sat together afterward, Vodaya rubbing salve into a scrape on Zenya's back, Zenya watching the sun dip from sight. "Here," Vodaya said, passing a pill bottle forward. "These are enhancers that I often use on patrol, when I am not training five-units. You need to focus."

"I *am* focused," Zenya said. It was a rare protest, but she was beyond tired.

Vodaya pressed a finger hard against Zenya's scraped back, making her wince. "I could have severed your spine if I'd wanted to. Take them as needed. Or don't. But fatigue is not an excuse."

Zenya pocketed the bottle.

Here is another letter that Zenya didn't send, a moment too fleeting (*too confusing*) to put into words:

She was late leaving her apartment after lunch one day, her head swirling with flight and distance calculations, so distracted that she nearly ran into a person loitering in the hallway.

It was the traitor Pava Genkolai.

"Excuse me," she said, and made to step around him.

"Wait." He blocked her exit. "I know she keeps you busy. I'll be quick."

Zenya should have walked away right then, but she hesitated. Up close he looked more sad than traitorous, a boy with dark, wounded eyes and heavily drawn brows.

"You're her favorite," he said, softly, rapidly. "But it won't last. She'll push you until you break, and use it as a lesson for the others. Ask them what happened to me."

Zenya bristled. "I did. You abandoned them."

Genkolai held up his left hand, the one that was mere skeleton. "This is why I left. When you disappoint her—and you will—she won't catch you when you fall."

Zenya stared at him, suddenly breathless. "She's preparing us for real combat," she said, more uncertainly than she intended. "Real combat *is* dangerous."

Genkolai lowered his hand. "I get it," he said. "Believe me, I do." Something over her shoulder caught his eye, and his face fell. "Just . . . try to keep some perspective," he whispered urgently. "Don't let her be your entire world." And he hurried away, eyes aimed at the ground.

Zenya turned, certainty already making her throat tight.

It was Winged Vodaya, of course, marching their way. She followed Genkolai's departure with a suspicious frown, then turned the force of that expression on Zenya. (This was another power of hers that Zenya found impossible to describe: the way you could desire her attention so badly and then dread it once you'd gotten it.)

Vodaya considered Zenya closely for a moment before offering, almost off-handedly, "He was a poor student. I wouldn't give him your back in the field."

Zenya had a million questions, but she boiled them down to one. "What happened to his hand?"

Vodaya looked past her, lost in thought. "A foolish accident during combat training. Knowing Genkolai, he still hasn't taken responsibility for it. It really is a shame. Now come with me. There's an assembly being called in the yard."

Zenya knew when a topic was being dropped. She followed Vodaya to the training yard, and what she saw there immediately drove all thoughts of Genkolai and his purported incompetence from her head.

The entire class was assembled, five-unit wedged against five-unit. Their Winged instructors all stood proudly to one side, presenting them to a tall figure standing in the sand.

It was Mecha Petrogon. The Voice of the mecha god. The leader of their sect. The man who regularly flew up through the mecha god's portal, and sat at her feet, and took down her wisdoms. *Mecha Petrogon!*

He was younger than she'd expected, mid-forties at most, but every one of those years had been a trial. Mecha Petrogon's hair was entirely gray, a subtle complement to wings and armor that swirled the mottled blue of a cloudy sky. He bore deep scars down both cheeks, and Zenya could not tell if either of his arms was original.

But even more striking than his appearance was his demeanor. Mecha Petrogon carried a stillness with him like a living thing, an armor more impenetrable than the hardest metal.

Zenya slipped into line beside her teammates (three exasperated looks slewed in her direction—as though she'd known the occasion!), but Vodaya kept going, past the rest of the trainees, past her Winged colleagues on the sidelines, all the way to Mecha Petrogon's side.

A faint glow emanated from his skin, and as he smiled at Vodaya, she seemed to take on some of that glow. She was his favorite, his confidante, superseded by his quadrant leaders in rank only—and that not for long. (Was that Winged Raksa glowering on the sidelines? How inappropriate.)

"Pava!" Vodaya called. "You have assembled today to hear the word of the Voice. Listen well: he speaks of your path to the sky."

"Thank you," Mecha Petrogon murmured. He gazed at her with fond approval.

Zenya warmed at that look (she was being mentored by the Winged who had earned that look!), and then Mecha Petrogon paused, more commanding in his silence than any other Winged at full shout.

He spoke:

"When the gods went looking for a new home, they traveled the whole of the earth, and everywhere they bickered. The earth god required fertile land to sow. The creator god required metals and glass. The scholar god wished for linen and wood. The mecha god would not settle for an indefensible space, and the worker god despaired because they could not find a home that satisfied the needs of one without dissatisfying the rest.

"And then they crossed the mountains Kelior, and they found a quiet valley populated by an industrious people. This valley had vast acreages of land suitable for cottons and crops. It had untapped veins of metals in the hills, hidden beneath forests of dense oakwood. There was natural water and temperate weather, and best of all: mountains on all sides, stark and steep and filled with murderous beasts, the few trade passages narrow and easily guarded."

Petrogon's voice rose. "The gods blessed our ancestors with divine technologies. They gave us the means to build this city, to fill and feed and defend it. They gave us the means to enhance our bodies, to worship through perpetual improvement, to remake ourselves in their image. And of all the implants and chemical augments we've developed over the generations, none is more complex, more refined, more *divine* . . . than a warrior's wings."

He paused. The yard was silent, every breath held, every eye wide.

Gravely, Mecha Petrogon said, "Radezhda thrives due to our vigilance. The mecha god's warriors hold the mountain. They hold the plains. They form a barrier between our farmland and the states who wish to take it from us. Lord Menegal and Sovereign Allia would see us wiped from the earth, but they will be forever thwarted, because they lack conviction, and because they lack our blessings. Radezhda has the strength of five gods, but it is the benevolent wisdom of the mecha god that prevails over the rest. She is the mother and the judge. The maker of law.

"Only the best of you will earn wings. The rest will find other ways to serve the mecha god—and make no mistake, those support roles are vital to our sect. Here in the training grounds, you will eat, live, and breathe with your five-unit. You will do everything your Winged asks of you, and more. But never forget: the life of a Winged warrior is a singular one. A warrior stands alone before the mecha god, and alone before her enemies."

He gestured to the east, to tower Kemyana and the mountains beyond. "And that is why your final test is solo flight. If you prove yourself worthy in study and combat, you will receive mech ports. If you prove yourself capable with mech ports, you will choose the color of your wings. And if you are one of the mecha god's chosen, then on the night of your graduation you will attempt first flight. You will climb Ruk Head Mountain alone, with only your wings on your back and a torch in your hand. If you reach Vitalia's Cliff by dawn—and not all of you will—then your ascent to the mecha god's service is only a leap away." He considered them sternly. "You will have no help from your five-unit. You will have no instructor waiting in the valley to catch you. Those of you who reach the top of tower Kemyana will be warriors. The others will fall."

Mecha Petrogon nodded to Vodaya, his part in this complete. She raised both hands to the audience. "What say you, trainees?"

They thundered with applause.

Zenya returned to work with renewed excitement, visions of Ruk Head Mountain behind every lesson. In no scenario did she imagine herself joining the failures on the valley floor.

She lived and breathed and dreamed of first flight.

Vodaya never explicitly told Zenya that she was a permanent member of the five-unit, but months slipped by, and the possibility of rejection lessened. Zenya came to understand that this was Vodaya's way—she gave the most of herself and expected the most in return, and she considered reassurances a fiction-of-the-moment. Would Zenya last? That was up to Zenya.

And all of this would have been enough. It *should* have been enough. Zenya's life stretched out before her, shining and orderly: an early graduation, bright wings of copper, a tour on the border to show her mettle before returning for good to the city. She would rise at Vodaya's side, from unit commander to quadrant leader, training her own students, showing her family that this had been her path all along—

But it wasn't meant to be.

Conflict came to the city as it always did: in the form of a thought experiment.

CHAPTER EIGHT

The tower is complete and tomorrow is the day—oh I wish my grandfather were alive to see this.

I have heard these stories all my life, but I am terrified. What if it is not what we expect?

—*Diary of an unnamed worker*

ZEMOLAI STARED AT SCHOLAR PYETKA, struck dizzy by the realization that history was repeating itself.

Her entire life was changing, and Scholar Pyetka was there once again, his presence even more unexpected than the last time. He was dead. He was supposed to be dead. She'd *assumed* him dead, because she had seen the bag go over his head and she had never seen someone again after they'd been bagged.

Not only was her former teacher very much alive, but he was about to lead an unsupervised scholar service, something she had been assured was not happening anymore.

Zemolai slipped free of the curtain but hung back, leaning against the cool comfort of the adjoining wall. She pressed her fist hard against the wound in her upper thigh, gripping the resonance chip tightly, unable to stop her thoughts from spiraling. It couldn't be him. Of course it was him. But how could it be him? He had to be coming up on eighty-five . . .

The lanterns flashed a simple pattern of blinks, and the crowd sat down on the floor, murmuring apologies to one another as they bumped elbows and knees. Galiana had found her friends, but she hadn't told them what she'd done yet—they were relaxed, oblivious, while she darted nervous glances toward the back wall. Zemolai stared back at her, offering nothing.

The lanterns stopped blinking.

Pyetka opened his satchel, and a woman with lime-green fingers hurried over to help. She scooped up handfuls of dried kilva fruit and walked through the audience, handing each of them two or three pieces of the chewy, shriveled hallucinogen.

Zemolai, so recently cleared of toxins, wasn't about to volunteer. She watched from the comfort of her shadows as the other attendees nibbled their kilva. Within a minute, they were relaxed and swaying where they sat.

Scholar Pyetka looked over the room, patiently awaiting their readiness. His eyes alighted briefly on Zemolai and flicked away again, so quickly she might have imagined it.

When everyone was sufficiently intoxicated, he sat down, crossed his legs, and pulled the mirror into his lap. It was a beautiful affair, an oval pane of glass two feet tall inside a wrought iron frame. He had taken a considerable risk, transporting such an artifact.

The assistant clapped her hands. "The Scholar will begin. Are you ready for his words?"

Zemolai abruptly remembered her questioning by Winged Teskodoy (*Did he show you heretical materials?*), and she tensed, struck by a sudden and irrational fear. Had there been more to that question than rote investigation? What if the works of the Heretic Scholar had resurfaced, carried for decades in the memory of the only remaining scholar to have glimpsed their contents before they were suppressed?

But what followed was an ordinary service.

Scholar Pyetka began to sing. His voice was thick, cracked, burdened by a lifetime of the struggle for perfection. The only evidence of his decades of drug use was the bright gleaming moons of his eyes and the smoke in his song.

He spoke god words, summoning words. The air hung heavy with them, and sweet, like bits of sugar-preserved fruit slices in air gone to jelly. Zemolai ran her tongue over the roof of her mouth, grimacing at the candy taste.

As Scholar Pyetka continued singing, slow and melancholy and insistent, the taste intensified.

A faint light appeared in the depths of the mirror. One by one the dark reflections of the audience members winked out, leaving only that wisp in a sea of black. The light pulsed in time with the old scholar's song, drifting closer and closer until it turned the entire surface of the mirror a milky, glowing white.

The mirror reflected another location now, a place high above the city.

A portal.

The audience hummed along. It was a discordant blend of fifty doped-up people who didn't actually know the words, but together they made a powerful backdrop. The air vibrated with their intentions, and the cataract glow of the mirror brightened. A thin, dark crack appeared in the reflection, and with that fingerhold established, it began to widen.

The portal to the scholar god's heaven eased open, and pain twisted Zemolai's stomach at the sight.

Twenty-five floors above them, hovering over the roof of temple tower Zhelan, the portal would be gushing with light, a clear sign to anyone paying attention that somebody was accessing the god's domain. In the mirror's reflection the light was muted, flattened. The images they glimpsed were a jumble of oversaturated colors, like three lantern slides stacked one on top of the other. The kilva fruit helped relax the mind and blur the eyes, allowing the optical trickery of heaven to snap into focus, but it wasn't the only way.

Zemolai had years of practice under her belt. It only took her a moment's concentration to parse the vision. Brushstrokes of amber on emerald—that was down. Hints of silver and scorch—that was up. On this plane, the portal was fixed in place. But in that other world, it drifted, as free and delicate as an errant soap bubble. It passed over a strange and beautiful landscape, showing them layers of color and texture and complexity beyond comprehension.

Translated by the mirror, the scenery was a series of vibrant blots, tragically lacking the scent and sound and divine sensation of entering the realm in body. This was a poor substitute for traditional rites atop the tower, but it was all Pyetka could muster from so far away. At the scholar's mournful urging—every note of his song a somber plea—the portal drifted higher, higher, skimming up a structure like liquid metal, a structure of intertwined struts writhing lazily in and around one another, a tower built like a snake.

And at the top, for the briefest moment, they glimpsed a smooth chamber, hard and semitranslucent—and *there*, just visible, blurred through the casing: the feet of the sleeping god.

Gasps and cries filled the room, interrupting the humming chorus. The portal dipped again, spinning out over heaven, moving too quickly now to convey any detail. Scholar Pyetka's voice rose, and the audience tried to salvage their part, but the ritual had already broken down. The mirror clouded over, sliding shut like a great eye, forcing everyone back to bleak reality.

And Zemolai's heart panged, after all these years, as though the damned thing didn't realize it was supposed to be dead.

When was the last time she'd glimpsed the scholar god?

Scholar Pyetka let the connection close and then gently set aside his mirror. He walked the room quietly, handing out the second bit of candy he'd brought along—this one a downer to speed up the metabolizing of the kilva fruit.

Pyetka murmured sympathy and reassurances as he went. The worshippers clutched his hands and let the tears stream down their faces, bereft at having gotten a glimpse of their god and then losing him again.

Zemolai knew that pain too well.

Now she shifted, uncomfortable, her hips like mismatched doll parts grinding in their sockets, and she struggled against a surge of emotion. A realization was growing claws and feathers in her chest, and she didn't dare name it or she'd give it life. She stared at her feet, breathing shallowly to let it pass.

In her peripheral vision she saw Scholar Pyetka approach, a slow shuffle of a walk, and when he was almost upon her, she said, "I don't need your candy, old man."

He laughed, husky after all that raw-throated singing. "You don't need anything, do you, Milar Zemolai?"

Her head snapped up. She searched his face, but there was no anger there, no resentment, if she could rightly interpret the flat discs of his eyes. She didn't know what she was looking at, but she didn't like it.

"That isn't my name," she said softly.

"No," he agreed. "You have no district anymore. But that doesn't mean you don't serve."

An unfamiliar yearning struck her then, though she didn't know for what. "How are you here?" she asked. A sideways question, clumsy. *How did you escape? How did you survive?*

"With great difficulty," he said curtly. "Are you here to take me in?"

Her thigh throbbed. Her fist tightened around the resonance chip. She said, "No."

Pyetka considered her a moment before nodding, accepting this possible untruth. She wanted to warn him then—to hold open her fist and beg forgiveness—but her tongue stuck to the roof of her mouth at the thought.

Instead, one of Galiana's questions sprang to her lips, unbidden: "Would they have taken me back, do you think? After . . ." After that day.

"No."

Zemolai winced. It was the answer that she had expected, but that didn't make it any easier to hear. "We talked about theory once," she said. "Right before I joined the mecha sect."

Pyetka paused, brow furrowed as he searched his memory. "Yes," he said slowly. "Your parents asked me to advise you?"

Zemolai swallowed. It was the moment her path had become clear, all those years ago, and she'd turned his words over in her mind a thousand times since—but for him it had been one fleeting conversation among many. "My father," she corrected. "We discussed an essay of Lemain's, about the nature of the self. He believed we are every person we have ever been, continually."

"Ah." Pyetka softened in understanding, and his pity was worse than his spite would have been. "We are always living with the consequences of our actions, and in that sense the past is never truly past, no."

"And what do you think?" Zemolai asked guardedly. "Are you the same person you were on that day? Am I?" She didn't know which day she meant—the conversation or the black bag—but it didn't matter. Both of them. All of them.

"You're asking if we change." Pyetka turned stony. "I certainly hope so."

Scholar Pyetka turned to go, and she should have been relieved to see the back of him, but Zemolai wasn't ready. Any moment now the audience would recover, and Galiana would spring up with a load of outraged bolt-babies at her side, and Zemolai would release the beacon still clutched in her fist, but before that happened she had to say one more thing.

"Scholar!" she blurted. "I'm—I'm sorry."

Pyetka paused. In that moment, shoulders hunched and face drawn, he looked every one of his eighty-five years.

"I never read them, you know. The works of Scholar Vikenzy," he clarified, as though he could possibly mean anything else. Zemolai was too shocked to correct him—*Heretic* Scholar Vikenzy. The thought experiment she had gone to such lengths to suppress. The reason the bag had gone over his head.

Pyetka continued, almost wryly, "I would have, believe me! But the opportunity never presented itself. I heard the same rumor as everyone else—that a student had turned up an errant copy, misplaced in the upper archives. That this student was planning to publish without the approval of the robed scholars. Scholar Lemain quoted Vikenzy many times, but even *he* stopped short of reproducing the full text." Curiously, he asked, "Was it true? Or was it a mecha ruse, an excuse to come after us?"

Zemolai unglued her tongue. "It was true," she said. "But it was destroyed."

"Ah," he sighed. "More's the pity." Then Pyetka jangled his bag and asked, "Are you sure you wouldn't like a candy? No? Then I really must go."

He retreated back to his assistant, and they vanished into the depths of the temple maze with a god-mirror and a depleted satchel, back to a life lived underground until the next safe gathering requested a service.

The quiet of his absence was broken by Rustaya's now-familiar shout: "*What were you thinking!*"

Zemolai had been discovered. The bolt-babies came running, still wobbly with the aftereffects of their heavenly vision. Galiana got there first and physically blocked Zemolai with her body. "She needed to see this!" she insisted. "*Trust me.*"

Her leg was burning and her chest aching as Zemolai turned Pyetka's words over in her head. He'd never seen the papers. He was the one who had been tasked with the catalog on that floor, she'd been certain of it. So how could he not have seen them?

"Why did you bring me here?" she demanded. Her voice was ragged—let them think it was anger and not grief.

"Good question," Eleny said tightly. She glared at Galiana.

Galiana swallowed. "I wanted her to see what their edicts have done on the ground." She twisted around, imploring Zemolai directly. "I wanted you to see firsthand what they force people to do: hide, worship in secret, subsist on the barest glimpses of heaven for fear of being labeled seditionists. It isn't right. You *know* it isn't right. But it's different knowing a thing and seeing a thing. And," she admitted, "I thought it would strike a chord, to see a scholar's service."

Zemolai shut her eyes. She reflected, for a moment, on what she *should* be doing. Because what she *should* be doing was subduing a room full of criminals, alerting high command, and fulfilling some last shred of duty to this city.

For twenty-six years, she had served the mecha god—more than half her lifetime spent aloft, on patrol, on *alert*, creating order out of chaos for a slumbering giant that barely knew she existed. She had done so with a single-minded devotion that left no space in her life for anything else. Saint Radezhda had given her life for the city—who was Zemolai to give any less?

But now it was over. She looked inside, and the will to fight these children simply wasn't there. The violence had worn thin a decade ago, *two* decades ago. Zemolai didn't know what remained in the hollow spot where purpose had lived, but it wasn't duty.

The truth of the situation threatened to overwhelm her then. She felt, deep in her bones, that as soon as she faced reality, she was going to lie down and she wasn't going to get up again.

But she realized, to her surprise, that she did not actually want to die.

There wasn't much point to living anymore, but she wasn't ready for the afterlife, either.

Quietly, Eleny said, "I know this isn't ideal." Not even close. "I know that a lot has changed for you very quickly, and you have no reason to listen to a word I say. But I am asking you to wait. Just wait, and let us explain."

It was a bit of a joke, telling her they held a leash and then asking nicely. They knew it, she knew it. *Stay with us, or resume a painful death*, that's what they were saying.

There was a third option, of course. She could let go of the resonance chip. Let herself be found, and taken home, and judged a second time, now with a passel of prisoners along for an apology.

She thought of facing the mecha god again—facing *Vodaya* again—and panic washed through her like a flash fire. Zemolai slumped against the wall, the weight of this decision too much to bear.

Are you here to take me in? Scholar Pyetka had asked. A matter-of-fact question. She could not stop the scholar sect from flourishing in secret. She could only abscond with one of its adherents in yet another act of petty violence that did nothing to solve the underlying conflict.

This internal debate was a formality, her head catching up with her gut. Zemolai had made her decision the moment she saw the light from the scholar god's portal. "Yes," she rasped. "I'll stay another day."

Eleny let out a breath. "Thank you. Now—"

"There's something you should know." Zemolai held out her hand. They startled at the sight of her bloody palm—disgust from Rustaya, confusion from Timyan, and then Galiana's dismayed realization as she recognized the resonance chip for what it was.

Zemolai said it anyway. "Mecha command knows I'm still alive, and when this goes cold, they'll come and find me."

Their evacuation was swift, the underground maze reduced to its simplest configuration. Zemolai emerged, blinking, into her first sunlight in untold days. Her steps felt wobbly, her head fuzzy. Everything around her was moving entirely too fast.

She twisted to look at tower Zhelan, the source of so many memories, both comforting and cruel. There were few outward signs of trouble—a broken brick here, a mismatched window there. Old injuries.

And far above, half-obscured by clouds at the top of the tower, was a shimmer of light: the portal to the scholar god's heaven. Closed now, but thrumming with power.

Timyan ran off with the resonance chip, wrinkling his nose at the sticky teardrop of metal. He would dispose of it away from the tower and then run back. Zemolai was too tired to argue—it was already too late. When the chip cooled, the ground team would come looking for her. When they found a bloody chip with no body, they'd tear the surrounding neighborhood apart.

The remaining bolt-babies led Zemolai only two blocks away, to the third floor of an abandoned factory. The building hadn't turned out a product since the war, and likely never would again. Everything useful had been stripped away and sold over the years, replaced by the debris of two decades of squatters. Empty chemical drums littered the perimeter of the broad space, the ragged holes in their sides evidence of amateur theft.

Galiana pulled a pair of monocular lenses from her bag, and she and Rustaya settled down beside the south-facing window to wait, spying nervously in the direction Timyan had run.

"It won't matter," Zemolai said. Was she defiant? Morose? The inability to nail down her emotions was maddening: one moment dreading discovery, the next moment desperate for it.

Eleny gestured toward a rickety chair and said, "Well, you can't keep walking around like that, so sit down."

Zemolai bristled. She wasn't about to be mothered by a younger woman. But she was dizzy, and her leg was seeping. She sat down.

Eleny produced a first-aid kit from her bag and meticulously arranged the contents on a clean towel, then pinned open the tear in Zemolai's pants and swabbed the skin around her stab wound. There was a gentleness to the big woman's touch, thoroughly at odds with the rough field dressings Zemolai was accustomed to.

"I don't have a topical painkiller," Eleny warned, brandishing needle and thread. Zemolai arched an eyebrow and Eleny snorted. "Just letting you know."

Zemolai hissed at the first push of the needle and was immediately washed in self-loathing. She'd had shrapnel removed from her chest. Broken limbs. Every kind of burn, cut, stab, concussive impact. And here she was wincing at a pinprick like a baby being inoculated.

Eleny worked swiftly but neatly, humming all the while. She never once looked up at Zemolai's face, and Zemolai would have been grateful if she didn't hate the woman on principle. By the time the cut was closed, she had herself under control.

"Hm." Eleny eyed her work critically and gave a short, satisfied nod. She wiped the skin clean, taped an antiseptic bandage over the top, and immediately threaded a clean needle to repair Zemolai's pants.

"The blood's ruined them," she said. "But no sense walking around with the cloth gaping like that, hm?"

Zemolai didn't answer. Soon after, Timyan reappeared, harried but unhurt. Eleny ran to check on him, leaving Zemolai alone again with her thoughts while the group crowded the window.

She waited. And waited.

The minutes ticked by. An hour's worth. A deplorable response time even under siege conditions, and these weren't siege conditions. The tension leaked out of the bolt-babies' shoulders. They began to whisper jokes, elbowing one another at each punchline. And Eleny cut a glance at Zemolai, a solemn look that clearly said: *you see?*

Quietly, slowly, the truth became undeniable: nobody was coming. There would be no Pava ground team, no Winged commander, no attempt to carry Zemolai's supposed corpse to her final resting place beneath tower Kemyana. Winged Zemolai was dead, and she didn't even rate burying.

If the rebels were aware of her impending breakdown, they chose to politely ignore it. They turned their backs on her, caught up in the debate over where to go next. Zemolai tried to tune them out, to work through the firestorm of her thoughts in peace, but their voices kept breaking through.

"We can't stay here."

"They're not coming for her, though . . ."

No, they weren't, and now she felt the world's biggest fool for thinking they would.

"They might. If anyone gets curious. If anyone happens to look. There can't be any trace of us here to make things worse."

"Then where do you suggest?"

She had stood in that chamber with her own blood squeezing from her fist, looked into Scholar Pyetka's eyes, and told him she wasn't going to take him away again. A truth only told by accident. The universe, laughing: *You couldn't if you wanted to.*

That was the part that burned the most: that it hadn't been in her hands to begin with. Zemolai wanted something, *anything*, to happen by her own choice. She'd been cast aside. She'd been picked back up. When was the last time she had set her own course?

"A common house. Or perhaps . . ." An alternate location suggested by whisper.

"With *her* in tow? What are you thinking!"

"Well, what other option do we have?"

There was always another option. Galiana had already presented the one she wanted most. *I thought it would strike a chord, to see a scholar's service.* It had struck all right, but not the way the young woman had intended.

"We have to leave a message for Karolin." Their handler, referred to only by the name of a worker district. Clearly code.

"Karolin is the one who—"

"Not until we have a plan!"

If she helped them . . . Zemolai grimaced. The fact that she was even considering the matter was more evidence of her innate corruption. She wondered if this potential for betrayal had been simmering in her blood all along, or if the poison had only been planted recently.

If she helped them, there was something else at the training grounds. Something she had wanted to recover for a long time.

Zemolai shut her eyes, considering how such a foray might play out. The list of potential outcomes was unanimously terrible. Death. Arrest. An arrest inevitably ending in her death.

But she heard Pyetka asking, *Was it true? Or was it a mecha ruse?* And she remembered a day so long ago when she had briefly wondered the same. Her doubts had been allayed at the time—but had the evidence actually been that compelling, or had she only accepted it because Vodaya accepted it? It was blasphemy to question the Voice. (At the time, she had not been the Voice.)

A warrior wasn't supposed to make decisions out of anger—she wasn't supposed to strategize under the cloud of love or grief or resentment or revenge—but Zemolai wasn't a warrior anymore, was she? She was increasingly unwilling to live her life based on what she wasn't supposed to do.

And she wanted answers.

Zemolai stood so abruptly, she nearly upset Eleny's cart of first-aid supplies. The rebels turned, eyes slewing to the cart and its assortment of scissors and needles, assessing the risk of deranged attack by sewing kit.

"I'll get you into the training grounds," Zemolai said. "The grounds, the armory, whatever it is, I don't care."

Eleny drew in a sharp breath. Galiana straightened up, eyes shining, ready to bask in the victory her scholar service tactic had brought to them.

Zemolai finished: "But only if I come with you."

CHAPTER NINE

How fiercely they argued! It was remarkable to us, who had assumed them all to be of one mind. We began to understand the
differences in their philosophies, and align ourselves according
to the passions of our own hearts . . .

— Fragment 23f, *the Dierka Mountain Scrolls*

Two years passed before any trouble reached Zenya's small slice of the world.

She hadn't left Pava once in all that time. (There had been a few letters scribbled to Niklaus in the first year: *My schedule is sure to lighten up next week; I'll visit soon*—a lie.)

Instead, she spent that time immersed in her work. *Reveling* in it. After an uncertain start, Zenya was excelling in combat and classwork. Every day she saw herself reflected in Vodaya's eyes and could almost see the wings on her own back. She was fifteen, and the rest of her life waited just around the corner.

So it was a shock when Vodaya held everyone back after prayer one morning, her expression grim, to tell them that trouble was brewing in Radezhda, and had been for months.

Mecha Petrogon alighted among them to deliver the news, his commanders circling high overhead. He eyed them carefully, these devoted children awaiting his word, and he said:

"The scholar sect is helmed by a heretic."

Zenya recoiled. This was a grave accusation, one that wouldn't be made without serious evidence. But she'd met Lead Scholar Brekkia herself, and they did not seem the type.

Petrogon continued over the sudden outbreak of whispering. "It has long been rumored that Heretic Scholar Vikenzy's papers are still being preserved in the archives of tower Zhelan. Lead Scholar Brekkia's predecessors swore they were destroyed—but scholars dissemble."

Zenya's heart sank as he went on. Whatever hope she'd had for a misunderstanding quickly vanished, because what followed sounded exactly like her childhood sect.

Scholar Brekkia had ordered a full survey of the archives—the first one in decades—and one of their students found a hidden trove of documents: assorted papers carefully bound together and padlocked shut. Rather than leave them there (*you gave a student every key on the ring*, Zenya wanted to say, *of course they would not leave them there*), the student had pulled the documents for personal research.

There were rumors now that a new theory was being written based on their contents.

A little thought experiment.

"Scholar Brekkia is allowing this," Mecha Petrogon warned. "They are letting the works of a madman recirculate—a man who doubted the most basic tenets of our belief. This *will* lead to strife. This *will* lead to innocent Radezhdeans dragged from the path of the five gods.

"Our only defense against the outside world is our united front. Our *only* defense! Saint Radezhda died to bring the people of this city together, and for hundreds of years that sacrifice has held us strong. But make no mistake, if the scholar sect sets us against one another, our enemies will storm our borders. They will destroy Radezhda, and take its towers for themselves—but only if we let them."

An entire generation of trainees leaned in to hear more—how they were special, how they were burdened with glory—and Mecha Petrogon gave them all that they wanted. When he left, the five-units clustered around their instructors, bubbling over with questions.

"How long do we have?"

"What must we do?"

Quietly, Zenya asked, "What *is* the new theory?"

Vodaya considered her for a long moment, unreadable. Finally, she said, "It's immaterial. Not only is it immaterial, it is heretical, and if I find out that any of you—*any of you*—are in possession of heretical materials, or entertaining these scholar theories, you will be cut from my unit and the Pava program entirely, do you understand?"

There was no time for alarm.

(That would come later: a long night awake in bed, wondering how rapidly things might have changed in the greater city; wondering how easily her bright-eyed brother might be taken in by agitators. She wrote to him: *have you heard about this?* He only answered: *you should visit.*)

The Pava trainees were told to prepare themselves, should the worst come to pass (this was a phrase repeated ominously every morning; opinions varied on what, exactly, the worst would look like when it arrived).

Vodaya was their island in a storm-laden sea. She praised them, and they glowed; she called for their bravery, and they felt themselves capable of fighting monsters.

Privately, Zenya was conflicted, half of her thoughts aimed homeward. None of the rumors that floated through Pava were any consolation. The scholars were denying the existence of Vikenzy's papers. Or they were already producing copies. Or this was all the work of a Rava State spy, embedded in the scholar sect to sow chaos and doubt. (Zenya almost preferred this version; at least it took the onus off Milar.)

Finally, she went to Vodaya to confess her worry. "I know it must be true," she said. "But how can it be true?"

Vodaya only said, "Come pray with me." She led Zenya down the hall, to a quiet room full of shrines, each one a semiprivate nook with a kneeling bench and an offering dish. There was one other supplicant there when they arrived, but at the sight of Vodaya she blew out her candle and left.

Zenya knelt beside her, shadowed by the deep silhouette of her wings, and tried to still the tremor of her own heart. She stared at the simple sculpture on the wall: a dagger held in a silver fist.

Vodaya said, "I know this is difficult for you."

Zenya turned, surprised at the soft tone. Vodaya's face was creased deeply, not with disappointment but with sympathy. "You love your family," she said. "There's no fault in that."

Zenya whispered, "I'm afraid. What if they've been caught up in all this?"

The candlelight caught in Vodaya's hair, illuminating the first strands of silver working their way out from her temple. "I admire your compassion," she said slowly, "but there is an important lesson here. Are you ready to hear it?"

Zenya nodded, unable to speak, and Vodaya said: "You cannot take on the weight of others' insecurities. As you grow, you'll learn that some people have a lack within their heart, a need they can't name, and they will cast about for anything to fill it. The scholar sect, though pious on their face, is tailor-made to attract such people. The truth is not enough for them; they continue to ask questions, to dig for another answer, and another, never satisfied. You know the truth, and you have forged your path accordingly. They have chosen theirs, and it is not your responsibility or your fault. Let us pray that they come around."

They prayed.

Zenya tried to take Vodaya's words to heart, but she couldn't stop thinking of those rumors, and her brother, and she needed her fears to be put to rest.

She found her opportunity eight days later. Word had spread that Mecha Petrogon was going to put forth an official demand at the Council of Five: he wanted unanimous approval before the publication of new histories.

Outrage from the scholar sect was to be expected, but there were murmurs of a demonstration being planned during the next council meeting, not from the scholars, but the engineers. The creator god's people had grievances of their own against the mecha sect, and were using this new strife to make their voices louder.

Mecha Petrogon was bringing a hand-selected five-unit to the meeting in a show of solidarity. One of his chosen was, of course, Vodaya, and that left Zenya free for the day.

"I trust you will all make good use of the downtime," Vodaya said wryly, and Zenya nodded because a nod felt like less of a lie.

Vodaya left, and Zenya's teammates dispersed toward lunch and leisure. Zenya muttered something about taking a jog, and then she grabbed her day bag and made a run for it.

It was a shock to leave the training grounds. A shock to walk roads that she remembered like a dream. For two years, her social circle had been restricted to a simple five-unit. The city outside Pava District was both familiar and very strange.

To get to Milar, Zenya first had to walk through Zavet, a worker district and this month's location for the open-air council meeting. Each sect, even the farmers on their sprawling land outside the city walls, had an amphitheater for politics and entertainment and entertainment-like politics. The workers' meeting place was modest in design: a half-moon of stone steps facing a broad stage. Upon that stage were five stone pavilions, each upon a raised dais—lovingly carved re-creations of the resting places of the gods the council members were there to represent.

Ordinarily, these meetings were sparsely attended. But Zenya slowed at the sound of commotion long before the amphitheater came into view. It was the chaos of a thousand voices striving and failing to synchronize. Three or four different chants competed for dominance, full of words like *food* and *family* and *fair pay*.

Two blocks away, she was forced to a halt. Hundreds of people stretched from the amphitheater entrance to the steps of a storage building across the street. Even more wended out of sight into the alleys on either side. Zenya couldn't recall a council meeting ever filling an audience, much less running out of room, and this one hadn't even started yet.

There were workers in their aprons and gloves, office girls toting handmade signs, kitchen staff waving wooden spoons with holes drilled through the center. Standing at intervals around the edge of the human mass, there were engineers on stilts, shouting encouragement through handheld amplifiers as they long-leg-walked back and forth.

She looked up. Yes, there they were: mecha warriors arranged on the surrounding rooftops, overlooking the proceedings with their wings outstretched.

Zenya's stomach turned uneasily at the aggressiveness of the display, and she took a long detour around the surrounding blocks to get past. By the time she reached Milar, the morning had dragged past noon, and her worries about the meeting were entirely supplanted by a thread of panic at the sight of her own front door.

What if nobody was home? (What if somebody was home?) She forced herself to knock before she could question why she felt the need to knock and then jumped back a step to wait.

Just when she thought her errand had been in vain, her brother's face appeared in the window: wary, then startled, then pleased—and then unaccountably wary again.

Zenya laughed nervously. "Are you letting me in?"

There was a pause, a far-too-long pause, before the door finally opened.

Niklaus stood straighter than she remembered. *Taller.* He wore his hair in a sleek, black knot, and he carried an air of gravitas that Zenya could scarcely reconcile with her memory of her little brother. He was barely fourteen and looked like a man.

"What are you doing here?" he asked.

"What's that supposed to mean?" Zenya exclaimed. "I'm visiting."

He looked behind her, as though expecting her to have brought company, and then he said, "Come on, hurry."

The inside of the house was nearly as she remembered it, the small changes more jarring than a renovation would have been (that picture was in the wrong place; these shelves were new; it was her home and it wasn't). Brother and sister stared at one another in the foyer, taking the same uneasy catalog of one another.

Then Niklaus sighed (sighed!) and poked her biceps. "Look at you. What are they feeding you?"

Zenya hunched with a self-conscious laugh. Combat training had thinned her out where she'd been round, and thickened her muscles where she'd been lean. It was another source of anxiety she didn't want to think about here. Every pound she weighed over the average slim-bred Pava was another pound of strain on a wing rig.

But Niklaus wasn't laughing. "Aren't you supposed to be putting down a protest?" he asked. "Off to strong-arm in the name of your Voice?"

Zenya drew back. "If you mean the council meeting," she said slowly, "Mecha Petrogon is there to speak . . ."

"With a little army of Winged, no doubt."

She nearly squawked. "As a show of support!"

"You mean show of force. It's an intimidation tactic—"

"That's not why I'm here!"

They stared at one another again, no longer the guarded cataloging but a raw assessment. Far more had changed between them than hair styles and muscle mass.

"Why then?" Niklaus asked. Unspoken, pained: *why now? Why not earlier?*

She hadn't meant to have this conversation in the foyer, but she tried anyway. "I should have visited sooner. I wanted to. It's been nothing but exercise and study and training and . . . that's no real excuse, except to say I really did mean to. I'm here now because I'm worried."

He nodded gravely. "What are they planning?"

"They?" Zenya shook her head. "I'm worried about *you*. I heard . . . there are rumors that someone has turned up the works of Heretic Scholar Vikenzy. Is it true?" She didn't know why she was asking. Of course it was true.

Niklaus searched her face for a moment, a whisper of desperate humor on his own, as though he were waiting for a joke to land. And then his expression shuttered. Too cautiously, he said, "I've heard the rumors, too. That's probably all they are. Rumors."

And Zenya was struck by the sudden, disorienting conviction that her brother was lying to her. That faint flush on his cheeks. The tilt of his shoulders. She'd been away for two years, but they'd spent every day together before that. She knew him. He was lying.

"Promise me you won't read them," she said, desperate and despairing.

Niklaus looked away. "Even if they do exist, they're only an old scholar's essays."

"Promise me!"

"I'm just saying, even if we find Scholar Vikenzy's—"

"*Heretic* Scholar Vikenzy."

"Yeah, sure. Heretic Scholar Vikenzy." He shrugged, annoyed. "Even if we find his papers, they're only one man's reflections. One opinion among many."

This sounded like a memorized talking point. Lead Scholar Brekkia was probably saying the same thing at the Council of Five that very moment, hands spread, imminently reasonable. There was a time Zenya would have felt the same.

"But there *is* a new theory," she said. "I know there is." *Don't lie.*

He nodded, jaw set stubbornly. "Yes. The scholars are producing a new volume of research on the origins of the Five. It is our legal and religious right to publish. It's nothing to do with Mecha Petrogon, and he has *no right* to interfere! Oh, Zenya—"it was a shock, to hear her familiar name after years of formality; and now his voice turned dreamy, the Nushki she remembered relating the contents of a new book—"they're letting me assist the catalogers. I've touched primary sources. Originals! The words of the saints, written by their own hands. Don't you miss it? Wouldn't you walk the archives, if you could?"

Zenya shut her eyes. She could feel the rasp of rag paper on her fingertips; could smell the familiar blend of dust and ink. She'd spent her toddlerhood under her mother's desk; her adolescence in the family library. Her teachers had all spoken so rapturously of those upper stories of the tower, where history was bound and preserved.

And then Niklaus said, "I have a draft. Would you like to read it?"

Her eyes snapped open. She should have said no, instantly and angrily. But oh, she wanted to know what she was supposed to be fighting against.

"You swear to me?" she said. "You swear to me this is not the heretic's work?"

"This is not the heretic's work," Niklaus said, and she knew he was being too specific, but she followed him down the hall anyway.

Niklaus entered his bedroom, where he stood framed against a backdrop of floor-to-ceiling books and papers, very much the scholar in his natural habitat. Zenya hovered inside the doorway, too jittery to take a seat even if there had been a spot cleared. For the first time in her life, she felt like an intruder in her brother's space.

"It's only a draft," he warned, digging around the chaos of his desk. "Scholar Pyetka invited me to give notes." He produced an unbound sheaf of papers and shoved them into her hands. His handwriting was a familiar scribble in the margins.

"Why are our gods and our gods alone accessible through physical portals?" Niklaus asked. "Why are they sleeping above Radezhda, when our neighbor states have only invisible gods to worship?"

He held up a finger.

"Because maybe they aren't gods at all."

Frozen as she was—faced with a horror she'd never imagined from a source she didn't expect—Zenya could only listen, speechless, as her brother outlined his mad hypothesis.

She thought: he'd always been prone to flights of fancy; eager to follow every silly argument to its furthest, least plausible end; susceptible to the new, exciting, and strange.

She thought: this is all my fault for leaving him alone.

In her hands she held a diagram: five figures in pods, connected by numerous lines and annotated with questions in Niklaus's cramped handwriting.

"Begin with one supposition," Niklaus said. "That the beings in the sky are from another place. Travelers. Then we ask: why would they travel? Perhaps they are not gods, but *scientists*, on an expedition. There is ample evidence that the metals we mine from the mountains Kelior are not native to the earth. So perhaps the metals crashed here, long before the mountains formed. Have our gods been here just as long? Or did they come here to mine it themselves?" He shrugged. "Either way, they came, but never left. They're sleeping, maybe waiting for a rescue vessel to reach them. It's possible that what we think of as heaven is their broken ship, and what we think of as portals are simply doorways. They seem divine, but only because the technology is so far beyond us."

Zenya flipped through the pages, faster and faster, hunting for the punchline that surely followed, the moment a metaphor was unveiled to collapse the theory back into doctrine.

Niklaus misread her expression. "Think about it!" he said. He began to tick points away on his fingers. "Who do you bring on an expedition? A researcher to conduct experiments and catalog findings—that's the scholar god. A botanist to grow food and test the feasibility of new land—that's the earth god. A mechanic to maintain the ship's equipment—the creator god. You need somebody to pilot and staff the other stations—the worker god—and you need some kind of security, especially entering unknown environments. The mecha god! Now, we *know* they were awake for a while, sharing technology and teachings. But some of the early writings, before the gods chose sleep, are really very odd, for instance—what? What is it?"

Zenya finally choked out, "Is *that* what they're teaching you?" She crushed the papers in her fists. "That there aren't any gods, just some idiots from another planet who got lost? Bloody Vitalia, Nushki! I'm not worshipping some—some kind of *alien security guard!*"

Niklaus grabbed the papers from her and began to smooth them out. "It's a *theory*," he said. "A thought experiment. Gods or aliens, what does it matter?"

"It matters to me!" Zenya was so furious she thought she would start screaming. "I'm devoting my *life* to this path," she said. "I believe in the way of the gods. I believe we each have a purpose and a place. And you think it's some stupid *misunderstanding?*"

Niklaus reached for her hand. She yanked it away. And now he was fully fourteen, rolling his eyes at his big sister's foolishness. "If you believe in the path you're following, it shouldn't matter who penned the text." He spread his hands. "Faith isn't believing in gods, it's believing in their wisdom."

She laughed—she couldn't help it. It was a short bark of a thing, a laugh pleading for a joke. But Niklaus had none to offer.

They stared at one another, stalemated, unable to reconcile this sudden incompatibility after a lifetime of agreement. She wondered: how could this have happened so quickly?

Subdued now, Zenya said, "I have to go back. But I want to keep talking about this. How about you write to me more often? Please?" She thought maybe, if nothing else, she could temper this. She could rein him in, so he wasn't only hearing one side of things.

Niklaus hesitated. Zenya wanted to take his hands in hers. (She did not take his hands in hers.)

"Fine," he said, and the word had scarcely left his mouth before the floor shook beneath their feet. Zenya's eyes widened in recognition—and then the unmistakable sound of an explosion reached them, rattling the books on their shelves.

She ran out of the house, Niklaus close on her heels. "Stay here!" she cried. There, from Zavet District: a billowing plume of smoke.

Zavet was transformed.

The air was filled with dust; the roads with fleeing protesters. Some were unscathed, others covered in weeping cuts, still others dragging bloody limbs, their faces rictuses of terror. Deeper within the cloud, blurrier forms lay still on the ground, including engineers still attached to shattered stilts and office girls in crumpled heaps beneath their protest signs.

Zenya had been in earthquakes before. She'd been in cleanup crews after fires and sealed windows against storms—but this was bigger, this was terrifying, this was beyond anything she'd ever seen.

She fought through the current of bodies, struck by stray elbows, tripping over discarded signs. Wails of pain sent her heart skyrocketing—pockets of silence were somehow even worse. She thought: maybe it wasn't the amphitheater. (Of course it was the amphitheater.)

The entrance to the public seating area was not clogged, as she'd expected, but damningly open. Those who could run had already done so. Zenya clambered over a pile of loose stones and into the arena. She saw:

Lead Scholar Brekkia with their leg a bloodied mess, leaning heavily on a knot of students. Farmer Udyll covered in dust and Worker Hyte with his arms full of lawbooks. Daises cracked, the metaphorical beds of the gods damaged beyond repair.

And at the epicenter: Mecha Petrogon trapped under the rubble of his pavilion. His head and shoulders were free, but his legs—Zenya's stomach turned. They were buried beneath two tons of granite.

His Winged entourage was struggling to dig him out. Zenya immediately sought out Vodaya—and there she was, laboring to his left. One side of her face was white with dust. The other side was red, blood running freely from a cut at her hairline, but she was alive, she was all right, there was no reason to panic. Vodaya hauled at a huge piece of stone, wider around than a human torso, and her shoulders strained at the weight. It came loose from the pile, and she jumped back, letting it roll away.

"*Vodaya.*" It was Petrogon, stretching out one shaky hand.

Vodaya froze, crouched over the next piece of debris. They stared at one another, a silent argument that only they could parse, and then to Zenya's shock, Vodaya said, "No."

He repeated her name, imploring, and she shook her head. She was visibly furious, turning away to grab another stone, but then Petrogon insisted, he summoned the Voice and pitched it to a terrible thunder: "*Vodaya, attend to me. Winged, disperse.*"

Zenya clapped her hands to her ears. Cries of protest rang out around the amphitheater. Petrogon's Winged paused, fraught, and then they *complied*, they actually stepped away and left him to the rubble—

And then she realized what she was seeing. Petrogon believed he was dying. None of his highest commanders were there, and he wanted Vodaya to hear his last words.

Vodaya knelt beside him, providing a privacy shield with her body. The city was still howling behind them. Pockets of activity coalesced around the remaining injured, with surgeons finally arriving with their hastily grabbed bags and seemingly all of Pava pouring in around the outskirts. Vodaya and Petrogon were a spot of stillness in the chaos, and Zenya could only imagine what Vodaya was going through, serving witness to her commander, her mentor, the man who had sponsored her wings and guided her up the ranks.

Vodaya drew back, her shock visible across the arena. Petrogon grabbed at her arm, insistent, sorrowful. He spoke a few minutes more, then fell back, and Vodaya rose to her feet.

The other Winged rushed in to continue the rescue attempt. They had regrouped during the pause and returned now with straps to haul the final stones away and a harness with which to carry Petrogon away to their own surgeons.

Vodaya walked—no, *stumbled* away, wearing an expression that Zenya had never seen on her before. There was a bloody handprint on her arm where Petrogon had clutched at her, shockingly red.

Zenya's paralysis broke, her worry for Vodaya overcoming her fear of being asked which direction she'd come from. She ran across the open ground. Breathless, she asked, "Are you all right? What happened?"

Vodaya stared at her. Through her. "He told me . . ." She was in a distant place, full of grief. And then she shook it off. Stiff and angry, she said, "He spoke privately, Pava."

Zenya shrank back from the heat in her voice. "Of course. I'm sorry."

Vodaya cast about the arena, looking for a target. "Look there," she said, pointing. Creator Talley, the engineers' representative, stood to one side with his partner, Vanyamir. In the midst of so much destruction, they were conspicuously uninjured. "Not even a scratch," Vodaya spat. "Talley stepped down from his pavilion minutes before the explosion, claiming he needed a consult with Vanyamir. The engineers attacked us today, make no mistake, and we will find all who aided them. Our investigation begins today."

It was hard to believe the engineers so ruthless—at a glance: one grandfatherly and petite, the other a stately older woman, gray hair twisted neatly behind her head—but Zenya wasn't about to argue. "Of course," she said again.

Vodaya fixed her with a burning glare. "Terrible times have come to Radezhda. This is civil war. By the grace of the mecha god, it won't last long, but lacking her grace we need everyone in fighting shape as quickly as possible."

Zenya nodded, too shocked to offer much else.

Something in her expression must have raised Vodaya's ire, because she added, "This won't be the last disaster you witness, and it won't be the worst. Learn how to live with it now, or leave. Do you understand?"

"Yes," Zenya said. She swallowed, her throat dry. "What about the scholars? Where do they stand in all of this?"

Vodaya paused, expression inscrutable, and then she cupped Zenya's cheek, her hand warm and smelling of copper. "I only have one thing to tell you, and then we get to work. Hm?"

She waited for Zenya to nod, and then she said, "I don't give a *shit* where the scholars stand, and neither do you. From this moment forward, we are a five-unit in true: four limbs and a head. I speak it, and I need it done. You aren't Milar Zemolai anymore. You haven't been that girl since you stepped inside my fight ring.

"You are *Pava* Zemolai. Don't you dare forget it."

This was the moment, though she didn't understand at the time: the moment that everything changed. Mecha Petrogon spoke his heart's deepest truths to Winged Vodaya, his mentee and confidante, his hope for the future of their chosen sect.

And she was never the same.

CHAPTER TEN

Such gifts they gave us! Things wonderful and strange . . .
   We asked: How have you come by such magics?
   And they laughed, and said: These are common technologies where we come from.
                    —Fragment 25, *the Dierka Mountain Scrolls*

T HE BOLT-BABIES didn't react well to Zemolai's proposition (why would they want a once-Winged warrior at their back during a risky mission?), but they tabled the argument until they could reach a new hiding place far from the scholar tower.

They settled on a common house, one of those last-resort living arrangements in Radezhda's border district. The district itself was a narrow slip of a non-neighborhood between Ario District and the northern city wall, oft-ignored. The house was less of a house and more of a compound, containing dozens of cramped apartments. Citizens of all ages and backgrounds roomed there, some for a few desperate days, and others for the rest of their lives.

This was a side of the city many preferred not to exist. All of the mecha sect's efforts—and they were continuous—couldn't eliminate the indecisive, the uninitiated, or the impoverished.

Zemolai would not stand out in this motley crowd.

They packed into the front room of a small apartment. It was sparsely furnished: a stained kitchenette, three rickety chairs, and a pile of moth-eaten cushions, a general air of secondhand despondency. Zemolai dragged one of the chairs to an isolated corner and sank down, her joints creaking in tune with the wood.

Timyan pulled out his notebook and consulted a scribbled chart. "If we're still on last week's patrol schedule, we have a good three, four days before these rooms are checked."

"More than enough!" Rustaya flopped down onto the pile of mismatched cushions, sending up a cloud of dust. Galiana unrolled a thin sheet from her pack, shaking it fastidiously to drape over her seat, but Rustaya hooked her by the leg and brought her tumbling down with a squeak and a protest: "Rustaya!"

"Let's unpack," they said. They flipped open their bag to reveal a neat row of glass bottles separated by rolled shirts.

"Don't tell me that's all you brought!" Galiana exclaimed, but there was a laugh behind the protest.

Giddiness filled the air. They had managed to slip a series of dire circumstances—escaping the tower, hiding underground with a Winged prisoner, dodging Zemolai's laughable attempt to bring a patrol down upon their heads—and now they were safe for a brief stint of shelter and companionship before they headed back into danger again.

Of course they'd brought drinks.

"We have planning to do," Eleny said sternly, but she didn't turn down the bottle that Rustaya shook enticingly at her.

"Here," said Timyan. He grabbed two and held one out for Zemolai, a half-smile forming. She hesitated, then took the bottle, nodding once in thanks.

"To Chae Savro!" Galiana declared. The others murmured agreement and took their first swigs. Zemolai pulled her cork and winced at the sharp smell that wafted up. It didn't go down smoothly, but it did go down, and the warmth hit her stomach like a punch.

"So," Zemolai said, trying not to cough. "When is this thing happening?"

Eleny gave her a rueful look. "Tomorrow night there's going to be a graduation ceremony atop tower Kemyana. That's our window, while the training grounds are minimally staffed."

Zemolai did a quick calculation and grimaced—if graduation was one day away, then it had been ten days since her judgment, with half that time spent berserk. An eternity ago and no time at all.

She also now understood the urgency that had driven Galiana to gamble on releasing her. One day away . . . they'd lost their minds.

"It's a terrible idea," Eleny declared. "Taking you onto the grounds. You know this."

Zemolai shrugged. "You could shackle me to a bed. I'll give you a head start before I start slamming the walls, but you'd have to get into the armory without me. What was your original plan? Another bomb?"

"Something like that," Eleny sighed.

"Let me work!" Galiana wriggled out of Rustaya's grasp and joined Timyan in the middle of the room. They sat down hip-to-hip, spreading their papers in a semicircle, debating whether to broach the training grounds via this entryway or that, periodically raising their drinks to toast old friends and damn their enemies.

Timyan's nervousness evaporated under her undivided attention. When Galiana smiled, he beamed. When Galiana laughed, he chattered on with full confidence, extolling the merits of a servants' tunnel with an easy door-code system.

They'd built in bypasses when they worked on the grounds—a chilling thought, but that was the danger of engineers in workers' guise, wasn't it?

Zemolai frowned at that. "Door codes are one thing," she said. "But minimal staffing isn't zero staffing. The first person to spot you will pull the alarm, and then every Winged in the city will come dropping down the side of tower Kemyana."

An awkward hush fell, and Galiana glanced at the others before answering. "Karolin has a team working on a systems upgrade. They can ensure that the perimeter alarms are disabled during the ceremony. The four of us—five of us, now, I suppose—can handle a few trainees on our way out."

Zemolai was struck silent for a moment at the depths of their infiltration. She was a hypocrite, she knew, entering the grounds herself and providing them the armory code, but what they were doing was a step beyond.

Almost choked, she said, "You've said that name before—Karolin. Who are they?"

"You know we're not telling you that," Eleny murmured.

"You understand this handler of yours is setting you up for failure, don't you?" Zemolai demanded. "Alarms or not, you're known fugitives. The mecha sect will pin this to you even if you do manage to slip through unseen."

"I'm aware," Eleny said calmly. "Better that they add this to our list of crimes than turn their suspicions on the training-ground workers."

Zemolai shut her mouth after that.

It seemed her life was determined to fold upon itself, following the pattern of her youth. Zemolai was studying the ways of a five-unit again, but this one was loose, undisciplined. Four limbs and a head: that was the proper arrangement. But this team was on its own, their leader little more than a code name, and they were four limbs with no notion where they were being walked.

As their plan coalesced and their bottles emptied, the conversation drifted inevitably and regrettably toward current events.

"Word is, there's a curfew coming," Galiana said.

"For what reason?" Timyan exclaimed.

"Trouble with day merchants overstaying their pass, apparently."

Rustaya brooded on their cushion pile, their drink in one hand, dissatisfaction radiating like spikes. When they were agitated, they tapped their implant fingers against a skeletal leg, *tata tat tat*. Occasionally they shouted an interjection.

"YEAH, IF YOU BELIEVE THAT BULLSHIT!"

Or:

"THAT'S WHAT THEY'D LIKE YOU TO THINK!"

And then Eleny would shush them, and Timyan would turn bright red and make that nervous grimace like he was about to have a stroke from the embarrassment of it all, and—oh bloody Vitalia, how did Zemolai end up in this mess?

They were comfortable. Boisterous. *Bonded.* They were Zemolai's old training unit, before she joined their ranks. And she was a slumbering bear at the back of the cave, trying to block out their camaraderie, their jokes, the relationships that emerged as they let their guard down.

Her mood worsened, aided along by Rustaya's truly noxious alcohol, and she turned her thoughts inward—always a mistake.

And then Galiana began drunkenly speculating about the service they had just seen beneath tower Zhelan. "What do you suppose is at the bottom? We always see the top of the landscape, the god's bed . . . what's below? How is there so much space if they're above us?"

"Are you a scholar now, too?" Zemolai interrupted. "How could you ask that?"

Galiana blinked at her, taken aback. "I want to know more about the nature of the gods," she said. "We all should."

"No," Zemolai said fiercely. "We shouldn't."

Nothing had changed. The engineers and the scholars still believed the gods could be understood with science and study, as though humankind was even meant to understand them. Their constant questioning of the moral order—their constant pushing and blaspheming—had brought civil war down on all of their heads, and for what? Nothing. The state of Radezhda today was worse than before.

But Galiana was unfazed. "Why are they sleeping?" she asked. "How long has it really been? Have we strayed from their intentions? We shape our lives by their teachings. Shouldn't we know more about them?"

"You don't know what you're talking about," Zemolai said.

"That is exactly what I am saying. We don't know—"

"I said, *you don't know what you're talking about,*" Zemolai repeated, and now she was angry, a week's worth of angry, two decades' worth of angry. "You all sit there spinning theories like the gods are a logic puzzle, like they aren't real, and alive, and sleeping above this city. I've *seen* my god. I've been in her *presence.* I've felt her *judgment.*" Zemolai's breath hitched, her back on fire with the memory.

The room had gone deathly quiet, all merriment ended. Timyan had one hand on Galiana's arm, urging quiet, but she insisted, "The scholar god values free thinking."

Zemolai shook her head. "Maybe the scholar god likes those games, but he's the only one. The earth god doesn't have *hypothetical* farming. The creator god doesn't ignore *math*. Do the mecha god's teachings leave room for dissent? No. But you insist on riling people up anyway, filling their heads with questions, pitting them against one another, leading them off their paths, and for what? So that idiot boys can ruin their lives, bashing their heads against the prescribed order, fighting and dying over nothing—" Zemolai stopped, choked up and furious.

"It's not nothing," Galiana said, but falteringly now.

Zemolai was struck dizzy. She couldn't tolerate the weight of this building over her head, the air dense with everyone else's breath, all of their eyes on her.

Eleny finally interjected, a soft but firm, "She's done for tonight."

Zemolai glared at her, pained and angry that Eleny could see it. Without another word, she dropped her drink and left for one of the bare little bedrooms at the back of the flat. It had one narrow window and a lone, wilted plant, and Zemolai climbed under threadbare sheets that had seen more bodies than she cared to know.

The dizziness soon subsided, but Zemolai could not bring herself to rise. She was thirsty, but her body would not cooperate. At first, she convinced herself it was physical exhaustion that kept her bedridden, continued recovery from her ordeal in the cage. But as one hour dragged into three, she knew that it wasn't only her body that needed mending. She lay awake, staring at the bare walls of her ten-by-ten, unable to move.

Sometime later, the door creaked open.

A weight pressed down the mattress at her back. Eleny didn't touch her, but the warmth of her body reached out, making phantom contact. "Take your time," she said softly. "What's done took decades. It can't be undone in days. Give yourself permission to feel it."

This was laughable advice, because Zemolai was currently feeling nothing at all, and she intended to *continue* feeling nothing at all for the rest of her natural life. She was only tired; too tired to bother explaining that she was only tired.

"Did you ever doubt?" Eleny asked. Soft, curious—far too familiar.

"No," Zemolai said swiftly. "Never." And then, a truth spoken to the wall: "It wasn't like this at the beginning."

She immediately regretted the clarification. She recalled those early days, the thrill of purpose and the glory of the god-light, when everything had been clear.

"What changed?" Eleny asked.

An image flashed before her eyes: Mecha Petrogon in the rubble, one hand outstretched. Zemolai shut her eyes. "I don't know."

"Either something changed, or it was always going to be like this," Eleny said, far too reasonably. "What happened? When did it go wrong?"

She pictured Vodaya, stricken, serving witness to what she thought were Petrogon's last words; Vodaya, staggering away with his bloody handprint on her arm. The dark days that followed.

"She never lied," Zemolai said, unable to resist the impulse to defend Vodaya, even now. "For all her faults, she never lied. Her whole life has been dedicated to the mecha god. All that's happened—it's in her name."

Eleny made a soft sound like *fah*, but she let the matter drop. An endless minute later her warmth slipped away, leaving Zemolai alone to contemplate the cracks in the wall.

The bolt-babies whispered long into the night. Their voices rose and fell, a gentle susurrus like a predawn wind, and it was to this almost-familiar lullaby that Zemolai tossed and turned, chewing over and over on the same old question until she finally fell asleep:

What really happened that day?

Zemolai awoke late the next morning—not refreshed, but no longer in the state of paralysis that had struck the night before. She shambled out to the common room to take her pill from Eleny, and then she retreated, wordless, to the shower room. She stayed under the hot water for as long as she could bear it.

The others were already packed when she came out again, looking only marginally worse for wear following their night of revelry. Galiana glanced at her nervously. Timyan wouldn't meet her eyes.

Eleny approached, gesturing her to the semiprivacy of the corner. "We need to talk about last night."

That tone! So condescendingly parental. "There's nothing to talk about," Zemolai grumbled.

"There *is*." Eleny dropped her volume, as though everyone else couldn't hear her all the same in this tiny space. "You're not in Pava anymore. We worship—really, we do—but our reverence doesn't look the same as yours. Why should it? Rustaya and I grew up in Chae District. Do you know what that's like? I was lucky enough to work on a breadline, but next door was a metal-stamping factory. That's where Rustaya lost their parents and later their legs—lost their *legs*, and was fitted with a mecha enhancement instead of a pension. Do you know what it's like, to wake up every morning and walk into the heart of the machinery that took your family, to be *beholden* to it, to live or die by the rations you earn from it?"

Zemolai glared at her. "Yes."

Eleny frowned. "I'm saying that you don't know what it's like out here, what it was like to grow up under your god's rule. They have questions, and they're entitled to ask them."

"You keep lecturing me," Zemolai growled. "As though I took your friend's legs, as though I passed any of the laws you've been bitching about. I was a child when I joined the mecha sect. I was raised for one purpose—"

"Well, you're not a child now," Eleny snapped. "So when was the tipping point? Was there one day you were innocent, and the next day complicit?"

For one bright, hot moment, Zemolai saw nothing but white.

"I already said I would go on your stupid fucking mission!" she shouted. "What else do you *want* from me?"

And Eleny barked back: "I want you to get your head out of your ass! I want you to choose where you stand! *You*, yourself. Not what you were taught. Not where you've been or what you've done before. Just what's right, right *now*."

They stared at each other, breathing hard, and nobody else in the room was even pretending not to listen anymore. They were fighting (like parent and child) like *animals*, and Zemolai was so angry she was about to back out of this entire misguided venture.

Galiana had been watching all of this with growing alarm, and she stepped forward with her hands outstretched. "Don't do this," she said. "Come on now. We've only got a few hours to prepare. How about—how about Zemolai goes with me?"

A small battle of wills, briefly fought. Rustaya and Timyan already had their bags hoisted—the only two smart enough to stay out of it.

Eleny nodded, and that was that. The group split in half.

It was a silent walk out of the border district. Galiana wore her hood up to cover her blue-green braids. She and Zemolai made a curious pair: the short, shrouded figure slinking alongside the tall, muscular woman with a scowl on her face.

They passed through a printmaker's row, and Zemolai was enveloped by familiar sounds: the rattle-clank-roar of the press, the shouts of the printer's assistants, the familiar industry of approved words being put to approved paper.

She'd spent many evenings in the corner of one of those studios, heavy muffs clapped over her ears as she practiced letters on her writing slate and her mother put in extra hours at the typeset table. And always, there had been Niklaus sitting beside her—growing up to the sound of knowledge, inscribed.

Eleny's words came back—*well, you're not a child now*—and Zemolai was angry all over again.

They left the printmakers behind and headed into a rundown stretch of specialty shops. Half the structures were crusted with overgrown vines, the other half with dirt. Galiana stopped at one of the more ragged storefronts. A broken wooden sign, illegible, was propped next to the weed-covered entrance. Two windows were boarded over.

It didn't inspire much confidence.

The crooked door made an unholy racket as it stuttered open, revealing an interior that was even shabbier than the outside. Dust lay a quarter-inch thick on half-empty shelves. The few pieces of mismatched furniture had bits of wood shoved under their feet to keep them level, and the entire place was thick with the nauseating scent of old milk.

The shopkeeper looked up from the front counter, blinking affably. He was, to put it mildly, one of the most heavily modified individuals Zemolai had ever met. None of his limbs were constructed of the same material. What was left of his natural hair was tinted in so many shades, it was impossible to tell its original color. His eyes were too big, his teeth were too white, and his back was sharply bent, like he had frozen up leaning over a worktable.

All the hallmark, excessive modifications of a druggist.

Zemolai looked again at the filthy and understocked shelves, sharply this time. It was difficult to believe this place was the source of the mechalin substitute. Surely, Galiana couldn't have been foolish enough to lead Zemolai here if that were the case . . .

"Faiyan or Quaser?" she asked.

The druggist flinched at the engineering names, his big orange eyes darting worriedly to Galiana. She sighed and leaned close to whisper in his ear. A code phrase to assure him Galiana wasn't a mecha prisoner come to turn him over.

"I was born in Faiyan," he admitted, in a gravelly voice. "Now, tell me why you are here."

Galiana said, "We need something from downstairs."

"Ah." He gestured for them to come around the counter, where he revealed an iron-strapped trapdoor beneath a faded rug. He hit a switch, and enormous security gates crashed down behind his front door and windows. Zemolai was equally impressed and irritated.

Engineers always had their little tricks.

Now they descended into the *real* shop, and it was clear this one was maintained with great care. Pots bubbled along every wall. Centrifuges whirred. An automated grinder was turning a barrel full of feska seed into powder fine enough to mix into comedown candies. Zemolai searched for some sign of her drug, but nothing was labeled, and damned if she knew what it looked like raw.

She eyeballed the druggist. He was slender, with enhancements only useful to a lab setting. Zemolai could overpower him easily. The trouble, as always, would be determining the truth of any confession made under duress. He could just as easily give her a recipe for poison, and she wouldn't know until she injected herself. She needed a test subject.

Oblivious to his impending abduction and drugging, the man shuffled up to Zemolai and peered into her face. "Let me look at you, let me look at you," he said, blinking rapidly. He gripped her chin for a moment before she yanked back, disgusted. Still, he seemed pleased by what he saw. "Remarkable."

"She was on mechalin for over two decades," Galiana said excitedly. "I really think we've got the mix down now."

"You must put me in touch with your producer," he chided. "I could double your supply."

"You don't make it here?" Zemolai asked sharply. Just like that, her plan collapsed, and she couldn't keep the frustration off her face. Galiana gave her a wounded look, which was even more aggravating. Had she really expected Zemolai to accept the situation with grace?

"No," the druggist said sourly. "I have tried many times to synthesize a comparable substance, but without success. It is a heavily guarded secret, isn't it, my dear?"

Galiana shuffled her feet and muttered, "The formula will be made public when the time is right." She flashed a sudden, fearful look at Zemolai, as if the danger had only just occurred to her. "I don't know the formula either, if that's what you're thinking."

The druggist tut-tutted. "Alas. Well, what have you come for today?"

"We need a sedative," Galiana said. Blatantly avoiding Zemolai's eyes, she muttered, "Something strong enough to knock out warriors in full gear."

"Oh ho! In the field now, are we?" His head bobbed appreciatively. "Give me . . . ten minutes to concentrate the dose."

He took off to another workstation and bent low over his tools. His spine clicked and stuttered to a ninety-degree angle, forcing his belly to pooch out over his belt.

Zemolai stared at the unnatural curvature of his back for a moment before turning all of her bubbling resentment on Galiana. "Is that your plan?" she demanded. "If a Winged attacks, you'll hit her with a sedative? You'll never get close enough to stick a warrior with a needle!"

"That's not the *whole* plan," Galiana said. "We have other ways to defend ourselves."

Zemolai almost laughed. "I've seen your gear. You have a handful of bolt-guns, knives, and now sedatives, and not one of those is going to protect you."

"We have—" Galiana abruptly shut her mouth, thinking better of whatever she'd been on the verge of saying.

There it was. "You have what?" Zemolai prodded.

Now the struggle on Galiana's face was something else entirely—not concerned, but calculating. In all the rush out of tower Zhelan and her arguments with Eleny, Zemolai had nearly forgotten that Galiana was harboring an agenda of her own.

Engineers and their tricks.

When Galiana spoke, her words were slow, carefully chosen. "I've been working on a prototype," she said, watching Zemolai's reaction closely. "A new kind of signal blocker. It's only effective for a few minutes, but I've got some ideas on how to extend its life—"

"Wait," Zemolai interrupted. "A signal blocker? What does that mean?"

There—a flash of disappointment. Galiana smoothed it away quickly. "A device that blocks electrical impulses. Anything mechanical that passes through the active field will stop in its tracks. Depending on the strength of the signal, I can affect up to a hundred-foot radius. The applications are . . ." Galiana paused. "What's wrong?"

"What's *wrong*?" Zemolai was aghast. "You could drop Winged from the sky! You'd kill them without lifting a weapon! Without coming anywhere near them, without even showing your *face*." The concept was dishonorable, offensive, *revolting*. Zemolai felt sick.

Galiana's expression shuttered. Zemolai had dismissed her as a clever but naïve farmer turned engineer, unaware of how her skills were being exploited by the rebellion.

Clearly, that had been a mistake.

"I know exactly how it could be used," Galiana said calmly. "This isn't a clean fight. It never has been."

Zemolai had heard so much in the past day—their codes, their spies—but it was *this*, a device that could knock a Winged from the sky, that hit her like a javelin.

"I won't have it anywhere near me," Zemolai said.

"What do you . . ."

Zemolai advanced, knocking Galiana back a step. "I won't have it near me. It isn't entering the training grounds. Do you understand, or do I have to say it more slowly?"

"You *just* said we weren't prepared to fight a Winged!" Galiana protested.

"And *you* said there wouldn't be any Winged there to fight!"

"Then why should it matter—"

Zemolai held up a staying hand. "You can bring your signal blocker, or you can bring me. Drugs be damned, if I die, it won't be as a complete coward."

They stood at an impasse. Faiyan hummed to himself at his workstation, oblivious. His back stuttered and clicked, rearing him up several inches, and he widened his eye lenses at a vial of tawny liquid held in front of an open flame. Galiana could have pressed her threat—it must have seemed an arbitrary line to draw, when Zemolai was already willing to aid their theft of combat weaponry. But that, at least, would garner a fair fight.

Galiana blinked first.

"Well," she said stiffly. "If that's how it is."

They waited out the druggist's work in silence. When he'd finished, Faiyan handed over a small wooden case of syringes in exchange for a bundle of cash and wished them well.

Galiana glanced at Zemolai once while they waited for Faiyan to lift the security gate from his front door, but she quickly looked away again, her lips compressed into a grim line. Zemolai was more than happy to have the bit of quiet.

Get into the training grounds, she thought. *Get in, get out.*

It was nearly dusk when the group came back together. Rustaya was to remain on lookout outside the compound, accessible by short-range coder.

They wore their tools, their weapons, their sedatives, their empty duffel bags. Eleny had arranged a covered vehicle to haul away their goods. It waited in an alley shielded from overhead eyes by a thick awning.

They were as prepared as humanly possible.

The worker's entrance was located a discreet block south of the training grounds, next to a shrine. The humble hut contained little more than a blessing dish and an icon of the worker god—everything that his followers needed to make their daily prayers before heading in to work.

"Are you ready?" Timyan whispered, and they murmured assent.

He led them underground, down a narrow tunnel connecting the shrine to a network of servants' byways. A pain had been building in Zemolai's gut all afternoon, unexpected and sharp. As soon as they left the surface, she had to fight to keep her breathing under control.

They were a few scant steps from entering the training grounds, where she had lived and bled for years, where all of this had begun. She was buffeted by memory, by guilt and by shame.

Are you ready? No, not at all, perhaps not ever. But readiness had nothing to do with it. She'd made a single promise: she would get them into the armory. After that, she had business of her own.

She knew when they crossed the threshold from city block to walled compound, though it only looked as if they'd passed from one dim, unremarkable hallway into another. It was a slight change in the tile perhaps, or the incremental rise in temperature as they strode beneath the god's devices powering the machinery above. Or perhaps it was just instinct and a once-Winged's unerring sense of direction in the dark. The open city was behind them.

Zemolai was home.

INTERLUDE

CONSIDER THIS:

In the beginning, there was a city of stone and sod, a people of humble means, a home in a valley of no consequence. And then the gods came.

What was Radezhda before the gods? It was not even called Radezhda—not until the attempted invasion by Rava State, and the death of the first saint, bless her memory. It was hardly even a city, not in any of the senses defined above. It was a disparate group of families scattered through a quiet valley nestled against the mountains Kelior. They farmed with stone tools. They lived in houses of wood and sod. Only much later, looking back, did we say: ah, that is where the city began.

Imagine this life. Imagine their wonder, when the sky filled with god-light, and those incomprehensible voices spoke for the first time. Five of them, each with their own preoccupation, each with their own set of gifts.

Imagine it.

Little remains from those early days. We have fragments of the Dierka Mountain Scrolls. Hints and whispers from the past—they were afraid, then they were not. They were dazzled by all of the Five, then they began to align themselves according to each god's teachings.

This we know beyond doubt:

The creator god required their followers to explore and innovate, for without engineers, there could be no progress.

The scholar god required his followers to study and learn, for without scholars, the city would succumb to the mistakes of the past.

The worker god required her followers to labor and maintain, for without workers, there could be no production.

The earth god required his followers to sow and reap, for without farmers, the city would starve.

The mecha god required her followers to protect and judge, for without warriors, the city would fall to the first aggressor.

Wonderful. Concise. But in practice, so much more complicated. We mined the hills and plowed the land and built machines we had never dreamt possible. We were united in worship, in ambition, in a belief that anything was possible as long as we followed the wisdom and guidance of the beings who had chosen us, above all others in the world, as their favored people.

If a city is a story, then ours was beautiful in its simplicity: *they came to us, they loved us, they showed us how to live.*

We defined ourselves by our gods!

And then our gods went to sleep.

CHAPTER ELEVEN

I beg you, give this another chance. It is the only just solution: appoint one representative of each philosophy to make
their cases in the public eye, and thereby arrive at a common
good . . .

—*Letter from Scholar Pierenski to Creator Stasia,*
re: creation of the Council of Five

O F EVERYTHING that might have happened after the bombing at the
Council of Five, the most startling was this:

Mecha Petrogon survived.

The news went through the city like wildfire. The Voice had come back
from the very edge of death, and Pava rejoiced, for he was truly blessed: the
mecha god's chosen representative in Radezhda, with work not yet done.

But he was not unscathed. Two weeks after his assassination attempt
(two weeks of rumors and fury and denials and threats flung back and
forth between sects), Mecha Petrogon was released from the surgeon's hall.

Word was, his legs had been destroyed, and he had been outfitted with
mechanicals.

Word was, he would speak to no one outside his inner circle.

No human, at least. The lights flashing above tower Kemyana were
a clear sign of where the Voice was spending his time. Mecha Petrogon
communed with his god for hours every morning, though he had not yet
shared what she said.

News flew fast and thick through the training grounds, trickling in through family members, through instructors, through unsubstantiated word-of-mouth. Protesters had stormed a bakery floor to shut down the ovens. Fights were breaking out in the bread-lines. A boardinghouse had burned down (nobody could agree where).

And then, a week after his emergence, Petrogon sent word to the border. His field leaders were ordered to return to the city. The mecha sect was going to retaliate.

Zenya was in her room when Mecha Petrogon called an assembly, but she hardly heard the announcement through the buzzing in her ears.

In her hands, she held a letter.

Dear Zenya, it said, as though it were an ordinary message on an ordinary day. *Dear Zenya*, as though it weren't another bomb, devised of paper and ink instead of wire and clay.

When a second knock sounded on her door, she shoved everything beneath her mattress and dashed out, hoping that the shaking of her hands wouldn't betray her.

She needn't have worried. Unlike the last time Mecha Petrogon called an assembly, proud and stern and urging them toward first flight, there was no cheerful chatter, no ribaldry, no smiles. Zenya slipped into place with her five-unit, and nobody spared her a glance.

Uneasily, she realized: it had not only been the trainees summoned that day. Around the perimeter of the yard stood the kitchen workers and tower staff—even the compound's lone engineering instructor, Faiyan Sanador. Zenya had been in his workshop for her first year, learning maintenance and repair. She'd laughed at his jokes when her teammates weren't looking, and felt relief at the normalcy of his tests.

Sanador wasn't joking now. He looked like he hadn't slept in a month.

"Eyes up," a Pava fifth-year ordered.

The Winged launched from atop tower Kemyana. One by one their knife-like bodies descended, framed by glorious wings in metallic blues and greens and copper and silver. Some circled into graceful landings.

Others dropped like bombs and caught air at the last possible second, a display of precision and power that left their audience dazzled.

Petrogon's field leaders spent their days flying the mountains beyond Radezhdean farmland, monitoring their enemies, destroying foreign foot patrols. *True* warriors, with elaborate brocade crests buttoned to the fronts of their vests and scars all over their arms.

The Pava team landed shortly behind them, Vodaya and Raksa included. The pair of them made a sharp contrast: Vodaya in her dusty leathers and silver wings, Raksa wearing dark cloth and brass. Vodaya looked grim—hadn't *stopped* looking grim, really, in three weeks.

And finally, Mecha Petrogon himself, landing hard on his new legs. He gave no hint of the pain his freshly bolted flesh must be causing him, but his cheeks were hollow, and his fists were clenched tight at his sides.

He said:

"Hear this. The scholars and the engineers are fomenting rebellion. The scholars continue to defend their heresy, and the engineers are using the conflict to advance their own agenda. They are demanding a regulatory commission in the Council of Five. They want *outside forces* to overview mecha protocols and city patrol schedules. As though *outside forces* would have any idea what they were reviewing. As though this is not a clear ploy to eliminate our vote."

Petrogon swept them all with his silver-tinted stare before declaring, "There will be a reckoning. This conflict ends with the resignations of Creator Talley and Lead Scholar Brekkia, and the surrender of all heretical materials in the archives. That is our goal, and it will be done."

They answered with thunder. "It will be done!"

Petrogon nodded, already pale from the effort of speaking. "Winged Raksa, come with me—we have more to discuss." To the rest of the yard he said, "Pava! Heed your instructors, and the introductions to follow."

Startled, Zenya looked toward Vodaya. She was ordinarily invited to stay after a meeting, but she was staring at the Voice with an expression bordering on hostility. Petrogon and Raksa launched back toward the tower without her, and she didn't breathe a word.

"Attention!" Winged Pilivar barked, dragging everyone's attention back to their visitors. "Know these warriors. Winged Shantar of the southeast quadrant, with seventeen years of service and one hundred ninety-seven combat incidents to his name. Winged Dietra of the southwest quadrant, with twenty-one years of service and two hundred fifty-two combat incidents to her name . . ."

Legendary, all of them, but the real sensation was at the end of the line. Four figures in crimson and black, from their boots to their vests to the two-toned magnificence of their wings. On their chests they bore row after row of grim insignia: wild animal fangs, long and pointed and carved all over in soot-blackened script.

These were the mecha god's Teeth: her top four warriors, to whom she assigned her severest judgments. When the god handed down a fatal verdict, the name of the condemned was carved onto a fang and handed to one of the crimson and black. Upon completion of this terrible duty, the warrior affixed the fang to their vestment as a mark of their unwavering service. The Teeth plus the Voice formed the most exalted five-unit of the mecha administration.

And these Teeth wore dozens of fangs apiece.

Winged Shantar spoke to the trainees first, his voice warmer than expected. "It is typical for warriors to begin their service on the border. In light of the current unrest, it is more likely that, should you ascend in the following months, you will be conducting safety patrols in the city. That is, of course, *assuming* you ascend. Our need for wings in no way undermines our standards for earning them." He gave them a stern look. "I see your excitement, but let me be clear: there is no honor in fighting your fellow Radezhdeans. Pray it doesn't come to that."

One of the Teeth spoke as well, but his instructions were significantly shorter.

"If you see us coming," he said heavily, "do not get in our way."

Vodaya pulled her unit aside immediately afterward, giving only a curt, "*Now.*" She led them across the yard, to a supply room none of them had been granted access to before.

The room was so full, they barely fit past the door. Every inch of shelving was crammed two boxes deep, and the center of the room was stacked chest-high with wooden crates. Zenya glimpsed weaponry and prosthetics, bandoliers and tool belts, communication devices as big as cinderblocks, flamethrowers and flamestoppers.

These were the toys of advanced Pava units.

"You are all on reserve now," Vodaya said. "From this moment on, we ready for war."

Vodaya gave them each a bright white badge meant to distinguish them in riot situations, and flare guns for when no warrior was in sight.

And she issued distress beacons. Beacons came in pairs, red and white. They were thin and knobby, like twigs, with a wire loop at one end for hooking onto clothing. Each pair was stamped with matching digits and had a flat edge on one side for etching names.

"These beacons are entangled," Vodaya explained, holding up one in each hand. "A godly technology. A gift to us. They are your final call for help when you are cornered and your defenses will not hold. Break your beacon"—she snapped the red beacon with one clench of her fingers—"and I will be alerted." The white beacon pulsed red, its smooth surface gone translucent.

"Take more than one," she instructed. "Split them between yourselves."

Vodaya handed out both pieces for inspection. The red twig was cool, almost damp. The white twig, on the other hand, was hot with proximity, almost burning to the touch. It would only cool when they drew it farther away from its counterpart.

It was a distress call and a simple tracking system all in one.

Vodaya went over more specifics, and Zenya listened with half an ear, staring at the weapons all around them. Weapons they might have to use against their fellow Radezhdeans.

"Pava Zemolai," Vodaya snapped. "Am I not holding your attention?"

Zenya jerked up. "I'm listening," she said, far too late.

Vodaya stepped into Zenya's space, towering and terrible with her wings hooked sharp overhead. "You've been very distractible lately," she said. "Are you having doubts? Is it too much for you, to be caught between two sects?"

"I'm not caught between anything," Zenya protested. "I'm a Pava trainee. Wholly!" Her face was burning (she was a liar, she had the papers stuffed beneath her mattress to prove it), but her face often burned.

Vodaya considered her with eerie indifference. And then she said, "I really hope so. Because there is a fight coming, and my unit will be ready when it does."

She meant it.

Just past midnight, scant hours after they had retired to bed, Zenya's unit awoke to harsh banging on the apartment door. Winged Vodaya entered briskly and made a quick circuit of the common room, hitting door after door until they stumbled out, expecting disaster.

"Support unit," she barked. "There's been an altercation at Rinko Pass. Our warriors are landing in shifts for repair. Move, move—no, Lijo, there isn't time to change clothing, try wearing more to bed—let's *go*."

They staggered out to the courtyard, where a series of lampposts cast overlapping circles of illumination on baskets of jumbled tools.

It was a training exercise.

"Load up, get to the repair station, fix what you find," Vodaya instructed. "*Go*."

They packed their belts from the baskets. They scaled a pair of ladders to a mock landing platform and mended practice parts: dented joints, broken feathers, slashed wires.

Vodaya waited for them down below. When they returned, she castigated them for their clumsiness, their slowness—a response time like that would mean a delay in repair shifts, and a delay in repair shifts could mean a warrior's death.

They returned to their apartment, heavy-limbed and dejected. "Can you believe it?" Dolynne grumbled. "Dragging us out of bed for this. Of course we'd be ready, if we were actually assigned to a repair station!"

Zenya nodded along, but she was shaken, ashamed, determined to do better. Vodaya had high expectations of them, but her criticism had always been tempered with praise. For two years Zenya had held her favor—to feel like a disappointment now was unbearable.

It happened again the next night. And the next. Their previous routine had been exhausting, but only *physically* exhausting. Adding sleep deprivation was torture. Everyone was foggy-headed, short-tempered, anger flaring frequently and unpredictably.

Zenya was so desperate for rest that she napped during the free periods she'd previously used for studying. When she did crack a book open, the words blurred, and she couldn't remember what she read. She wanted to work; her body wanted to sleep.

And her body was winning.

Zenya staggered through her lessons, every missed step and lost scuffle driving Vodaya wild with disappointment. She'd snap her fingers, shouting, "Wake up, Zemolai. Wake up!"

Wake up. Wake up. Stand straight. Open your eyes. *Focus.*

Zenya was finally driven to her nightstand drawer, in which she had long ago secreted Vodaya's bottle of enhancers: the small purple pills used by warriors on long patrols. The pills Zenya had thus far disdained to use, preferring to rely on her own abilities.

She swallowed the first one dry.

Within minutes, her aches faded and her posture straightened. The fog lifted from her brain. Her body hummed with energy. When Vodaya arrived at their door, some two hours before midnight, Zenya was still awake and impatient to get started.

"How can you be smiling?" Romil groaned. Zenya shrugged, guilty.

In the yard, she scaled the repair station and started her project before anyone else had finished assembling their tools. The drug was lighter than she had expected, a boost, bubbling and bright and clarifying. She almost laughed at the strength in her limbs.

It was Pava Lijo who snapped first. He sat down hard, a half-assembled tool belt in his hands, and cried, "I'm not going up that ladder. I can't."

Zenya hesitated in her work and peeked over the edge. Vodaya stood facing the platform. Of the rest, Zenya could only see bed-mussed heads and angry-set shoulders.

"There are injured warriors waiting above," Vodaya said calmly.

Dolynne put their hand on Lijo's shoulder, their belt abandoned in the sand. "You have to let us sleep! What good are we to anyone like this?"

"That is exactly what we are out here to determine," Vodaya said. "What *good* are you?" She gestured toward the platform. "Look. Zemolai is doing just fine."

This sparked an incredible backlash. The other trainees babbled over one another, their frustrations spewing forth like overdue geysers. Vodaya had praised Zenya in front of them for two years—heaping compliments on her work ethic, her lengthy answers, even her posture and physical appearance—and they'd always smiled and held any good-natured teasing till later.

There was nothing good-natured in their expressions now. Everything else evaporated in the crucible of endless fatigue, and what remained was pure resentment.

"We're supposed to be a team!"

"We're *constantly* fighting for second-best."

"She isn't even Pava, she's from *Milar*, aren't you worried that she's from Milar—"

Zenya shrank back on the platform, her heart pounding. For two years she'd been expecting this to happen, and oh, it was crueler for the long wait.

Vodaya waited patiently for the outburst to slow. "Are you finished?" she asked, and they fell silent. Zenya couldn't imagine what grueling exercise Vodaya would assign now.

But Vodaya didn't tear into them for insubordination. She didn't even yell. She said, "You are correct. I've pushed you far enough. It is necessary for me to know the limits of your endurance. It is necessary for *you* to know. In the field, it will be up to you to gauge your condition and know when to reach out for help." Vodaya smiled. "I am proud of your perseverance. Go to bed. You've earned it."

They stuttered out apologies, thoroughly embarrassed now that they'd gotten what they wanted. Only Romil glanced at the platform before slinking from the yard, too quick to read.

Zenya did not climb down right away. She completed her task, stubbornly stripping each wire and twisting it into place. The delay gave her time to package her hurt and tuck it away, and by the time she descended the ladder, she was calm, even if her eyes felt hot.

Vodaya waited with her arms crossed. "Tell me what you're thinking," she said.

Zenya tried to speak evenly. "They're right to be upset. Tonight I . . . I took an enhancer. I think I might have given up soon if I hadn't . . . cheated." The word was a ball of medicine wax, noxious and clinging to her teeth.

But Vodaya only smiled, gentle and affectionate—the first hint of her old self since the bombing. "Zemolai, Zemolai. What did I say was the purpose of this exercise? To know your limits. Between the two of us, I confess I needed to know something else: what each of you would do when you *reached* your limit. Pava Lijo fell to the ground and cried. The others used his failure as an excuse to retreat. But you saw it coming and chose to get through the task at all costs. Come here."

And then Vodaya opened her arms and tugged Zenya into an embrace.

Zenya resisted at first, shocked by the physical contact. She couldn't remember the last time she'd felt a gentle touch (Natulia, perhaps, half a lifetime ago). But Vodaya was warm and her arms were strong and it was easier to lean in than to pull away. Tears pricked Zenya's eyes. She blamed exhaustion.

"You are wholly committed to reaching your goal," Vodaya said softly. "The Five have their disagreements—and that is all this is, a disagreement overdue for correction—but in one thing the gods are united: they desire, above all else, for their disciples to choose a path. And so you have."

Vodaya leaned back far enough to look Zenya in the face. "Let them be angry. You and I know what's important."

Zenya swallowed hard, and smiled back, and tried to keep the guilt off her face.

She still hadn't told Vodaya about the letter.

Zenya should have stopped writing Niklaus after the bombing. She *knew* this. But he had become more committed to his ludicrous theory by the day. He went on and on about the free flow of information and the god-given right to blaspheme, as though that weren't a slap in the face of the divine. She was desperate to talk him out of it.

Show some respect, she'd begged—he could question his own god, but why interfere with anyone else's? *Saint Radezhda died to unite this city.* This only provoked a three-page rant insisting the mecha sect was trying to control acceptable modes of worship, something that Zenya knew was categorically untrue.

Their correspondence ended with the letter she had failed to report. A single envelope, bulging at the enclosure, a sheaf of papers inside that began, *Dear Zenya, READ THIS.*

Zenya had only skimmed a few sentences before realizing what it was—a transcription of Heretic Scholar Vikenzy's essay, in her brother's handwriting—and then she screwed her eyes shut and crumpled the pages in her fists. Her heart pounded and bile burned the back of her throat. That he had sent her *this*, that her own brother would violate her boundaries when he knew exactly where she stood on the matter—!

And worse, she wanted to look. After all the rumors and the fighting and the fear, she had to wonder: was this the evidence the scholars were hinging their deranged theory upon? Had Heretic Scholar Vikenzy stumbled upon something that he believed was proof of the gods having other-worldly origins?

That the paper contained lies (or, at best, bad scholarship), she was certain. And it was tempting, *so tempting*, to meet the scholars on terms they understood: to read this paper, and write an argument against it, deconstructing Vikenzy's points one by one. Zenya had tried and failed to explain this to her Pava fellows: that the scholars loved their thought experiments, and only a proper discrediting would shake their interest in this one.

But Vodaya's exhortation echoed in her head—*if I find out that any of you are in possession of heretical materials, you will be cut from my unit and the Pava program entirely*—and she couldn't do it.

She should have burnt it, but she couldn't bring herself to do that either. There was still a hint of the scholar within her, queasy at the thought of destruction (control it; bury it in the archives; but don't burn it!). She hid it instead, *all of it*, his letters and the heretic's paper alongside, beneath a floorboard in the kitchen pantry. It was a terrible trip in the dead of night.

Zenya wrote back to Niklaus, lengthy and imploring and furious. She had not read it; she would not read it; he must never send anything like it again!

And Niklaus stopped writing.

A month passed without a word, and at first Zenya welcomed the break (what horrible thing would he send next?), but then worry set in.

The city went eerily quiet in that time. Vodaya gave her five-unit one night's reprieve after their repair station meltdown, and then she picked up a frenetic pace once more. Zenya took enhancers daily. She suspected her teammates had caught on, because almost overnight she was surrounded by focused, energetic competition after months of leaving them gasping in the dust.

But at the back of her mind was Niklaus, always Niklaus. A month of silence, and every time Zenya snuck out to the mail office, the man behind the counter gave her a more ominous look than before.

She had to know whether he was all right.

Zenya found her opportunity during the next war meeting, hastily called on a late afternoon after news of a factory strike. Petrogon always held these meetings in open air, at the base of the god-tree atop tower Kemyana. There his top Winged debated strategy beneath the portal's glow—a solemn reminder that the mecha god could cast judgment at any point during the proceedings.

Vodaya grimly informed them, "This will be a long one. Get some sleep."

And Zenya ran for it. She told her teammates that she was fetching food. Nobody protested. Why would they? She barely spoke to them outside of the training ring these days.

It was nerve-wracking to exit the Pava grounds, nerve-wracking to walk through the gate with her head held high, praying she wouldn't be stopped by a guard and asked difficult questions. But what she found outside Pava wiped all that from her mind.

Radezhda was a city transformed. Gone were the corner vendors. Gone were the clothing lines and flower chains that had linked the buildings across district boundary lines. Gone were the daytime pedestrians strolling the city's many bridges, now empty and scattered with aging piles of trash.

Milar District was unrecognizable. Half the homes were shuttered and abandoned, and the other half were in an uproar. The sight of shattered windows and acid-etched graffiti quickened Zenya's step until she was nearly running. She turned onto her street, hardly daring to breathe around the knot of fear in her throat.

Zenya's home was in ruins.

She froze on the sidewalk. The garden was buried under a mountain of broken furniture. One of the library windows was smashed. A bookcase hung through, the contents of its shelves vomited into a mildewing heap on the earth. It was shocking to see books abandoned without rescue, left to die in the elements like the unwanted parts of an animal carcass. It was a house gutted like a wild boar.

Zenya broke into a run. The front door was ajar, and she didn't know what she feared worse: finding something terrible or finding nothing at all.

"Nushki!" she called. "Tomel!"

The interior of the house had been ransacked, bitterness and anger scrawled across the walls in charcoal and paint. Zenya skidded into the back hallway—and drew up short, gasping, facing down the length of an antique sword.

The sword bearer trembled and dropped his arm. It was her father, looking as awkward and inexperienced as could be expected. "Zenya," he said wearily, "why are you here?"

"What happened?" she cried.

"What do you mean, what happened?" He shook his head. "Bands have been ransacking scholar homes for weeks. They came early this morning while we were at a service."

Dread settled in Zenya's stomach. "Where's Nushki?"

"He's packing," he said, and now she saw the rings under his eyes, the gray in his hair. The last two years hadn't been kind. "If there's anything of yours you still care about, you should take it now. I don't think there'll be much left next time they come around."

Something crashed outside, down the road. Tomel retreated, sword banging against his boot—and what was he thinking, grabbing that old thing off the wall? It would snap at the first strike! They weren't even in style with real warriors, and her father was anything but.

She bit back the urge to yell—they needed help, *protection*, and they hadn't even sent *word*—and followed him down the hall. There, at last, Niklaus was in his room. He sat on the edge of his bed, surrounded by a mess of books and clothes and all the little trinkets he'd accrued through the years.

Zenya waited until their father had retreated back down the hall before hissing, "Was it that damn paper they were looking for?"

His head jerked up. His cheeks were too hollow, his eyes too bright. "Not unless you were the one who turned me in."

"No," she said swiftly. "Never. But Nushki," and now she began to plead, "who gave it to you? Does Scholar Pyetka know? He was always more sensible than—"

"Did you read it?" he interrupted.

Zenya shook her head, almost violently. "Of course not. I told you I wouldn't!"

Niklaus was the ghost of Natulia in that moment, mouth set in the same disappointed lines. Defiantly, he said, "Nobody gave it to me. Those rumors you heard were true—a student *did* turn up Vikenzy's missing paper. It was me. I realized what it was right away and made a copy of my own, because I knew this was going to happen: the scholars would spend a decade debating whether to print it, and the mecha sect would lose their minds."

Zenya groaned. "Oh Nushki, how could you!"

He shrugged, his shoulders still angry-set. "Our purpose is to study! Knowledge for the sake of knowledge! Not knowledge locked away. If

Brekkia doesn't see that, I don't care. And I'm not the only one who thinks so."

"How many people have it now?" she demanded.

"I put the original back," he said, which was hardly an answer at all. "I asked too many questions. I'm assuming that's where the rumors got started. But I won't tell them where I found it, so don't bother asking."

"I can't believe—" Zenya stopped, more confused now than ever. "Wait. Why would the scholars be split on this? They're literally fighting for the right to publish this stupid theory."

Niklaus huffed a breath. "We're talking about two different things, meathead! Listen: the scholars are working on their new theory, yes—don't give me that look, I don't care—and Lead Scholar Brekkia ordered every floor to run a catalog in search of supporting documents. I found Vikenzy's paper in my department, completely unrelated—" He paused, turning thoughtful. "Well. They aren't mutually exclusive . . ." He stopped again at the look on her face. "Fine! What I'm saying is, the fight that's happening now is going to happen no matter what. I won't be silenced on this."

Voice shaking, Zenya said, "I can't have any part of it."

Niklaus's face crumpled, but only briefly, before he recomposed himself. He nodded angrily, then wedged one arm beneath the mattress, groped around, and pulled out a bundle of papers. Zenya's letters, with Zenya's postal lockbox number scrawled across the top. "I'm sorry," he said, "I should have burned these sooner."

She made a faint sound of protest, but her feet didn't walk her forward, and her hands stayed firmly on her elbows. She watched him empty a metal wastebasket and crumple her letters into it. She watched him rummage in the wreckage of his desk, watched him light the match, watched her words of affection and sympathy begin to smolder. And it was a relief, an undeniable relief.

"Where are you going?" she asked quietly.

He paused, gazing into the flames. "There are rooms open in Quaser."

"Nushki!" The engineering district was the heart of the conflict. Zenya was about to protest further (they could come with her, they could beg succor at Pava, she could find them a safe house far from the fighting—!), and then it fizzled out on her tongue. She already knew the answer, but she asked anyway, too sad to do anything else. "You won't come with me, will you?"

"To Pava? No." He turned quiet. "And you won't read the paper."

"No."

They stared at one another then, over the uncrossable gulf of his bedroom floor. They had tried to keep this from happening—for two years they'd tried—but their paths were about to diverge irreversibly, and they both knew it. Zenya pictured it for a moment, her baby brother chasing heresy in the middle of a war zone, no means to send for help when he realized where he'd gone wrong.

And then she remembered: she still had one recourse available. Zenya dug into her bag, so abruptly it set Niklaus frowning. There, at the bottom: her spare distress beacons, issued a month prior. After the incident during repair-station training, she had been too mortified to ask one of her teammates to swap with her.

Niklaus wrinkled his nose at the sight of mecha tech.

"Just take it," Zenya said. "Do you know what it is? You know how it works?"

He only sighed. "Yes."

Zenya snapped the string. She pocketed the white beacon and left the mate in his hands. "If you need me, you don't hesitate," she said.

"Zenya . . ."

"I swear," she said fiercely. "Don't hesitate. I'll come running if I can't come flying."

Niklaus hesitated, searching her face. And then he nodded. They hugged goodbye and pretended it might not be for the last time.

CHAPTER TWELVE

She gave us these glorious schematics, these designs we could never have dreamed of, battle arts and wisdoms beyond compare. But I am a flawed man, unworthy . . .

I fear that in following the very tactics she has taught us, I am betraying her.

—Diary of Mecha Vitaly

ZEMOLAI HAD ENTERED the training grounds a thousand times, but never from underneath.

The servants' tunnel was antiseptically clean, lined floor-to-ceiling in pale-green tile and glowing faintly under a string of safety lights. Gaping doorways opened root-like paths through the earth: badger tunnels to the kitchens, the laundry, the empty sleeping quarters.

Sensor-locked doors blocked access to the surface, but Galiana didn't even blink. One minute with a pair of pliers and a short-range coder, and she had typed in their bypass code, circumventing the most technologically advanced security system in Radezhda.

They climbed a narrow staircase to the kitchen. The room was dark and gleaming, every surface ceramic or chrome. The staff had been requisitioned uptower for the festivities following the graduation ceremony, leaving the space eerily silent.

During Zemolai's student years, most trainees had only ever glimpsed these worker spaces through the food-counter window, if they even felt inclined to look. Zemolai glanced toward the pantry door, an unforgiving block of insulation stone as thick as the barrier to an underground vault. Everything was exactly as she remembered.

She shook off her impatience. First, offload the bolt-babies, then return alone.

Galiana led them along a winding servant's path, keeping to the shelter of an inner hallway for as long as possible. Their target was at the opposite end of the compound, accessible by a single set of armory doors.

("You'll want the central equipment chamber," Zemolai had explained outside. "That's where extra gear is stored for the field leaders—"

"The good shit!" Rustaya had shouted, before peeling off for lookout duty.

"Yes," Zemolai had said. "The good shit.")

Easy enough, in theory, except they had gone as far as they could indoors. They had to exit the building and dart twenty feet around the edge of the training yard, where Zemolai would have to get them through the next sensor. For a few brief moments, they would be exposed to the sky.

Timyan eased the exterior door open a scant inch and slipped a right-angle monocular through the gap. Anyone walking directly past would spot it immediately, but from the heights of the tower, it would be an invisible blip of shadow on a long, dust-spattered wall.

"The yard is empty," he said softly. "But there's a light at the main gate."

They waited, breath shallow, hoping this departure would be the last. Zemolai struggled to keep her temper in check, stuck in place till Timyan gave the go-ahead. It galled her to wait on somebody else's judgment. She glanced up and down the empty hallway, hypersensitive to the barest sound of movement. She'd never seen the grounds so empty.

It was full of ghosts.

"It's clear," said Timyan, and they streamed out in a thin line, like a malicious band of beka birds racing for the water's edge. Timyan and Eleny ran with empty duffel bags bouncing against their backs, Galiana ran with her tool belt clattering like a stampede, and they all stormed the vast quiet of the open courtyard.

The moon shone like a searchlight. The dust smothered like a choke bomb. Zemolai stepped into the past, perfectly preserved. There were the obstacle courses, the ladders to nowhere, the sand pits and the fight rings. There was the storehouse, a later addition, now a burned-out husk, not secure after all. She looked up, to brightly lit tower Kemyana, to all of its ardently cobbled levels reaching higher, higher, where they stopped at—

She tore her eyes away, dizzy. Pain flared in her shoulders. Would she still be here when the portal opened? Did she *want* to be?

When Zemolai turned back, she was chasing after two bolt-babies rather than three. Galiana had peeled off the group and was running clear across the yard in the other direction.

"Where is she going?" Zemolai hissed.

Eleny only threw her a quelling gesture.

And then they were across the yard, concealed by the high wall of the compound and a narrow awning over the armory doors. The doors were twice their height, massive slabs of metal and wood carved top to bottom with the glowering figures of Winged Zorska and Winged Orlusky. Both were depicted pre-sainthood, furious and surrounded by the sharp geometrical glory of their wings. These were doors that a Winged could march through without pause.

"Where is she going?" Zemolai repeated.

Timyan looked away, but Eleny was unfazed. Calmly, she said, "You've got your business, and she's got hers. You said you could get past this door, didn't you?"

There was no time to argue, not with their backs so exposed. Zemolai gave in with an angry huff. She considered the sensor a moment, this one a green box with a glass pane on top. "I need a screwdriver," she said curtly. "Maybe some pliers."

Eleny handed over the tools, eyebrows raised quizzically. Zemolai shifted subtly to block her movements, admitting ruefully, "I lied when I said I had the code. It changes frequently. But trainees have their tricks, too."

She unscrewed the box from the wall and let it dangle from its thick cluster of multicolored wires, squinting through the shadows to make them out. Not much had changed over the years—there were more than a few patches visible already. The trouble with training mecha kids to be security experts was that they learned how to bypass anything they could build.

Zemolai loosened four of the patches and began to rearrange the wiring. If she cut the connection entirely, it would remain locked. What she needed was for the sensor to read her palm chip . . . and then neglect to pass that information to the security office.

She screwed the box back into place and flexed her hand over the glass. There was a slight pause, just long enough to make her think the fuse had blown, or her chip had been destroyed during the mecha god's judgment, or the alarm was more sophisticated than before—and then the lock gave way with a soft sigh.

"Good work!" Eleny flashed her a grin. She and Timyan walked in first, shifting their duffels toward the front of their bodies.

Zemolai saw the change in their body language half a second before she saw the cause.

She was two steps behind, slow as molasses, eyes adjusting to the indoor light, and forty feet away, down the only clear aisle in the overcrowded room, a man was closing a wrought-iron cabinet door and turning at the sound of their entry: a man wearing nothing but crimson and black, from his boots to his vest to his wings tucked back like charred and bloody bones.

A Tooth.

Zemolai rolled left, slamming the giant door shut behind her, aware with thoughtless instinct that their only chance of survival was here, indoors, where the warrior was grounded. The sky was their enemy. The sky meant their death.

Eleny and Timyan moved, but they didn't have the same reaction time. They were workers by training, spies at best, utterly unprepared for a fight with any Winged warrior, much less the mecha god's own Tooth. They dropped their duffels but didn't run for cover. They didn't know this vast tangle of a room, the climbing points, the dead ends, which storage cases were bolted down and which would tip over and crush them.

The Tooth charged, swift and merciless, storming down the forty-foot aisle with both hands coming up from his sides: in one a knife, in the other a net-gun. Capture or kill, it made no difference to him. There was no legitimate reason for workers to enter the armory. There was no legitimate reason for once-Winged Zemolai to be alive and inside the Pava training grounds.

He did not even need to speak.

Zemolai heard Eleny's involuntary cry of terror and Timyan shouting, "Wait!" as though a Tooth would pause for an explanation.

High ground, high ground. Zemolai forced her way down a side aisle, one that was too narrow for the Tooth to follow. She blurred past crates of all the assorted weaponry available to mecha warriors: the batons and daggers and throwing knives, the bows and crossbows, the knuckle gauntlets and elbow blades and spiked boots, the experimental mechanicals capable of launching tiny projectiles at immense distance and speed.

She heard them grappling, all three in a close-quarters boxing match, and two on one was *nothing*, they needed *ten* on one, they needed *one hundred*. Zemolai had seconds to act. The Tooth knew she was in here. He knew that she was the only real threat in the room and that she was circling to his right.

Zemolai heard the percussive release of the net-gun. Eleny cried out. Timyan shouted something defiant—a waste of breath. The Tooth's wings clattered against a metal cabinet, the first sound to give Zemolai hope. Mecha wings were durable but not indestructible. The Tooth was off guard, to be so clumsy.

She scaled the sturdiest shelving unit she could reach, feeling like a fresh-faced trainee climbing ladders—except that when a trainee slipped and fell, they probably weren't going to break a hip. The top of the shelving unit was packed as full as the rest of the room. Zemolai crushed something soft beneath one knee, struck something pointy with the other, nearly sent a box of throwing knives sliding to the floor.

She had one gasped-breath moment to absorb the scene below her:

Eleny was tangled in the net, one hand outstretched, fingers clawing through the rope. Timyan stood over her, but he was losing ground, about to trip over her body, barely blocking the Tooth's attacks with a half-body shield he'd scooped up from the floor. The Tooth was a machine, ruthlessly pressing Timyan back, striking the shield with his hunting knife with unflagging determination, one well-timed blow away from upsetting Timyan's footing.

The Tooth heard her coming. He held Timyan at bay with one arm and raised his knife in the other to skewer her on the way down. But his turn radius was limited, and his wings crashed boxes from their shelves. He didn't have the mobility of open air.

Zemolai jumped.

Or more like Zemolai *plummeted*, a hailstorm of weaponry falling with her, and she purposefully overshot her mark, expecting the Tooth to lean back to catch her, expecting the Tooth to expect *her* to have better aim.

They split the difference. The Tooth caught her in the arm, a long thin slice as Zemolai dropped onto his back, her elbows hitting his shoulders, her knees braced against the small of his back, her body caught tight between the pinch of his wings. The Tooth roared, furious at this violation, stabbing aimlessly over his shoulder and just missing her eye.

Timyan grabbed the Tooth's knife arm and held on for all he was worth, but even the full weight of his body barely dragged at the warrior's enhanced strength. In grabbing the Tooth, Timyan had lost his shield, opening the side of his body to a series of furious punches. A couple more of those would rupture a kidney.

While Timyan weighed the Tooth down and Zemolai scrabbled one-handed for the wing port release on his back, Eleny rolled her netted body toward the shelving units—specifically, toward the debris that had followed Zemolai down from the top shelf. She grabbed hold of a small throwing knife and cut at the ropes, nightmarishly slow at first, and then faster and faster as she gained room to maneuver.

The Tooth flexed his wings, opening them a foot and then snapping them back in, keeping Zemolai off balance. He tried to shake Timyan loose, but Timyan twisted with the motion, his back to the Tooth now, holding the man's arm away from both of them. Zemolai locked one arm tight around the Tooth's throat, but she was slippery with her own blood, barely tilting the man's head back.

Eleny kicked free of the net and dove for her discarded duffel bag, digging frantically through the top pocket.

Zemolai groped at the Tooth's wing port release, her goal simple and ruthless: rip a wing loose, get her hand into the sensitive wiring of the port itself, and bring him down through pain compliance.

She didn't get that far. Eleny lunged forward on her knees and stabbed her syringe into the Tooth's thigh. He kicked her in the gut, but she curled around the blow and depressed the plunger on the druggist's high-concentration sedative.

The Tooth screamed in fury. It wasn't working. There was too much mechalin going through his system, he was going to knock them loose and tear them limb from limb—

And then his rage did their work for them, hurtling his drugged blood through his heart and his arteries and straight to all those vulnerable little transmitters in his brain. The Tooth staggered. Fell. Eleny scrambled out of the way, but Timyan collapsed beneath several hundred pounds of muscle and metal and Zemolai to boot.

Zemolai climbed out from between sharp metal feathers, shaky on her feet. "Get up," she ordered raggedly. "Hurry."

But Timyan was trapped beneath the Tooth, only one arm and part of his face clear of the crimson and black. Eleny tried to shove the Tooth off him, but she couldn't do more than shift his shoulder.

"Gotta move him in pieces," Zemolai said. Blood flowed hot and sticky from her arm as she worked, bright red dewdrops smearing across metal and leather. She disengaged the lock at the base of his spine. The cylinders in his back ports whirred obligingly, and she dragged each wing off his limp body.

Timyan crawled out from beneath the Tooth, breathing heavily and flexing his limbs. He looked up at Zemolai. "Is there any rope in here?"

It was a shock to hear this from Timyan, of all people, seemingly the meekest among them. But the bolt-babies had continually surprised her. Zemolai glowered at him, disapproving—but she still gestured to the left.

Eleny caught on a second later. "This isn't what we came for!" she protested.

But it was too good an opportunity to resist. The rebels had come seeking an advantage, hadn't they? They were never going to get another run at a Tooth like this.

Zemolai considered foiling them. Standing her ground the way she had with Galiana. But she looked down at the Tooth and felt nothing but disgust. He'd been felled by a pair of unprepared workers and a half-broken ex-Winged in mechalin withdrawal. She knew exactly what the Voice would say in this situation:

He deserved whatever he got.

"He has a resonance chip in his thigh, same as I did," Zemolai said briskly. "You have two options. First, you can leave it where it is. A Tooth comes and goes on his own schedule. If he was arming up tonight, then he was about to go out on a mission and likely won't be missed till tomorrow. It's unlikely anyone else will access the armory tonight and notice this mess. They'll all be reveling till dawn."

"But the chip is trackable, isn't it?" Eleny asked doubtfully. "I'm not sure whether Galiana has anything to block it."

"Your second option is to dig the chip out. In that case, an alarm will sound immediately, and every Winged in the city will hunt you down to find him. Up to you."

They chose the first option.

Even without his wings the Tooth was strikingly heavy, but together they got him trussed and gagged and off the floor. Zemolai patted him down for manual distress beacons and found none. A Tooth didn't call for backup. He *was* the backup.

There was no time to put the armory back together, but they padlocked his wings and the worst evidence of the fight into a storage crate to slow the investigation down.

Next, they had to get the Tooth out of the training grounds.

The only way out was the way they'd come in: across the open training yard, around the hallway, through the kitchens, and out the worker tunnel; where, if nothing else had gone wrong, a covered car was waiting for their weapons haul. They had a heavily modified warrior to carry, and nothing but the deepening night to conceal them.

They crossed the yard like mice in the kingdom of owls: just trying to stay lucky. The tower was an exclamation mark at their backs, pointing its accusation for anyone who'd listen. An eternity of seconds later, they reached the relative safety of worker byways, and they only knocked their prisoner's head once or twice on the way out.

The alley was still empty. Another bit of luck, but one that wouldn't last. They hoisted their sleeping cargo into the car and darted back through the servants' entrance, quickly sketching out the details of their new plan.

"Call Rustaya," Eleny told Timyan. "Tell them to get down here and be ready to drive. We can fill a duffel apiece while Galiana finishes with—while Galiana finishes."

Timyan already had his short-distance coder in hand. They had agreed to radio silence except in case of emergency, but this certainly qualified. Timyan tapped out their message in a bit of memorized code.

Zemolai stopped when they reached the kitchen.

"What is it?" Timyan said. "We have to keep moving."

"I've gone beyond what I agreed to do," she said. "You already knew I had my own business here. I'll meet you at the car."

Eleny obviously wanted to argue, but they were out of time.

Zemolai waited till they were out of sight, and then she jogged to the great stone door of the pantry. It opened lightly, on well-oiled tracks. Everything inside was exactly as she remembered: clean, precise shelves at neurotically right angles, hundreds of linear feet of bags and boxes and cans. Enough to feed a hungry fighting force and all its attendant staff for weeks under siege.

She winced at the thought of another Zemolai long past, furtively entering this dark room, crawling into the farthest corner to pry up a floorboard with her bare fingers. Her memory had the far-off tang of myth, a story told to herself at night, worn to a high gloss over time.

Now she lifted up that same old wooden board and wedged her hand beneath, grimacing at the dusty damp and half-expecting to lose a finger to some mutant vermin grown large on filched enhancers.

Her fingertips brushed paper, and it was like an electric jolt to her nervous system. She drew out the bundle: more than two dozen letters tied with twine, nibbled a bit around the edges, but basically intact. A lump rose in her throat.

It was in here: the answer. Or *an* answer, one answer to a single question out of hundreds, but it was one that had worried her for decades. What had Niklaus been trying to tell her?

Zemolai tucked the letters inside her vest. She knelt another moment on the floor, inexplicably out of breath again. She told herself it was the enclosed space (definitely not fear) and not fear (clearly, it was only the enclosed space).

"I'm all right," she whispered, just to break the awful silence with a human voice. "I'm alive. I'm here. I'm all right."

And then an alarm sounded, shrill and unmistakable. One, then two, then all the interior courtyard klaxons blared in furious panic, and thunder quickly followed: the thunder of every gate crashing down over the training ground exits.

The whole plan was going to shit.

Zemolai was off her knees and running through the kitchen before she could think twice. The wail of the klaxon set her blood pumping. Her response was programmed deep, like wires through her bones.

She dashed through the dining room, abandoning the rebels' carefully crafted route. A pair of double doors led directly to the training yard, and Zemolai threw them open—to a complete disaster coming her way.

The perimeter alarms were going off.

The ones that weren't supposed to be connected tonight.

The raucous noise was punctuated by strobing pink and purple lights. A plea to the tower: if you can't hear us, then *see us, see us*. The outer gates had sealed. The inner doors were chiming a countdown, soon to join them.

Eleny and Timyan were racing across the yard, staggered out from one another, weighed down by their duffel bags. Galiana appeared next, the stricken look on her face a sure sign of guilt—wherever she'd been, whatever she'd tried to do, she had triggered this—but without the extra weight of the armory on her back, she was catching up to her teammates quickly.

They were in flat-out escape mode, not even detouring into the shelter of the inner hallway—which was smart, since it was about to lock down and trap everyone inside.

Zemolai registered their terror almost as an afterthought. Her attention was focused past them, all the way across the yard, on the twin figures stepping out of the commander's quarters.

Mecha Vodaya. A slip of darkness framed by shining silver wings. And at her side another Winged, a young man with garish green and yellow feathers, her new protégé, fresh and adoring: Winged Mitrios.

In the dull calm at the back of her mind, Zemolai knew that Vodaya was *always* the last one to leave. She was *always* finishing some other work first, because her work was more important than the pomp and ceremony of graduation.

That was at the back of her mind. The front was a firestorm of rage and hurt and resentment and jealousy and fear, and Zemolai wanted to fight, wanted to hurt, wanted to rip somebody apart with her hands and her teeth and the force of her fury. She would never succeed, and she wanted to die trying.

But Vodaya locked eyes with her across the yard, and Zemolai froze in place.

CHAPTER THIRTEEN

The gods say they are not withdrawing from us, they are only tired and need rest, but who can believe that? The workers blame the farmers, the engineers blame the warriors, on and on, they will tear one another apart before this is done.

Oh, I cannot take it! We've brought this on ourselves!

—*Diary of Scholar Pierenski*

Zenya's life, until this point, had balanced on a wire. Her family (Niklaus) on one side. Her chosen sect (Vodaya) on the other. Two obligations kept carefully, desperately apart.

It was all falling to pieces.

Another month had passed, and the conflict had only grown worse. Every time the fighting slowed, there was a factory explosion, or a sabotaged power grid, or another street demonstration devolving into violence. Production lines were disrupted. Trade was stalled.

New weapons appeared with disturbing regularity: projectiles, bombs, hidden blades. For years the engineers had resisted designing such tools for the god-appointed warriors of the mecha sect, and all the while they'd been stockpiling such things for themselves.

And then pamphlets were found circulating in the worker districts, printed in defiance of both scholar and mecha leadership, announcing a public reading of the work of Heretic Scholar Vikenzy. The chaos was brief. Two dozen agitators were arrested, six injured, and an unknown number scattered from the meeting place, but there was no sign of the heretic's paper.

Winged Pilivar's team did not rest until they had traced the origin of the incendiary pamphlet: Milar Niklaus, likely aided by his father, Milar Tomel. Agitators from the scholar sect bent on converting naïve workers to Vikenzy's brand of divine denialism.

And once Niklaus and his father were discovered missing, their home vacated in secret a month earlier—at that point, it was only a matter of time before their sole living relative, Pava Zemolai, was brought in for questioning.

Zenya stared at the evidence spread out on the floor before her.

The pamphlets were all painstakingly handwritten in thick blue ink on cheap yellow paper. The text was provocative, detailing the purported crimes of their mecha captors, and encouraging a live demonstration, the details of which would be described in person at the reading. (It was an audacious loophole: a reading was not technically publication.)

By the time Zenya reached the final exclamation mark, the world around her had faded to a distant buzz. The text was infuriating, criminally misleading, a betrayal of everything she was working to preserve. And she would have recognized that handwriting anywhere.

She finally forced a response out, cracked and close to wobbling. "I don't know anything about this. I—I've lived in Pava for over two years."

She was in a small, windowless room, kneeling upon the ground in supplication pose. Winged Dietra loomed over her, no less intimidating for having left her wings outside, radiating disapproval from every sharp angle. "When was your last contact with your family?"

"I . . ." Zenya thought fast, struggling to recall if anyone had seen her exit the grounds that last time. What would her roommates say if they were questioned? What piece of truth could she use to obscure the rest? "We used to exchange letters."

"Used to?"

"My brother—Milar Niklaus—we both became busy. We fell out of touch months ago. You can check with the mail service." The last was blurted too defensively, she knew.

"There are many records at our disposal," Dietra said coolly. "The mail service included. Why didn't you mention these letters to your instructor?"

"The contents were unremarkable."

"And where are these letters now?"

"Discarded. I had no reason to keep them."

Dietra's lips thinned at that. "You knew about the situation in the city."

"The situation, yes. I didn't know my family was involved." It was a simple lie, to hold so much weight. Dimwitted ignorance wasn't flattering, but it wasn't betrayal either.

Winged Dietra kept at her for another twenty minutes before bowing out. Zenya took a deep breath and waited. And waited.

The minutes ticked by, and even taking into account that every minute felt like an hour, she thought more time had passed than necessary. Was another Winged going to take Dietra's place? Zenya struggled to think of something, anything else, but there was nothing to distract her. If she stopped worrying about the Winged, she'd start thinking about Niklaus, and if she thought about him, she would burst into angry tears.

When the door opened again, it framed a familiar set of wings.

"Follow me," Vodaya said. "Or would you rather stay?"

Zenya hastened after her. They passed Winged Dietra, who watched pensively with Winged Raksa at her side. Raksa leaned down to whisper in her ear, and Dietra glowered at him.

It wasn't until Vodaya and Zenya were crossing the training yard, safely distant from the grand hallway and its many spying doorways, that Zenya said, "Thank you, I didn't know how long they were going to—"

Vodaya spun, staggering Zenya to a halt. "Don't think me a fool," she hissed. "I maintained your ignorance in this matter. I'd like to believe it. But don't imagine for one second that you can lie to me. I know you visited your family. I know where you are at all times. You are *my* responsibility. Your actions reflect on *me*. Do you understand that?"

Zenya stayed silent. There was no correct answer today.

"Winged Dietra is my quadrant leader," Vodaya said. "She trusts my judgment, but there are limits to all things. You have to prove your loyalty beyond a doubt, Pava Zemolai. Beyond a *doubt*. If you want to earn back the trust of your peers—if you want to stand pure before the mecha god when it comes time to beg your wings—then I advise you to proceed carefully. Do you understand?"

"Yes," Zenya said.

Vodaya gazed past her. She looked incredibly tired, and for a moment the truth crowded Zenya's teeth. She *did* have information, vital information, because if Niklaus had found the papers during a routine catalog, then he had done so under Scholar Pyetka's supervision, and Zenya knew that floor of the tower like the back of her hand. She tried to imagine what they would do with that information and swallowed the words back down.

And then Vodaya nodded to herself, coming to an internal decision. To Zenya, she spoke with the finality of law. "Stay in the compound, where I can vouch for your whereabouts. Take no correspondence. Commit to your studies. And whatever I ask of you, I expect you to do it."

Over the following weeks, Zenya sank into a prison of her own making. If she'd been eager to impress Vodaya before, she was now desperate to prove her presence more valuable than her expulsion.

It meant performing flawlessly. It meant relying ever more heavily on her bottle of pills. It meant studying like her life depended on every correct answer, and it meant following every one of Vodaya's orders without hesitation.

A small blessing: the extra work kept her away from home, where her five-unit took great pains to exclude her from every conversation. After her interrogation, they'd become mistrustful, dismissive when they acknowledged her at all.

It grated (she deserved it). But she deserved it (oh, it grated).

Zenya had enough to worry about with Winged Vodaya. "You're distracted!" she'd shout, throwing practice knives at Zenya's legs. "You're wasting my time! I thought you were better than this!"

Days went by in which Zenya said little more than *yes* and *I'm sorry*, and then she came home to her teammates and repeated *yes* and *I'm sorry*, and then she hid in her room for the night and practiced new ways to say *yes* and *I'm sorry*, and then in the morning she put them into effect and they didn't help, not one bit.

And then, after weeks of hitting all of her marks and saying everything she was supposed to say, Zenya found herself the recipient of some genuinely positive feedback. The words came like blessed rain after a long drought.

"Don't think I haven't noticed the extra hours you commit on your free day," Vodaya murmured. It was an unseasonably warm afternoon, and she was stripped down to a sleeveless tunic and light breeches. They'd been sparring, alone, like the early days.

She put an arm around Zenya's shoulders, her bare skin sun-roughened and thinly veiling the ropy muscles beneath. Even Vodaya's affection was a reminder of her physical power. She said, "It may seem as though I push you harder than the others—that's all right, don't deny it—but you know I only have your best interests in mind, yes?"

"Yes, of course," Zenya said quickly.

Vodaya smiled. "You've come a long way since Milar." This close, the lines in her face were in sharp relief, equal parts laugh and frown, etched deep by a dozen years in the sky. They creased with sympathy as she said, "I know you are having trouble with your teammates. Don't worry about them."

"It's hard not to," Zenya admitted.

"You only need concern yourself with my opinion," Vodaya said firmly. "And in *my* opinion, you've done what you need to do to separate your professional and personal lives. What else could I ask for?"

The contrary little voice at the back of Zenya's mind whispered, *there's nothing else you can ask of me, that's* everything—but she shoved it away just as quickly.

Vodaya clapped her on the back and resumed her fighting stance, limbs loose and unfettered by stress. It was a *good* day, and on good days, Zenya could see her entire future taking shape, a straight path from training to graduation to service in the mecha god's honor. On days like this, Zenya could practically feel the wind against her wings.

Of course it couldn't last.

An older trainee, Pava Senkai, burst into the yard, her hair a tangled mess. "Winged Vodaya!" she gasped. "You're needed by Winged Pilivar."

"What is it?" Vodaya was on alert now, her easy warmth vanished.

"Creator Talley is dead."

Creator Talley, the engineers' representative on the Council of Five, was found dead in his home the day before he'd planned to put forth a vote of no confidence in Mecha Petrogon.

The cause of his death was unclear, but it didn't matter. Overnight, protests turned into riots. Fist-fights turned into street brawls. The engineers took down an electrical tower and plunged entire neighborhoods into darkness. The workers couldn't work. The traveling merchants had no products to trade.

Creator Vanyamir—Talley's former partner, his second-in-command, the most likely candidate to take charge of the sect—covered the city in propaganda, throwing up flyers as quickly as mecha patrols could tear them down. She traveled underground, rabble-rousing in the deepest and poorest worker burrows.

Her description circulated the training grounds: white-haired, bony thin, a face lined by sixty-three years of hard tinkering and hate. It was entirely possible, they whispered, that she had killed Creator Talley herself to generate outrage.

Winged Raksa led a ground team into Faiyan District, looking for Creator Vanyamir's printing operation. He found armored suits. Weaponized vehicles. A warehouse packed with dishonorable inventions meant to elevate untrained amateurs against the god's chosen warriors.

The discovery ushered in a new conflict phase. Mecha Petrogon formed city patrols and did not consult the Council of Five about their use. He deliberately summoned militant border five-units into Radezhda and assigned them to the engineer districts. As more violence erupted, he expanded control to the scholar districts.

Three weeks passed, and half the city was under siege.

Trapped as she was in the training grounds, Zenya could only piece together the situation through secondhand reports. Quaser and Faiyan were the main battlegrounds. The residents had sealed the windows of the tallest engineering buildings with metal shutters, locking creators into their labs and everyone else into the street. There were rumors of an even greater defense system being constructed underground.

The top of tower Lizmanya was constantly flashing with godly light as the engineers begged knowledge and guidance through the creator god's portal. The light carried so far that she could see it all the way in Pava on a dark night.

Was the creator god encouraging their behavior, or ignoring it?

Zenya was three hours into much-needed sleep when an intruder woke her, shaking her roughly by the shoulder. Zenya flailed for a moment before recognizing Pava Senkai.

"Where's Vodaya?" Zenya mumbled, struggling loose from her sheets.

"Working," Senkai said curtly. "And so are you. Repair station, level ten."

Adrenaline snapped through Zenya's system. This wasn't an exercise. They were going to tower Kemyana! She grabbed her tool belt, moving more by instinct than thought, but as soon as she stood up, pain exploded between her temples, doubling her over.

Zenya supported herself with her hands on her knees, head low. She breathed long, circular breaths, thinking through the pain. For three days she had been riding hard on the edge of sleeplessness, regularly popping enhancers to stay focused. Three hours of sleep hadn't been nearly enough time to leech the drugs from her system.

Hangover didn't begin to cover it.

Zenya took another pill, fumbling clumsily at the cap. She promised herself she would drink copious amounts of water and take a few days off from the pills as soon as this assignment was over.

By the time Zenya reached the tower elevator, she was pain-free and raring to go. The rest of her five-unit fidgeted anxiously around her, their eyes glassy-bright with drugs of their own, but they weren't three days deep like she was.

They reached a staggeringly large balcony on the tenth level of the tower. Baskets of parts were stacked head-high on all sides. The floor was striped in oil slicks. The wind was freezing.

Senkai drew Zenya to the end of the balcony. "Have you used one of these?"

Zenya shook her head, squinting against the wind to examine the workstation. A long metal beam extended from the balcony railing, rigged up with a belt-and-pulley system. A sturdy delivery bucket bobbed at the end, swaying, waiting, over the dark city.

"Basic haul line," Senkai said briskly. "Crank here to bring the bucket in. Unload, then immediately send it back out. My advice? Rotate stations and keep one of you at rest. That gives you a quarter of your time on your ass, a quarter of your time freezing on the haul line, and the rest doing repairs. Lavatory's down the hall. Better to use it when you can."

There were lights in the distance, bits of the city furiously illuminated between patches of residential darkness. All of it scored by the sounds of combat.

"Somebody will contact you periodically from resupply," Senkai continued. "Know what you have and what you need at all times. They'll be here and gone quick."

A figure swooped by, rapid and terrible. He came down like a hawk diving for the kill and snatched up the payload with a force that set the whole delivery beam shaking. Without a word of acknowledgment, he disappeared back into the city.

Senkai patted Zenya roughly on the back. "Stay focused," she said, and left.

She *left*. It was their first time in the field, and they were completely on their own.

Zenya took a deep breath and pushed the panic away. There was a commotion coming, a furious beating of air like a flock of birds fleeing a storm. The night sky was awake and hurried and needful, and it swept Zenya's hair back from her face like a god's cold breath.

Civil war flew at them, wearing metal wings.

They fell into a rhythm. They had to. Zenya rested one hour in four, and she found it worse than working continuously. Every time her energy flagged, she swallowed another pill, all too aware that each dose was slightly less effective than the last—and that the longer she waited to crash, the worse it would be.

But it was that or fail, and she would not fail.

The haul line was the worst of it. Zenya stood at the balcony's edge for an hour at a time, squinting into the dark sky and wondering which flick of movement would resolve itself into a warrior bearing an anvil's weight of broken equipment for the bucket.

Dawn came, and the harsh sunlight was worse than the cold. Smoke curled up from Faiyan and Quaser. Distant figures circled the battlefields, darting down in synchronized attacks. Sometimes they flew back to Kemyana with a prisoner struggling inside a net, one torn rope away from plummeting to their death.

Night fell. Romil's hands shook. Dolynne had a steady flow of tears down their cheeks, which the others politely ignored. They worked till their fingers bled, switched shifts, burnt out their muscles for a while instead, rested briefly, kept going.

Dawn came again, and with it a spasm of despair.

A fresh-faced Pava appeared in their doorway with cold food and a request for inventory. "Eat quickly," she advised. "There's word the Quaser wall is cracking."

"When are we being relieved?" Lijo begged.

The Pava said, "Soon." They always said *soon*.

Zenya was halfway through restocking a bandolier when she noticed a strange sensation against her thigh. She scratched at it absently, shifted in her damp clothing, assumed it an itch born of too many hours chafing against the same sweaty seams. But it wasn't an itch.

It was heat.

Her breath stopped. She knew the shape of it. She knew what it meant. She managed to finish packing the bandolier before begging a lavatory run.

Zenya closeted herself in a stall and reached into her pocket with trembling fingers.

The distress beacon pulsed weakly, flashes of emergency red beneath its translucent shell. Every beat of warmth was an accusation. A challenge. A plea for help. Niklaus.

I'll come running if I can't come flying.

In her state, she wasn't even sure she could run.

Zenya lurched back to the balcony like a marionette with half its strings cut. Everything on the repair station was cast in bright relief. The oil slicks. The haggard tear lines on Dolynne's face. The shimmer of sunlight on the delivery beam.

Zenya waited, every second a blow to the chest, until the Pava returned with their supplies. She had barely begun to unpack when Zenya shouted, "When is our relief coming?"

The young woman glowered. "Soon, I said."

Zenya strode forward, saw the woman's eyes widening in surprise, saw her teammates sitting up to startled attention as she grabbed the Pava by her shoulders and yelled, "We've been working for two days straight! You want us to drop in our tracks? To patch a pair of wings wrong and send a warrior tumbling out of the sky? We're done! Get somebody up here!"

"Get your hands off me." The Pava shook Zenya loose, disgusted, glowering—but also, *there*: a strand of pity. "You should be ashamed of yourself," she said.

She strode off. But she hadn't said *no*, and she hadn't taken her cart.

Dolynne slapped Zenya on the back, making her startle. But they only laughed. "Who'd have thought it would be you first? You saved me the embarrassment!"

The others joined in cheerily, but Zenya scarcely heard them. All her focus was on the ticking clock, the pulse of warmth against her thigh, the wordless insistence of the distress call—the thought of her brother in so much danger, he'd resorted to using mecha technology.

"I have to go," she said hoarsely, and just like that she destroyed their goodwill.

Dolynne recoiled. "Our replacements aren't here yet."

"I have to go," Zenya repeated, backing away.

"We don't know if she's actually getting anyone!"

"I'm sorry." Zenya staggered for the exit. Their outrage was drowned out by the roar in her ears—but it wasn't her heart pumping, it was the grind of overheated metal as a Winged careened toward the balcony.

It was abandonment of the worst kind. Desertion of her post in the middle of a crisis. Vodaya would never forgive this.

Zenya stared at the oncoming warrior, at the light washing like liquid over his wings. This was what she'd wanted since she was old enough to realize it was possible. For a chance at flight, she had ground her body to pieces, endured isolation and exhaustion and insult.

But it wasn't only the joy of flight that had drawn her. It was an unshakable belief in the merit of the mecha god's directive: *In word and deed, become the protector.* Niklaus's distress burned against her thigh. She had made a promise.

Zenya fled the balcony and left her calling behind for the sake of fulfilling it.

She hurtled down the interior stairwell, terrified of who she might encounter in the elevator bays. The steps were punishing, the pain a welcome distraction. A door waited below, and once it locked behind her, there would be no coming back.

Zenya took one step outside—and stumbled against the outer wall, dizzy and shaking. She could barely focus her eyes.

It was the mechalin comedown that had been stalking her since before her shift began. She felt it bubbling up her throat, the hot-cold panic of a drug crash, and she knew she had already wildly exceeded her daily dosage, but what other choice did she have?

She dug the bottle out of her pocket, shook out the very last pill, and dry-swallowed it.

It took several agonizing minutes for the drug to take effect. Zenya breathed through the protesting clench of her stomach, painfully aware of her body's sluggish response, and then lurched off the wall, the distress beacon clutched tightly in one hand.

For a moment she clung to the foolish hope that Niklaus and Tomel had hidden in Chae. Or Zavet. Maybe they were short on supplies, or needed medicine, and Zenya was the only person they could trust.

But the thought was fleeting, a waste of time. She knew exactly where the beacon led.

Zenya dashed through empty streets, an entire city in hiding, following the hot-cold pattern of the distress beacon and irrationally wishing she'd had the forethought to steal something more cutting-edge.

She reached Faiyan first, and the destruction there took her breath away.

Roofs caved in. Streets like rivers of glittering glass. And everywhere: trails of dried and drying blood. There were surgeons digging in the rubble alongside survivors in tattered clothes. Youthful protesters sat in rows on the sidewalk, their arms bound, their eyes bubbling angry or plain vacant. Wingless guards stood watch over the rows, waiting for prisoner transport.

Zenya took this in at a run, panic pumping fresh energy to her legs. She ran past shouts and tears and mournful wails, and the deeper she penetrated the district, the more volatile the scene became. Here, protesters were still being pacified, dozens tangled in nets, dozens more tangled hand-to-hand with ground patrols. Deeper still, and it was *real* fighting: knives clashing, clubs swinging, screams ragged with dust and fury. Zenya veered to avoid the thick of it, skirting an abandoned laboratory, glancing through the windows and then wishing she hadn't.

There's word the Quaser wall is cracking.

She saw it long before she reached it: a horror. The engineers had built an enormous dome, a mechanical wonder of interlocking metal plates that came up in two halves and snapped shut over the district. It was half a mile across and five stories tall, with the top of tower Lizmanya emerging from a cutout in the main seam. The tower windows were armored, impenetrable unless the Winged were willing to damage the tower itself.

Zenya paused, swaying on her feet. She saw Winged converge on the dome. A dozen of them brandished hooks and crowbars, and a second wave flanked them with real weaponry.

Panels slid open on the dome's surface, and cannon muzzles peeked through. They fired simultaneously, a great booming recoil of fire and smoke and cannon shot. The panels slid shut, and the Winged landed hard, working at the seams with their crowbars.

She thought: it must be so dark in there.

She thought: it must sound like the world is ending.

The Winged pried at the main seam with dogged strength, a long line of them working in furious coordination. More panels opened, and the engineers fired their weapons. One of the cannonballs hit its mark, smashing through a warrior's left wing and striking another in the chest.

Before the tiny victory could gel, a new figure appeared in bright crimson wings. He landed hard and shoved both arms through one of the closing gaps. Whoever was strapped inside the cannon station never had a chance. The warrior tucked his wings tight and plunged inside, and the panel snapped shut behind him.

The Teeth were here. And one had breached the dome.

Zenya ran toward it because there was nothing else she could do. Surely Niklaus had some plan—a message outside the dome that only she would understand.

She never found out. Whatever the Tooth did inside, he did with ruthless efficiency. An almighty mechanical screech sounded, and one side of the dome began to collapse. The panels folded down, one row behind the next, metal screaming, *people* screaming. The cannon stations set under the roof disconnected, and their operators plummeted inside steel cages.

The wall hit the ground in an explosion of metal and dust. As it began to clear, the scene turned gruesome. Dozens of Winged darted into Quaser, and the district cracked open beneath them like the innards of a split turtle. Foot patrols poured out of neighboring alleys. It was chaos at street level, nobody sure whether to fight or seek shelter, and all trampling one another in their haste.

Zenya clambered over the collapsed wall. It had originally fit into an enormous trench circling the district, but it had fallen haphazardly, sticking up in jagged slices.

Fights broke out all around her, workers and engineers and scholars and warriors only distinguishable by the quality of their protective gear. Zenya wore nothing thicker than her leathers. She carried nothing more dangerous than her knives. She ran wildly, without thought. The beacon dragged her onward, so hot she thought its pattern would be burned into her skin.

She neared a lab: three stories tall, metal and glass. Arrows poured from windows on the top floor. One struck a Winged, but she broke the shaft sticking out of her arm and kept going. There were four, no, *five* Winged coming, and they each carried a smoldering green orb: fire bombs, full of shrapnel and a volatile oil that could not be doused with water.

The Winged aimed their bodies boots-first and kicked back whoever was behind the shutters. They shoved their bombs through the gaps and launched back into the sky.

The detonation blew heat and glass over the street. The world reverberated with the crash of shrapnel inside, dents bowing out metal shutters like they were infected canned goods. Screams above, screams below, it all added to the chorus of a district crumbling to pieces.

And the beacon had gone dead in Zenya's hand.

Later, it only came to her in flashes, brief and painful images that she doused with denial and distraction and drugs. She remembered:

Ripping a pair of ground-level window shutters loose with her bare, bleeding hands.

Running through the dark building, floor by floor. Screaming their names till she couldn't recognize her own voice. Bodies, in a pile—

Staggering out into painfully bright sunlight. Escaping Quaser. Crying in the street.

It was all fractured, gruesome half-recorded memories with missing pieces. Zenya had been holding back a mechalin crash for hours, for *days*. Her body shook. She could barely see, but she traced her steps anyway, like a beacon was calling her back to Pava.

There was a good chance they'd refuse her. There was a good chance she'd die convulsing outside the main gate, her five-unit and all their neighbors standing atop the wall to get a good look at the traitor Pava Zemolai. *Milar* Zemolai.

Zenya ran home anyway, because she didn't know what else to do.

Later, she would not remember how she got back to the training grounds, only that she did. She reached the gate and found she couldn't take another step. She cast about, desperate, willing somebody, *anybody*, to find her. A guard walked out to check her credentials, and she couldn't even speak—but he took one look and understood exactly what was happening.

The guard called for help, fuzzy words on a buzzing breeze. Zenya sank to the ground. She felt hands on her arms and legs. She caught scattered words—*withdrawal* and *berserk* and *containment*—each one spoken with more urgency than the last. Then a dark space, a narrow space, thudding steps threatening to split her head in half.

They thrust Zenya into a containment cage. She curled up on the ground, hot and cold, hot and cold. Somewhere in the night she went mad.

When the cage door swung open again, Zenya was exhausted, sweat-soaked, starving—but lucid. Vodaya knelt at her side, wingless, silhouetted against the faint light of the hallway like a temple icon come to life. Zenya tried to sit up, but she was too weak.

"Shh, come here," Vodaya said gently. She pulled Zenya halfway into her lap, cradling her head, washing her in the warm scent of leather and dust. Through chattering teeth, Zenya gasped out the worst of it: they were dead, they were dead, she tried to get them out, but they wouldn't listen to her, and now they were dead.

Vodaya was commiseration and comfort, confessor and absolution. She rocked Zenya through the worst of her crying, and then leaned down, and kissed her forehead, and said, "We will get through this, Zemolai. We will get through this. Stay with me, and I will never leave you."

CHAPTER FOURTEEN

These were terrible times. We were made animals by our grief. The truth is that we would have done anything to make them want us again.

—Fragment 39, *the Dierka Mountain Scrolls*

MECHA VODAYA STRODE ACROSS THE YARD, and the wrath on her face was paralyzing. Zemolai stood pinned in place by it.

And oh, Winged Mitrios. So young and strong. He had looked up to Zemolai for so long, and she had repaid him with what—jealousy? Childish resentment? Now he approached with a look of furious conviction. It wasn't just anger—it was eagerness. It was the fierce desire to prove himself. It was *glee* that this opportunity had presented itself when he was in the presence of his idol.

It was a feeling Zemolai knew too well.

"Go! Go!" Timyan yelled. Zemolai could barely hear him over the alarms. He and Eleny still had their duffels bouncing heavily at their sides— fools, in their panic, failing to drop the extra weight. Galiana pulled ahead of them, nothing but her tool belt to slow her down, her arms pumping tight against her ribs. Warning bells chimed over the dining room door. Any moment, the lockdown procedure would activate and seal them off from escape.

And still Zemolai couldn't move.

Winged Mitrios launched upward, kicking up a sandstorm. Vodaya didn't even blink. She strode through the cloud like a knife, her eyes burning solely for Zemolai, and Zemolai knew that look too well. It was outrage, *betrayal*.

As though *she* were the injured party.

Mitrios drew two weapons from his hips, and neither one held a net. They were bolt-guns, shining silver and bulky with expanded ammunition chambers. He gave no warning, made no request for their cooperation or compliance.

With pure exultation, he fired. One bolt struck the ground, burying deep. The second sliced through the meat of Galiana's calf, sending her into a shock-faced stagger. She tried to yell for help, but it was only a gasp, and the others didn't hear.

Mitrios fired the rest of his bolts in a long line, aiming for as many of them as possible, and the shots came so rapidly they seemed to land all at once:

Three in Eleny's back, *one two three*, like a plant sprouting new shoots.

One grazing Timyan's arm, splashing a line of blood nearly black in the emergency lighting.

And the rest buried in the wall beside Zemolai's head, landing like punches; a cluster of instant deaths narrowly dodged.

Galiana ripped a large metal sphere from her belt and threw it to the ground. It landed with a weighty thud, and she kept running without looking back. She missed the sight of Eleny falling face first into the dirt, the bolts quivering in the flesh around her spine, the duffel of mecha weapons landing hard at her side.

But Timyan didn't. Zemolai saw the realization dawning terrible on his face, the split-second debate: was he close enough to stop, could he save her, was she still alive, or would he only doom himself at her side? *Should* he doom himself at her side?

Mitrios cast aside the empty guns and angled downward. He meant to attack the rest of them directly. Their only grace was the long head start they'd had running across the yard, but Mitrios would close that in a matter of heartbeats.

Galiana reached Zemolai first, grabbing her by her lacerated arm and shoving her backward, and it was the pain that finally broke her paralysis.

Galiana pulled a small remote from her belt, and belatedly Zemolai realized what it was she'd thrown to the ground: her prototype signal blocker, meant to kill electrical impulses in Winged mechanicals.

The device she had explicitly promised to leave behind.

Galiana hit the switch. A brief flash of light emitted from the sphere and then sputtered out. Zemolai had one heartbeat of fear (hope?) as it appeared to fail—and then Winged Mitrios flew through the invisible energy field, and every mechanical implant in his body went dead. He gasped, his wings outstretched and motionless, and tumbled from fifteen feet up. He fell with all the weight of his wings on top of him and crashed in a heap in the sand.

But Vodaya . . . Vodaya strode right over the signal blocker without missing a beat. She glanced once toward Mitrios, disdain curling her lip. A red light flashed on her breastplate—no, *through* her breastplate, like her armor was made of glass and her heart had caught fire. The light pulsed three times before fading.

Vodaya stared at Zemolai, her wings flexing defiantly around her body, and she would not stop.

Galiana groaned and shoved Zemolai through the door. Timyan hurtled in after them, tears streaking his cheeks, constricting his chest, and Zemolai caught her last glimpse of Vodaya stepping over Eleny's body, only ten yards away and moving quickly.

"Come on, *come on.*" Galiana fumbled at her remote, panic-fingers making her clumsy. On her second try, she hit the right sequence. The small sphere exploded, shredding any possibility of the Winged reverse-engineering her prototype.

The lockdown chimes spat their last warning, and a great metal barricade plummeted over the dining room door. Klaxons continued to wail throughout the compound, but they were muffled, distant thunder. The three of them had only a moment to stare at one another, coming to grips with how rapidly everything had fallen apart.

The interior lighting strobed. The next phase, room-level lockdown, was imminent.

Zemolai turned to Galiana and yelled, "What the hell happened? *Where were you?*"

All the blood had rushed from Galiana's face, but she flared up defensively. "We don't have time for this."

"You said the alarms would be disconnected!"

"I know what I said, but we have to go *now* before those gates drop!"

Galiana took Timyan by the arm, but he only stared at her. Stared *past* her, to the doors, through which Eleny was either dead or breathing her last.

"We have to go!" Galiana shook him hard.

"Yes," he gasped.

The gate over the kitchen entrance rattled in warning. They limped between dining tables, droplets of blood marking a gory trail behind them. Galiana dragged Timyan toward the door, toward the lights strobing ever faster, toward the first squeal of a rarely used gear turning in its mount, toward escape.

And Zemolai . . .

Zemolai stopped. She saw the gate cover pop open and the metal plates unfold. She saw Galiana pull Timyan's head down to duck through, and she saw the brief moment of confusion and alarm when Galiana looked back to find her lagging.

The gate crashed down, sealing off the dining room from the kitchen.

Galiana pounded on the other side. Her voice came through muffled: "Zemolai! Don't move! I'll get you out!"

But Zemolai had already turned away. Toward the other gate, the one that separated her from the training yard. Beyond it stood certain condemnation.

There was a perverse comfort in that. A *certainty*. Zemolai had only ever wanted to be certain.

And then, as though her thoughts were a distress beacon of their own, a new sound pierced the ongoing wail of the alarms: a short, sharp bell, chiming in bursts of four.

There was a live-speak radio hanging next to the door. It was ringing.

Zemolai drifted toward it with a dreamlike lack of control. She was clammy all over, faint, before she even lifted the receiver to her ear, but her limbs moved of their own volition, succumbing to the force of long habit.

She listened, hardly breathing, to crackling static, and then a husky voice said, "Once-Winged Zemolai. There's no use running from me."

Her voice cut like a surgeon's saw. It was the Voice of the mecha god making her demands. Zemolai was turned to stone by it, as surely as Saint Orlusky was felled by the basilisk.

The Voice dropped in timbre, and now it was only Vodaya ringing clear through the receiver. "Zemolai," she complained. "How could you do this to me? I brought you up. I trained you. I sponsored your wings. Have you been working against me this whole time?"

Zemolai couldn't seem to control her legs. It was that voice, that voice she had been trained to obey without question for so long. It was also guilt, because Vodaya was right to be furious. Zemolai had failed the mecha god. She'd been punished fairly for it. And in return she was assisting a worse betrayal.

Her instinct was to explain herself, to beg forgiveness. The words swelled up in her throat in a wash of bile, painfully bitter. She wanted to leave, but she couldn't, not unless she could make Vodaya understand.

She started to say, "I never . . ." and then faltered, overcome.

A soft sigh on the other side.

"This needn't be the end," Vodaya said, so silken and clear she could have been standing at Zemolai's side. "The mecha god passed her judgment. You accepted your punishment. As far as I am concerned, that means you have a clean slate. That is what you want, isn't it? A way to prove your loyalty? A way back into the tower?"

God help her, it was.

Zemolai glanced at the far gate, where the rebels had fled. Where they might very well have escaped altogether, their stolen goods and her imitation mechalin in hand.

"Yes," she said. She spoke faintly, clutching the receiver like it was a lookout post in a storm.

"Then prove to me you still serve the mecha administration," Vodaya said. "Give me the rebels responsible for the storehouse bombing. But first, tell me. What did they come here for?"

Resistance flared in Zemolai's breast, a little voice protesting: Vodaya had cast her out, had left her to die, had taken her *wings*, and now she wanted to wipe the slate clean, pretend it had never happened and move on the way they *always* moved on, with Vodaya content and Zemolai grieving over whatever she had lost this time—

And then the little flame guttered out, because she owed so much to this woman, even if it had ended badly.

"Weapons," Zemolai said roughly. "They have a stronghold nearby." She hesitated, then added, "And they've captured a Tooth. I could arrange his escape . . ."

Vodaya snorted. Briskly now, she said, "If one of my Teeth can't overcome a handful of workers on his own, then he's worthless to me. No. Deliver him to this stronghold of theirs, and we'll follow his resonance chip." She paused. "Winged Mitrios is recovered. If he catches you, I won't intervene."

The line went dead. Zemolai put the radio back just before she heard a muffled shout from the kitchen: "Stand back!"

The gate exploded inward, showering the room in bolts and metal sheeting. Galiana thrust her head through the gap, harried and fearful. "Zemolai!"

"I'm coming," Zemolai muttered.

Metal screamed behind her. Winged Mitrios was attacking the lockdown barricade. Possibly, he had fetched a saw. Or possibly, he was so enraged that he was ripping the panels apart with his bare hands. A Winged gone berserk wouldn't feel their injuries for hours.

Zemolai climbed through the wreckage of the doorway. She passed a pile of cleaning supplies, the hasty ingredients for Galiana's door bomb. Her arm was still bleeding from the Tooth's attack, the pain bright and sharp (much deserved).

Galiana led her through the kitchens at a limping run. "I have a plan," she said. "I can get us back to the servant's tunnel."

"Everything is sealed," Zemolai said. The sterile expanse of the kitchen counters stared back at them with stubborn apathy, refusing even the promise of sanctuary.

"Not everything." Galiana yanked open drawers until she found what she wanted: a heavy meat knife with a wicked edge. She led Zemolai to a short, narrow hall. Timyan was there, slumped against the wall. Blood streaked the tiles where his injured arm leaned, stark red against all that clean ceramic. Zemolai recognized the look.

He was shutting down.

Several yards past Timyan, the hall dead-ended at a chest-high grate mounted into the wall. The grate covered an enormous trash compartment. Load it up, shut the grate, and send each massive load tumbling to the incinerator on the bottom floor.

"We'll burn," Zemolai protested.

"We won't." Galiana dropped to her knees. She tapped the wall in a few places, listening closely, and then stabbed one foot to the right of the grate. The knife wasn't designed for construction, but she sawed steadily in a lop-sided circle till she'd done enough damage to rip a chunk of plaster loose. Behind the ragged, head-sized hole, a series of pipes and tubes disappeared up into the wall, rusty and untouched.

"You're kidding," Zemolai said.

Galiana plucked a wrench from her tool belt, her face set in stubborn lines. "I'm unscrewing the gas line," she said. "There's a sensor in the incinerator that will register the leak and shut off the gas, extinguishing the flames."

"And if it doesn't?"

The barricade screeched in protest as Mitrios continued his assault. Any moment, it was going to fail.

Galiana heaved on the wrench, fighting a coupling that had rusted in place. It gave in abruptly, almost tumbling her to the ground. She jerked the two lengths of pipe apart and gas flowed out, staining the air with its acrid stench. There were no additional alarm bells, no way of knowing whether the leak sensor was working.

The kitchen barricade finally fell, unleashing the full wail of the alarms. The thunder of boots came next, and it wasn't two pairs but a dozen. Mitrios had found reinforcements, and they weren't likely to be trainees.

"Climb in, climb in!" Galiana was hastily reattaching the gas pipes.

"How do you know it's off?" Zemolai demanded.

"It's off! It's probably off!"

"Eleny is dead," Timyan said, still staring at his feet. "We left her. She's dead."

Galiana spun around, grabbed him by the shoulders, and yelled, "Fall apart later!"

Winged Mitrios is recovered. If he catches you, I won't intervene.

Fuck it. Zemolai climbed inside the trash chute. The staging chamber was a five-foot cube, forcing her into an awkward crouch. The floor bowed slightly with her weight. It was only two metal flaps that met in the middle, a hatch geared to drop open at the close of the grate. Heat seeped through her boots. The air was muggy with it.

Timyan crowded in beside her, a menace with that damned duffel still on his back. Galiana gave one last twist of the wrench, sealing the gas pipe. She leaped inside—they could hear the kitchen door slam open, hear the oncoming storm of armed warriors—and she pulled the grate shut, triggering the hatch beneath them.

Zemolai gasped—or tried to. The air was torn clean out of her. There was nothing but hot wind and metal walls and loose limbs flailing as they tried to streamline their bodies and failed. The chute curved, dropping them into a slide rather than a free fall, and the darkness was streaked in old trash and the smell of char. They hurtled toward the incinerator, bouncing painfully, here and there glimpsing the light of another floor's chute connecting with theirs.

Galiana let out a sound halfway between squeak and scream. They hit the bottom in resounding succession, and Timyan groaned as he landed on his duffel bag. The fire was out, praise the Five, but the grate was still burning hot and streaked with the char of the previous load. The air was full of ash and dagger, choking them.

And the maintenance hatch was shut, locked from the outside. They were in a dazed heap in a locked chamber, and their skin was about to start sizzling through their clothes.

"Move!" Zemolai braced her back against the wall. The metal surface burned through her shirt, burned against her spine, and for a moment she was paralyzed, breathless, her mind thrust back to the sight of that enormous hand descending through the god-portal, gripping her entire body, melting the metal in her wing ports with a pain like death—and then she kicked hard at the hatch, again and again, until the hatch gave way.

They scrambled into the incinerator room, gasping and shaking and patting themselves down for burns. The room contained little more than the burn chamber itself, a blackened metal behemoth stretching wall to wall and tapering into the ceiling like a hellish smokestack.

Hoarsely, Zemolai said, "They'll see your hack job on the wall. They'll know we came down this way."

"They can have fun following us." Galiana slammed the hatch shut and then turned the gas on full force. She hit the sparker, and two dozen gas jets burst with flame, hungrily rising up through the grate.

It was a short-term stall, but they needed every second they could get. Zemolai didn't entertain any illusion that Vodaya would save her. Either the rebels were caught today, or she had Zemolai as a potential insurgent in their ranks later. Vodaya hadn't become the Voice without learning how to extract a victory from every outcome.

By now there would be Winged, flying circuits around the training grounds, covering any possible escape route. Zemolai could only pray their servant entrance was far enough outside the perimeter to escape immediate notice.

They exited into a long hallway. "This way," Galiana said, turning right. ". . . I think."

"You *think*?"

"It's been a long time, and we didn't overlap much with the trash crew!"

They took it at a limping run. Timyan breathed harshly, and it wasn't just physical pain wracking his body. His same grief was waiting in the wings for Galiana, but for the moment, at least, she was focused on the crisis at hand.

At last they crept outside, into the shadowed alley. Zemolai's heart hammered against her ribs, and she stared up at the awning, waiting for a barrage of bolts to shoot through, but nothing came.

Their car was still there, a hulking machine with a half-cylinder arch of canvas concealing the dangerous cargo within, and Rustaya poked their head out the front. "Thank the saints—now get the fuck in!"

The Tooth was trussed and unconscious in the back. Timyan shoved his ill-gotten duffel next to the body, and Galiana clambered over both.

Rustaya's eyes widened at their bloodstains. "Where's Eleny?"

Timyan shut his eyes. Galiana kept hers firmly aimed out back.

"*Where's Eleny?*"

Galiana said, "She's meeting us at the safe house. Go now, there'll be Winged all over the district any second."

Rustaya frowned at that, but dutifully turned the engine. The gentle whir of machinery may as well have been a firecracker screaming their location to the sky, but when they pulled into the street, there was no hail of bolt-fire waiting.

Zemolai crouched in the narrow space beside the Tooth. His face was turned to the floor, his back barely rising with each shallow breath. He was illuminated in flashes as the occasional streetlamp penetrated their front window, a slumbering monster in crimson and black. Zemolai shoved him over just enough to give him adequate airflow, then settled in for the ride.

They hurtled down deserted streets. From the sheltered backseat, Zemolai only had the tension in Rustaya's shoulders to indicate when anyone crossed their path. The sirens of the training compound had wound her nerves tight, but as the bells faded into the distance, she found the quiet even more unsettling.

Galiana kept busy with the Tooth. She rigged a signal dampener around his thigh using the components of a small radio blocker in her gear. It was a clumsy device, hastily attached to a wide leather belt, and only a small blinking bulb indicated it was active. But it *was* active. The Tooth would appear to be out of range of the tracking chamber, for now.

She turned to Zemolai and Timyan next, producing a med kit from beneath her seat. Zemolai held a hand out, stopping her. "We have to talk," she said, low and angry.

Galiana wouldn't meet her eyes. "We will. But not now." Silently, she went about her work, slathering the laceration on Zemolai's arm with med gel, then applying a bandage. She glanced up now and then, furtive, but Zemolai never made a sound.

It took an hour, a good number of alarmed grunts from Rustaya, and an echoing drive through what Zemolai could only speculate to be a tunnel. Her unease grew at that. Where was there a tunnel wide enough to grant a full-sized vehicle clear passage?

They rode in silence, sweating from the heat of the machinery beneath their seats. There was a reason few people used them, preferring to work within walking distance of their homes.

But what else could you expect from a work of the creator god? All of their innovations came with drawbacks. The engineers thought they had a closer relationship to their god than anyone else, because the creator granted inspiration in the form of schematics. Their leader returned from each visit in a state of ecstasy, barely lucid, and she scribbled what she had learned in a mindless frenzy, filling sheet after sheet with diagrams and calculations, upon completion of which she collapsed, catatonic for days after being so blessed.

Engines and electrics, short-distance coders and live-speak radios. For those who could acquire it, daily life was powered by invention. But the creator god had also imparted the knowledge necessary to design bolt-guns and armor, cannons and bombs, battering rams and projectile nets.

And, of course, wings.

"We're here," Rustaya said, blessedly interrupting that train of thought, and at long last they emerged from the vehicle and back into the night.

They were no longer in Radezhda.

Zemolai squinted in the starlight, trying to make sense of her surroundings. Dozens of wooden stalls extended in both directions. An open-air market, shuttered for the night.

This was farmland. The rebels had a hiding place outside city walls.

"Help me," Galiana huffed, trying to drag the Tooth by his shoulders. Zemolai joined her reluctantly, and the Tooth slid to the ground between them, dead weight.

"Timyan, *please*," Galiana begged. He unfolded himself from the bench and crawled out, a machine running out of power. He dragged the duffel by one strap, as though loath to touch it.

With much cursing and grunting, they hauled the Tooth into the nearest wooden stall: a decoy structure concealing yet another trapdoor. This one covered a simple staircase.

They didn't take much care getting the Tooth downstairs.

Half a dozen lamps lit a warm space roughly ten feet by fifteen. The main room was stuffed with contraband, including a cache of scrolls and codices clearly salvaged from a scholar's library. There were plush chairs and plush blankets; pedestals carved into prayer hands spread to cup an open book; a knee-high statue of the scholar god asleep on a bed of paper. All of it illegal. All of it achingly familiar.

"Back room!" Galiana ordered.

The second room was smaller than the first, containing a few bare cots and a stack of musty blankets. They deposited the Tooth and retreated to the main space, where Zemolai promptly took herself to a corner and sank down, letting the adrenaline run out of her limbs, letting the pain take its place, averting her gaze from the coming meltdown. She had her own pain to cope with.

There was only one other door, and it led to an even more cramped washroom. There was no place they could avoid one another, and nothing left to distract them from what had happened.

Rustaya drifted back to the stairwell, peering up worriedly. "Which way was Eleny coming from?"

"We have to contact Karolin," Galiana said, pacing the floor, avoiding the inevitable. She'd acted bravely this entire time but was a coward at the last, eyes trained on her feet, shoulders hunched as though she could deflect the question.

Rustaya turned rapidly between Galiana and Timyan, more alarmed every second. "Where's Eleny?" they asked, and Timyan shook his head, wordless. Galiana said, "We should have left a marker for Karolin on the way. Do you think they'll check tonight? Maybe I should go now." And Rustaya repeated, *"Where's Eleny?"* except this time they were terrified, because they knew the answer, and they needed to hear it, but they didn't want to, not really, and then Timyan shook his head again, and Rustaya began to cry, and Zemolai sank down tighter in her corner and struggled to ignore them, because she had already heard this song too many times to count, and she didn't want any part of it now.

CHAPTER FIFTEEN

All victorious warriors share these common principles: *belief*
and *commitment*.

Belief in their god. Commitment to their commander. Belief
in moral authority. Commitment to discipline.

Hold tight to these, and you will know no grief, no fear, no
hesitation.

                          —*The Collected Wisdoms of Saint Vitalia*

ZENYA HAD NEVER experienced such pain.

She couldn't run from it. She couldn't fight it. It was a steel bubble
buried deep in her chest where the surgeons couldn't reach, and it was
growing larger every day, pushing out her heart, her lungs, her ribs.

Her mother's death had been painful, but complicated—the woman
a distant figure, defined more by what Zenya wanted from her than by
what she ever gave. But her brother? It was a grief she'd never even contem-
plated, except for the vague, morbid fantasizing of every would-be fighter:
if anybody hurt my family, I would get revenge. Except there wasn't anybody
to revenge herself upon. Tomel and Niklaus—they'd sided with anarchy.
They'd hidden in siege territory, vowing sedition. They were casualties of
a righteous attack.

Nushki, the steel bubble cried, and she swallowed against it, struggling
for breath.

She couldn't revenge herself upon the Winged who'd dropped the
bombs. She couldn't revenge herself upon the Tooth who'd breached the
building. She could only fight the rebellion that had seduced her family.

Her despair felt like a hunger for victory.

By the time Zenya emerged from her hellish stay in the containment cage, the siege of Quaser was over, but there was plenty of work to be done. Pockets of resistance flared up in violent skirmishes every few days. The Quaser survivors had gone into hiding, moving and regrouping as quickly as they were routed out.

Now when Vodaya went into the city, she took her five-unit as a ground team. They followed tip after elusive tip, driving knots of fugitives into the open for a wing team to subdue. These places were dark and desperate—a perfect focus for Zenya's rage. She volunteered for the dangerous point position more often than not (a meager apology for abandoning her team at the tower), but found little more than wet and pleading faces behind each door.

"You have no right!" they cried. Or: "This is blasphemous!" Or: "Please, please, please, I have children—" "—a mother—" "—a lover—"

A brother?

In the weeks following the siege of Quaser, Zenya devoted herself wholly to the fight, and it was only in the very heart of combat that she felt any purpose. On every mission she was first to her post and last to leave. In the lulls between missions, she hit the training grounds, working out alone after hours and creeping home well after the others were asleep.

Zenya cautiously eased back into enhancers. This time she paid careful attention to her pacing and dosage, charted her symptoms, and eased off when she felt the beginning tickles of madness at the edge of her vision. She reduced her nightly sleep to roughly four hours, an unavoidable window just before dawn.

Pava Romil was the first one to take her aside when he caught her dressing for combat on a free day. He was the only one who had offered her a friendly word since her breakdown.

"Don't you think you're taking this too far?" he asked, pitching his voice low, as though everyone else weren't listening intently outside the kitchen. He had one hand on her elbow, as though she were a flight danger.

"*Too far?*" Zenya shook her elbow loose. "You're all trying to hit your basic marks, but your marks won't matter for shit once you're out there—

and I mean really *out there*, not this filthy ground cleanup we're doing. You're still acting like a student. I'm acting like a warrior."

"No warrior does this!" His voice rose, the illusion of privacy abandoned. "Look at yourself! Bloody Vitalia, I'm surprised you haven't turned *blue.*"

"I know *exactly* what—" Zenya stopped. Took a breath. "I don't have to explain myself to you." She turned her back, so she didn't see him leave the kitchen. She only heard the faint murmur of a question from Dolynne in the next room, and the exclamation mark of his answer.

Instead of slowing her down, the incident fired her up. She didn't get back till after midnight, her clothing sticky with sweat, her hands raw from endless ladder drills. More than ever, Zenya felt alone. None of them had given up a goddamned thing to join this sect.

And none of them had lost anything to this fight.

One month passed. One month to the day. Zenya awoke that morning, burning with recognition at the date. She remedied a pounding headache with a tall glass of water and a pill, but a deeper dread stayed with her long after the painful edge of withdrawal had been sawn off.

In the afternoon they went hunting. Zenya was spearhead again, leading her five-unit into a series of tunnels below an engineering lab. Witnesses had spotted late-night activity in a nearby alley, widely understood to be the entryway to an underground bunker.

Except this wasn't a bunker. It was a damned gopher burrow. Zenya turned each corner with her heart in her throat, scanning the shadows for signs of movement. Her five-unit trod carefully, but they were loaded with gear. If anyone was here, they knew trouble was coming.

They found half a dozen storage rooms, all stacked with supplies. It was sickening to realize how long the engineers must have been stockpiling for this. A civil war planned down to the sacks of beans. The team fired bolts into each door and its adjoining wall, padlocking them shut to block rebels sneaking up from behind.

The main tunnel ended at a round wooden door. It moved an inch, revealing a thick chain and a strip of darkness. Lijo and Romil surged forward with a metal battering ram. They struck once, twice, and sent the chain and thick wooden splinters flying.

"Face to the wall, face to the wall!" Zenya barged through, shouting orders, her breath too hot behind her face guard, her eyesight narrowed by her helmet.

There were ten of them—maybe a dozen—too many people for this space, a mob on the verge of panic. Three stood in front with weapons, the metal glinting when it hit the light from the tunnel. They'd been waiting in the dark, preparing an ambush like cowards.

"We haven't done anything!" a woman screamed, but a pair of bolt-guns went off, their projectiles striking armored chests and bouncing away.

Chaos reigned in the small space, some figures huddled toward the back, some on their knees, the rest throwing everything they could get their hands on: empty guns, hard fruits, even goddamned rocks like they were farmers chasing off wild dogs. A sharp grunt behind her—Lijo?

Zenya pushed forward shield-first, and her team quickly adjusted into exit formation. They formed a curved wall, scooping the crowd toward the door, giving them no recourse but to spill out into the hallway. They pushed with their shields, herding people like animals.

The rebels clutched at side doors and found them locked. They staggered forward, hurling back tears and abuse, until they hit the rung ladder. Some raced up willingly, desperate enough to think they had a chance. The rest had to be crowded, had to have their legs smacked with batons, had to be shouted at, louder and louder, till they obeyed.

A thrill of fear raised Zenya's heart rate as she climbed the ladder after them, but she found everyone being contained exactly as planned. Vodaya and Winged Pilivar cast down nets from above, while Pilivar's five-unit blocked the mouth of the alley.

Zenya's unit had completed their part, but they waded into the fray anyway to hasten the cleanup. There were howls and tears, but whether they fought back with hidden weapons or just panicked and failed to obey orders, the result was the same: bloody bodies, weeping friends.

And Vodaya was magnificent. She draped herself in the trappings of war and burned like a star. When Zenya emerged from the dark, she saw only Vodaya shining overhead in her silver and leathers, her dark hair bound tight, her strong hands clutching the sigils of their work.

When Vodaya fought, she fought with the hand of the mecha god at her back.

Ten rebels were netted. Three dead. One more on their way to death. Zenya leaned against a scarred brick wall, surreptitiously trying to overcome a wave of dizziness while Winged Pilivar led her unit away to fetch the prison wagons.

Winged Vodaya landed in the alley. High color stained her cheeks. "Excellent job," she said. "Pava Dolynne, that was quick work blocking the door. Pava Lijo, see to that shoulder." Lijo nodded, one hand pressed to a wound between armor plates.

Vodaya said, "Pilivar's team will load up the prisoners. We return to Pava."

The team was more than happy to oblige, but Zenya hesitated. It was only for a fraction of a second, a quick self-balancing, but Vodaya's sharp eye caught everything. She strode over to Zenya and grabbed her by the chin. "When have you last eaten?"

"This morning."

It was a lie. They both knew it was a lie. This close, Zenya could see every line on Vodaya's face, and they betrayed a sharp disappointment.

"I don't want another collapse," Vodaya warned. "I don't have time to nurse you again."

Zenya shook free of her grip. "I know my limit," she said. And she *did*. She was close now, just the very edges of her vision flickering, but Vodaya didn't need to know how close, because Zenya had it under control.

"Pava Lijo was struck in the shoulder," Vodaya said.

"I know."

"Nothing should get past your front line. Not even a rock."

"I *know*."

"The spearhead is a position of trust. Your five-unit trusts you. *I* trust you. Excelling isn't enough. In this life there is luck, or there is perfection, and a warrior doesn't rely on luck."

The other trainees stood beside their prisoners, resignedly waiting out the tirade. Zenya stared hard at the insignia on Vodaya's breastplate: a silver fist clutching a small bird. She only hoped it would be over before Winged Pilivar's five-unit returned with the carts.

"If this is too much responsibility for you, tell me now," Vodaya said. "When I agreed to take you back, I assured Mecha Petrogon that you were worth a second chance. I assured him that you were worth the extra investment of my time."

Zenya knew better than to protest. Objections crowded behind her teeth, but if she let them show on her face, she would only bring on a longer lecture. Real warriors knew how to control their emotions. There was no place in the mecha sect for oversensitive scholars who cried over every bit of constructive advice.

So Zenya kept her thoughts behind a mask, and after Vodaya said her piece, she agreed and apologized and returned to work.

Vodaya hadn't finished making her point. When they returned to Pava, she ordered everyone straight to the yard, no refreshment, no change of clothing. Combat training.

"We're the last line of defense," she said, circling the fight ring. "That means constant vigilance. That means unpredictability. The call to arms is the call to arms. You answer, whether you're rested, whether you're fed, whether you're clean. You answer and you fight."

She set them one-on-one, two-on-two, three-on-one. Any combination to keep them guessing, calling victors or announcing change-ups without warning. Lijo was pale-faced and sweating, but didn't dare ask to be excused.

Vodaya stalked Zenya around the ring, calling out flaw after flaw. "Your shield arm dropped. Too late! Lose the shield. If he's got a knife, you're dead."

Or: "Focus, Zemolai! You followed his feint and left yourself open to Dolynne. The enemy doesn't step up nicely one at a time."

Or: "These aren't games! You don't get to tap out and collect partial points. If you aren't hamstrung by now, it's because you're fighting a pair of infants. Switch!"

Zenya launched herself at Romil before Vodaya had finished barking her instruction. He deflected Zenya's first attack, knocking her arms aside and landing a blow to her ear. Humiliated, she spun low to take out his legs, but Romil was ready for that too. Every failure to breach his defense made her even wilder, and the wilder she got, the worse she performed.

Zenya screamed her frustration and full-body tackled him. The scream startled him—he hesitated a fraction of a second too long, and she took him to the ground. In a flash, they'd gone from combat to street fight, dirty wrestling with no rules and no escape.

"Dammit, Zemolai!" he choked. He thrashed beneath the elbow on his throat but couldn't break loose.

The mood in the ring changed. The rest of the unit faltered, and Vodaya didn't even yell at them to continue. All eyes were on Romil and Zenya.

"Fight me!" Zenya screamed. Her world narrowed to this single impulse. She wanted his fists. She wanted every bright starburst of pain. She wanted to be destroyed in the ring. She *needed* to be destroyed in the ring.

For an endless minute they brawled in the dirt. They rolled clear out of the circle, but nobody called for the match to end. Now it was Romil on top with a knee in Zenya's gut. Now it was Zenya again with a fist in his hair. Around they went, until Zenya's strength crumbled beneath weeks of poor sleep and drug use. She landed flat on her back and let him strike her in the face.

It took three strikes for Romil to realize the fight had ended. He reared back, breathing hard, horrified at the sight of Zenya bleeding from the nose and crying. She didn't even raise her hands to cover her face. She just lay in the dirt in the bright afternoon sun and wept.

"Zemolai—shit—" Romil rolled off her body. He reached for her hand, but she didn't move.

"Lesson over," Vodaya said curtly. "Back to work in the morning."

Lijo started forward from the sideline. "You can't expect—"

"I don't expect," Vodaya snapped. "I order."

They left. Zenya hardly noticed. Her chest was hitching, and she couldn't catch a solid breath. Her body was coming apart from the inside. She must have miscalculated a dose or misjudged the time. She was going to go berserk on the spot, and Vodaya would have to drag her down to a containment cage, and that would be the end of it, she was done in the Pava program.

Slowly she realized it wasn't an overdose. The symptoms were all wrong.

Zenya was hot and cold, and her hands were numb, and she couldn't control her body—but her thoughts were perfectly clear, *more* than clear, they were clamoring: she couldn't go on like this, she was a failure, first a failed scholar and now a failed warrior, and if she couldn't handle one afternoon of combat training she'd never survive in the field, she'd never be worthy of wings, this was all for nothing, she had nothing, she *was* nothing . . .

Vodaya knelt at her side, just out of reach, her wings half-spread and cupping them both in their shadow. She watched, calm, while Zenya sobbed in the dirt, and when she spoke it was very soft, the voice of an animal trainer trying to soothe a spooked pet. "You know I'm only trying to help you?" she said. "You know I only want you to reach your full potential?"

It was worse than an insult. The apology that Zenya babbled out was laced in despair. "I'm so sorry—you have to find somebody else—" She couldn't even get her resignation out with dignity.

Zenya braced herself for the final dismissal—*Yes, go, stop wasting my time*—but Vodaya said, "Nonsense." She slid one arm beneath Zenya's shoulders and slowly raised her to a sitting position. Zenya slumped within the warm crescent of her body, too bone-weary to resist.

"You are one of the best students I've ever had, Pava Zemolai," Vodaya said, and the affection in her voice was almost enough to get Zenya sobbing again. "Let me show you something."

Zenya stood on trembling legs, sniffing blood. Her panic subsided slightly beneath the familiarity of following a command.

Vodaya unrolled a carry harness from her belt. She held it out with one eyebrow raised in invitation.

She was offering flight.

"Yes," Zenya breathed. Even now, in the face of her failure, the desire overwhelmed everything else. She stepped into the leg straps, trembling, and lifted her arms around Vodaya's shoulders. Vodaya clicked the loose ends of the harness onto the corresponding hooks on her back rig and tightened the straps, pulling Zenya snug against her body.

"Hold on," Vodaya murmured, and launched them both into the sky.

A spasm of grief struck Zenya, twin to her joy—this might be it, the closest she ever got to wings. But she laid one cheek against Vodaya's chest and soaked up the glorious rush of air over her face. The harness bit into her thighs, punishing and satisfying.

The fight ring dropped out from beneath them, and they rose beside Kemyana at exhilarating speed, past the wide base levels of stone, then brick, then wood and plaster. They continued past metal and glass, those shining beacons of modernity, the tower itself a living illustration of their progress toward self-perfection.

Every floor they passed stripped some of the weight from Zenya's shoulders. By the time they reached the roof, she was relaxed, almost giddy, but Vodaya didn't stop there. They coasted over the elaborate swirls of colorful brick and into the grasping arms of the god-tree itself.

"Oh, god," Zenya gasped.

"Yes," Vodaya said.

Vodaya set down in the heart of those dark, gnarled branches. The portal glimmered three feet over her head, a slender seam of white light barely two feet long. Zenya gaped unabashedly. She had never been this close to a portal. Her heart hammered so hard, she thought she'd pass out.

Vodaya tugged up one side of her vest, revealing a small port above her hip bone. She produced a mechanical cord from an inner pocket and plugged one end into her side. The other end went into a similar port embedded in the blackened skin of a nearby branch.

Vodaya began to murmur in the god's language, words like thunderbolts shaking the fabric of reality. It was unthinkable, impossible, she wasn't the Voice! If Mecha Petrogon knew—if anyone saw them—

The portal elongated gently, like a stretching cat, and Zenya could no longer think of anything else. It widened, pouring out a strand of that glittering light. Zenya's eyes watered uncontrollably, but she kept them open wide, soaking in every detail.

She saw vibrant colors, an endless variety of greens and yellows and blues; she saw twisting shapes, incomprehensible from this angle, pure beauty.

"Hold on," Vodaya repeated. She unplugged her port and gently spread her wings within the confines of the tree branches. She flapped once, twice, and carried Zenya upward.

The portal resisted them for a moment, bending and stretching like an invisible membrane. Zenya wanted to thrash, to fight that suffocation, but Vodaya held her tight and pushed through.

And then they were in the god's realm. It was overwhelming. Crushing. The air was sweeter. Everything was bathed in white light. It bounced from every surface, painfully harsh.

Zenya's eyes were accustomed to the fluctuating swirl of a multicolored sky. This place was too bright, too clear. She struggled to untangle the sights around her, sharp as knives.

"Unfocus," Vodaya whispered, and even her voice was different here, a soft musical chime. "The more you struggle, the less you'll see."

Zenya wanted to cry with frustration. How could she *not* focus on their surroundings? But she had read about the optical trickery of the god's realm. She almost laughed to remember it now: a diagram in a book, flat and lifeless and absolutely nothing like the reality.

She took a deep breath and let her sight drift, seeing *past* her surroundings, letting her peripheral sight creep in. Slowly, painfully, Zenya's eyes adjusted. The world around the edges of her vision clarified, and she gasped, automatically focusing on an orange-yellow vine. Her vision blurred, and she wanted to scream, but she reached deep for patience and tried again.

This time it came more quickly. Tentatively, with her eyes blurred and her attention on the periphery, Zenya peeked at the world of the mecha god.

Vodaya carried her up through a dense jungle. It was an endless expanse, no horizon in sight, packed with twisting, slender posts bursting with plant life. Up close, the posts appeared porous, *spongy*, softly colored like young wood, dappled in shadow where they were even visible through the dense vegetation growing around and between them.

Strong braided vines dripped with colorful appendages that might have been flowers, or fleshy seed pods, or whisker-like needles, or the downiest feathers. All of it was gigantic, god-sized, including spiky fruits the size of Zenya's leg and blossoms like gaping mouths large enough to swallow her whole. There was nothing beneath the greenery but a gently swirling fog, obscuring any hint of land below.

Even here, in this sacred space, Niklaus's voice intruded on her awe. *What does the mecha god need with a garden?* he whispered. *Are you rising through heaven or a botanist's experimental food supply?*

She shoved him away. Niklaus and his incessant questioning. Where had it gotten him?

The portal wandered off, and they were left wholly alone in a silence so intense it vibrated in Zenya's ears. There was no wind, no movement of air at all, and yet Vodaya continued to rise with only the mildest of wing strokes, navigating carefully to avoid the loops of plant matter haphazardly connecting posts.

They rose because the sky wanted them to rise.

This would have been enough, this brief minute soaring through heaven, but Vodaya pressed upward, and now Zenya could see the distant top of the garden canopy: not intertwined branches and leaves but a curved metal platform. This she had glimpsed before, and if Vodaya hadn't been supporting her, she would have fallen into the endless abyss.

It was the mecha god's place of slumber.

Panic clutched her, a sudden instinct screaming *Run, run, this sight wasn't meant for your eyes.* But they rose past the edge of the platform and set down on the surface, dense but not hard like metal. Vodaya unclipped the harness, and Zenya clutched at her shoulders, terrified to let go.

Vodaya laughed softly, musically. Up here the air was even clearer, the light even sharper. It played tricks on Zenya's eyes, throwing her in and out of focus. Vodaya was her only frame of reference, but even Vodaya looked different in this light. Her skin glowed, dark and translucent, the faint pulse of an artery in her neck. Her hair was washed silver, her armor painfully bright, Zenya's blood on her vest crystalline.

Vodaya gently turned her around, and Zenya was crying again—had she ever stopped? These were clear tears now, cleansing tears, and she knew if she didn't let them out, she'd swell and swell until she burst at the seams.

She looked upon the vast metallic shimmer of the platform. Its surface rose and fell in gentle waves. There was no forest of gargantuan botany up here, only the endless white sky, the silver platform, and the raised dais at the center of it all. Vodaya gently pushed her forward, one step at a time, until they came within twenty feet of it.

The figure resting there was a giant, fifteen feet if she was an inch, ensconced within a corona of pearly light. Zenya could barely make out the form within the protective bubble. She glimpsed an impression of limbs— and the languid rise and fall of a chest. A small voice whispered, *You should not see the face of a god*, but oh, she wanted to.

Vodaya spoke quietly in Zenya's ear. "This is your purpose." And she repeated words that Zenya had heard many times. Warriors made weapons of themselves to be wielded by a divine hand. The remaining Four relied on the wisdom of the mecha god to keep them safe, and so the mecha god reigned supreme: four limbs and a head.

A soft red light pulsed near the foot of the dais, startling against all that pearly white. A complicated design ran around the base of the god's cradle, and the longer Zenya looked, the more colorful it appeared. Embedded in the chrome were carvings of staggering beauty, faceted like gems and running the gamut from metallic to mineral. From this distance, she could barely make out their shapes. The strange red light blurred everything around it.

Zenya stared, mesmerized, and didn't even realize her eyes had refocused until her temples began to throb. A corresponding warmth thrummed in time at her back, and Zenya twisted around to see the cause.

Two flickering Vodayas faced her, overlapping in the middle, one smiling and one utterly blank, a terrible sight, bone-shaking—and then Zenya clarified her vision, banishing the blank twin, and it was only that smile remaining, fervent and warm.

"This is what we're fighting for," Vodaya said. "Stay by my side, and one day you'll take your place at hers."

Peace came over Zenya then. A radiant calm. Vodaya could have cut her loose. She could have ignored the pitiful sight of her trainee falling apart. Instead, she had given Zenya something wondrous, something beautiful, something that justified every difficult moment they'd spent together. Vodaya loved her, really and truly.

And Zenya had something she could give in return: a gift to the sect that had taken her in and a blow to the sect that had taken her brother, an act so stark that nobody could question her loyalties again.

"I know where they found the works of Heretic Scholar Vikenzy," she said, "and I can lead you there."

INTERLUDE

A FTER THE GODS retreated, blame was laid upon every head. The fighting was immediate, intense. There were documents destroyed, a terrible crime born of terrible grief. We know these things, but our knowledge is a skeleton of the truth.

To preserve their fledgling community, the people of the city not-yet-called-Radezhda divided themselves according to worldview: they lived in separate neighborhoods, they held separate worship. A fragile truce. They were no longer the scattered villagers they had been before the gods' arrival, but they had not yet built the city we know today.

They were sibling districts finding their way forward after a tumultuous youth, each with its own notion of how to proceed.

Two sects put their focus on service, for the farmers and the workers take solace in the good they do their fellows. Two continued the quest for knowledge, for the scholars and the engineers desire answers to all things. And the warriors . . . the warriors locked in place and tried to keep everything as it was, a house undisturbed, waiting for its master to come home.

But all of them agreed on this: they longed to see the gods again (for comfort; for answers; for instructions), and so they built towers to the heavens.

The towers are not the concern of this paper. Their construction is well-documented and their schematics thorough. It is the frenzied time period beforehand that is shrouded in debate: the circumstances of the gods' retreat.

Why did they leave us?

The warriors believe we were not pious enough; the engineers believe we were not clever enough; the workers believe we were too lazy. Even the farmers murmur an inscrutable story about a poor planting season so egregious that their grandparents' grandparents hoarded jelly jars until their deaths. These reasons are frustratingly vague, even when they are bafflingly specific. (The scholars consider ourselves neutral parties, mere observers and collectors of facts, but make no mistake: we blame the rest.)

It is amazing to me that this pivotal moment in our history, this *defining* moment—the retreat of the gods from humanity in favor of perpetual sleep—is in such contention.

It is amazing to me that so many of our ancestors were present at this monumental event, and yet our records are so scarce, our interpretations so varied.

What really happened?

And if a city is its history, what does it mean when we forget the past?

CHAPTER SIXTEEN

Four limbs and a head, that is the way we are taught, the way we live every day of our lives, training together, eating together, speaking long into the night before we sleep.

They did not tell us how it would feel to lose a limb.

—*Diary of an unnamed disciple*

ZEMOLAI TIGHTENED ONE HAND around the laceration on her forearm and squeezed.

Galiana had assured her that she was on a bare minimum dose of their imitation mechalin, but her stomach was trying to climb out of her throat like she was on the verge of going berserk, and her thoughts were ricocheting wildly, trapped in the training yard—

(Because she'd frozen, she'd *frozen*, one look from Vodaya and she'd been helpless, unable to defend herself—)

And pain was the only thing keeping her grounded, so she squeezed her arm again.

Galiana paced the other side of the room, talking rapidly through her next steps. She would leave a marker for Karolin, then resolve any stock needs while she was out. Did anyone need anything? Did anyone need anything?

Timyan and Rustaya clung to one another, tearfully sharing their first memories of Eleny: her kindness, her fierceness, her devotion—remember when she smuggled Savro his shots, remember when she stole that girl's paperwork and doctored it, remember the night we met? Remember? Remember? Remember?

And Zemolai couldn't stand to listen—

(Because again, in the dining hall, one word from Vodaya and she couldn't refuse, she could hardly draw breath without permission—)

"Maybe I should go now," Galiana said. "Do you think I should go now?"

Rustaya cried, "Don't you care? Didn't Eleny mean anything to you?"

Galiana gasped. "I'm not—I'm just—We have to make sure we're safe before—"

(*SHE WAS A COWARD. SHE WAS A COWARD. SHE WAS A COWARD.*)

Zemolai curled in on her pain, raw with it, bitterly angry. She had just begun to face the possibility of life without wings. Life on the ground. Life *underground*. Life without Mecha Vodaya dictating every mission, every chore, every minute of every day. It was a colorless existence down here, *yes*, it was humiliating, *yes*—but it was a relief to be free of Vodaya's endless demands.

Wasn't it?

Self-loathing choked her at the thought. Her feelings toward Vodaya were irrelevant. This was about the sect, not her relationship to the Voice. If Zemolai didn't hold the rebels accountable, then she really did deserve the mecha god's dismissal.

Across the room, Timyan held Rustaya tight with one arm and gestured imploringly at Galiana with the other. "We all loved Eleny. We all care." He went on and on, spouting all the clumsy justifications a penitent told at a wake. "Leny believed in the worker god's service. She really believed we can transcend through self-sacrifice. That we serve ourselves by serving the greater good. Our—our humanity is our capacity to care for humanity. We—"

"Oh, for the love of the Five!" Zemolai cried. "Look at yourselves! This has nothing to do with your god's path. It has nothing to do with transcendence. Your boss sent you in there to steal some gear, and your friend got killed, that's *it*."

Rustaya was geared to fight, but Timyan held them back. Galiana's breath came shorter, her face crumpling with the effort to hold back the flood. Timyan held open his free arm, and Galiana finally ran to his embrace. Her crying was all the more raw for having been held back. He kissed her face, over and over, whispering platitudes.

Zemolai pressed hard on her bandage and tried to drown out the sound of the bolt-babies consoling one another. With trembling fingers she reached inside her vest. She stroked the brittle edges of old paper and thought she might vomit.

She felt punched by their grief. Pummeled by it. There was no single person left in this world for whom she would grieve the way they were grieving. Timyan and Rustaya were reciting anecdotes like prayers, with Galiana as their witness. Eleny had been both leader and friend, respected and loved. Never feared.

For twenty-six years, Zemolai had operated by a simple philosophy: entanglements made life too messy. They interfered with your work, muddied your convictions. Hormones lied. Family left.

But deep down, she knew better. She was over forty years old, and she had nobody.

Zemolai shut her eyes and fixed in her mind the glory of flight, wordless and pure, the wind a cleansing force over her face, her arms, her body. When nothing else in her life had made sense, when she had committed acts that haunted her nights or made mistakes that haunted her days, there had always been the sky waiting to whisk her away. Serving from the tower would not be the same. It wasn't flight, but surely it was better than this rough scrabble life on the ground.

The Tooth thrashed in the next room. They heard the clatter of metal—the cot crashing to one side. Everyone held their breath, waiting for a storm of violence to erupt through the door.

The sounds subsided, but the Tooth wouldn't be contained forever.

Over and over now, Zemolai's head swam with questions. Would Vodaya really forgive her? Would Vodaya let her back into the mecha god's service?

Could she?

Galiana slipped out before dawn to leave their message for Karolin (*safehouse, casualty, prisoner, please advise*).

Nobody had done more than doze, propped up in armchairs or piled up like puppies on the floor, jolting awake at every stray thump from the next room. By the time the aboveground market geared up for the day's business, they were all red-eyed and resentful, buried deep in their individual miseries.

They waited for hours, until their stomachs were growling loud enough to fill in for conversation. Galiana finally broke the vigil. "I'll get food," she said, untangling from her nest. "Zemolai, why don't you come with me?"

Zemolai's initial impulse was to refuse, to curl up and continue dying on the hard floor, but her fatigue evaporated at the memory of those wooden stalls above. It would be useful to gather more information about this place. And Galiana was overdue for providing answers.

"Let's get you a new shirt too," Galiana said. She dug up an old cloak to throw over Zemolai's shoulders. Held carefully, it covered the worst of the flaking stains on her clothing.

They climbed up into the market, where an entirely different world had unfurled.

Almost every stall was open and bursting with wares: fresh fruits and vegetables, bolts of handwoven fabric, woodware and wickerware and beaten metalware. The land surrounding them was drastically flat, with only a handful of low wooden buildings visible to the north and the looping cityscape of Radezhda to the south.

A farming market. And apparently a hiding place for sedition.

It was a bitter blow. The farming community had been neutral since the beginning of the conflict, humbly providing sustenance to the city without taking a side. Zemolai didn't delude herself into thinking anyone here was ignorant of their collusion. Not one of the stall owners or their customers batted an eye at the sight of two filthy, grown women emerging from underground wearing cloaks over bloodstained clothing.

Galiana led her to a long, low building that would have appeared to be a storage barn if viewed from the air. It extended two or three hundred feet, and what appeared to be cheerily painted wooden siding was actually overlapping sheets of bright green metal, like a reptile's scales. It was a fortress pretending to be a barn.

A crude figure of a human body was painted on the scaly siding, the fingers on both hands spread defiantly wide. It was an allusion to an old children's song. Every neighborhood's children liked to put their own sect first, so the version Zemolai had grown up with went:

Scholars, the eyes, look to the past,
Creators, the brain, plan far ahead,
Workers, the back, keep it all running,
Farmers, the belly, keep us all fed,
Mecha, the fist, protect all the rest,
These are the Five, joined to the end.

This figure had no fists.

A side door let them into a spacious receiving area with comfortable chairs, washbasins, and tables loaded with refreshments. A handful of residents in sun-faded tunics were resting there (farmers, Zemolai would have guessed, but who knew anymore), and they nodded congenially before returning to a game of dice.

Galiana took the leftmost hallway, a wide corridor dotted with open, arched entryways to additional brightly lit chambers. She stayed close to Zemolai's side, pointing out the services they had cobbled together under one roof. "Visitor's tour," she whispered with a nervous grin.

There were three build chambers in which engineers were teaching farmers how to construct and maintain automated threshers. Zemolai glimpsed half-finished machines with legs sticking out from underneath, and an engineer with hair gone white as chalk, laughing as she called out the next instruction.

There was a library, only a scant dozen shelves so far, but free to access and growing by donation. The first tentative attempt at a purchase list was pinned next to the door, titles scrawled hopefully in handwriting of varied skill.

There was a doctor on site, and a teacher of letters holding class with students ranging from the prepubescent to the elderly. Regardless of how many people sat in each room, regardless of what they were learning or how, one thing was the same: they were alight with the heady buzz of optimism. There was an entire miniature society bubbling up beneath the public face of Radezhda, its first spindly growths of economy and public services reaching for the sun.

And it was so bold. The building was right there in the open, barely masquerading as produce storage. It was a testament to how deeply the farming community had been taken for granted these past years, because they'd clearly lost all fear of a surprise inspection by the mecha administration.

That, Zemolai thought, was about to change.

Galiana described it all in rapturous delight, her grief temporarily forgotten in the light of her new world. "This is only the first of our public works barns," she said wistfully. "The goal is to have one within a half-hour cart ride of every farm family in the countryside. There isn't any reason they can't have access to the same services that we do in the city."

They had a new vision for Radezhda. One that better incorporated the values of the sect they all relied upon to feed them while they pursued other endeavors. The earth god shared indiscriminately. He encouraged families that spread like roots, the branching tendrils of one bush tangled so tightly with those of its neighbors that one couldn't be pulled up without ripping loose all the topsoil in between. To the earth god's people, the fate of one was the fate of all, and the strength of community was measured by the health of its weakest members.

Nice for farmers, Zemolai supposed, but the mecha god had to take a decidedly more pragmatic approach. Warriors required a minimum standard of competence. The notion of covering for an incompetent colleague was ludicrous. Better to eject him before he put others in danger. To the mecha god, weakness was weakness.

They thought their utopia was scalable? Nonsense. A hundred people could be brought to a consensus on the common good—*maybe*. A thousand people couldn't even begin to agree on a *definition* of common good, much less how to achieve it.

Galiana stopped in the library and began digging through a shelf of engineering texts. Softly, without meeting Zemolai's eye, she said, "Eleny brought all of us in, but she grew up with Rustaya. Her family took care of them after their parents died on the factory line. They met Timyan later." A ghost of a smile tugged at her lips. "Timyan was teaching underground reading classes for worker kids. Can you imagine? They hit it off right away. And then I came in from the farms for schooling, like I said, and I met Eleny. What she told me . . . I couldn't resist. I followed her right out of there, and then I fell in love with Timyan and Rustaya, who I wouldn't ever have met otherwise. Eleny was . . . she was just so passionate. You couldn't tell her no."

Zemolai tried to keep her hackles up. She didn't want their stories. She didn't want any more reason to hesitate over what she needed to do.

"Don't try to distract me," Zemolai said. "What happened back there?"

Galiana hesitated, and then there it was again: that look. The calculating expression that slipped out now and then in between the nervousness and the affability. Zemolai had seen it in the druggist's shop, and at times during their conversations in the containment cage, always when Galiana was about to gauge her reaction to some odd piece of information.

"When we were running," Galiana said slowly, "Mecha Vodaya walked through my signal blocker like it was nothing."

Zemolai frowned. "So your toy didn't work, who cares? You know that isn't what I'm asking."

"But it *did* work," Galiana said. "You saw what happened to the other warrior."

"Mitrios. A baby with wings. *Tell me where you were.*"

Again, disappointment. Galiana expected this to mean something to Zemolai, but what did Zemolai care about the dabbling of engineers? It was a distraction from a truth the woman did not want to face: that she had set off the alarm that summoned her friend's death.

"It doesn't matter where I was," Galiana said. Then, with a challenging tilt of her chin, "Where did *you* go?"

They stood there in stubborn stalemate for a moment longer before Galiana turned back to her book selection. Zemolai felt a sudden weight on her chest, as though the letters hidden there had turned to stone. And then irritation flared. She was letting herself be distracted again. Her mission was to divide and attack. Create an opening. Unblock the Tooth's beacon and bring Vodaya's forces here.

"Do they know?" Zemolai gestured angrily toward the door. "The farmers and the rest of your defectors. Do they know that you're building your new society on the same brute force you despise in the old one?"

Galiana turned, startled. "What are you talking about?"

Zemolai shrugged, as though her blood wasn't racing. "The Tooth. You brought him here to be tortured."

"Well. *Questioned* . . . ," Galiana said uneasily.

Zemolai laughed. "That's another word for it, yes. There's only one way I know to break a warrior, and it's mechalin withdrawal. It'll take all evening to get him delirious, longer if he dosed right before we caught him, but I doubt that. By the time Karolin gets here, he'll be ripe."

It was something the Winged didn't like to acknowledge. Mechalin made their enhancements possible, but it was *also* an exploitable chink in their defenses. The Tooth was well aware of his position here. If he couldn't see a way to escape, he would try to kill himself.

"You saw what it was like for me," Zemolai pressed.

"Can't we talk about this later?" Galiana said. She had three books clutched to her chest, and her eyes were rimmed red.

"It starts with dizziness, *emptiness*, like a hunger," Zemolai said. "You've caught the worst chill of your life, but you're also feverish, sweating through your clothes, so hot your brain starts to misfire. Your thoughts ricochet and repeat—and that's the best time to get something coherent out of a captive, by the way, before they start vomiting."

"Zemolai," Galiana said tightly.

"The pain kicks in, like nothing you've ever felt. All your nerve endings are on fire, the worst of it in your ports." Just saying the words thrust Zemolai back into that cage, and she couldn't help rolling her shoulders, shaking off a phantom ache. "Your body betrays you, rejects your machinery, thrusts you back into the weak shell you were born with. It's enraging, that pain. It's humiliating. You've spent years, *decades*, exerting control, and over the course of days you lose it entirely. By the time you go berserk, you're more animal than person, flinging yourself against the bars of your cage because by then breaking bones is preferable to sitting still."

"*Zemolai*," Galiana pled. "Why are you telling me this?" She was trembling, fingers gripping the books like they were a shield. She hadn't slept any more than the rest of them, her grief new and raw.

Guilt flared, and Zemolai angrily tamped it down. She was kicking the vulnerable, yes.

No better time to do it.

"I want to make sure you know exactly what you're a part of," she said. "I'm sure it's been nice, to get this far without getting your hands dirty, but you should understand the nature of information gathering." She gestured at the library shelves. "This little barn of yours is cute, but it's built on the same bloody bones the mecha sect has buried."

Galiana swallowed. "It isn't the same."

"Yes, it is."

"Part of our mission is to *liberate* the Winged. We need answers, yes, but Karolin can save the Tooth from mechalin, same as we did for you . . ."

Her denial was half-hearted at best. "You don't believe that," Zemolai said curtly. "A Tooth would rather die. You'll never turn a Winged of rank. Hell, you found me cast out, dying in the street, and you still think it's necessary to keep me on a leash."

It was the right screw to turn. Galiana blanched. She opened her mouth—to protest, no doubt, to insist yet again that the situation was temporary, that Zemolai would *definitely* be handed the keys to her freedom soon and *not* held hostage or interrogated for inside information—but she snapped her teeth shut on the urge.

"Let's go," she whispered instead.

They stopped in one more room for clean clothing and blankets. Galiana thrust them into her pack with hardly a glance for sizing.

Zemolai ignored her on the return route. She shrugged noncommittally when they stopped at a hot lunch stall and Galiana tried, with open desperation, to solicit her opinion on the food choices. Fortunately (unfortunately), cold silence was a tactic that Zemolai was painfully familiar with, and even over the course of a short walk, she felt the other woman descending into contortions over it.

There was something both satisfying and depressing about inhabiting the other side of this dynamic. She wanted to stop (hadn't she always hated this?). She also wanted to push the knife deeper (hadn't she earned it?).

Timyan and Rustaya barely stirred at their return, each of them sunk into an overstuffed chair, their fingers loosely twined between the armrests.

Zemolai dropped her borrowed cloak and took a medical kit and her new shirt into the washroom. It was a small, dingy space with a burnished metal mirror, one heavy lantern, and a washbasin with a hole punched through the bottom for drainage. At least they'd stacked a crate of sealed water canisters beside the basin rather than tapping into some dodgy local pipe system.

She peeled her shirt off. The bandage around her forearm had dried out and wedded itself to her flesh. Even after she moistened the cloth, it was a laborious removal, but she found healthy flesh underneath, no sign yet of infection. She dabbed away the fresh welling of blood and left it to air-dry while she rag-washed the rest of her exposed torso.

The washroom door was a polite fiction. Zemolai could hear almost every word muttered on the other side, and her self-ministrations slowed at the first flash of an argument.

"Who cares what Karolin does to him?" Rustaya burst. "Let him rot! How many names do you think are carved on his fucking vest?"

It was Galiana's fault, of course, chewing over Zemolai's accusations as intended. Her rejoinder was swallowed by Rustaya's bitter laughter. Timyan murmured something conciliatory and was brushed off with equal disdain.

"We have questions," Rustaya insisted. "The Tooth has answers."

"But *torture*?"

The argument revived with even more force, three voices overlapping in passionate and increasingly strident disagreement—and this time, no motherly figure of compromise to calm them down.

Zemolai applied a new bandage to her wound, taking care to apply a liberal amount of antiseptic gel. She shrugged into the clean shirt. Between button one and button six, the altercation turned tearful, with Galiana begging for quiet and Rustaya belligerently raising their voice.

Zemolai stared down at the sink, suddenly dizzy. This was what she'd wanted, yes? Seeds of doubt. Levers to pull. It was how Vodaya operated: keep everyone off-kilter and squabbling, and then carry on with her own plan while they were distracted. Zemolai knew she could finish this right now if she wanted. She could slip into that back room, disable the dampener around the Tooth's thigh, and wait for aid.

But Scholar Pyetka was in her thoughts again, asking in that matter-of-fact way, *Are you here to take me in?* She had decided to spare him then, and to spare the tower. A moment of weakness when she thought all hope was lost.

Lemain believed that you are every person you have ever been—that is what he'd said, all those years ago. Zemolai was continual and simultaneous. She had always been the girl who wanted the sky and always would be. If there was a way back into tower Kemyana, she had to take it.

Still, she hesitated.

And then: a hard knock on the door at the top of the stairwell, a quick pattern, predecided. Karolin was here. She had managed to overthink her way into missing her window of opportunity again.

Zemolai took a steadying breath and stepped out of the washroom. The bolt-babies stood in a cluster, each of them red-faced with their prematurely halted diatribes, stricken with defiance and guilt in equal measures.

And facing them: a person who could only be their elusive handler.

They were mid-remonstration. "I sent you there *covertly*, not to alert the entire fucking sect—" and then they caught sight of Zemolai, freshly tidied, locally garbed, but in no way mistakable for a farmer.

"And what," they demanded, "is *this*?"

CHAPTER SEVENTEEN

Do not seek to slow our work with your doubts. If we abide by
their teachings, then our actions are pure, and if our actions are
pure, then nothing we do is immoral so long as it is in service
to the greater good.
        —Winged Orlusky, *address to the Council of Five*

O N THE MORNING that Zenya betrayed the scholar sect, a gentle rain
was falling, barely more than mist. She would dwell on that mist
later—steady, unavoidable, but far too light to wash her clean.

The mecha sect approached at dawn. They made no valorous statement
of war. They gave no battle cry at the gate. Mecha Petrogon had granted
them leave to omit all honorable notice, a dispensation made for grave circumstances. They did not want a last-minute attempt to smuggle Heretic
Scholar Vikenzy's papers from the tower.

Winged Dietra and Winged Shantar led the containment effort by air,
ready to halt any attempt at evacuation. Vodaya led the ground team, with
Zenya on point.

She gave them the gate keys. She gave them a map of hidden doors
and secret passages, branching hallways stacked with incoming books. She
marched them into the twenty-second-floor archives, where Scholar Pyetka
had asked her brother to assist in the tower-wide cataloging project, on
the hunt for an entirely different heresy than the one he found.

It was her brother she was thinking of when Pyetka looked up from
his desk. Pyetka's hair was beginning to thin (Niklaus's never would).

His eyes were taking on their first hint of silver. He was sitting there in the robes that Niklaus had longed for since toddlerhood, working quietly and comfortably on a cushioned chair as though there weren't children fighting and dying in the streets for words he had helped to write.

There was a smile on his face when the door first cracked, a welcoming expression, *Who has come to visit my stacks today*, but it faltered at the sight of Zenya, and then fell at the sight of the armed team behind her.

Later, the official documentation would say: *Winged Vodaya's team questioned the suspected heretic Scholar Pyetka.*

But it was less of a questioning, and more of a plea.

"*Tell me*," Zenya said. "Tell me where Heretic Scholar Vikenzy's papers are. Don't make us tear this room apart."

"Oh, Zenya," he said (and that was it, though she didn't realize; that was the last time she would ever hear her familiar name spoken aloud). "What have you done?"

"Tell us," she repeated. And now she could hear the fighting in the halls: the rest of their ground team, borrowed from Winged Pilivar, versus the scholars, mounting an inadequate defense.

"It is only a rumor," Pyetka insisted. "They do not exist."

Vodaya made a curt gesture. Romil and Lijo surged forward, black bag raised, and Pyetka was terrified (of course he was), and the last look he cast at Zenya was full of grief.

The bag cinched down. He was dragged away, struggling ineffectually at the grasp of two strong youths. And Vodaya asked, briskly, "Where is it? You've used their systems. Where would it be?"

But Zenya had known, long before they walked into the room, there was far too much here to search. The room contained hundreds of thousands of individual pieces of paper. They were bound into books, foldered and boxed, stacked on shelves, tucked in drawers. Niklaus had found Vikenzy's work by accident, going through this enormous room one sheet at a time, and he had left it there secure in the knowledge that it would take a miracle for somebody else to find it the same way.

Pyetka knew. He had to know. He had been Niklaus's mentor, his direct supervisor, the first person Niklaus would have asked his prying questions.

But if Pyetka would not talk . . .

"We have to burn it all," Zenya said.

She felt it (the uncrossable line being crossed; the gate slamming shut behind her, ensuring her forward march), but if there was a part of her that balked at the unholy destruction about to occur, it was quelled by the relief that this was it—this was the end of the temptation that had killed her brother.

The walls here were stone; the room as good as a kiln. One bottle of accelerant was smashed against the ground, a spark was lit, and within moments they were slamming the doors against an unbearable heat.

Half a dozen scholars broke through Winged Pilivar's blockade. They threw themselves forward, screaming, desperate to enter the furnace—a sure death, but a grave shared with the knowledge they'd sworn to protect. They scrabbled; they lost; the mecha trainees dragged them away, saving their lives as surely as they were ending their way of life.

When Zenya stepped out of tower Zhelan, the mist was still falling, and it turned the ashes on her skin to mud.

It was the end of things, or the beginning, or only one sorry step on a long path. In the wake of the burning of the archives, Zenya had no limits. She had done the worst thing she could think of.

When Vodaya came to her that evening and said, "Your combat training is complete. I'm pulling you from your unit," Zenya followed her and didn't look back.

Vodaya led her up into tower Kemyana, to a darkened hall on the twenty-fourth floor. She threw open a nondescript door and ushered Zenya inside.

It was a small room, but tidily furnished, with a bed and a kitchenette and even a little shrine smoldering with extinguished incense. A bookcase was already stocked with the works of Vodaya's favorite saints.

It was perfect.

"You know the next step," Vodaya prompted.

Energy twanged through Zenya's nerves, and she stood to attention.

"A training port," she said. The only way to learn how to control a prosthetic was to plug one in. Vodaya was talking about wing prep, the advanced Pava engineering course.

"I want you to sleep here," Vodaya said briskly. "My personal quarters are through the adjoining door. You will work with me in the field and attend on me when I am in the tower, but otherwise you may set your own study hours for port training. Do you understand?"

"Yes." It took all of Zenya's willpower not to break out in an undignified grin.

"Good, because there is one other thing." Vodaya considered her carefully. "I am going to trust you with something, Zemolai, because I believe you truly understand the nature of the mecha god's directives, and because you have proved yourself to me today. But this is a matter of great secrecy. What I say to you now cannot leave this room."

"I understand," Zenya said.

Vodaya stepped closer, lowering her voice as though somebody might be lurking nearby. She said, "Faiyan Sanador is collaborating with the engineers."

Zenya drew back, shocked. She pictured her old engineering instructor, grumbly and focused, interested in nothing other than mechanics. To think, she had felt a rapport with him—another transplant from a non-mecha sect, using his skills to aid the Winged. Apparently not.

Anger washed through her. For two decades Sanador had been part of the Pava school curriculum. "When did he turn?" Zenya asked. Then her thoughts slewed toward her own situation, and she added, "Who will take over the port training program?"

"Nobody is taking over the training—yet. I need more information before I bring this to Mecha Petrogon's attention." Vodaya opened the bottom drawer of a small writing desk. She withdrew a mechanical device and placed it in Zenya's hands.

A transponder. Wired all over like one of Faiyan Sanador's programming boards.

"I want you to take this to Sanador's chamber," Vodaya instructed. "He has a private live-speak radio there, which is not wired through our communications grid. I already monitor his physical correspondence, but I suspect he is using live-speak to avoid a paper trail."

This was not at all what Zenya had expected. She frowned. "You want me . . ."

"To spy on him, yes." Vodaya considered her gravely. "This is a delicate situation, Zemolai. You will study with this man—your training must continue, and despite his questionable loyalties, he is still our resident expert and dedicated to his craft—but you will also be watching him for signs of disloyalty and monitoring his radio when he is out of your sight."

Zenya was no stranger to subterfuge. She had spent years preparing for this life in secret (an easy trick, admittedly, when one's parent paid minimal attention), but one of the comforts of the mecha sect was how brutally candid the expectations were. Their moral code was clear-cut. They announced their intentions and followed through. Spying was something else entirely.

But routing out a traitor engineer was nothing in comparison to what Zenya had already done. She said, "I won't disappoint you."

Vodaya smiled. "I am happy to hear that. Take care of it tonight. To-morrow, you have an appointment with the surgeon."

Sanador had a meeting that would keep him away, Vodaya said. Where, with whom—that was none of Zenya's business. She crept through the training grounds with a transponder and one of Vodaya's spare access codes and prayed there would be no traitor engineer waiting for her at the end of the hall.

When Zenya dashed into Sanador's quarters, using one of Vodaya's own override access codes, her heart was fluttering like it had wings of its own. Sanador's bed was piled in blankets. His walls were covered in reli-gious leaflets and inspiring quotations scrawled directly on the stones in black paint. Papers spilled from end tables and a broad oak writing desk. It felt like a violation to look at this mess, even more so to pick through it.

She found the device wedged beneath his bed. It was a long, shallow rectangular box—odd proportions, custom-built to conceal. Wires ran to the wall, presumably connecting to the power grid, but an additional box was attached halfway along the cords. Vodaya had described this as a type of scrambler, allowing Sanador to use the power grid while blocking intercepts.

Zenya wired in the transponder, as instructed. She tried to view it as an exercise. An assignment. An order. If she felt queasy about what she was doing—well, it hadn't been her decision, had it?

As Winged Zorska would say: she was only the hand on the blade.

The next day she reported to the surgery hall, trembling behind a brave façade. It was what she wanted—had wanted, would always want—and it was terrifying.

Surgeons were a strange bunch, simultaneously revered for their skill and distrusted for their lack of pure ideology. They worshipped both creator god and earth god, combining tech and natural remedy with wild abandon. Country doctors worked in farmland; faith healers in purist corners of the city; but in this hall, where the need was situated firmly between the chemical and the mechanical, true surgeons were indispensable.

"Pava Zemolai, please."

Zenya took a deep breath and followed. Her surgeon was a small, round woman with delicate fingers and enormous eyes. She said, "I recommend the left flank. Easy to reach for maintenance, but out of the way if you sustain injury to the torso."

"Whatever you think best," Zenya said, nervously pulling her tunic over her head. The air in the hall was bitingly cold, and her skin rippled with goosebumps. The operating table stood only three feet off the ground.

A hygiene assistant provided a pillow, a set of restraints, and a bite block scored with teeth marks and vaguely smelling of antiseptic. She set down a tray full of syringes—all medical solutions adapted from the gods' teachings. Paralytics and pain relief; protections from infection, hemorrhage, and the myriad complications that plagued doctors' halls outside of Radezhda.

They looped restraints over her hips and shoulders, but once the paralytics kicked in, they were unnecessary. Zenya was awake but immobile when the surgeon made a small incision in the flesh above her hip and propped it wide with a wound spreader.

Zenya bit her rubber block and tried to breathe through it, unashamed of the tears blurring her vision as the surgeon teased out a set of nerves and attached them directly to wires. She tried to imagine herself somewhere else, anywhere else—and there was one place that made the hurt worthwhile. The light of the mecha god's heaven had eased her through many sleepless nights, and she clung to the memory again now.

This was pain with a purpose.

The surgeon bent sideways, her eyes level with Zenya's. "You are doing very well, Pava. Do you see this?" She held up a small metal cylinder, bristling at one end with connections for the wires. "The finest modern engineering. You will have nearly the functionality of the full-size port, albeit at a lower energy capacity. So, no heavy lifting, eh?"

Zenya wanted to shout, *Just finish! Give me the tutorial when I'm not gaped open on the operating table!* Perhaps her eyes conveyed it well enough, because the surgeon completed her work without further digression.

It was a long while shuddering on the table before the paralytic left her system. Rawness radiated out from the surgery site, and Zenya clung tightly to the bag of painkillers, antibiotics, and suppressants the surgeon had left her. With shaky triumph, she grinned at the bandage wrapped around her abdomen.

Zenya had her first rudimentary mech port. She was one step closer to wings.

Two weeks passed. The surgeon inspected her for signs of infection and then gave her approval to begin practicing. Gently, at first! Do not overstrain! As though she were tempted—for once, Zenya found her heels dragging at the thought of her next step.

Faiyan Sanador's workshop was just as she remembered, bursting with tool racks and parts bins, crafting stations and cutting boards, anvils and forges, sheet rollers and presses.

The back door opened, and Sanador walked in. He had changed over the past months. He was quieter, paler. He did not look like a traitor, but who did?

At the sight of Zenya, he smiled. "I should have known you would be the first one through my door."

She tried to smile back, after a brief internal war (she longed for praise—but she should not want it from a traitor—but she should not look like she thought he was a traitor—). The silence stretched between them, uncomfortable.

"This way," Sanador finally said, and he led her into an adjoining room: the tech chamber. The tech chamber had five walls, each equipped with a communications board, a book of defunct security codes, and a table of small mechanical devices. It was set up for an entire five-unit to study at once, but Zenya had left hers behind.

Sanador gestured at the equipment. "The function of your training port is twofold," he said. "First, we will practice connecting with systems. Second, and more importantly, I will assess your ability to direct basic motor functions."

Zenya shifted nervously at that, her hand hovering over the still-painful, half-healed wound on her abdomen. The thought of failing at motor functions was terrifying. To come so far in combat training only to be stymied by the very technology that defined the sect? Unimaginable.

"I want to start now," she said.

Zenya hurried through basic hygiene (how to sanitize open ports, how to seal them, how to share cords safely), and then basic access (inserting plugs, setting security signatures, connecting to communications). These were passive skills, talentless, just steps on a checklist, and she waited impatiently for Sanador to give her something worthwhile to work on.

"Pace yourself," he murmured, but this *was* Zenya's ordinary pace. She was anxious, hurried—and, yes, a little selfish. One day soon, Sanador would be arrested, and port training would be thrown into chaos while a new candidate was scouted. Zenya wanted to be far enough along to continue on her own when that happened.

So she worked, and she watched him, looking for the evidence that

Vodaya needed to raise her suspicion with Mecha Petrogon. And it hurt when he praised her; when he made a mechanics joke; when he laughed. Was no one trustworthy?

Wherever Zenya went, she carried a receiver in her pack, the bulky twin to the transponder she'd installed in Sanador's room. She tried not to think of it when she was in the tech chamber, taking advice from the man whose downfall she was planning.

As the weeks crawled by, Vodaya began to press her. "What have you seen? What have you heard?"

"Nothing," Zenya said, over and over again. "Nothing."

"Fah." Vodaya would turn back to her work, a dismissal colder than the wind off Ruk Head Mountain, and Zenya would return to her room for the night, alone.

This was only half of Zenya's daily life.

Vodaya had also given her a call beacon, a modified version of a distress beacon, which could be used repeatedly at short distances. At any time of day or night, if the device grew hot on Zenya's hip, she dropped what she was doing to attend on Vodaya.

And in exchange, a new world of inner-sect politics opened to her. When Vodaya was not on rotation in the city, she was locked away in meetings. War meetings with Mecha Petrogon. Strategy meetings with her quadrant leader. Informal meetings with any Winged willing to engage her on the subject of city security.

Vodaya and Raksa clashed with increasing ferocity atop tower Ke-myana, often with Mecha Petrogon standing between them. He watched them spit and strut, absorbing their arguments with grave patience before making his wishes law. He strode a middle ground between their demands, to the satisfaction of neither, but as the conflict wound down, he began leaning toward reconciliation.

Vodaya followed Petrogon back to his quarters when one particularly volatile war meeting ended in his flat-out refusal to grant her another ground team. Zenya stood stiff and uncomfortable outside his door while Vodaya continued making her case.

"A campaign of appeasement will ruin our momentum," she insisted.

"We've made our point," Mecha Petrogon said, and there was steel beneath the words. "The engineers are cowed. They are willing to reconcile. Production suffers while we fight."

"It's a ploy!" Vodaya said. "They want us to lower our guard. If you convene a new council, it will be the same fight on a new field, only now their sect garners sympathy from the earth god's people. While we're distracted in debate, they'll entrench themselves underground."

"Vodaya, my ground intelligence is extremely thorough. You have to trust my judgment on this. The city needs to focus on healing now."

"Give me command!" she insisted. "You can return to the council and deploy your quadrant leaders back to the perimeter, and I will be your city security. If the engineers are cowed, I need do nothing. But if they are not . . ."

Mecha Petrogon sighed, a strangely ordinary sound to hear from the mecha god's own Voice. "When I say this, I mean it in the most constructive way possible," he said. "Vodaya, your dedication is admirable. But you need to understand the difference between the glory of necessary battle and battle for the sake of glory. Your obsession with preemptive action is why you will never be made Tooth."

Zenya's breath caught at the blunt criticism. It had been this way between them since the bombing—tense, combative. Zenya wondered, not for the first time, what had really passed between them that day.

Vodaya emerged in a predictably foul mood. "Do you have something for me yet?" she demanded.

Zenya shook her head. Vodaya's lips thinned. "You've been playing at ports long enough today," she snapped. "Combat skills degrade when they aren't maintained. Clean communication cords won't save you from a knife in the kidney."

It would be a grueling bout in the combat ring. Vodaya never removed her wings for these sessions anymore. She rained hell from the sky, and Zenya waged a desperate defense from the ground, and it was a terrible afternoon not worth remembering afterward.

It happened, at last: Faiyan Sanador deemed Zenya ready for motor control.

The practice device was a mechanical hand, clenched tight around the thick, worn cable protruding from its palm. Her goal: open the fist. Easy. Yes?

Zenya plugged in, giddy at the tingle of awareness where the cord entered her abdomen. She tried to imagine what it would feel like when it was her entire back. She took a deep breath, cleared her mind, and visualized the fingers uncurling . . .

Nothing happened. Zenya made an angry sound.

"*Patience*," Sanador murmured. "Even an ordinary prosthetic takes time to master, and that's when the brain's impulses are traveling familiar paths. Unnatural appendages are another skill entirely. In this exercise, the appendage is familiar to you, but the pathway is not. Wings will be another step beyond this, alien to the body in both respects."

Zenya knew this, but it didn't make the learning curve any less frustrating. She was used to deciding, then doing. Study, memorize. Practice, improve. She didn't just . . . *fail*!

To her surprise, Sanador pulled a chair up next to hers and sat down. "Zemolai," he said gently, and she knew that tone—it never went well. "You push yourself too hard. Port training is a long course of study. You don't need to stay up late, or take pills, or self-castigate." He hesitated, then added, "Is there anything you'd like to talk about?"

Oh, what a wonderful liar he was. The compassion on his face! As though this weren't a clear ploy to extract information from her. Was he fishing for damaging information on Vodaya? Petrogon? The content of their war meetings?

There was a true answer, unusable. *I'm in a hurry; you'll be arrested soon, and the mecha sect does not have a second engineer on staff.*

She said, "Do I have permission to use the tech chamber this evening?"

The mood was broken. Sanador sighed, leaning back. "Stay as long as you like," he said. "I'll see you tomorrow."

At last he left, and Zenya shut her eyes, feeling her way back to the steady ache of her port. The plug was right there, a dense lump of dead metal shoved into her side. The wires leading out of it were strange, living things, ripe with potential, voids waiting to be filled. Her temples began to throb, and her own hands clenched and unclenched reflexively.

Maybe if she . . .

Zenya tried and tried, sometimes feeling a tingle that might have been connectivity, more often feeling like she was about to burst a blood vessel in her head, and every time failing miserably. Not even a twitch.

If she couldn't even open a hand, how would she manage the complexity of wings?

Zenya slammed the training toy back on the table and sat there for a long time with her furious thoughts. It was late, and her stomach was growling mercilessly, and her painkillers had long since worn off, but she was damned if she was going to go home now. *Have you heard anything?* Vodaya would ask, and then, disappointed, scathing, *Are you even making progress with your port, or are you failing at that, too?*

She refocused. She tried again.

It was nearly two hours later—when Zenya was trembling with exertion and pain and the many tendrils of self-loathing that lurked beneath them—that, at long last, a single finger uncurled from the fist.

She was so shocked, she gasped; the first sound the room had heard in hours. And then she laughed at her own shock and laughed at the sudden simplicity of the connection. Of course, there it was, there it had been all along! She opened and closed the fist, beaming all the while.

And then an odd chiming sound interrupted her triumph. It was high-pitched, unfamiliar—and she realized it was the receiver, chiming in her pack beneath the chair. Faiyan Sanador was making a call.

Zenya hastily dragged the device out and hit the audio switch, tuning in mid-conversation.

Sanador was abrupt. "You have to stop asking me questions."

Another voice whispered through the speaker, made tinny and flat by the imperfect technology. "We're in difficult times," it said. "I'm not going to judge you for your part in it. I only want you to hear my argument before you do anything further."

Zenya froze, placing the thready voice to a face.

It was Winged Raksa.

"I've told you already," Sanador said, "it's nothing to do with me."

Zenya snatched up the nearest pen and flipped over a page of study notes, cursing herself for not having paper at the ready. She scribbled down the gist of what had already been said, and Raksa continued, oblivious to the spy on the line.

"I know you met in secret last week. You can't convince me that was a social call."

Sanador demurred, his mumble almost entirely consumed by static. But Zenya could sense him weakening. He hadn't called Winged Raksa on an illegal line only to tell him off.

"I can protect you," Raksa insisted. "I have the ear of Mecha Petrogon. With your help I'll have the leverage I need to end the threat to your people. We want the same thing."

Zenya transcribed the words automatically, but her mind was divorced from her hand, spiraling off into all possible interpretations of that promise. None of them were good. She waited breathlessly for Faiyan Sanador's response, hanging onto his words almost as eagerly as Winged Raksa himself must have been.

"I won't discuss this over wires," Sanador said finally.

"Can you slip your overseer?" Raksa asked.

"Yes." With reluctance, the engineer admitted, "I have another exit."

They settled on a time and place, away from the compound and only two days away. The receiver went dead, and Zenya finished scrawling her notes. She considered the ink-splattered page for only a moment before dashing out of the workshop. She ran for tower Kemyana and spent an eternity in the lift before reaching Vodaya's floor and bursting into her quarters.

Vodaya emerged from the loft before Zenya reached the stairs. She was halfway down with a bolt-gun drawn before recognizing her own trainee.

"What?" she demanded.

Zenya thrust out the paper, terribly out of breath. "The transponder. A call."

Vodaya continued to scowl as she read. Then she reached the end, and her entire body twanged straight with excitement. "Go on, then," she urged. "Get dressed."

Zenya drew back. "Now? Where are we going?" She had expected this to be one piece of evidence in a pile; a case made before Mecha Petrogon, and let *him* decide their next actions. They had two days before Sanador and Raksa's meeting to gather more information.

But Vodaya grinned, ghoulish in the dim light, and said, "We are going to arrest Faiyan Sanador ourselves."

CHAPTER EIGHTEEN

I am not telling you to abandon your optimism, I am saying do not let it fool you to complacency. We must keep weapons of our own. We must prepare for the worst.

For if a day comes that the mecha god desires more power, she will stop at nothing—and therefore neither must we.

—Letter from Creator Vanyamir to Creator Talley

THE BOLT-BABIES' CELL LEADER, the long-awaited Karolin, was not at all what Zemolai had expected. They were short and stout, with thick, curly hair and a fixed expression of parental concern. The nicks around their neck hinted at glass-factory work, but their demeanor seemed better suited to telling bedtime stories in a nursery school. They carried a pair of old satchels, green and covered in buckles, like something a grandfather would tote around, but Zemolai did not think they were full of candies.

"Explain," they said. Their attention hadn't budged from Zemolai, who casually leaned against the wall and returned their appraising stare.

Timyan kept one hand on Rustaya's arm, silently urging his impatient partner to let him take the lead. "We found her after we left tower Kemyana and cleared her system. She helped us breach the training compound . . ."

"You didn't mention any of this in your report."

Timyan said, "We thought it better to be cautious. We couldn't risk it being intercepted."

Karolin grunted acknowledgment, but their look at Zemolai was anything but forgiving. Timyan summarized the timeline from there: their successful acquisition of one duffel of weaponry; the presence of Mecha Vodaya and Winged Mitrios on site.

Karolin cut him off. "And now they'll be scouring the grounds for your access point. You're lucky you even escaped."

"Not all of us," Rustaya snapped. At Karolin's blank look they gestured angrily around the room. "Eleny. Eleny didn't come back."

Karolin nodded. "I see that. I'm sorry."

"Are you?"

Karolin's paternalistic façade dropped, and the real guerrilla war veteran stared back at them. They said, "Eleny understood the risks. You all do. Or did your years of scrubbing pots convince you that you were ordinary kitchen workers all this time?"

"That isn't what—"

"You knew a posting in tower Kemyana would be dangerous. You knew you might be discovered at any time."

"This isn't about our cover being blown!" Rustaya yelled. "This is about the fucking alarm systems, which you said would be disabled!"

"I gave you accurate information," Karolin said coolly.

"Accurate? *Accurate?*"

Fate, or rather the Tooth, intervened.

His scream was muffled, but his tone came through clearly. He was awake, and he was prepared to murder the first person who gave him a chance.

Karolin's eyes glittered. "We'll talk about this later," they said sternly. They set one of their grandfatherly satchels by the door and hefted the other one into their arms. "I'm going in now. Don't interrupt me."

It was the purpose for which the rebels netted the warrior, but their feelings had evolved considerably over the course of their long wait.

"They're lying," Timyan said softly.

"What if they aren't?" Galiana asked. "What if I . . ." She looked stricken. *What if I got Eleny killed?*

The three of them huddled together in a corner, whispering through their options. It wasn't a complete breakdown of cell structure, not yet, but it was coming. They had all the discipline of the truly principled: easy targets for disorder when they disagreed on a point of conduct. There were a lot of ways to be wrong. Nobody could agree on the best way to be right.

Muffled curses from the next room told them the Tooth was ungagged. Karolin's voice was a persistent murmur beneath the warrior's recriminations. Patient and unyielding.

Zemolai didn't need to hear the Tooth's words to know the script. Under ordinary circumstances a Tooth would be impenetrable. Nothing but cold silence and a plan to escape. The fact that they could hear his voice at all meant the last trace of mechalin had left his system, and he was succumbing to a feverish rant.

Karolin only needed time, but they didn't care to wait. The rebels knew when the nature of the interrogation changed by the screech of metal dragging across the floor. The Tooth thrashed and fell from the cot with a meaty thud.

And then the ranting came, louder than ever, peppered with words like *god* and *traitor* and *destroy*.

And then furious screaming.

And then *less* furious screaming, and a voice dropping to a ragged hush . . .

And then new resistance, fresh ranting, the cycle starting over again.

They sat in horrified silence and listened to Karolin torture their prisoner. Timyan looked nauseated, Rustaya unsettled, Galiana firm-lipped and staring at her hands.

They showed some practicality, at least. As angry as they were, they didn't interrupt.

"We could cure him," Timyan whispered.

Galiana grimaced. She glanced at Zemolai, who had just laid the situation out for her so neatly in the barn. "Karolin is accelerating his meltdown, not easing it."

"I just mean . . . after . . ."

"He's an assassin," Rustaya said abruptly. "A fucking murderer."

The Tooth screamed again, plunging them back into an icy silence. Zemolai shut her eyes and leaned her head against the wall. It felt good. A nice hard surface to hold her up. She gave it a tap with her skull. Another. How hard would she have to hit her head to block all of this out?

She'd held no illusions about what would happen to the Tooth when they captured him, but she'd expected more from herself, some emotion when confronted with the reality of it. She even knew what his name had been before he was called up into his current, nameless rank: Winged Vedelsen. He was a veteran, having flown his first missions as Tooth when Zemolai was still in training. A slight change in career path and *she* could have gone for the crimson one day.

If Zemolai hadn't fucked up her life over Chae Savro's fucking scholar idol, she'd still be flying, and the rebels would be dead. And if she hadn't tagged along on their suicide mission, they never would have overcome the Tooth.

But Zemolai heard his torment and was wholly numb to it. She wondered when she had stopped caring. It had been long before her judgment. Long before Chae Savro.

The Tooth screamed. She did nothing.

Karolin emerged with a vacuum at their back. Cold and deathly silent. They looked decidedly less grandfatherly with their shirtsleeves rolled up above bloody fists full of syringes. A light sheen of sweat coated their face.

"You can't stay here," they said brusquely. "The situation is far too volatile. Dispose of the Tooth's body within city limits. Find new lodging, and I'll send for you later."

Nobody moved. Testily, Karolin said, "I meant *now*. Get moving."

"What did the Tooth say?" Rustaya asked.

"You know better than to ask me that," Karolin said. "It's no concern of yours."

"But it is." Rustaya turned steely. "Eleny died for that information. Was it worth it?"

"Yes," Karolin said curtly. "Now. Do what I've said. I'll make sure that your new friend gets settled at the barn."

And just like that, Zemolai's nerves were singing. There was a knife on her hip, but Karolin might be hiding something worse. The duffel bag was close, but it was unlikely that any projectile weapons were preloaded. The rebels were an unknown quantity. She'd have to take their leader down first and then see how they reacted . . .

Galiana shot forward. "We called you here for the Tooth, Karolin. That's it."

"You should have told me you had a Winged days ago," they said. "Be grateful I'm willing to overlook that."

Galiana folded her arms, and the gesture almost hid the way they trembled. "Zemolai stays with us," she said. She cast about for support from the others. Timyan wouldn't meet her eyes. Rustaya looked like the whole thing was a bitter pill in their mouth.

Galiana took Timyan by the arm. "Tell them! We didn't cure her so she could vanish into a black box. What are we fighting for, if it isn't the right to choose our own paths?" Desperate, she played her best card. "You know *exactly* what Eleny would say."

"That's enough," Karolin snapped. "This isn't your decision."

They reached into the satchel they'd left by the door and produced an ankle shackle. It was braided steel with a ceramic interior, pulsing lightly like an activated distress beacon.

A tracking device and a chain combined. Zemolai's eyes narrowed. She'd used such devices herself. They were practically indestructible, another little gift from the creator god. When activated—either by the entangled companion piece or when the shackled individual left the field of influence—the tracker clamped tight as the teeth of a bear trap.

Once that device locked around her ankle, she wasn't leaving again. Not alive.

"I'm not wearing that," she said, too abruptly.

She should have stalled. Her only objective was to disable the dampener Galiana had placed around the Tooth's thigh (wasn't it?). She could do that with a shackle on, and once Vodaya was here, she'd have access to the mecha administration's finest pet engineers. They'd have it off in a flash (wouldn't they?).

The truth was she didn't know if Vodaya would release her. *If one of my Teeth can't overcome a handful of workers on his own*, she'd said, *he's worthless to me.* She had never afforded Zemolai any more lenience.

"Put that away," Rustaya said. They were gruff, annoyed at being backed into this corner. "It was our decision to pick her up. We'll be responsible for her."

Karolin laughed. "That's a poor joke."

"It's not a joke. We made a commitment—"

"This isn't about commitment. This is about—"

"We'll dispose of the Tooth. We'll wait for your next instructions. All we ask—"

"This isn't a negotiation!"

Rustaya persisted, raising their voice over Karolin's. "All we ask is some time to decompress, Zemolai included—"

Karolin's face burned hot. "*Winged don't defect.* You brought me here. She knows my *face*. The first chance she gets, she'll turn us in, and if you think I'm going to let that happen—"

They charged forward a step—and halted, faced by a line of three younger fighters. Timyan and Rustaya might have had their reservations, but they would always stand by Galiana.

That was what happened when you let your fighters have families.

A few well-placed words, and Zemolai had guilted Galiana into her corner. A few well-placed words, and the rest of them had fallen in line behind her. Zemolai couldn't have planned it better.

But it didn't feel like a victory. It felt dirty. It felt like spy work, and Zemolai had never achieved anything good through spy work.

"You're either part of this movement, or you aren't," Karolin insisted. "If we let them pit us against one another, we *lose*, do you understand? You don't come and go as the work suits you. You don't decide which orders to follow. You sure as shit don't pick a *Winged* over your own cause."

"I'm not moving," Galiana said.

Karolin tensed, as though about to charge—and then they considered Galiana more carefully. Zemolai knew that sort of look. It was the wind shifting before a storm.

"This is your fault," Karolin told her, with barely leashed fury. "This isn't some matter of principle. This is about *you*, and your obsession with god-light. That's where you went, isn't it?"

Zemolai zeroed in on this—the answer, finally, to her question.

Galiana shook her head, her face gone pale. Karolin persisted, "Yes, that's it. You went digging where you weren't supposed to, and you set off an alarm. You got your own friend killed over this idiocy, and now you're putting your trust in a Winged to prove your point."

"Stop it," Rustaya warned.

Karolin gestured at Zemolai and laughed. "Did Galiana tell you why she's really keeping you around? Her little project?"

"It's not . . ." Galiana faltered. She looked toward Zemolai, full of fear.

Something hard formed in Zemolai's chest then. She stared at Galiana, thinking again of all the dissonant little moments that had thrummed between them before. Galiana asking something. Galiana wanting something.

"I swear to the Five, Karolin," Rustaya growled. "If you don't get out of here . . ."

Karolin glared at each of them in turn. "Keep your pet for the time being, but do what I've said. Dispose of the Tooth. Stay away from the barn. I'm coming back here at sunset, and if I find you dawdling, you'll all be shipped over the mountains in chains, do you hear me?"

They nodded, and held their breaths, and stood steady and silent until the trapdoor slammed shut.

It had worked. Karolin was gone.

Timyan collapsed against a wall, boneless. He said, "Did we just do what I think we did?"

"It'll be fine," Galiana said, a touch stridently. "We'll need to keep a low profile till they calm down, that's all."

Timyan covered his face and groaned.

"We'll finish this business with the Tooth, and then we'll find a safe house," Rustaya said. "One of ours, not one they've arranged. The important thing is that we stay together."

Galiana nodded, but without the same conviction. "I'm sorry," she whispered.

Timyan flicked a miserable glance at Zemolai. "You'd better be worth this."

"She isn't," Rustaya said bluntly. "But neither was Karolin." They limped toward the back room.

"What are you doing?" Timyan asked.

Rustaya glared. "We have a job to do, don't we? Let's hurry before Karolin comes back with a sack full of shackles and a five-unit at their back."

Timyan followed them, quietly discussing the logistics of fetching another vehicle, leaving behind Galiana and Zemolai and a secret the height of a tower in the air.

"What did Karolin mean?" Zemolai asked. She kept her voice tight, low. Her body hummed, ready to fight. "What were they saying about god-light?"

Galiana looked up, shiny-eyed and desperate. "I meant what I said. We didn't pick you up to put you in a new cage. We're building something different, I swear. Everyone free to choose their path."

"You keep saying that," Zemolai snapped, "but it isn't true. You've already got me shackled, and you've made it damn clear you don't trust me with the key. I hope you weren't relying on Karolin to stock my drugs, because if so, you've just cut me off. *What did they mean?*"

"I don't . . . I didn't . . ." Galiana's breath came quickly. She was holding off tears. When she spoke again, it was so softly, so miserably, Zemolai almost didn't hear it. Four words, four whispered words, and she said the only possible thing that could have distracted Zemolai in that moment:

"You don't need them."

Zemolai blinked. "What did you say?"

"The drugs. You don't need them." Galiana swallowed, looking toward the back room, toward the people who had just put themselves in danger on her behalf, who had just taken responsibility for keeping Zemolai in check. She spoke quickly, before she could change her mind. "You only needed two days' worth to flush out your system. We've been giving you a placebo since then."

Something white and hot flooded Zemolai's thoughts, and she lurched forward. Galiana stumbled back, eyes wide, and Zemolai wanted to grab her, wanted to shake her, wanted to throw her to the floor.

"You're telling me this *now*?" she shouted, and she didn't care who heard, fuck them, fuck these babies and their games, fuck everybody who had ever put her on a leash. The entire miserable week flooded over her, every decision made under duress, an illusion of autonomy. She'd gone back to Pava, she'd broken the last of her principles, she'd come face-to-face with Vodaya again and crumpled like an infant, like a coward, she'd practically *begged*.

She wanted to storm the back room right then and there. Rip the resonance chip from the Tooth's leg and shatter it. Forget subtlety. Forget keeping them in the dark. Just let the Winged come and burn this rat's nest into the earth.

"You're right," Galiana said, and now she *was* crying. "If I have to threaten you to make you help us, then I'm no better than they are. I don't *want* to manipulate you. I want you to see there's another way." She wiped at her eyes. "If you stay, do it of your own choice. If you won't, then go now, while everyone's distracted. I'll deal with the consequences."

Zemolai froze. Violence, she was always prepared for. Manipulation, bribery, threats—for all of those, she had a response.

Galiana was offering her a choice.

A terrible choice, a choice offered too late, a choice between going alone into a world that hated her or fighting the only world that had ever accepted her. But it was still a choice.

For days, she had watched this little group, hardly able to believe they could handle their fake jobs, much less their real ones. Her fury was easy. Her resentment was comfortable. They were a welcome distraction, familiar feelings to cling to, because if she peeked behind the curtain, she'd find they were masking something else entirely: the crack in her shell.

That day in the workers' quarters, when she had foolishly let Chae Savro run off with his idol, she'd attributed her poor judgment to age, sentimentality. But deep down, she knew it had been something far worse.

Regret.

Regret for her years of service to a violent cause. Regret for the lives she'd ruined. The people she'd killed. Regret for the destruction of her childhood faith. She had let grief and anger drive her to extremes, and when she'd come out the other side of it, gasping and bloodied, she'd been too invested in Vodaya's new world order to turn back.

It was regret for doing what she was told. For letting herself be molded, for *watching it happen* and continuing forward anyway, because the only way to stop was to admit it had all been for nothing.

Zemolai had never been flawless, however hard she tried. Perhaps, if she hadn't made so many mistakes, she would have seen the cruelty in Vodaya's methods earlier. Instead, she was cursed with perpetual uncertainty, the nagging conviction that she had, in fact, deserved every minute of it.

The recriminations? Only constructive criticism from a superior. The isolation? Only a way to limit her distractions and push her toward her full potential. The long shifts, the difficult assignments, always demanding that Zemolai give more? It was only because Zemolai was *capable* of more. Vodaya had explained herself at every step of the way, and it had always made sense at the time.

And yet Zemolai was still so *angry*. Angry then. Angry now.

She'd heard Vodaya's voice over the kitchen radio, and she'd folded, immediately. She'd been obedient for too many years to shore up her spine in a matter of days. But the incident had gutted her. It was humiliating. Transparently pathetic.

Galiana waited. Frightened and repentant.

Zemolai was supposed to murder her. If not directly, then by proxy, because Mecha Vodaya wanted it. Vodaya, who'd cast her aside when her usefulness ran out. Vodaya, who'd left her to die. Until Zemolai reappeared in a valuable position, at which point Vodaya didn't hesitate. Didn't show a bit of remorse. Just cracked the whip once more, expecting immediate compliance.

Zemolai was never going home again. Vodaya was never going to *let* her go home again. Not even in the humbling capacity of a support team.

The admission—held at bay this long by exhaustion and desperation and longing—turned her willpower to ash. The force that had been driving her forward blew away, and all that remained was hollow panic.

Zemolai teetered on a precipice, and for the first time in her life, she had no idea what waited below. So often, she had simply taken the leap. With wings of wood and paper, with wings of metal, with no wings at all.

But every one of those times, she had been secure in her purpose. She had not hesitated, because she knew (or *believed* she knew, with a ferocity that felt like truth) what was going to happen next.

This time, she needed something more before she jumped.

Abruptly, she spun away from Galiana. She drifted to the back room on legs gone weak with shock, and Galiana rushed after her, sickly beneath her tan—though what she planned to do if Zemolai attacked the others was anyone's guess.

Timyan and Rustaya had cut the Tooth's ropes and arranged him with some dignity on the floor, but Karolin's work was too thorough to disguise. Their technique had been straightforward and gruesome: pump the Tooth full of comedown drugs, heighten every sensation to the point of agony, and then go to work with something sharp.

It wouldn't have taken much to get him talking after that, though whether it was usable information was another story.

Zemolai crouched beside the Tooth's mangled body, ignoring her audience. She was supposed to disable the dampener around his thigh. If she did, an alarm would sound at tower Kemyana. At least one elite five-unit would descend on the market, perhaps two, and they would lay waste to everything they found here. The farmers' stalls. The community barn. Every survivor would be rounded up and arrested. New edicts would be passed to regulate the movements of the earth god's sect, and open fighting would begin again.

Zemolai lifted a bloody flap of fabric that had slid over the homemade signal dampener.

She heard Galiana's sound of dismay and looked up. They stared at one another over the corpse of the Tooth, the threat clear, the question even clearer. Zemolai said it anyway. "Tell me what you really want from me, or I end this now."

Silence descended, brittle, everyone wondering if they had just made the biggest mistake of their lives.

"I lied," Galiana said faintly. She glanced at Timyan and Rustaya, both frozen, waiting for her next move. "Back at the training grounds. The device I threw down. It wasn't just a signal blocker. I . . ." She swallowed, still stalling, even as the clock was ticking down on Karolin's deadline. "The engineers are trying to harness god-light. Have been, for quite some time."

A terrible feeling spooled in Zemolai's gut. The same feeling she'd had all those years ago, when her brother handed her a sheaf of papers containing a new scholar theory: *I am about to learn something terrible.* She said, "You can't."

Galiana shifted nervously. "God-light is incredibly versatile. The heavens are powered by it. The gods use it to read our bodies, to overload our electricals, to pierce the veil between their realm and ours . . . and we think it's replicable. That is the amazing part. At least, we believe it to be, at least in parts . . ."

"*Galiana,*" Timyan urged.

"Right." She stared down at her hands. "What the engineers *don't* believe is that they aren't *first.* They don't think it's possible another sect could beat them at engineering. But after working in tower Kemyana, digging into your security systems . . . Zemolai, those technologies didn't come through us. I thought you were hiding it from me, but you weren't lying, were you? You didn't have any idea what I was asking about."

"It isn't possible," Zemolai said. "I would know." She felt dizzy. Destabilized. A harsh buzzing had begun in her ears. "God-light isn't—it isn't earthly. It's divine, not quantifiable, not something that can be captured in a machine. It's not technology."

Weakly, Galiana tried to reassure her, "It's still a *godly* technology . . . as are all the secrets bestowed on us by the gods . . ."

Zemolai shook her head. "This is different. This is . . ." This was everything she believed in: that there could be a single truth, inviolable, that the gods alone held a special ability to see into the hearts of humankind and judge what they found.

Galiana said, "I've been experimenting with a signal blocker, using what we know about god-light, thinking, oh, we could use it to stop anything the mecha sect throws at us, we could see into your systems, short-circuit any lock, make any Winged malfunction. And you *saw* that it worked. You saw it take Winged Mitrios down. But Mecha Vodaya just . . . deflected it. It didn't work on her." Galiana tapped her chest. "She had a device behind her breastplate. Its glow made the metal *translucent*. That isn't anything we know how to make."

It was painful to recall. Vodaya striding through the courtyard like an avenging saint. Vodaya crossing the energy field like it was nothing, her breastplate flashing red. Zemolai had seen that flash before and never questioned it. Why would she? The Voice had technologies bestowed directly by the gods, be they nobody's business but her own.

Faintly, Zemolai said, "You think she can block god-light. That would mean . . ."

Galiana nodded. "God-light overrides electrical impulses, communications, radar, *everything*," she said. "If she can block that, it means nothing can broach her mechanicals, her implants, hell, even her heat signature. Not even the mecha god could read her. She's a blank slate. You see? The mecha sect is way ahead of us. They've already mastered god-light."

A blank slate.

Zemolai pictured Vodaya standing in the light of the mecha god's judgment, shining pure and clean, only her heart beating red, red, red.

How long?

When Vodaya had closed their borders, she'd stood in the mecha god's light to ease the concerns of her unit commanders. When she'd forced through identification policies and trade restrictions and religious declarations, she'd preemptively summoned the god to judge her, to forestall internal protest.

Twenty-six years Zemolai had followed her orders. *Twenty-six years.*

How many times had Vodaya vanished into the god's realm for hours, *days*? She always came back with long scrolls of paper covered in her tight, feverish handwriting, edict after edict, precision law-making that slotted perfectly into her previous commandments, always tightening the belt a little bit more, for everyone but her chosen few.

Stay with me, and I will never leave you.

Vodaya had taken her to heaven.

Twenty-six years.

A scream was welling up inside of her, bubbling up and bubbling up. None of it had come from the mecha god. None of it.

This was it: the precipice. And Zemolai was going over the edge.

"I'm sorry," Galiana said. "I don't know how long she's had it . . ." A feeble offer of hope, *perhaps this was only a recent development*, but her hope was misplaced, because:

"I do," Zemolai said hoarsely. She shut her eyes, remembering. "The mecha sect is decades ahead of you, Galiana. If it makes you feel any better, they did have the help of an engineer. I was there when she got her hands on him—I just didn't realize it at the time."

CHAPTER NINETEEN

And I realized, then, that this was an integral part of the call-
ing. It will ask things of you that you never thought yourself
capable of—and you will rise to the occasion, or you will die.
—Saint Orlusky, An Account of Mount Feralai

THEY MOVED on Faiyan Sanador before dawn.

It was a tiny operation, only Zenya and Vodaya and an ankle shackle—
for Sanador's security, of course. He was awake in his bed when they
entered, oddly frail beneath the blankets, his white hair gleaming in the
dim light from the hall. He lurched up at the sight of them, gasping and
wide-eyed, but he wasn't surprised. Miserable, but not surprised.

"I want to see Winged Milarka," he said. His overseer.

"That time has passed," Vodaya said coolly. She held out the shackle.
"Gather your things."

He sat on the edge of the bed, unmoving, and Zenya tensed. She didn't
want to hurt her instructor. But he was a traitor, she reminded herself. A
hopeless gearhead. He was collaborating with Winged Raksa to undermine
the war effort.

It didn't come to that. Faiyan Sanador quietly gathered clothing and
toiletries, holding each item out for Vodaya's approval before tucking it
into a bag. He changed into tunic and pants, his body thin but wiry with
strength. His scars spoke to a lifetime of improvements: chest, knees, one
of his hips. He even had a small port on his abdomen, a twin to Zenya's.

Sanador attached his own shackle. He didn't bother asking about the range of movement. Instead, he asked Zenya, "Has she told you her plans?"

"Don't speak to her," Vodaya snapped. "Or you'll get a gag to match that shackle."

He marched out between them, shuffling like a reprimanded student. Zenya was all nerves. Sanador's quarters were in one of the farthest cogs from trainee housing, a cluster of single-room apartments for support staff. He only needed to shout to bring everybody running, and Vodaya had made it clear she wanted this arrest to be discreet.

They nearly made it.

A supply door opened, and a boy stepped out carrying a basket of parts balanced on one hip. He had a metal skeleton for a hand.

Pava Genkolai. And he understood immediately what was happening. "Let him go," he said. His bravado was undercut by fear.

Faiyan Sanador sighed, a sad sound, and Winged Vodaya said, "Come here, Genkolai." Her hand hovered over the thin loops of cord attached to her belt.

Genkolai took one look at her face—his former instructor, his superior, physically fearsome and ruthless—and he ran. He dropped the basket and took off in the opposite direction at a flat sprint.

"Go. Stop him." Vodaya kept hold of Faiyan Sanador's elbow, as though she weren't the more logical option to talk Genkolai down. When Zenya hesitated, she snapped, "He's running to Winged Raksa. Show me you can handle this. *Go!*"

Zenya chased Genkolai without another thought. There was only the hard impact of dirt under her feet and the eerie predawn hush all around them. He didn't scream for help. Wherever he was headed was a straight shot through the yard.

She caught him near the obstacle course. He was slowed by a block of hurdles, nearly invisible in the dark, and Zenya snatched at the back of his vest. Furiously, she whispered, "Genkolai, listen to me!"

He pivoted immediately and struck her across the face. Zenya reeled, shocked by the sudden escalation, and he pressed his advantage, landing a rapid series of hard-knuckled punches in her gut, her ribs, the freshly scarred flesh around her mech port. The last one made her gasp in pain, but she finally got her arm up to deflect the next assault.

And all throughout, Genkolai said, "You won't get away with this— Vodaya will stand before the mecha god—I'll see you both caged—"

He'd gone mad, or Raksa had filled his head with sedition. Zenya didn't care which. She clung to him, landing the occasional blow of her own, but he was fighting like his life was at stake. His next punch landed on her jaw, and Zenya's grip turned to jelly. She staggered, vision blurring, and Genkolai bolted.

Zenya turned, expecting Vodaya to come to her aid, but the yard was empty. She'd already vanished from the grounds with Faiyan Sanador.

Genkolai reached a door. He fumbled at the sensor, clumsy in his panic. Zenya had seconds before he vanished into the interior.

She shook her head clear, letting rage burn through the fog. Genkolai was irrational. Violent. Misled. Vodaya was counting on her to take care of this.

Zenya ran after him, her head pounding, her side stitching up where he'd struck her port. Genkolai ripped open the door and darted inside, but he didn't keep running. He tore at the control panel on the other side, exposing a tangle of wires underneath, and Zenya realized he wasn't trying to escape her.

He was trying to set off an alarm.

She was only fifteen feet away. Ten. He saw her coming. His mouth opened, but he never got a chance to protest. Zenya hit him at full speed, a hard tackle to the core, and he shot back—

Into open air. It wasn't the main hallway, but a stairwell, a worker byway to underground storage. They plummeted together, Zenya's head buried against his stomach, bouncing and crying out at the impact of every sharp stone step.

They landed in a heap. Zenya's ears were ringing. Her shoulder ached. It took three attempts to sit up, and when she did, the vertigo nearly made her heave. The only source of illumination was starlight, and it barely sketched out the prone body beside her. Beyond him was only darkness.

"Genkolai," she whispered. He didn't move. She groped around until she found his face, thinking to give him a quick slap—and her hands came away sticky.

For a moment, her thoughts were blank. She almost put her hands out again, because there had to have been a mistake, that was no face—and then the reality of what she'd done roared up, and she was shaking, shaking. She broke her distress beacon in half, and when help didn't appear, she smashed it against the floor, she tore at the wires, she cried.

Zenya waited in the dark for a long time.

When the meager light was blocked at the top of the stairwell, she nearly fainted. But it was Vodaya's familiar silhouette against the stars; Vodaya's familiar step descending casually, without haste.

Her eyes held a faint, silver glow, washing out Zenya's night vision. She looked over the scene, forbidding in her silence, until finally, in a voice as cool as glass, she said, "Go to my rooms. Stay there. Breathe word of this to no one."

Vodaya returned home just after dawn, and Zenya was a wreck. As soon as she heard movement in the loft, she bolted upstairs, desperate for good news. Genkolai's head injury had been less severe than she thought—a trick of the dark, perhaps—

Vodaya calmly stepped away from her wing hooks. She rolled her shoulders with an audible crackle and said, "My wings need cleaning."

"What happened?" Zenya cried. "Is Genkolai alive? Does he know it was an accident? I only meant to hold him—"

Vodaya crowded forward, suddenly fierce. "This night never happened, Zemolai. Faiyan Sanador has gone missing. So has Pava Genkolai. That is all you know, and you will not even know it until after *I* am informed of the situation. Do you understand?"

Zenya stared at her, speechless, her thoughts stuttering out of control. Genkolai was dead. Genkolai was dead.

"Swear it to me," Vodaya insisted.

"I swear it," Zenya whispered.

Vodaya nodded, thoughtful. She gestured to the edge of the bed. "Why don't you sit down? I think you're more upset than you ought to be. The boy was a traitor." She gestured again. "Go on, do as I say. I'm going to trust you with sensitive information, and I want you sitting for it. I must warn you, it will be distressing. But I believe it will ease your conscience."

Zenya sank down. She couldn't imagine anything absolving her of Genkolai's murder, but, oh, she was desperate to be wrong.

"I had a long, interesting conversation with Faiyan Sanador just now," Vodaya said. She leaned against the bare patch of wall beneath her wings so that, even detached, they extended dramatically to either side of her. "It confirmed my worst fears. You have to understand, Zemolai. The mecha god deserves your devotion, but there are imperfections in her worldly administration. *Exploitable* imperfections."

She paused, ensuring she had Zenya's full attention, and then dropped her bomb. "Winged Raksa is working with the engineers, and his goal is not reconciliation. He intends to remove Mecha Petrogon from the Council of Five and give the engineers a total victory."

Zenya recoiled, horrified. "But *why?*"

Vodaya glowered. "Bribery? Corruption? I don't know his mind. But the engineers would form a new government in which the mecha god's people are subservient to the other Four. They want to remove our teeth, if you will. We would be primitive beasts, a mindless fighting force deployed on the whim of a vote."

"Surely, the mecha god wouldn't stand for that . . ."

"The mecha god sleeps," Vodaya said bluntly. "As they all sleep. She knows what the Voice tells her. If Petrogon is removed, and Winged Raksa is installed as our next Voice . . ."

Then the mecha god would know only what Raksa saw fit to tell her.

Vodaya stepped out from the enclosure of her wings. "There is a battle coming," she said, fervent and secretive and darkly excited. "A glorious endgame. Faiyan Sanador believes the engineers are marshaling the last of their forces, but I can't afford to tip my hand until I know where they are hiding. Do you see now why I require your discretion? When I go to

Mecha Petrogon I must have incontrovertible proof, evidence he cannot deny." She raised a hand to Zenya's cheek, warm and rough and smelling of dust.

"And then?" Zenya whispered.

Vodaya smiled. "We destroy them."

Zenya swallowed an extra pill the next day, but her work still staggered to a halt.

She was supposed to master a practice wing next—a miniature replica with ten individually wired feathers. Zenya stared at it till she thought her eyes would bleed, unable to keep focused for more than a second or two. By the time she could no longer ignore the hunger cannibalizing her stomach, she had haltingly nudged only two feathers.

A warrior couldn't afford to be distracted. A warrior responded to changing battle conditions before the change even registered in her thoughts, and a warrior *certainly* didn't spend the entire fight agonizing over the first opponent they'd struck down.

Zenya fled to her room, burning with failure, and escaped into one of her books. She read until the panic had subsided and then started taking notes.

It was an engrossing text—too engrossing. Hours later, Zenya was torn from her reading by the sound of an argument. Her head swam with the words of Saint Kelior—*a philosopher proves their mettle in ink, a warrior in blood*—and the sound of wings snapping shut struck her like a gun bolt.

She shot up from her desk, ready to run to Vodaya's defense, but she heard no call for aid from the other room. Zenya hovered by the door, uncertain, while the confrontation unfolded.

Winged Raksa's voice seeped through, muffled but furious: "Where are they?"

Vodaya murmured in response.

"You know exactly what I'm talking about! Faiyan Sanador has gone missing from his quarters. So has Pava Genkolai."

235

Zenya's heart lurched. But Vodaya was unfazed. "How unfortunate," she said. "Do you suspect your trainee of abetting the engineer's escape?"

"Tell me where they are," Raksa demanded.

"I've always maintained it was a mistake to have an engineer on staff. Now look. Corrupting a Pava trainee? How disgraceful."

"The war is over!" Raksa shouted. "You are the only one trying to carry it on!"

"It will be over when they capitulate," Vodaya said sharply. "Not before."

"Mecha Petrogon made his decision. You can't fight him any more than you can fight the will of the mecha god."

"The mecha god doesn't condemn him. That does not mean she condones. You should know the difference by now."

The accusations flew thick between them after that, too quick for Zenya to parse, until Raksa stormed out. The room went quiet once again, a silence like a knife.

Zenya fractured further over the ensuing weeks. Vaguely, she was aware that the fighting had slowed in the city. Vaguely, she was aware that the protests had dwindled. Radezhda was exhausted and looking for reasons to reconcile. There were even rumors that the Council of Five might convene to negotiate a truce.

And yet she remained locked in her own head, replaying the fight with Pava Genkolai over and over, obsessively trying to determine another way it could have ended. If she had only realized where he was standing . . . if she had only tried to talk him down first . . .

She made no progress with her mech port. She could hardly focus long enough to read, much less manipulate an unnatural limb. She still attended on Vodaya during Petrogon's war meetings, but her nerves twisted tighter every day that passed without Vodaya making her move. Vodaya's verbal battles with Winged Raksa grew ever more volatile but came no closer to a resolution. That horrific night seemed forgotten.

And as the streets quieted down, Winged Raksa's case gained support.

"Saint Radezhda gave her life for the cohesion of the Five," Raksa said. "Our purpose is to protect the people of this city from external threats. Every day that we fight our own people, we are drawing resources away from our borders."

On that point, he had the ear of all four quadrant leaders. Their combat units had been spread thin to cover shifts on both sides of the wall, and they were wearying of the double front.

"The answer is to end this. Decisively," Vodaya countered, and her clipped tone betrayed her impatience. As usual, the two warriors had drifted toward the patch of earth beneath the god-tree, circling one another like they were gearing up for a practice bout.

"Yes," Raksa agreed. "By making a joint public statement following a reconvening of the Five."

Mecha Petrogon stirred, brooding as always by the trunk of the god-tree. "The meeting will occur," he said carefully. "The outcome is yet to be decided."

Vodaya jabbed a finger at her rival. "Winged Raksa has done nothing but press the engineers' interests!" It was the closest she had come to publicly denouncing his motives yet, and Zenya held her breath, waiting for his response.

And Winged Raksa admitted, "I have been in contact with members of the creator sect."

Not a few gasps burst from the audience. The quadrant leaders scarcely moved. Raksa's superior, Winged Shantar, looked ready to arrest him on the spot.

But Mecha Petrogon was unsurprised. Nothing, it seemed, was enough to ruffle the Voice's calm. "Explain yourself," he murmured.

Raksa nodded, looking shaky at his own daring. He said, "The individuals I contacted were in Creator Talley's inner circle. Upon Talley's death, Creator Vanyamir overruled them in favor of her own aggressive politicking. They want to make peace, according to Creator Talley's original wishes, but they are afraid to confront Vanyamir without a guarantee of our support."

Vodaya charged forward. "That is the vilest lie—"

Mecha Petrogon held up a hand, silencing her. "What are their intentions?"

"They desire new leadership," Raksa said. "Creator Vanyamir is addicted to conflict. She is determined to see us stricken from the Council of Five. She would make us into an external security force, subject to their instructions."

Zenya's brow furrowed. It was the very conspiracy that Vodaya believed to be underway—but Raksa claimed to be on the other side of it.

"She won't hear reason from her subordinates," Raksa continued. "She is barely in consultation with the creator god and refuses to transcribe their words when she does ascend. Alone, her opponents don't feel capable of resisting. But with our cooperation, there is the possibility of forging a truce without her."

He stepped back, and the rooftop burst into debate. The quadrant leaders were keen to end the civil conflict and refocus on the border, but their warriors were split. Younger and full of fire, they desired peace in theory, but envisioned it being won at the end of a bolt-gun.

And Zenya . . . Zenya were two hearts packed into one chest. She couldn't stop looking at Vodaya, who had gone tight-lipped and silent. Zenya was offended on her behalf. She *felt* Vodaya's fury and mortification at being shunted aside in the discussion.

If Winged Raksa was telling the truth, they could see a peaceful end to this war in weeks. Maybe days. Zenya wanted it to be over so badly, she found herself longing to believe him.

But if Winged Raksa were telling the truth, it also meant that Vodaya was *wrong*. It meant that she had found evidence of the engineers' plans, and evidence of Raksa's communications, and then had been so thoroughly overcome by her own zeal that she misinterpreted them.

It meant that Zenya's fight with Pava Genkolai had been over nothing.

The meeting ended abruptly. "Disperse," Mecha Petrogon ordered. "Winged Raksa, remain with me. *Only* Winged Raksa."

The rest of the Winged responded promptly, launching from the rooftop in competing flurries of wind. Vodaya hesitated for only a moment before complying, but in her posture Zenya could read every unspoken protest.

Zenya rode down with the other Pava attendees. The air was electric, but they all knew better than to discuss the contents of a war meeting, even amongst themselves.

Zenya hastened to Vodaya's quarters. The balcony doors were still open, and a cool draft spilled down from the loft. She found Vodaya upstairs, de-winged, brooding in the large chair beside her bed.

Vodaya looked up expectantly—and then blew out an impatient breath. "Yes, yes. You wish to discuss Raksa's flagrant deception. I'll admit it, I was shocked at his boldness, but I shouldn't be. His confidence is limitless."

"Mecha Petrogon seemed to believe him . . ." Zenya said.

"Ha! As though the Voice would ever let you glimpse his thoughts."

The question burst out before Zenya could stop herself: "What if we're wrong?"

Vodaya's expression sharpened, and Zenya's last chance to backtrack evaporated. "Excuse me?"

But it was like a holy spirit had taken Zenya's tongue. She babbled, "What if Winged Raksa is telling the truth? What if I misinterpreted his call from Faiyan Sanador? What if the information Sanador gave you was incorrect?"

"It wasn't incorrect," Vodaya said softly.

Zenya couldn't stop. "We have to tell Mecha Petrogon what we know! He can stand Winged Raksa before the mecha god and—"

Vodaya shot out of her chair. Zenya hardly had time to duck before a book of verse flew past her head, dense and leather-bound and previously holding a place of prominence on Vodaya's side table.

"And *what*?" Vodaya raged. She marched forward, eating up Zenya's retreat. "What's your plan, Pava? Are you going to tell Mecha Petrogon that you arrested one of your instructors without his order? Are you going to tell him you murdered another Pava trainee, but now you regret it, because you *do not trust my ability to conduct an interrogation*?"

"That isn't what I meant!" Zenya exclaimed, but it was too late. She backed down the stairs, flinching away from a barrage of books and knick-knacks and bottles of oil that shattered against the rails.

"You won't breathe a word of this!" Vodaya shouted. "You'll do what I tell you to do! After all I've done, you'd still take that vile, traitorous deceiver's word against mine—get out, get out!"

Zenya ran to her room, where she listened, paralyzed, to the sounds of petty destruction through the adjoining wall. Vodaya shoved furniture, threw plates. Zenya had never heard anything like it. She was riveted, bunny-rabbit scared.

There was a moment of silence, in which Zenya's heartbeat began to slow . . . and then the door slammed open and into the wall, a crash like a thousand volts to the nervous system, and Vodaya stood there in a blaze of self-righteousness.

"Get back here," she ordered. Her hair was unkempt, her vest unbuttoned. "I'm not finished with you."

"I don't . . ." Zenya trailed off, breathless, holding tight to the edge of the desk behind her.

It was the wrong answer. "Yes, you do!" Vodaya snapped. "Grab your cords."

Zenya automatically reached for her port equipment, too dazed to protest. "But what are we doing?" she asked.

"*You* are going to begin manipulating wings. Real wings, not that useless shit you've been playing with. And *I* am going to see if my time has been worth anything."

Zenya was so startled, she dropped her bag. "I thought—the surgeon said our practice ports aren't designed for—"

The look on Vodaya's face was murderous, but she abruptly calmed down, and the calm was worse than the shouting. She took a moment to fix her buttons, one silver fist sliding neatly into place after another. She said, "Do you really want to find out your limits *after* spinal surgery? Hm? Do you think I want to waste a set of wing ports—the materials, the production, the surgeon's *time*—on a trainee who hasn't demonstrated whether or not she can operate them?" Vodaya slid the last button into place and spun on her heel. "Grab your fucking cords."

The sitting room was a wreck. Vodaya's plush furniture had been shoved out of its careful arrangement; her paintings knocked from the walls; her books swept off tables. Zenya passed these signs of tempest, and a hard knot swelled her throat shut. She had seen Vodaya in combat training. She had seen Vodaya on patrol and on arrest teams.

Zenya had never seen Vodaya lose control.

It was a long, dreadful climb up those stairs. The loft bore fewer signs of temper but contained something far worse: Vodaya's wings on gleaming hooks. Zenya's stomach heaved at the sight of them. She couldn't possibly—!

But that was precisely what Vodaya had in mind. She took Zenya by the shoulders and thrust her toward the wings. Zenya only gaped at them.

"Come on then," Vodaya said impatiently. She lifted Zenya's shirt, exposing the practice port. She forced a cord into the port, ignoring Zenya's squeak of discomfort, and ran the thick braid of wiring to the leftwing mount. "There," she said. "I'm only connecting you to one. Do you think you can handle a single wing?"

"Yes," Zenya said faintly. A bald lie. She couldn't even manage this test in miniature.

Vodaya stood back, arms crossed. Zenya had no idea what she wanted. She suspected it was five percent more than she was capable of, regardless of how much she was capable of.

But she took a breath, and tried to cease her trembling, and reached out along that tenuous line of wiring and godly mechanics that linked hot nerves to cold metals, and breathed life into their joints. The wings were enormous, hungry reservoirs demanding to be filled, and Zenya's skin goosefleshed at the thought.

She didn't want to do this. A hot ache bloomed in her side as the cord sent demands back through her port, and she *didn't want to do this.*

"I don't think . . ." she said.

"Do it or get out," Vodaya said.

Zenya shut her eyes tight, struggling to focus on that thin connection. The wings were a looming presence behind her back, about to snap shut and consume her like a carnivorous plant seizing a fly. Dizziness washed over her. She braced her legs against it. She told herself it was only one wing. If she managed even minor control, Vodaya would be satisfied and let her go.

"You're concentrating too hard," Vodaya said. "If you have to think about it, you're not acting reflexively. If you're not acting reflexively, you don't adjust course quickly enough. You miss your mark. You crash."

Zenya could *feel* her way through the wing, but it was bulky, unnatural. Like trying to lift a limb that had fallen asleep—the flesh dense and numb, blood just beginning to flow back to blocked nerves, nerves beginning to tingle again but painfully, painfully! Her body grew clammy with the effort. She started shaking.

"This is what you've been working toward," Vodaya said. "The *only* thing you've been working toward. I've supported you. I've spent thousands of hours guiding you. Was it all for nothing? You're either a scholar or a warrior, Zemolai. You cannot be both."

The feedback from Zenya's port was unbearable. Her entire side was aflame with it, the pain creeping toward her spine. She called on muscles she'd never had, *demanded* her body funnel energy into bloodless metal. And still the wing was lifeless, mocking, greedily absorbing her efforts and giving nothing back.

Delirious, she wanted to scream, *What are they made of, what did the gods give us, this is no substance of the earth, this is like nothing mechanical I've touched—*

Instead she warbled, "This port . . . it's not meant to . . . it's not strong enough . . ."

"Don't make excuses!" Vodaya snapped. "You're blaming your circumstances. Take responsibility. *If* you receive wing ports, *if* you are granted a wing test, you will get *one* chance to leap from that mountain. Do you hear me? There won't be any midair adjustments. There won't be any second chance if the weather is poor or your equipment needs tinkering. You'll be ready or you'll die."

Zenya struggled to control herself. Just the primaries. If she could just ruffle the primaries a bit, spread a few feathers at the very end . . . She couldn't flex a joint, she *knew* she couldn't flex a joint, but if she could make some token show of progress—

Zenya's knees buckled. She shrieked, "I can't!"

"You have to!" Vodaya shouted, but Zenya collapsed. She scrabbled at her side, her hands uncooperative, everything tied up in the monster at her back. Vodaya knocked her hands away and said, "Get up."

Zenya groaned and slipped further, one elbow coming down hard on the wooden floor. Vodaya shoved Zenya onto her back, a painful position with the cord pulled taut between her flesh and the wing. Zenya struggled to get loose, to unhook herself, to *end* this, but Vodaya pressed down on her shoulders and said, "Then give up being Pava. Just give up."

"Please," Zenya gasped. The wings framed Vodaya's face, upside down, unnatural.

"Are you giving up?" Vodaya demanded.

"No."

"Are you giving up?"

"No!"

Zenya's vision blurred. Her body cried for mercy, but there was Vodaya, furious and disgusted, and she couldn't let it end like this, in humiliation and defeat, if she passed out now it was over, she was finished here—and then, right there, framing Vodaya's face like a crown:

The fluttering of feathers.

Zenya slumped, crying, her electrical connection tenuous but continuous. Vodaya looked up and smiled, the expression tight. She sat back on her heels, and Zenya waited, unable to control the quivering of her limbs, for Vodaya to grant her permission to disengage.

But then a heavy fist beat on the front door. A muffled voice called Vodaya's name, and her nostrils flared at the interruption.

"Not now!" she yelled.

The knocking grew louder, the voice insistent. Vodaya stomped to the edge of the loft. She leaned over the rail and called down, "Come in then!" She glanced back, almost like it was an afterthought. "I'm done with you."

With a soft groan of relief, Zenya unplugged the cord from her side, but she couldn't seem to stand. She breathed fast and shallow, waiting for her port to cool, waiting for the blood to return to her numb limbs.

The door opened. Vodaya's posture abruptly straightened, and she descended the stairs to her sitting room without looking back.

"I'm surprised to see you on this level," she said coolly.

A familiar voice responded, "Sometimes these conversations are better held in private."

It was Mecha Petrogon.

Zenya's hearing sharpened, some of her pain buffered by surprise. The Voice had entered Vodaya's private quarters through the interior hallway. Which meant he was wingless.

"I've caught you at a bad time," he said.

"Redecorating," Vodaya said curtly.

"Mm. I'll be quick, then. Vodaya, I am allowing Raksa to continue his correspondence with the engineers. I do not want your interference or your provocation."

"Bloody Vitalia!"

"Vodaya . . ."

"No! He's the worst person to represent our interests . . ."

Zenya held her breath, exhilarated and horrified at the sound of Vodaya arguing with the Voice of the mecha god. This was the perfect opportunity for Vodaya to air her real concerns, but she and Petrogon were arguing as though all those words had already been said and buried.

He cut in on Vodaya's tirade, his tone gentle and chiding. "You can't keep antagonizing Winged Raksa. We have enough to fight without fighting each other."

Vodaya made a derisive sound. "If Raksa has his way, we won't be fighting anyone."

"That is the goal," Petrogon agreed. "But I didn't come here to relay Raksa's concerns—or to debate them." He grew stern. "Where has Faiyan Sanador gone?"

Vodaya turned cagey. "Somewhere safe. We wouldn't want him to be roped in with his old friends, would we?"

"I need to see him."

"You will."

"*Now.*"

A pregnant pause followed. Zenya tried to roll to her side, but her abdomen cramped and she fell back, panting. One little flutter of feathers, and she was an absolute wreck. Fresh tears sprang to her already puffy eyes.

"He's been detained," Vodaya finally said. "But if you are that in need of repair, I'm sure I could make an arrangement."

"You aren't his gatekeeper," Mecha Petrogon said sharply.

Vodaya laughed. "For your sake, you'd better hope I *am*. Come along then, Voice. Let's go clear your throat."

The door slid shut with a decisive clack, and Zenya was alone on the floor of the loft, nothing but Vodaya's wings to stare at while she recovered control of her limbs.

CHAPTER TWENTY

I am tired of waiting! We deserve an explanation, and we deserve it now! Let us build our way up to their very doors, let us find them where they are sleeping, and let us demand the answers that we are due.

—[Attribution missing], *address to the Council of Five*

"WHERE IS Faiyan Sanador now?" Galiana asked. The bolt-babies had listened quietly while Zemolai related the least shameful parts of the engineer's arrest (cowardly, perhaps; but they did not need to know about poor Genkolai today, or the interlude in Vodaya's loft that she had spent so long trying to forget).

"I don't know," Zemolai admitted. "Dead or locked away. Why did he build it for her? How did he manipulate god-light so long ago, if the engineers are only beginning to tinker with it now?" She shook her head, brooding. "There's only one person who knows, and I doubt she's going to tell us."

"This is so far beyond us," Timyan whispered.

An uncomfortable silence fell, and then Rustaya said, "I don't want to be the asshole here, but we are running out of time to get rid of this thing."

They were still crouched over the Tooth's corpse. Karolin would be back when the sun set, and they'd made it clear that they wouldn't return alone.

Zemolai retreated inward, boneless, while the others turned back to the immediate problem. She grasped wildly for a steady thought and came up empty. The thought of Vodaya deceiving the mecha god was overwhelming, unbearable—and it was all painfully circumstantial, wasn't it? The sort of evidence she would have scoffed at in a trainee's report. But it *felt* true, and as she dug through the sands of her memory, one disconcerting thing after another seemed to fall into place, made explicable by this single additional fact.

And then it came to her, all at once like a heavenly vision: a plan. A foolish plan, a reckless plan, but it filled her with a sense of purpose, stronger than anything she'd felt in years. She felt righteous. She felt *right*.

Zemolai abruptly wheeled out of the room, heedless of their reactions (Galiana called her name; it didn't matter). She felt lighter than air. Bird-boned. But there were a few things she needed first. Zemolai worked quickly, sensitive to the growing time constraint.

By the time she returned to the back room, the others had agreed on a course of action. Timyan and Rustaya were spooling rope. Galiana was gathering sheets from a cot. It didn't matter. Whatever they were doing wasn't enough.

Zemolai dropped a half-empty duffel bag to the floor, loud as a bolt-gun shot. The other half of its contents were firmly strapped to her body—her thighs, her waist, her back, every weapon pointy or barreled and ready for mayhem.

"Bloody Vitalia!" Galiana squeaked.

"Load up," Zemolai ordered, and now she was on firmer ground, now she was back to form. She dropped into a crouch beside the Tooth's body, sending Timyan and Rustaya rearing back. A dizzy spell hit hard, the finality of what she had done crashing over her like a narcotic.

This was it. This was her life now. Chae Savro had been a mistake, the Pava raid misguided, but this was a choice. There would be no forgiveness, no peace, no quiet death in a gutter. Vodaya would hunt her down and destroy her for this.

She stared at the Tooth. His crimsons and blacks had only deepened in shade following Karolin's ministrations. His face was uninjured, all of its scars long healed, all of its lines old and deep-set. He was older than Zemolai by a handful of years, his strength and vitality extended by numerous prosthetics, implants, and chemical enhancements.

But she'd outlasted him. He had done everything right, and he was dead anyway.

She rummaged in his pockets, snatching a bloodstained set of mechanical cords. Anything of potential use she threw into the duffel bag.

She opened his vest and found the heavy chains of animal fangs from which the Tooth got his name. Seven rows of steel links burst with evidence of his long service. Mountain wolf and wildcat and brown bear, from fresh pearly white to age-cracked yellow, each one inscribed in tiny, precise lettering. Zemolai ran her fingers over them, dozens of assignments, each one a bloody victory in the mecha god's name. Every neighborhood was represented, though the names skewed heavily toward Quaser and Faiyan, Chae and Verolai.

Milar.

Zemolai ran her fingers over a fang that was nearly as long as her palm, ripped from the jaw of a mountain bear. It was yellowed with age but still so smooth the soot-blackened carvings stood out in sharp, damning relief. She remembered a day long past. Another time her future had branched before her, only for one of those branches to be brutally, abruptly cut off.

"Zemolai?" Galiana's voice pierced the fog, and it was clearly not the first time she'd spoken. She was fuzzy around the edges. Concern wrapped in a dark cloak.

"What?" Zemolai asked thickly.

"What are you *doing*?"

Zemolai snapped back to herself. Tightly, she said, "I'm stopping her." She didn't need to elaborate on which *her*. Galiana's eyes widened.

Rustaya shook their head. "Didn't you hear Galiana? She's untouchable."

A fever was taking her again. Zemolai was hot from her head to her toes. "The mecha god doesn't know what she's doing," she said. "This isn't the mecha god's will. If we disable her signal blocker, we can expose her."

"We can't," Timyan squeaked. "We don't know where it is—what it is—how to destroy it—"

But Zemolai did.

She remembered a light. Vivid and red and pulsing in time with the beat of Vodaya's heart. She remembered a day when all had seemed lost, and Vodaya had made it right again. There had been a moment when she stood in the mecha god's light and showed twin faces: one smiling and one utterly blank. A mask. A signal neatly blocked.

"I know where the power source is. Where nobody would ever dare look." Zemolai considered them gravely. "It's in the god's realm, embedded at the feet of the mecha god."

Understanding crackled through the room like a live wire, but they resisted it. They weren't willing to believe where she was going with this. Zemolai didn't care. She was alight with purpose, and it was a glimmer of sunlight after a season of dark. "Come with me or don't," she said. "The mecha god has to know. She has to see what's happening."

"You've seen her response," Timyan said. "We've all seen it. Your god stirs at every reckoning, and she doesn't care."

"I don't believe that," Zemolai said fiercely. "You heard Galiana. She's been blocking the god's sight." *She.* Zemolai couldn't even say her name. "The mecha god knows what the Voice tells her, and the Voice has been *lying.*"

"It's a theory!" Galiana cried. "It's only a theory!"

But Timyan leaned forward, intent to understand. "All this time? You really believe Mecha Vodaya has been deceiving your god for decades?"

"Yes," Zemolai said, and the certainty of it made her feel faint. She pictured another morning long past. She remembered the look on Mecha Petrogon's face when it all turned against him. "You don't know her. She's capable of anything."

Fiercely, Rustaya said, "And yet you followed her this entire time. You beat us. You rounded us up. You enforced her restrictions. All of that. *All* of what you've done. You're admitting that it's all been for *her* power and not the path of your god?"

Bile rose in Zemolai's throat. She felt flayed alive, exposed down to her bones. If she said it out loud, that made it true. But she had given up everything else: her home, her family, her peers, her vocation. She couldn't give up her god.

It had to have been for something. Even if she had been mistaken. Even if she had been lied to, and her life spent on the wrong course. It had to have been for the right reason.

"Yes," she said roughly. "All of it, yes."

"Exposing her now doesn't change the past," Rustaya said. "This won't make up for what you've done."

"No," Zemolai agreed softly. "It won't."

In a small voice, Galiana said, "You're going to fight her."

Zemolai tried to imagine it and flinched. No. She couldn't face Vodaya directly. Zemolai was broken, wingless, stripped of all enhancing drugs. Vodaya was the greatest warrior of their age. She was honed to near physical perfection. She had their god's will wrapped up in a device upon her chest.

And, too painful to admit aloud: even now, even knowing all of this, Zemolai couldn't stand before her and resist. At the first sound of Vodaya's voice, her body would betray her. It was too well-trained.

"No," she said gruffly. "I can't fight her. But I've seen the power source, and I believe we can destroy it. After that, let the reckoning come to her as it will."

"This is too big for us," Timyan protested. "We have to hand this information over to the engineers."

"No," Zemolai said.

"We don't have the resources to handle this on our own! Let's find Scholar Pyetka. He'll have contacts further up than we do. We can explain about Karolin at the same time."

"*No.*"

Galiana had been standing to the side with her face in her hands. She lowered them now, miserable. "She's right," she said.

"What do you mean?" Timyan asked.

Galiana looked at Zemolai while she spoke. "If we hand this over to the engineers, they won't destroy it. They'll want to re-create the technology for themselves and install their own liaison to the mecha god—maybe even the other gods, as well. So Zemolai won't tell them what it looks like—isn't that right?"

Zemolai inclined her head. "Correct."

They had a torrent of counterarguments. There was no way of knowing how many Winged were on-site, no way past upper-level security measures, no way to ascend unseen. They'd never make it to the roof of tower Kemyana. Even if by some miracle they did, only a Voice could travel through to the gods' realm.

"You want us to break into tower Kemyana?" Rustaya demanded. "After what just happened in the training compound? We've been compromised. People know our faces. Not to mention yours!"

Zemolai said, "Then we've only got one chance, haven't we? Better hope we don't bump into the wrong person."

"How would you open the portal?" Timyan asked.

"I know the words," she said shortly. "The mecha god will let me in."

His brow furrowed. "How do you—"

"*She'll let me in.*"

"Okay. Maybe." Timyan frowned, but he let Zemolai's outrageous claim slide for the moment. "And once you're in, what then? We've seen her realm in mirrors. It's a forest. It's built for wings."

"Flying would be easier," Zemolai admitted, and for a moment the thought was utterly debilitating—she would never have that option again—but she shoved it aside ruthlessly, to be dealt with later. "The posts are porous," she said instead. "A small team with climbing gear could scale them before anyone realized what we're doing."

"How could they *not* realize?" Timyan cried. "*Maybe* we could avoid the tower workers, and *maybe* we could fight off a handful of Pava, but where will the Winged be?"

"Gone."

"Gone *where*?"

"They'll be looking for the Tooth. The resonance chip, remember? We get his body across town, disable the dampener, let the signal ring clear." The rest of the truth was on the tip of her tongue (*they'll come, because I promised*), but she bit it back. "It has to be tonight," she said. "Tonight is first flight. Most of the Winged have been off duty all day, reveling with the graduating Pava trainees. They'll escort them to Ruk Head Mountain, and they won't get back till near dawn. The remaining contingent will go after the Tooth."

"Even if the tower is miraculously empty," Rustaya said, "and I don't believe you on that—how do you plan to get inside, much less up to the *fucking roof*?"

Zemolai shrugged, steady as the summer sun. "I was thinking I would just walk in."

She let the furor run its course before raising her voice and pointing at Galiana. "You. Think you can code a mech port?" She lifted the hem of her shirt, revealing her long-unused training port.

Galiana's jaw clacked shut. "Oh," she said. "I might be able to forge a code, if that still works . . ."

"It still works," Zemolai said, with more confidence than she felt. It had not burned during the mecha god's judgment, anyway. "And you don't have to forge anything. I know one that won't have been flagged. We swipe in, we take an elevator."

Galiana turned to Rustaya with her eyebrows raised. Nervous energy singed the air between them.

"This has to be unanimous," Rustaya warned. "This is more dangerous than our raid on the training grounds. We're not certain what we'll find at the top. I'm not even sure how we'd get down."

"And the alternative?" Timyan asked.

Galiana sighed. "Ditch the Tooth. Hide deeper in the countryside maybe. Try to reconcile with Karolin. Or leave Radezhda for good. Not that I think we'd make it far into the mountains."

"They killed Eleny," Rustaya said. "They won't stop until they've got all of us."

Timyan rubbed his hands over his face. "Shit," he said. "Shit, shit, shit."

Zemolai shoved one boot against the bag of weaponry and sent it sliding toward them, filled now with such a fervor, she could have been god-lit herself and washed the room in white. "We aren't running away," she said fiercely. "We aren't hiding. We aren't giving up.

"We're going to end this. We're going to storm heaven itself."

INTERLUDE

YOU WILL EXPECT, by now, that I have a theory.

Of course I do. Hundreds of opinions have been written on this topic already. Hundreds more will follow mine. The question haunts us: *why did the gods go to sleep?* We pray, we beg, we preach it from every saint's day stage. We argue it in council meetings till the sun sets, and then we table the discussion and promise to gather again next month to shout about it some more. The ritual is dressed up in formalities so we do not feel like children, always squabbling over the same old hurt.

It was you, we are saying. *It was your fault. Do things my way, and we can fix this.*

But there is another answer, one that sidesteps the question entirely. A truth we would rather not face; a truth we are so loathe to admit that we would rather destroy one another in an eternity of fighting than voice it. What we do not want to admit is this:

There *was* no defining moment. There was no betrayal. There was no crime so great the gods had little choice but to turn away from us.

It is a simple answer, and deeply unsatisfying. It *must* have been something we did, we insist, because if it was something we did, then we have the ability to control the outcome in the future. We simply will not do that again!

But the gods lost interest. They retreated. That is all. They left an entire city desperate to pinpoint how it went wrong, and did not bother to offer any consolation. We have spent generations obsessed over who was at fault, how it may be reversed, how we must prove ourselves the next time, but we are arguing over the wrong thing.

The real question is not *what did we do to make them leave?* but *how could they leave us so easily?* How could they shower us with gifts, with knowledge, with the burning light of the heavens and the monumental weight of their love, only to take it back again?

Because it *is* a weight. It is a burden, to be singled out in this way, to be chosen above all others in the world, to be granted a spot at the side of our idols. What would we do to keep the affection of a god? The answer is anything, anything.

And what does it mean for them to witness our devotion—our desperation to please, our prayers and our tears—what does it mean for them to look upon our grief and then shrug and turn away?

I am afraid we can draw only one conclusion, a terrible truth, difficult to bear:

The gods do not love us, and never have.

CHAPTER TWENTY-ONE

She does not speak to me anymore. Why? Why? The creator
god speaks to their disciple, of this I am sure. He returns with
his head full of plans, but when we sing the words? She only
shows her fist. I know I should not compare, but oh my heart is
jealous. I am a flawed man.

—*Diary of Mecha Vitaly*

ZENYA RECOVERED in silence from her ordeal in the loft.
Vodaya didn't mention the incident. She didn't ask how Zenya was
doing. The next day proceeded as though nothing had happened, and so
did the day after that. The longer the silence curdled between them, the
more a single thought nagged at her:

She had to leave Winged Vodaya.

(Years later, so many years later, when Zenya was called Zemolai and
could scarcely remember a time when she wasn't—she would lie about
this.

Eleny would ask: *did you ever doubt?*

And Zemolai would answer, swiftly and decisively: *no, never.*

But there had been a moment, this moment, when things could have
gone differently.)

The thought of leaving made her feel sick. It was barely even a thought,
just a mad impulse originating deep in her gut. She prodded gently
around the edges of it, afraid to think too far ahead because whenever
she did, she spiraled into panic. *What will I do where will I go who else will
take me what will she do if I—*

But she kept reliving that moment in the loft. Vodaya holding her down. Vodaya hurting her. It hadn't been a training exercise. It had been pure frustration taken out on the nearest target. It had been cruelty for the sake of cruelty. Pava Genkolai's warnings came back to her with bitter hindsight. *Don't let her be your entire world.*

When Zenya was alone, the decision was clear. She would confront Vodaya. Demand an explanation. State her case and request a transfer.

But as soon as she saw Vodaya, her mouth went dry, and she was overcome with uncertainty. She thought of Genkolai, and she wanted to scream. She thought of her family and wanted to weep. She imagined leaving, giving up her chance at wings, and finding out Vodaya had been right all along, and the panic attack hooked so deep she thought she'd suffocate.

Just a little longer, she thought. Just a little longer, when the timing is right.

Despite his claims of indecision, Mecha Petrogon seemed hellbent on reconciliation. After every war meeting, he held Winged Raksa behind to discuss strategies regarding his communications with the rogue engineers.

Which only set Vodaya on her own private warpath.

Whenever one of Vodaya's black moods hit, she dragged Zenya into the city on fact-gathering missions. After the destruction of Quaser, survivors had scattered to small settlements throughout the city. Zenya marched from settlement to settlement, documenting residents, relationships, and missing persons. When Vodaya found an incongruity in one of Zenya's interviews, she returned to the settlement herself to continue the interrogation in her own style.

Zenya stood watch outside of these meetings. She didn't need to listen in to guess what Vodaya's style was like, and she didn't ask questions when Vodaya emerged with fresh-scrubbed hands and a glint in her eye.

"Why not confront Raksa now?" Zenya asked, after one of these horrors. "Have him arrested! You have Faiyan Sanador's testimony. Surely that will hold enough weight with Mecha Petrogon to call the mecha god?"

But Vodaya yelled, "I will *not* bring Sanador to the tree!"

They did not bring Sanador to the tree. Zenya complied, but she didn't understand. (Really, how could she have guessed?)

Nearly a month into these investigations, Vodaya found what she was looking for.

Zenya was waiting outside a common house when a bloodcurdling scream came from within. She raced inside and found a violent tableau: two young women tangled with Vodaya, slashing at the warrior with kitchen knives. A gaping armoire indicated where the second one had been lying in wait.

The ground-level receiving room was the only place in the house that could accommodate a Winged in full gear, but it didn't give Vodaya much room to maneuver. Her face was already sheeted in blood, the source unclear. Zenya grabbed the closest woman around the throat and hauled her back. Vodaya seized the other woman's wrist and twisted. The bones snapped. The woman screamed, and her knife went flying. Vodaya slammed her to the floor and turned to Zenya, her expression ghoulish through the blood pouring down her cheekbone.

Zenya struggled to disarm her own opponent, but she was wrestling the woman from behind and getting slashed across the forearms. A few well-angled slices skidded off her vambraces and reached flesh.

Vodaya scooped up the fallen knife and stabbed the second woman in the chest.

It was an ugly death. Zenya held tight to the thrashing body, held on through her gurgling, wheezing panic until the woman lost enough blood to pass out. Zenya let her slide to the floor and stood over the body, breathing a little too quickly.

When she could manage to speak again, she gestured to the first woman. "Is she . . . ?"

Vodaya pursed her lips. "Not yet. Stay by the door. Make sure I'm not interrupted."

It was worse than Zenya had imagined. Brutality during a fight was haunting, but at least it came with the caveat of self-defense. What happened next was torture. Vodaya struck the woman, cut her, twisted her broken hand until she passed out, and then slapped her awake again and dragged her through the blood of her fallen companion.

"Where is it?" Vodaya demanded. "I know you have a weapon. I know everything. Your friends will die for nothing. Tell me where it is."

A wild urge took Zenya. To object. To leave. If there was ever a moment to draw a line, to stand on principle, to put her mistakes behind her and confess all to Mecha Petrogon, this was it.

But the woman began to talk.

"You can't stop what's coming," she panted.

"Mm," Vodaya said. She twisted the woman's broken hand and prompted a wheezing scream that could barely escape its cage of broken ribs.

It took a scant few more minutes to transform defiance into desperation. "I don't know, I don't know," the woman cried.

"You have an insider," Vodaya said calmly. "You have corrupted one of us to your cause, and you are relying on that person to smooth your way. Tell me."

"I don't know."

"Tell me about the weapon."

"I don't know!"

"Vodaya," Zenya whispered, but Vodaya shot her a look so venomous it shriveled the rest of the question in her throat. The warrior pummeled her victim into the floor, asking calmly, then asking angrily, till the woman was weeping like a broken thing.

"Who is it?" Vodaya asked. "Who is it? One word will end this."

And then, finally, blessedly:

"Are you in contact with Winged Raksa? Is Raksa helping hide the weapon?"

"Yes," the woman gasped. "Yes, yes, yes. Raksa."

It was over quickly, and Zenya breathed a sigh of relief. The feeling was short-lived, however, because as soon as they had stepped out of the woman's hearing, Vodaya rounded on her ferociously. "If you ever interrupt me again, I will cast you out of the Pava program. Do you understand me? Do you understand the significance of what we just heard?"

"Yes," Zenya said, though it was the first she'd heard of a new weapon. "I only . . ."

Vodaya stopped inches from Zenya's face, crowding her back with the looming threat of her wings. "You only *what*?" she demanded.

Zenya couldn't look at her. She stared at the dead women instead and mumbled, "I'm not sure that she knew what she was saying."

"Listen to me very carefully," Vodaya said. "This is our purpose. To root out threats to Radezhda. To stop them. You don't get to decide as you go what you're willing to do to accomplish that. You know we need more evidence of the coming incursion. This is it."

"But Mecha Petrogon . . ."

Vodaya stabbed one finger into Zenya's chest. "Mecha Petrogon has strayed from his calling," she spat. "Years of peace have made him cowardly. We are living in difficult times, Pava Zemolai, and I foresee even more difficult times ahead of us."

Zenya wanted to argue, to defend Mecha Petrogon. She clamped her teeth shut, but her doubt was writ large on her face.

"There's a fight coming," Vodaya said. "The commanders are stubborn, but they'll understand my foresight when it does."

"I believe you," Zenya whispered miserably.

"No, you don't." Vodaya's eyes narrowed. "But you will soon. I'm delivering a formal challenge to Petrogon."

Zenya recoiled. "You're challenging Mecha Petrogon? Not Winged Raksa?"

Vodaya huffed. "It's not enough to root out a single weed. Mecha Petrogon has been taken in by Raksa's lies. It shows a fatal failure in judgment." She wiped the dead woman's knife clean on the back of an armchair and added it to her belt.

"I will submit my challenge," Vodaya said. "And in three days' time, we will lay our souls bare before the mecha god and let *her* judge which of us has the purest heart. Then you'll see who is right."

Zenya did not witness the challenge itself, delivered in private at a war meeting atop the tower, but she heard whispers of it afterward. Mecha

Petrogon walked away without speaking a word, they said.

A silent war waged as the Winged and their support staff aligned themselves in advance of the soul-baring. Raksa stated his support for the Voice in no uncertain terms, and Vodaya's opinion of them both was abundantly clear.

News streamed in from the city, all of it conflicted. There was peace on the ground. Or the fighting had resumed. Or a festival of healing was planned around the reconvening of the Council of Five. Or that same festival was the cover for an insidious attack.

The mecha sect needed clarity. It needed a Voice who could overcome all challenge.

Three nights of anticipation, and the third day bloomed dark purple over a shamelessly eager audience. The soul-baring didn't take place till dawn, but a crowd had formed on tower Kemyana's rooftop shortly after midnight.

Vodaya spent her final hours in contemplation. Zenya fluttered around her own room, unable to sleep. She tinkered with her mech port, read her saints, rearranged her meager belongings, and waited. She tried to put disloyal thoughts out of mind.

In the predawn hour, they ascended: Zenya by elevator and Vodaya by her own wings. The rooftop was packed, and Zenya had to muscle her way to the front. If the worst came to pass, Vodaya would need help getting down.

Vodaya and Mecha Petrogon stood side by side at the base of the god-tree. All four quadrant leaders stood in front of them in full armor.

A Tooth alighted in their midst, driving the first row of onlookers into the people behind them. She carried a mechanical cord: bright green with silver plugs at either end stamped in archaic symbols. She marched forward slowly, the cord thrust forth like a bloody sacrifice. Maybe, at one time, it had been.

The audience held its breath, rapt, as the Tooth plugged one end of the cord into the back of Mecha Petrogon's neck and the other end directly into the trunk of the tree.

The quadrant leaders began to sing.

They raised their voices in harmony, sharing the words normally sung by the Voice alone. It was jarring to hear that music from such ordinary throats. Would the mecha god respond? The Voice was connected, but the Voice was being challenged, and the mecha god could be fickle. One day, she might refuse.

But not today.

Godly light spilled forth from the portal, brighter than the coming day, and the crowd erupted in soft cries of wonderment and relief. Zenya basked in that light, her eyes blurring with tears. She struggled to maintain her composure, to be a worthy attendant, even as the light forced her to consider all of her own flaws.

Vodaya and Petrogon glowed in the god-light, and the soul-baring began.

"Do you believe the citizens of Radezhda were chosen by the woken gods to carry on their legacy?" asked Winged Shantar.

"Do you pledge your life to the protection of all Radezhda's citizens, regardless of sect, regardless of piety, regardless of their history with the law?" asked Winged Dietra.

Around and around the quadrant leaders went, prodding Vodaya and Petrogon to declare their most cherished beliefs.

Vodaya's refrain was simple, pious: "Become the protector. Enforce her edicts. Judge the wicked and reward the penitent. Uphold the laws of city and state."

Petrogon's was equally rooted in truth: "Our purpose is not to rule, but to uphold the laws of city and state."

The god-light filtered into Mecha Petrogon's body and illuminated a good soul. His skin shone translucent, and his heart was just visible, a glow within the glow, red and true.

When the Winged asked questions of law and tactic, Mecha Petrogon cast only the faintest of shadows. They flickered through his torso almost too quickly to catch, veins of darkness snaking out from his heart and vanishing into his limbs. His reservations were as expected: he held moderate views on prisoner detention and the extent to which the mecha god's judgment extended to conflicts between citizens. There was nothing Petrogon had not already expressed publicly in his calls for reconciliation.

It was an admirable performance, one that any Pava or Winged could aspire to.

But Vodaya was beyond admirable: she was immaculate. No matter how she was questioned, her body shone pure in the god-light. It was like she had never had a disloyal thought in her entire life.

Mecha Petrogon remained stoic while his own minor flaws were illuminated, but at each one of Vodaya's flawless recitations his gaze grew sharper. Angrier.

"I have no more questions," Winged Shantar declared, and the rest in turn agreed.

Their audience waited uncertainly for the verdict. Nothing had been revealed that they didn't already know.

Petrogon spread his hands, a conciliatory gesture, and raised his voice to the crowd. "Radezhda is a spoked wheel, weakened by the removal of any rod. We are more powerful together. That is what Saint Radezhda believed. That is what she died to defend, and that is why our first objective must be reconciliation."

"We aren't finished until the city is safe!" Vodaya exclaimed. "This is our purpose: to protect the citizens of this city, even from themselves. *Especially* from themselves." She returned to her favored refrain: "Has the mecha god ever opposed one of my decisions? Ever failed to uphold my justice?"

"I don't disagree with your theology," Petrogon snapped. "Only your methods."

"They are one and the same!"

In the crowning light of dawn, their wings glittered and flashed, flexing and snapping with every angry twitch of their shoulders. For a moment, it seemed as though the fight would turn physical.

Soft cries from the audience drew their eyes upward. All this time, the portal had been wandering that strange mechanical forest, across hills and waves of silver, to the mecha god's place of rest atop the broad metal platform and the fog-enveloped figure of the goddess herself.

Now, barely visible through the pearly glow: the mecha god's fingers twitched.

Was she stirring?

If she was, would she extend the hand, or the fist?

The mecha god's light continued to flow, steady and unyielding, the harsh white of it bleaching color from everything it touched, and her devotees waited breathlessly for the first sign of a lie.

Vodaya turned to the audience. "You have seen what I believe," she called out. "But I am only one warrior. What do *you* believe? Do you believe we are fulfilling our pledge to this city? Do you believe our citizens are safe? Do you believe they *feel* safe?"

Petrogon was furious, his heart bleeding black, but Vodaya wasn't finished. "This fight isn't over!" she proclaimed. "I have been working on the ground. I have been confronting our enemies in their deepest hiding places. They are *not* cowed. They are *not* repentant. They are stockpiling supplies against another siege, against *us*. These are not the actions of a people prepared to reconcile. They are planning a final assault, utilizing all the skills of their most cunning engineers. I have presented my evidence to Mecha Petrogon privately, but he will not listen. If he has any fault, it is his optimism, his belief that our enemies still share with us a common value. But *ours* are the core values of Radezhda. If they oppose us, then they are no different from the enemies who crowd our borders."

Mecha Petrogon turned on her, held back only by the cord linking him to the god-tree. "I accepted your challenge, Vodaya, and I have fulfilled it. This isn't the place for conspiracies!"

"This is *precisely* the place," she hissed. "This is the *only* place."

"We're finished," Mecha Petrogon snapped. "My orders stand. We are reconvening the council, and you will be lucky to retain your patrol status." He gestured impatiently at the Tooth who had delivered the mechanical cord, but the Tooth looked past him, to the quadrant leaders. And the quadrant leaders were listening to Vodaya.

"I have one question for you," Winged Vodaya said. "One question, and we can leave here today without doubt." She spread her arms wide, encompassing Petrogon, the god-tree, the gaping portal overhead, the audience surrounding them. "In all your years of service, in all your years as the Voice—have you truly served the will of the mecha god?"

All eyes were on Mecha Petrogon. It seemed a simple enough question to Zenya. Petrogon had stood in the god's eye many times and never provoked her ill will. But some deeper understanding passed between the two Winged. Vodaya was calm, triumphant. Petrogon looked . . . frightened.

"Vodaya—" he warned.

The god-light abruptly brightened, overwhelming in its intensity. Zenya gasped. There, barely visible through all that light—

The mecha god stirred, like wind through a fog.

Her right hand lifted slowly toward the portal, slender-fingered and grasping. The crowd cried out and swayed and prayed a hundred different prayers. A young man fainted. And then the mecha god's fingers pushed into their world. Her wrist stretched the portal three feet wide, a giant emerging over the scorched branches of the god-tree.

Petrogon tensed as though he might run, but he was still tethered to the tree. He watched the great hand coming for him and visibly braced for his fate.

She touched his head with a single luminous finger. The light washed him clean—until it didn't. Mecha Petrogon's heart beat hard within the translucent shell of his chest, pushing veins of color out, spreading shadow like an infection.

The mecha god searched for signs of disloyalty, and she found them.

His head snapped back; his jaw gaped wide. The mecha god caught his body in her hand, and still the shadows spread: disloyal, disloyal, disloyal. Her hand closed tightly, enveloping him from his wings to his knees, only his feet shaking freely at the bottom.

Reverent cries turned to horrified screams. The crowd pressed back from the reckoning, one panicked breath away from stampeding off the roof. Metal squealed, a gut-turning sound of wings deforming under enormous pressure.

They all heard when the resistance of metal gave way to the resistance of bone. Mecha Petrogon's wail abruptly stopped. Blood sizzled and spit and dripped like magma from between the mecha god's fingers, and she opened her fist.

The thing she held was hardly human. It dropped to the bricks with a sickening thump.

The hand tilted, hesitating over Vodaya.

She stood beside Petrogon's mangled body with her head held high, a picture of perfect stoicism framed by her wings and the branches of the god-tree. Zenya held her breath, bracing for the worst—

But . . . Vodaya glowed. The light had never stopped, and Vodaya had not flinched. She was silver from the crown of her hair to the soles of her boots, a gleam so bright that it hurt Zenya's eyes to look directly.

Only Vodaya's heart flared vibrant in her chest, bloody and crystalline, keeping a drumbeat like thunder. The mecha god could find no fault in her.

And Zenya was filled with shame.

She thought back to the loft, chewing through the memory as she had so many times already. Except the more she pictured it, the more she doubted her recollection of what had happened. She'd provoked Vodaya with her insubordination, after all.

If Vodaya's motives were pure, then her treatment of Zenya was exactly as she claimed: a training technique designed to bring out her potential. It had worked, hadn't it? Zenya *had* moved the wing.

Vodaya truly believed every word she said. She was Saint Radezhda on the mountain, a woman become a city become a myth. She was Orlusky, she was Zorska, she was Vitalia, she was every saint who'd held a pass, held the line, devoted herself body and soul to the god that protected them all.

She shone with the light of heaven and ended all doubt.

Surety settled over Zenya again, and it was a relief. It was shoulder-loosening and heart-swelling and true. This was what her brother had never understood: the sheer relief of placing yourself in the hands of someone who knew what was best for you; who made the decisions you did not know how to make. To be a hand on the blade.

It could have, should have, ended there, but then a terrible noise arose at the western end of the rooftop. The crowd jostled and turned, a great clumsy beast with too many limbs, and the cause rose—impossibly—into view.

There were five enormous wooden ships flying toward tower Kemyana. They were flat-bottomed, like river barges, fifteen feet wide and bristling with armored bodies. Each one bore four vast mechanical wings, monstrous caricatures of a warrior's. They were bulky, utilitarian, unrefined. With every wing stroke, their gears screeched and whined, loud and ungainly.

The engineers had built war machines.

Fear crackled through the air—but it was buttressed by outrage. *Fury.* The fight had come to their very door. Their place of worship. The engineers meant to cripple the administration tower, cut off access to the mecha god herself—and after the mecha sect had spared engineering tower Lizmanya. It was the perfect opportunity, the *only* opportunity, to eliminate the entire top tiers of the Winged hierarchy before a counterattack was launched.

And there was no way they could have known everyone would be assembled on the rooftop this morning.

Not unless they'd been informed about the challenge.

Vodaya addressed the panicking crowd, and her voice rang with delicious anger. "This is it! The engineers are launching their final attack! If we defeat them now—and we *will* defeat them now—the war is over. They have nothing else left!"

She launched herself into the sky, still glowing and god-lit in the morning sun, and she pointed to the oncoming engineers, only five hundred feet distant and closing in fast. "Winged, to your formations! Today, you fight for your home! For your god! For your city! Today, we decide what Radezhda will become!"

CHAPTER TWENTY-TWO

First the workers said they had run out of mortar. Now they say they have run out of clay. I do not care! If we cannot continue with brick, we will continue with wood! The only thing that matters is that we reach the heavens, and we will do so *by any means necessary.*

— [attribution missing], *private correspondence*

THE DAY was swiftly ticking down toward sunset. Zemolai and the remaining bolt-babies prepared to invade tower Kemyana.

Rustaya ran off on a hasty supply trip. They needed a cart and climbing gear, and Rustaya was in the market for a more specialized set of legs. Timyan parceled out their existing weaponry, nervously counting and re-counting as though he could generate a different rig by sheer force of will.

That left Galiana to recode Zemolai's mech port. It was an unpleasant procedure, requiring her to tug on wires linked directly to Zemolai's nerve endings in order to reconfigure them inside the wall of the port. Zemolai sat in a chair with her left arm propped loosely behind her head, stripped down to her breast band. Galiana crouched at her side, working in the combined glare of three lanterns.

"Sorry," Galiana kept saying. "Sorry. Sorry."

Zemolai sat uncomplaining. It gave her something immediate to focus on instead of letting her thoughts spiral madly into the future.

"Are you sure about this code?" Galiana asked, pliers poised. "I know the pattern used to generate codes for workers. I could get us most of the way up without setting off any flags."

"I'm sure," Zemolai said. Dryly, she added, "Mecha Vodaya can go anywhere she wants."

"Vodaya!" Galiana squeaked, nearly dropping her pliers.

"I've made adjustments for her before," Zemolai said. "The code's real."

"Real or not! How are we going to get away with that?"

Zemolai shrugged. "I only need it to work once."

The reality of what they were doing hit Zemolai in waves. One moment she was calm. The next, a dark cloud seized her limbs and stole her breath. Her life had been spent shoring up a lie. She was rejecting all of her training in pursuit of a flimsy hope, the hope that the mecha god was righteous, that the mecha god would see her true.

And if it wasn't a lie after all? If it wasn't just Vodaya, but the path itself that was toxic, and had been all this time? If there *was* no ethical way to serve a warrior god?

The weight of doubt threatened to crush her chest, and Zemolai hastily pushed it back. She couldn't afford doubt right now.

She would know the truth soon enough.

Galiana twisted the last wire into place and tested the connection on a small coder. The engineering was sound, at least. Zemolai's port did indeed transmit a code. Unfortunately, there was no way to find out if it would work on the right sensors until they tried it.

"Thanks." Zemolai pulled her shirt on and buckled her gear into place. "How far out do you think Rustaya is?"

Galiana considered. "Not long. Maybe twenty more minutes, if they weren't delayed."

Zemolai started for the door. "I'll be back."

Galiana jumped up. "Wait! Where are you going?"

"Not far."

"But we're about to leave! How long will you be gone? What if Karolin comes back early?"

Timyan rose from his work as well, but what were they going to do, tackle her? Zemolai said, "When Rustaya gets back, help them load the Tooth. I'll be here when I need to be here. Borrow your cloak?" She snatched up Galiana's traveling cloak and swung it around her shoulders. It wasn't perfect, but she wouldn't immediately appear to be a walking arsenal.

She climbed upstairs, exiting into the open-air market, and began looking for a shrine marker.

There, by the entrance: a bit of painted wood that had seen better days.

Zemolai set off, hugging Galiana's cloak tight. A handful of worshippers were walking toward the metal stairwell beside the marker, ready to make their final offerings before heading home for the night. Zemolai slipped in among them, careful to carve some distance around herself, and descended into the tunnel below.

Down here, the walls were intimately narrow and dimly lit. The air was scented by a dozen competing sticks of incense: some stale, some fresh, all combining to tickle the nose and sting the eyes.

There were more elaborate shrines at the center of the city, in which entirely separate tunnels had been dug for each god. This one was modest: a single circle with curtained alcoves dug out of the walls on either side. Zemolai walked lightly around the packed-dirt route until she found an open alcove. She ducked inside and pulled the curtain shut.

The narrow space contained a small, padded bench for kneeling and a tidy set of carved copper idols mounted to the wall. A dagger, a gear, a book, a hammer, and a bundle of barley. Simple and direct.

Zemolai leaned against the dagger and muttered a wry apology. "I'd kneel, but then I'd never get up again."

She'd walked here with a million pleas whirling through her head, but now, faced with the prospect of confession, Zemolai hardly knew what to say. "I haven't prayed in a long time," she started. Her breath hitched. This was foolish. A waste of time.

But then the words were there, like they'd been waiting beneath her tongue the whole time.

"I've made mistakes," she said. "I've been a fool, sometimes on purpose. What I'm about to do . . . it doesn't negate what I've done, but if anything is going to change, it has to start here, and I'm the one with the best chance of changing it."

She paused again, her right side cool against the metal of the blade, her left side still thrumming hot from Galiana's tinkering. "Protection and judgment. I still believe that. I still believe we need warriors, guardians. Shields. But . . . who are we shielding, if it isn't the other Four?"

The dagger bore silent witness. The mecha god never answered. Not in words.

"Please," Zemolai whispered. She pressed her forehead to the gleaming blade. "Please help me do what's right."

She waited until there was no time left to wait, and then she returned to her new five-unit and prepared for battle.

It was another cold wind night, and Zemolai approached tower Kemyana for what might be the last time.

Halfway across Pava District, they could hear the sounds of celebration ahead. Every balcony on the tower was lit, but it was only an illusion of a full house. The lights were a beacon, a clear end goal for the nearly Winged attempting first flight. The partying, though loud, was confined to the trainees who had been left behind.

They'd abandoned their cart and the body of the Tooth in Karolin District—an irony not lost on any of them. Zemolai did not relish the thought of drawing trouble to the quiet worker district, but it was the farthest they had estimated they could travel before the Tooth's newly undampened resonance chip set off an alarm at the tower.

It would be obvious, Zemolai told them, when the search team set out. They had to be within running distance of a tower entrance when that happened.

They approached from the south, giving the training grounds as much berth as they could. As Kemyana grew in size and sound and splendor, Zemolai couldn't help dwelling on how long it had been since she had approached the tower at ground level. And even then, it had never been like this—scurrying through the dark, avoiding the entrance for Pava worshippers in favor of the less-trafficked delivery side. Why would Winged

Vodaya be entering the ground-floor farm supply? It didn't matter to an automated sensor system.

The night sky was dense with cloud cover. They crouched in the shadow of a residential bridge and watched the tower lights flicker.

Minutes passed at a crawl. They waited, breathless, until Zemolai began to worry that Vodaya would not fetch her Tooth tonight after all. Her plan hinged on the fact that Vodaya thought her warriors were heading toward a rebel stronghold. She had to send all of her strongest fighters after the Tooth. She *had* to.

And then:

"*There*," Rustaya said. Balcony doors crashed open on the thirteenth floor. Winged launched in rapid succession, catching updrafts to their preferred altitudes and then shooting out across the city.

"Go," Zemolai said.

They broke cover and scurried like mice to the delivery door, enormous and strapped with thick bands of metal. Zemolai fumbled at the sensor, briefly fearing that it would take palm chips only, an upgrade incompatible with her decades-old tech—but there, on the side of the box, she found an opening for direct contact. Zemolai slipped the Tooth's cord into her abdomen and plugged in. The response was immediate.

It was a cruel sensation, to feel the warmth of solicited energy in her side, so much less than what she once controlled. Zemolai's breath hitched. Deep down, she hadn't known how the old port would respond, but the door unlatched with a sharp clack. Mecha Vodaya could go anywhere she pleased.

Inside, they squeezed between rows of shelving until they reached another door, another sensor, and in moments they were in a hallway.

Zemolai shut her eyes, mentally reorienting. "Turn right," she said softly.

The hallway was long and dark and gently pulsing with music. Only one thin wall separated them from the Pava revel in the grand hall. While the new graduates climbed Ruk Head Mountain, their peers prayed with their bodies. They stomped and chanted and fought and kissed. They sang songs for the victors and drank for the dead. They entreated the mecha god with the sweat of their bodies and the joy in their bones.

Zemolai resisted the urge to peek inside. She desperately wanted to look at this new generation of trainees, hopeful and fresh-faced before the grind. They were all strangers to her, pulled up the ranks during her years on the border. None of them knew a life before Vodaya was Voice. None of them knew Radezhda before the war. And none of them knew how drastically the course of their lives might change tonight.

Would they adapt? Or would they forever resent a city that was taken from them just when they were on the cusp of ascending?

Everyone in tower Kemyana had a story within several degrees of her own. They'd been born to this, or they'd swapped sects; they'd fought and bled and yearned their way toward wings. If not for a few chance events, Zemolai would still be among them.

Would Scholar Pyetka have considered it chance or simply more evidence that the world was cyclical and ever-folding? He would say that Zemolai had forever been the woman she was now, in this tower, taking this stand—she only hadn't known it yet.

The hallway ended with an oversized staff elevator. Zemolai ushered everyone inside and dragged the gates shut. Wordlessly, they all drew weapons from their sides. The elevator rose smoothly, the slow chime of the control panel the only indication of their progress.

Zemolai shut her eyes briefly, mentally preparing for the next step. Staff elevators only reached the twentieth floor. There, they could transfer to the private elevator built for Winged and their attendants.

They reached the top without stopping, and Galiana let out a soft sigh of relief. Timyan dragged the elevator gate open.

There were three workers standing in the dimly lit hallway, waiting to take the lift back down. They froze at the sight of three heavily armed criminals and a disgraced, once-Winged warrior brandishing a knife.

Zemolai lunged forward and grabbed the first one by the shirt. She twisted her knife and struck them sharply with the handle rather than the blade, one hard knock to the side of the neck. The worker gurgled and lost balance.

The second worker backpedaled from the attack, but Timyan and Rustaya were on him like hounds. "Somebody—help!" he shouted, and the last word ended on a grunt as his feet were swept out from under him. Rustaya rode him to the floor and clapped a hand over his mouth, while Zemolai administered a more effective blow to the back of the first worker's head.

Galiana emerged from the elevator, bolt-gun up. She aimed at the third person, but she waited too long and gave up her bluff. She wasn't willing to shoot an old coworker to ensure their passage. He spun away, and Galiana lunged after him.

Zemolai's mark passed out—still breathing, at least—but the one Timyan had tackled was thrashing up a ruckus with his boots.

"Oh, bloody Vitalia," Zemolai snapped. She shoved Timyan out of the way. It took three hits to knock that one out. Alive, but no promises about concussions.

Galiana let out a strangled shriek. The last worker had tackled her, straddling her waist and frantically smashing her bolt-gun hand against the tile floor. Zemolai ran down the hallway, watching the bolt-gun fly from Galiana's grip. The man lunged for the weapon—and Zemolai hauled him back by the collar of his shirt. A minute later there were three unconscious bodies in the hallway.

Galiana sat up, cradling her hand. Three of her fingers were crooked and streaked with blood. She tried to flex them and gasped, her face going sallow like she was about to faint.

"Are you all fucking incompetent?" Zemolai hissed. "Do you not understand what we're *doing* here?"

"*Shh!*" Timyan looked fearfully toward the elevator.

They paused, straining to hear any sound of approaching footsteps. There was nothing.

"I'm sorry," Galiana whispered.

Zemolai took a deep breath, forcing back the tidal wave of recriminations that threatened. They weren't warriors. She had to keep reminding herself that *they weren't warriors*. They didn't act like warriors in a fight, and they wouldn't respond like warriors to a rebuke. She didn't think that she could muster the familial, encouraging warmth of Eleny, but if she could keep her own head on straight, they'd follow.

They were a bunch of stupid bolt-babies, but they were *her* stupid bolt-babies now, and she was going to get them through this.

Galiana fumbled with a bandage and a pair of painkillers while Zemolai trussed up the cleaning crew and cast about for a hiding place. The twentieth floor was all living quarters, which made nearly every single door in the hallway a potential disaster.

"There," Rustaya said. The fourth door down had the silhouette of a worker's hammer burned into the wood. A supply closet. They dragged the workers inside the cramped space and shut it tight.

Zemolai recognized the jittery looks in their eyes. They were rattled, and the longer she let them dwell on it, the worse their reaction times would become. But it was far too late for second thoughts.

"Move. Now," she ordered. She put a hand under Galiana's elbow, and Galiana looked up at her with naked remorse.

Zemolai muttered, "I'm sorry for shouting," and received a wobbly smile in return.

The next elevator was large enough for Winged guards to escort prisoners uptower for judgment. Zemolai's ragtag crew looked insignificantly small in one corner, and she fought the sudden urge to push them out, send them back to the staff elevator, send them anywhere but here.

But as much as it killed her to admit it, she didn't think she could do this alone.

So she plugged herself into the control panel, flipped the switch for rooftop access—and let her hacked port do its work.

This time, none of them lowered their weapons. Zemolai thought she heard Rustaya breathing the words to a prayer. It wasn't worth asking them to repeat it.

The ceiling spun open like a flower overhead, and they emerged onto the deserted rooftop. Lanterns flickered at regular intervals all around the tower's edge, reducing the colorful brick patterns to shades of shadow and light.

The god-tree was a dark, hulking mass at the center of all that lamplight. Its gnarled branches made slashes of negative space through which no stars were visible.

In the distance, the flames of the new graduates had inched farther up Ruk Head Mountain. One or two stragglers were still below the mid-point of the path—doomed, if they didn't hurry. Dawn was hours away, but senior Winged would assemble on the rooftop before that to await the arrival of any successful first flights. Zemolai's window to act would close soon.

"I've never been this close to a portal before," Galiana said quietly, and the night sky seemed to swallow her words whole.

"We're about to get a hell of a lot closer," Rustaya muttered. They rolled up the wide hems of their trousers, revealing the thick pistons and hooked feet of their climbing legs. They made some adjustments to the feet, extending the teeth that would help them keep a grip as they free-climbed. The prosthetics, filched from the community barn stores, were considerably more powerful than their previous pair. If any of them fell, Rustaya had only to lock their legs to become an unmovable anchor from which the others could swing back to safety.

Assuming everyone's harnesses worked.

Assuming the posts weren't so porous that Rustaya's feet shredded them, dumping everyone into the fog without end.

Zemolai's mouth was dry. She led them to the base of the tree, where a small silver mech port was still embedded in the trunk, almost swallowed whole by encroaching growth. Zemolai ran her fingers around the edge of it, picking loose obstructive flakes of bark, feeling vaguely sacrilegious for scratching at the god's own tree.

"It's beautiful," Timyan said.

Zemolai looked up. The portal shimmered pale orange against an inky sky. It was a living thing, a fickle and otherworldly connection between the realms. This close, she could glimpse little flashes of light and color as the portal skimmed its way through the other world.

Even a glimpse was devastating. Zemolai's legs turned to jelly. Better to throw herself from the tower right now than face the mecha god. She'd been deemed unworthy once already, cast down, destroyed. It was madness to appeal to the god again, pure desperation. One touch of the light would reveal her reason for being there, and—

And Zemolai still didn't know what that was. At some moments, she was convinced she was here to stop Vodaya's abuse of power: simple, altruistic, righteous. At others, she wondered if this was a final pathetic attempt to ingratiate herself to the god herself, a final prostration.

Which motive would the god prefer?

The tree was warm beneath her hand, thrumming with anticipation. The rebels stared worriedly at her. Fumbling, she produced the cord again. Before her shaking hands could betray her, she plugged herself into the tree.

Warmth. Invitation. A rumbling, snapping, living vein of electricity the likes of which she'd never felt before. Zemolai was filled by it, moved by it, anchored to the spot and floated by it. She never wanted to leave. She couldn't bear another second.

"Are you ready?" she asked, in a voice like sandpaper. She cleared her throat. "As soon as that portal opens, we'll be visible to the entire city. We have to be on the other side before they get here."

"Yes, yes," Galiana said. "We're ready."

Zemolai shut her eyes, and the words came to her unbidden. She had them memorized: god words, ritual words she'd heard so many times over the years—words that most of them assumed only the Voice could speak, or a convocation of high-ranking Winged under extreme circumstances. But Zemolai knew the truth: that Vodaya learned them long before she was authorized to use them, and it had all worked the same.

Were the words just ceremony, designed to inspire awe? Were they encoded voice commands that triggered a mechanical response? Or did they truly awaken a sleeping god?

It didn't matter. Zemolai said them now, and they felt like candied rocks in her mouth. The consonants tumbled over one another like eager puppies, the vowels slippery with intention. She spoke the words, and energy flowed into her side, the opposite of what she'd expected. She'd expected to be drained dry, consumed, cast aside like an empty husk, but the god-tree was generous and giving, it filled her with a heat that eased her aching joints.

There was a soft gasp from Galiana, and Zemolai opened her eyes. The portal slid open, only a few feet wide but more than enough to illuminate the tree and the four people huddled nervously below its branches. They were cast in sharp relief, a marauding crew with wide, frightened eyes and rainbow hair. Above them, an alien forest stretched up toward a silver dais.

Tears coursed down Zemolai's cheeks, her first tears since she'd emerged, whole and broken, from the rebel cell's containment cage. The portal was opening for her. The mecha god was not turning her away, not yet. She thought she would break down right there, give up, leave this place for good and be satisfied with this shred of victory. To go any further was to invite humiliation and defeat.

"Is that enough?" Galiana asked, and the warble in her voice broke some of the spell. "Zemolai, do we go?"

Zemolai rubbed at her cheeks. "Yes." She unplugged the cord from her side, careful to leave the other end attached, though of course that was another ritual of unclear worth.

Rustaya aimed their grappling hook carefully and fired. The hook sailed perfectly through the center of the portal and caught hard in the crook of a knot of foliage on a slender post. Rustaya tugged once, twice. It held. They had to move quickly, before the portal began to wander again and either cut their rope or dragged it from Rustaya's hand.

Rustaya braced one foot against the trunk of the tree and wrapped their arm in the knotted rope. They gave Timyan a short, sharp nod, as though this was all perfectly ordinary. Only a bit of mountainside hiking.

And then a furious voice called out, "Traitor Zemolai! Release your hold on the god-tree! Turn around and face me, if you have a shred of honor left."

Winged Mitrios descended to the roof, rustling the lantern light with his passage. He landed hard on the bricks behind them, armed and ready to kill.

CHAPTER TWENTY-THREE

It is not what I expected. *She* is not what I expected. I don't
think I dare write it down, even here.

—*Diary of Mecha Petrogon*

ZENYA FROZE in the face of the oncoming attack for one horrifying
moment—and then her training stuttered into gear. She swung toward Vodaya, who was still raining orders from above. The warrior glowed
with purpose, with violent and self-righteous delight.

Beneath her, the quadrant leaders shouted words of relinquish and clo-
sure over the clamor of a horrorstruck crowd. Slowly, sluggishly, the mecha
god drew back to her realm, back to her pearly fog and bed of steel. Back
to her perpetual slumber. Safe.

Vodaya pointed at members of Pava five-units and shouted, "You, level
twelve! *You*, level fourteen! Zemolai, the rooftop."

There were six balcony repair stations on the west face of the tower, and
more than enough bodies present to fill them.

A familiar voice asked, "Do we have a post yet?"

Zenya turned, startled. Pava Romil stood behind her with the rest of
her former five-unit pressed tight around him. Dolynne gave her a short,
grim nod.

It was the wrong time to feel happy, but Zenya had to fight off a grin.
"Rooftop defense," she said. "We don't want a single boot to hit these
bricks, understand?"

"Understood!"

The elevator was opening for a new batch of evacuees. Zenya ran for it, yelling over her shoulder, "Fan out! Clear the roof! I'll be back with supplies."

She rode down to the nearest armory, grabbed a weapons bag, and raced back. On the roof again she slowed, only briefly, as she passed the god-tree. The body of once-Mecha Petrogon oozed red in the dirt: vulnerable, undignified, cautionary. Even disgraced, he deserved full death rites for his service.

But later, later. Everything later.

There were only twenty Winged in the air. Twenty warriors against five ships, each of which carried at least two dozen fighters on its deck. It shouldn't have been a challenge, even at those numbers.

But what the engineers lacked in martial prowess, they possessed in cunning. Their soldiers were covered head-to-toe in gleaming armor. Their ships bristled with cannons and net-guns and experimental projectile weaponry. They had built shells of bravery over their skins, and now they considered themselves worthy opponents of the mecha god's chosen warriors.

Cowards, every one of them.

An elderly woman stood at the prow of the lead ship: Creator Vanyamir, one of the few fighters not hiding her face behind a helmet. She raised a great golden amplifier to her lips and shouted, "Lay down your weapons! Lay down your weapons and be spared!"

Dolynne pumped their fist defiantly in the air. "Never!" they cried, and the cheer rippled out across the rooftop.

Boat met body four hundred feet from the tower's edge. Dozens of grim-faced, would-be warriors gripped swivel-mounted guns on the forward decks.

The engineers opened fire, perforating the air with bolts. The Winged dodged, swift as eels through water, but dozens of bolts hit the tower, shattering glass, clanging off metal, burrowing into the lower levels of wood and plaster with reverberating impacts.

"Arm up!" Zenya ordered. She passed weapons down the line, knives and grapple guns and spare bolts, and for a moment everything was normal again. Even Dolynne shot her a grin, flush with nerves and glee.

And then they waited. The fight was out of range. They were a final resort, backup in case a ship survived against the Winged—but what could they do against a fighting force that could defeat a sky full of mecha warriors?

Zenya watched as the Winged coalesced into the battle formations she had spent endless hours studying. They darted in and out, testing the engineers' defenses. The powerful movement of the ships' wings created unpredictable air currents—the only force keeping the Winged at any distance, lest they be felled by the turbulence.

Wind whipped fiercely at the edge of the roof, stinging her eyes and making a riot of her hair. She knew all the branching possibilities for each unit's next move, the many ways they could respond to the enemy's actions—and the many ways they could *not* respond, in order to stay out of one another's way.

And she couldn't do a thing from here.

Above it all flew Vodaya. Here and there, she darted into the fray—shouting instructions to unit commanders, lobbing knives, tapping out warriors for reload. Winged Shantar bellowed an order, and his warriors fired back on the lead ship. A handful of shots found gaps in the engineers' armor—the exposed hollow of a neck here, the thin line of a shoulder joint there—but for every person who fell, another stepped into their place.

The lead ship launched another volley, and this time they aimed high.

"Down!" Zenya shouted. She ducked behind the raised lip of the rooftop. Stray bolts battered the bricks, and screams broke out behind her. She twisted around in time to see the last group of worshippers squeeze into the elevator, dragging a young man with a bolt between his ribs, his blood a scarlet shriek against the bricks.

Pava Lijo fired back, an angry rejoinder, and Romil shouted, "Save your stock!"

Zenya's eyes caught on the god-tree again, with its miserable compost slumped on the roots. The tree was scorched and scarred, its branches so tough and denuded they barely responded to the wind. Zenya's heart twisted at the thought of their enemies striking the tree. Battle was the purview of the mecha god, yes, but not *here*!

A furious scream snapped her attention back to the sky. Winged Pilivar was caught in a net, and she plummeted, dangling over the side of a ship. The engineers who'd caught her braced themselves against the railing and hauled with all their might, but they couldn't lift the struggling warrior onto the deck.

And then a stray bolt caught one of the engineers in the eye, a perfect shot through the slot on his helmet. His hands went slack, and the other two engineers lost their grip.

The ropes slithered over the rail, and Winged Pilivar vanished from sight.

Zenya was too shocked to cry out. Pilivar had always led them flawlessly in ground missions. She was cool-headed, precise. Unstoppable.

And now she was dead.

The ships dodged closer to the tower, and Creator Vanyamir bellowed through her amplifier. "We are your neighbors! We are your kin!" She wore no helmet and carried no weapon. She led her comrades purely by her defiance and her fury of conviction.

But she had left an opening at her back.

Winged Vodaya gave no warning. She came down sharp, feet first, like a bird of prey, and bore Creator Vanyamir to the deck. The golden amplifier flew overboard, sketching the sky with one glittering arc before vanishing.

Vodaya had nothing but a pair of knives in her hands. She slit Creator Vanyamir's throat and spun toward the rest of the crew—all twenty of them, who now realized their guns had limited rotations, built to fire outward. They scrambled for hand-to-hand weaponry, outrageously unprepared for onboard fighting, and in those precious seconds of disarray Vodaya launched her real assault.

She killed them all.

The ship was locked on its trajectory, a hundred yards away and closing in fast on the tower. Zenya watched, breathless, as Vodaya sprang to the controls. She shoved the dead pilot aside, pulled levers, ripped at wires—and the ship abruptly banked left.

Bodies tilted over the edge, raining the street below, and the ship crashed into a supply building, the roof exploding beneath the onslaught of metal and wood. The damage was shocking. Horrific.

But the lead ship was down.

Zenya screamed with triumph as Vodaya regained altitude, dripping blood and blazing with satisfaction as she shouted orders to her closest commanders. Her victory was rousing, but it was also short-lived. The remaining four ships still bore direct paths toward the tower.

And a new threat appeared from the west.

A dozen small craft rose up into view from behind a water tower. They were miniaturized versions of the airships, carrying only two fliers apiece. The pilots had strapped themselves into canoes with wings, one manning the controls and the other on weapons.

The first boat screamed into the fray, and the backseat fighter lifted a projectile—dark green, spherical, nothing Zenya recognized. He ignored the Winged rising up into his path and aimed past her, toward the tower. The ball hit—and exploded in a spray of fire and shrapnel to the right of a repair station.

Zenya gasped. The engineers had bombs, and they were targeting support staff.

The bomb boats ducked and dodged, but they floundered on choppy waves, fighting dozens of competing air disruptions from the ships and Winged above.

The engineers had co-opted flight, but they hadn't trained for it, not really. *Maybe* they'd managed a handful of dangerous, furtive practices on cloudy nights. Maybe. They hadn't been raised to fight in the air, where an enemy could attack from left, right, ahead, behind, above, below.

They were going to fail, of that Zenya had no doubt. But how much damage would they do first? The engineers were losing more fighters than the Winged, but they had dozens more to start with. Engineers and scholars graduated by the hundreds every year. Whatever their losses today, they could replenish by expanding their academic programs in the coming spring.

Whereas this was an entire generation of warriors at risk.

Zenya leaned over the roof's edge, desperately tracking their progress.

Another dark green bomb soared through the air, and fire exploded at the base of a haul line. The edge of the balcony fell in crumbles of stone, and the Pava who had been working the line fell with it.

Zenya cried out with a hundred other voices.

"Who was it?" Lijo shouted. Zenya shook her head. The angle was too sharp for her to tell.

Eight bomb boats and three airships remained. There were a few bright scholar symbols visible in the fray, defiantly glued to the side of some of the bomb boat pilots' helmets. It so easily could have been her brother's face peeking out through one of those helms—but instead of making Zenya hesitate, it made her furious. Look where they had been leading him. *Look where they had left him.*

A bomb boat broke for the twentieth-floor repair station.

"There!" Zenya shouted. Romil was closest. Two of his bolts glanced off the wings, useless. A third struck the bomb clutched in an engineer's hands, and it detonated, blowing his arms to pieces and destroying the back of his pilot's head.

The boat veered sharply. Another fully crewed airship plunged alongside it, felled by a boarding party. Four of the five Winged who had boarded the ship escaped, but the fifth—a blur of solid blue wings and armor—was trapped. The ship missed the base of the tower by scarcely a block, exploding through a pair of flat-roofed houses.

Two family homes, demolished. If anyone had failed to evacuate, they were dead.

Vodaya and two other unit commanders fell back to the tower to confer. Zenya grabbed Romil by the shoulder. "Hold the line!" she ordered, and he nodded, grim, before she dashed toward the commanders.

She found an argument underway.

"We have to draw them away before Pava is destroyed!" Winged Ferriar shouted.

"They will never stand down," Vodaya said. "This won't end until every one of them is dead and burned."

"Then we should disable them," Winged Ferriar persisted. "We can take the ships. Fly them out of the district."

"No *time*."

"Look down! Entire homes crushed, entire—"

"This isn't the time for weak stomachs," Vodaya snapped. "Don't you understand? They knew we were convening today. Their corruption is spreading into our very ranks. Destroy them. I do not want a *single seed* left to sprout."

Ferriar growled, but peeled off to spread the word. Disagreement could come later. For now, Vodaya held the field. For now, the objective was simple: take the engineers down by any means necessary, regardless of what waited below, and *keep them off the tower.*

Vodaya spotted Zenya and snapped, "Zemolai, to me!"

Zenya ran to her side. "We've lost a repair station. We need to set up flags—maybe bring up an extra line of gunners—"

"Yes, yes, very good. I need you to do something for me." Vodaya pointed toward the god-tree. "Somewhere on Petrogon's body is a small mechanical device, light blue, hexagonal in shape. Find it and hold it for me."

"Right now?" Zenya exclaimed.

"That's an order, Pava," Vodaya snapped.

She launched without waiting for a response. Why bother? There was only one acceptable answer. Zenya hooked her bolt-gun to her belt and ran for the tree, all too aware of the open target of her back to the western sky.

"Oh, saints," she breathed. The reality of Petrogon's mangled body was almost too much for her. She tried to see it as an anatomical doll—one with far too many joints and half its stuffing pulled out.

His armor had been pinched and warped, slicing into his body like a bent can. Zenya wrestled open the buckles on his side and stripped the blood-slicked plating off, and what she found beneath was even worse. One terrible search later, she found the device, half-buried beneath his ribs. It slid free with a sound that made her shudder.

The hexagon was oddly dense, one surface pebbled with round glass bulbs now broken or cloudy, the other side flat. There were grooves on the back, and Zenya hesitated a moment before realizing why they looked so familiar. They resembled the wires and nodes inside the programming boards of Faiyan Sanador's mechanical maintenance course, except these were carved rather than wired in place.

Zenya pocketed the strange device, filing her questions away for later.

As she stood, a ragged voice shouted, "*You!*"

Winged Raksa hit the bricks behind her, and she fell back. He was disheveled, filthy, his brass wings smeared red. He charged at Zenya like a berserker, but his eyes were as clear as ever, and his face was flushed with ordinary anger, not madness.

She looked past him for help, but Vodaya was gone, the Winged were all engaged, her five-unit was clustered together at the farthest edge of the roof, screaming and shooting down at an oncoming bomber. She and Raksa were alone at the base of the god-tree.

"I have to get back to my post," Zenya said. She tried to dart around him, but Raksa was quick. He grabbed her by the vest and shook her.

"How did she do it?" he demanded. "How did she defeat Mecha Petrogon?"

CHAPTER TWENTY-FOUR

We lost seven faithful to the shimmer before she roused and gave us the words to enter safely. She asked: why did you keep trying, after the first?

And when we had worn ourselves out with joyful tears, we said: we love you more than we fear death—how could we stop?

—Diary of an unnamed disciple

THE REBELS faced Winged Mitrios, weapons drawn. Light from the portal shone through the branches of the god-tree, sending shadows like living things snaking across the bricks.

Winged Mitrios stood between two of those jagged stripes, lit up brilliantly. He was fully recovered from his encounter with the signal blocker, and appeared all the more furious for the humiliation.

However: he was also standing on his own two feet and peering carefully at the shadows. Maybe one good thing had come from Galiana's nefarious tinkering—fear of another electrical shortage might keep him from attacking by air.

Engaging on the ground was far better than fighting against a warrior in flight, but Zemolai needed him to come closer if she were going to engage at all—and they had to settle this quickly.

Winged Mitrios remained a stubborn twenty feet away, bolt-gun aimed at Zemolai, while he delivered his verdict—long, and likely long-rehearsed. "Your first crime was paid in full, once-Winged Zemolai. You faced the mecha god's judgment. She cast you down but let you live. Did you feel gratitude for her leniency? Regret for your actions? No! You joined the traitors you swore to protect against, you helped them break into the training grounds, where *children* sleep, you helped them steal weapons, weapons that will be used against your own colleagues, you—you attacked a *Tooth*. You delivered him into captivity. You murdered him!"

He grew more and more strident, but he did not step forward. Zemolai struggled to remain impassive. He was right, after all, and the anger that had pushed her this far wasn't enough to ease her guilt for those very transgressions. Mitrios's outrage, his inability to comprehend how a Winged could go so wrong—she couldn't fault him. In a different timeline she would have been the self-righteous defender on this rooftop, delivering an equally self-righteous speech.

And she found herself suddenly, ludicrously, painfully unwilling to fight him.

"You don't have the information I have," she said, knowing it was pointless and trying anyway. She heard the soft rustling of cloth behind her: the rebels getting antsy, weighing their options.

Mitrios ignored her, continuing his script. "And even that wasn't enough for you!" He gestured at the god-tree, his entire body stiff with rage. "You've come to the holiest heart of our sect—to do what? Close it. Close the portal *now*."

The fear in his voice was real—and Zemolai suddenly understood his reason for grandstanding. He could have descended from the sky without warning. He could have shot every one of them before they had time to mount a defense. But he didn't understand how they had opened the portal, and he was trying to look strong while stalling till help arrived.

And time was in his favor. It was the rebels who needed to push this to a confrontation before their window of opportunity closed.

She risked the briefest glance behind her. Their climbing rope still dangled from the portal, the loose end held tightly in Rustaya's fists. Even though it had been Zemolai's plan, the sight of a hook lodged into one of the god's own trees was outrageous, disorienting. Galiana was poised beside Rustaya with another grapple-gun tucked beneath her arm. With her good hand, she brandished a bolt-gun. Timyan was also armed, but his hand was trembling, his eyes blazing.

Rustaya didn't know that this was the Winged who had killed Eleny, but Timyan and Galiana did. And they weren't looking for reconciliation.

Zemolai knew her words would fall on indifferent ears. She knew that similar words, spoken to her in the flush of her youth, had done nothing. *Worse* than nothing: they had pressed her tighter to her convictions.

But she had to try.

"You love her," she said. "You respect her, and you fear her, and you love her."

Mitrios looked taken aback. Defiantly, he said, "Yes, I do."

"She tells you that you're the best she's ever trained," Zemolai said. "Even better than me, right? Even better than the kids who came between us. You're more talented, you work harder, she's never seen such devotion." She swallowed hard. "She tells you that you're better than your peers. That they aren't as serious as you are. That they aren't going to get nearly as far. Maybe you'll make quadrant leader. Or Tooth! You believe her, don't you? And you're terrified that you'll fail."

Mitrios paled. He said, "You're the failure. You just refuse to accept it."

These warnings, coming from Zemolai—who was a failure, yes, *undeniably* a failure—were like raindrops tossed at a hurricane. She wasn't going to change anything. She wasn't going to change *him*. But the words were hot coals in her lungs, and she had to spit them out.

She inched forward as she spoke, crossing distance and time. "She gets angry when you make a mistake, so angry, because you're supposed to be better than that, right? So you ignore the evidence in front of you—that she really *is* demanding the impossible—because you *believe* her. You mold yourself to what she wants, because she tells you that's what you are."

Mitrios wavered. It was only a flicker of acknowledgment, a tiny window into his world of love and despair, but Zemolai knew she'd found the chink in his armor, that she'd struck hot meat below.

In that moment, Zemolai was not thinking of their mission in the god's realm, currently hanging by a rope. She was thinking: *I wish I had chosen to leave.* She was thinking that it never should have been one and the same, raising children and warriors both. How could you convince someone to leave a path they'd been told was right all their life? How could you face being wrong when leaving meant leaving your friends, your family, and your sense of purpose all at once? One single person could not be god and mother and commander, but that is what Vodaya had been to her, and it had left Zemolai no other life to fall back upon.

Here she had a chance, she thought, to change one person's mind before it was too late—before the choice was made for him, before his path fell to pieces and he came to think: *I wish I had* chosen *to leave.*

But then a great deal happened at once.

The first bolt came from behind Zemolai—from her left, from Timyan—and struck Mitrios in the chest. Mitrios returned fire reflexively, but the impact thrust his shot wide, missing Zemolai by a few inches. It hit Rustaya instead, a solid collision, and they cried, fell over—and let the rope slither from their grasping hands. Timyan screamed.

Galiana lunged for the rope. Zemolai lunged for Mitrios.

He launched upward, instinct overcoming his fear of another signal blocker, and Zemolai hit him square in the gut instead of the chest, her arms coming around in a tackle. They grappled—Zemolai for better purchase, Mitrios trying to get an arm around her neck—and she managed to knock his bolt-gun in the air, a glint of silver arcing, arcing, disappearing past the lamplight. His fist struck her side, hard as a sack of rocks, but the damp wheeze of his breath at her ear told her the bolt in his chest had hit something important.

She only had to hold on.

Shadows flickered through the god-light, casting Mitrios's face in and out of stark relief. Galiana called out a shrill warning: "It's drifting!" The portal moved slowly, lazily, wandering upward and away from the grappling hook and tugging the rope with it. Rustaya was heaped, motionless, at the base of the tree.

Timyan appeared in Zemolai's peripheral vision, angling for another shot at the warrior. "Move," he said.

"Don't shoot," she snapped. Mitrios twisted into a defensive position, wings cupped partially around the pair of them like shields, Zemolai's body blocking his head and torso from attack. She had weapons she could reach for, but that wasn't how she wanted this to end.

Timyan again shouted at her to move. Mitrios smashed his forehead into Zemolai's face, igniting starbursts in her vision. He was solid muscle, new to wings but fresh from combat training. He was Zemolai at peak form, before decades of hard wear had wrecked her knees and back. His blood was pumping with mechalin, and hers was as clear as rainwater. He only had to get the right leverage, and he could snap her neck on the spot.

Zemolai reached between them and grabbed the protruding end of the bolt. She twisted hard, felt it grinding between ribs. The sound he made was more gargle than shout.

Not even mechalin could dampen that. Mitrios went weak in her arms, and she tore out of his embrace. He fell onto his back, half-propped up with his left wing lodged against a brick.

Mitrios wheezed and clutched at his chest, his leathers going darker with blood. Every attempt to rise only hastened the spreading stain, and rage distorted his features, so hot it should have cauterized the wound.

Zemolai knew exactly what she would have done in his situation: get back on her feet and keep fighting. Crawl if she couldn't walk. Reach the bolt-gun and fire into their backs as they climbed the god-tree.

So she took that option away. She raised one booted foot and brought it down hard on his left knee. The joint gave way with a sickening crack, and he wheeze-screamed again.

"Now will you let me through?" Timyan demanded, and his anger was full of tears.

Zemolai grimaced. "No." She knelt down, slapping Mitrios's weakened hands away from his belt. She patted him down, tossing his knives out of reach.

"I need some help here!" Galiana called desperately. She was on her knees next to Rustaya, one arm beneath their shoulders, the other still wrapped in the dangling rope. The portal tugged gently, nearly bowling her over.

"Go," Zemolai instructed.

Timyan looked back, clearly frantic to reach Rustaya. But he aimed the bolt-gun at Mitrios. "He killed Eleny."

"I know what he did," she said.

Trembling now: "Don't take this from me."

Zemolai shifted forward, once again blocking the shot. "This will never end if we keep taking one limb for another. He was defending his home." She pressed her hand against the butterfly-fright of Mitrios's heart and whispered, "Please, Timyan."

She thought he would disobey, and she wouldn't have blamed him. But Rustaya groaned, thick and miserable, and Timyan's nerve broke. He ran back to the tree.

Zemolai continued her body search, again swatting away Mitrios's feeble attempts to hold her off.

"There's . . . no hope for you now," he wheezed. "You're . . . damned, Zemolai."

She found what she was looking for in his vest: his distress beacon, slick with blood. Her heart sank, though she was hardly surprised. It was already snapped in half.

Mitrios laughed at her, bitter and victorious. "I broke it . . . before I set down. She's coming. Kill me . . . or don't. It won't stop her."

Zemolai dropped the beacon. She wiped her hands on her pants and rose. "You'll understand eventually, or you won't. I'm sorry."

"Don't—" He tried to roll after her but he was too weak. Instead he continued his wet, gasping threats.

Rustaya was conscious and nestled in Timyan's arms. A bolt protruded from their left-side gut. They were pale, made even paler by the white light, and responding to Timyan's whispered assurances with small nods.

"This is fixable," Galiana said, with a note of desperation. "There's a surgeon four blocks from here." She kissed Rustaya on their cheeks, forehead, lips, repeating, "This is fixable. This is fixable."

Zemolai grabbed the rope from her. It was pulled so taut that when Zemolai stood up, it lost six more inches through the portal and wouldn't come back. She said, "Mitrios cracked his beacon when he got here. She's coming. We have to move."

"This is my fault," Timyan said, stroking Rustaya's hair. His voice was choked. "I shouldn't have—I didn't think—"

"We have to *go*," Zemolai said.

Timyan glared up at her. "I'm not leaving them here!"

"Then stay. I'm going."

"Wait!" Galiana cried. "The climb—Rustaya was supposed to go first, to anchor the hooks—"

"Then I'm climbing without hooks."

Galiana looked at her partners, and at her mangled hand, and at Zemolai, and back at her partners. Timyan said, "You want to keep going, don't you?"

"I—" She blinked back tears, looked up at the portal. "It's—we've come so far—"

"There won't be a harness," Zemolai warned. "I'm not tying us together. I don't even know how far the portal is from where we need to be. What about your hand?"

Rustaya gave her the out, in the end. "Get the fucker," they gasped.

Galiana's jaw firmed. She nodded. "I'm going."

"Then *move*," Zemolai ordered.

Galiana touched Timyan's arm. "I'll help you get them into the elevator," she said. "But then you have to *hurry*. You haven't got much time to clear the building, and so help me if you don't get them there in time—"

Timyan stopped her with a kiss, and then they were both crying, and Zemolai thought she would have to catapult herself off the tower to speed things up. But Timyan and Galiana finally got Rustaya onto their feet. They staggered for a moment, their face going slack, but they remained conscious. The surgeon would scream at Timyan for moving them in that condition—provided they made it to the surgeon.

"Wait for me," Galiana said, sliding under Rustaya's arm.

Zemolai growled in frustration. She snatched up Galiana's forgotten grapple-gun and said, "Be back at my side when I start climbing."

They stumbled toward the elevator, past Mitrios gargling some caustic threat. Zemolai squinted up into the portal. The first hook was only visible at a sharp angle now. She didn't trust the rope to hold both their weights, but she also wanted Galiana to stay as close as possible during the climb. She was all too aware, how quickly their paths might diverge in the strange, tangled forest.

Nothing for it. She fired. The second hook hit a knot of foliage only two posts from the first one and not much farther down. It would have to do.

Galiana ran back to her side, out of breath and wiping the tears from her face. She took charge of the second rope. "Zemolai," she said nervously. "This *is* going to work, isn't it?"

Zemolai only said, "We're almost there." She planted a boot on the side of the god-tree and hauled herself up to the flat space between branches. She was hardly aware of Galiana following. All of her attention was on that slice of god's realm open overhead, pulsing steady as a heartbeat.

Zemolai used branches for footing until she couldn't touch them anymore, and then she gave all her weight to the rope. They had tied knots at regular intervals, and now she used them as footholds to drag her tired body into the sky.

Her hand touched the membranous sheen of the portal, and she had a moment of panic—it wouldn't budge, or it would wait until her face pressed tight and let her smother, or it would wait until she was halfway through and then abruptly close around her chest—but the membrane gave way, like pushing through water, and Zemolai climbed through.

The lazy drifting of the portal had tugged the rope out to a forty-five-degree angle, and as soon as she got a knee through, Zemolai fell over the edge. She clung tightly to the rope and swung through air dense and strange, air that didn't whistle past her face. She struck the side of a great spongy post hard enough to knock her breath out.

For a moment there was nothing but color, riotous color, bloody reds and jewel greens and dark chocolate browns warring for dominance, burning her eyes, assaulting all her senses. Zemolai blinked and blinked, and *there*, yes! The world came into glorious, heartbreaking focus.

She was in heaven.

CHAPTER TWENTY-FIVE

Would you let them take this city from you, these things you have built, these wonders that are your birthright? No! To our final breath, we must fight! We do not yield! Say it! We *do not yield!*

—*Saint Radezhda's final speech, Battle of Three Gates*

"WHAT DO YOU KNOW?" Winged Raksa demanded. The city was practically on fire behind them, ships and bomb boats firing at the heart of their sect, and he was standing beneath the god-tree, *still* looking for ways to undermine Vodaya.

"I know what I saw today," Zenya said. "You saw it too!"

"You're hers, entirely." His eyes unfocused, as though he were steeling himself to a decision.

Zenya saw the moment his resolve hardened, an ugly look, an animal brutality. She opened her mouth to scream, but she was too late. Raksa's hand shot to her throat and squeezed.

He marched her to the roof's edge, and her team was right *there*, only twenty yards away, but their backs were turned, and the battle was roaringly loud, and everyone else was fighting and killing and dying in the air over Pava District. Zenya tried to pry his hand loose, tried to claw his face, tried to reach one of the bolt-guns on her belt, but Raksa was a well-oiled machine, refined over twenty years for one purpose, and he gave her no opening.

"I'm sorry it's come to this," he said, and his regret almost sounded genuine. "But the entire city is at stake."

Her throat was collapsing beneath his fist, her body weakening, her blood pounding in her ears. Raksa took a few running steps toward the roof's edge, enough to launch both of them past the balconies and emergency ladders, past the barest possibility of hitting an overhang or a haul line—

And he let go.

Raksa vanished toward the battle without a backward glance, a mere passerby, a non-witness to a tragic accident, one more death among many that day, and Zenya fell.

She twisted and flailed, the wind battering her in cruel imitation of flight. She cast about for anything, *anything*, refusing to believe this was the end, refusing to give up until her body hit the ground.

And there, like a prayer answered, a bomb boat darted through the line of defense, streaming blue smoke out of its back compartment.

Zenya didn't think. She angled her feet down, knees bent to take the impact, praying madly that the trajectory wouldn't change. The bomber looked up at the last moment, eyes widening in disbelief, but her fate was locked. Zenya landed hard, legs buckling, and the lightweight boat dipped with her weight, nearly tipping her off the back.

The pilot overcorrected, and she was thrown forward instead, into the back of the bomber. Zenya drew a bolt-gun from her hip and pressed it into the soft spot between the bomber's helmet and back armor.

She fired.

The bomber slumped forward over her bag of explosives, and the pilot jerked the controls sideways. Zenya hit the railing hard, and her next shot went wide, glancing off the pilot's shoulder pad.

The pilot flinched away with a scream. He locked the controls and turned in his seat to fight her, his big brown eyes fearful through the gaps in his helmet. A scholar's symbol was pasted to the side, and Zenya was disoriented (*Do I know him? Do I know him?*), but she didn't recognize the boy inside the armor.

They grappled desperately, twenty floors above the earth and rising. "Let me go!" he cried, and it wasn't the voice of a self-righteous rebel but a frightened youth.

Zenya shoved the bolt-gun beneath his chin and pulled the trigger.

The moment seared itself into her memory; a portrait stamped with a branding iron. His eyes were wide and pleading, then glassy and gone. A nightmare that would return later, much later. But now, Zenya shoved his body aside and grabbed at the controls. She almost screamed in frustration, her bruised throat clenching against the impulse—whatever he had done to lock them on course, she didn't see a way to undo.

Zenya couldn't slow the boat down. She couldn't land it.

And she couldn't let it hit the tower.

She clambered halfway onto the wing, one foot hooked behind a rail. The wind whipped even more fiercely there, and exhaust poured from an engine in the undercarriage. Zenya shot the joint point-blank with her last three bolts, but they barely made a dent. She leaned harder—

Her weight did it. The joint snapped, and the boat swerved right, far harder than she'd expected. Zenya whipped away from the tower and out of grapple-gun range before she could gasp. Her stomach heaved. The pilot's body slid past her, nearly knocking her loose.

The boat sped straight for the heart of the battle, a wild conglomeration of airships and bomb boats and Winged flinging knives. An opportunity flashed toward her, quick as lightning: an airship about to cross her path overhead. Zenya swept a grapple-gun from her belt and fired upward. An impossible shot, a desperate shot—a lucky shot. The hook caught in the underside of a wing joint.

The airship sped east, the bomb boat west, and Zenya was jerked into the open air, legs streaming out nearly horizontal to the earth. She shrieked. The bomber spiraled out of control behind her, crashing through a residential rooftop and exploding in fire and dust.

Zenya's shoulder sockets wailed in agony as she dragged her body upward, one foot, then another. A pair of bolts whizzed by—too close—and she pulled her body beneath the dubious cover of a wing. She clung to the hull, the toes of her boots shoved into the ridges of a scaly protrusion, her arms trembling. Screams and battle cries erupted above her. Warriors had boarded the ship.

A delirious urge to laugh nearly overwhelmed her. This was ludicrous, insane. It was exactly what she'd wanted! To be soaring through the air in the middle of the action! But she was *supposed to have wings when it happened*.

Zenya had one more grapple-gun on her belt, and she cast about wildly for a target. The ship was still barreling toward the tower, nearly in range, *maybe*, with luck, but at any moment the Winged would take the controls and divert course. She had to go, *now*.

Zenya braced herself for the jump—

And then she saw Vodaya.

Vodaya was turning the controls of another bomb boat, two dead bodies slumped in their seats. She bent her knees to launch free when another Winged approached, coming in swiftly from behind. *Winged Raksa*.

He hit Vodaya with both boots, square between her shoulder blades. She collapsed over the control panel, and Raksa shot a net-gun, tangling both her wings.

He was forcing her down with the boat.

Zenya cried out, but the sky swallowed her voice. Surely somebody else would see this, she thought, *surely*—but then she realized: Raksa didn't care. He was within sight of the repair stations, the rooftop Pava, and any Winged who looked their way. He would be caught, judged, executed. But Vodaya would still be dead.

What happened next wasn't even a decision.

Zenya jumped, a straight shot from hull to bomb boat, but the boat veered with Vodaya's thrashing against the control panel. Zenya was overshooting the mark.

She grabbed her last grapple-gun mid-flight, knowing in the calm at the center of her heart that she could aim for the tower and save herself, or aim for Raksa and almost certainly die.

A single image came to her, searing hot: Vodaya at the center of the god-light, righteous and pure.

The shot was good. Her hook caught on Raksa's right wing, wedged tight in the joint against his back port. He twisted, unable to reach it, and for the second time in a handful of minutes Zenya found herself dangling by a rope.

Except this time, she hadn't caught anything nearly as sturdy as an airship, and her weight jerked Raksa off the boat entirely—away from Vodaya, but into a free fall.

Raksa and Zenya spun out of control. The world flashed rapidly: ground-tower-sky, ground-tower-sky. Raksa spread his wings to catch air and stabilize the descent, then drew them tight to speed past Zenya, struggling to dislodge the hook and cut her loose.

Somewhere in all that desperate maneuvering, Zenya found herself dropping toward his back. The impact knocked the breath out of her, but she latched on tightly, both arms around his shoulders. The hook was still lodged in place, trapped beneath her body, the gun lost and dangling at the end of its rope far below.

"Let go!" Raksa roared. He tried to throw her loose, battering his wings against her sides, lurching wildly. Zenya held tight with one arm. With the other, she fumbled at his ports.

Raksa threw them into a fresh spin. Zenya caught enough breath to yell, "Traitor!" He righted them again, but they were falling, only ten stories from the ground and falling.

"Look at what she's *doing*," Raksa pled.

The pain in his voice was real. Raksa truly believed that his cause was just. That Vodaya was wrong. That the mecha god must be shackled to the will of the other Four. Zenya hurt for him then, for his misplaced conviction.

But he was still a disciple of the mecha god, and the mecha god's people did not give up.

Zenya found the disengage lock against his spine. She hit it.

For a split second they were suspended in the air—and then Raksa dropped out from his wings, and Zenya was left clutching the damn things like ship's anchors. She felt more than saw them fall away from her. Her arms pinwheeled instinctively, uselessly, slicing through wind, through void.

She had nothing left. No tools, no tricks, no words of wisdom from the bloody saints, no athletic techniques from combat training, nobody to blame but herself. She was six floors up. Five. There wasn't even time to pray.

The mecha god heard her anyway.

Another body struck hers midair. Zenya was sightless for a moment, gasping, half-convinced she'd crashed and was dead. But a strong pair of arms wrapped tightly around her waist, and a familiar body pulled her out of free fall.

Zenya saw their mingled shadow swoop along the debris and body-laden street as Vodaya sank, corrected for the extra weight—and then began to rise.

They ascended at dizzying speed, past repair-station balconies and Pava trainees whooping with delight. They came up over the lip of the rooftop and then glided back down, to the safe and secure expanse of solid brick.

Zenya tried to keep her feet, but at the touch of a firm surface she collapsed. There was still work to be done—a battle to be fought—but she was shaking and chattering and reliving the entire confrontation with more intensity than she'd felt when she was in the middle of it.

Vodaya knelt over her, bloody-dusty-glorious, and said, "Take a deep breath, Zemolai. Take another. Look at the sky. We've done it. The last ship is coming down."

Zenya turned her head. It was true. In the midst of her own chaos, she'd missed the chaos surrounding her, and in that short stretch of time the Winged had destroyed all the bomb boats and were now united against the final airship.

Tears sprang to her eyes. Vodaya had saved her. She'd saved Vodaya. Tower Kemyana was safe. The rebellion was broken. Pava District was half-destroyed, but the battle was won.

"It's over," she whispered.

"Yes," Vodaya agreed. "You did wonderfully." She stroked Zenya's hair, and her gaze drifted left, to the patient silhouette of the god-tree.

"It's been a difficult path, hasn't it?" she murmured. Her fingers were warm on Zenya's scalp, her voice warm to Zenya's ears. "Sometimes you considered giving up. Giving in. It's all right, you can admit it."

"Yes," Zenya whispered. She smiled, trembling, as though a smile could soften the reality of those moments.

"But you didn't," Vodaya said firmly. "You are still here beside me. And there is no doubt in my mind that when it is time for your first flight, you will ascend that mountain like you were born to it, and the mecha god will welcome you with open arms."

Here, at the end of the terror and rage—this was the Vodaya who had drawn Zenya to the sect. This was the leader she wanted, warm and encouraging, fierce and noble. Soon they would have to rise and deal with the aftermath of the battle, but for this moment the crashes and cries were a thousand miles away, and it was only the pair of them together on the bricks of tower Kemyana.

"Imagine it," Vodaya said softly. "Soaring across the sky. Defending your city in her honor. We hold dominion here, Zemolai. We are the heralds of a new era of peace and prosperity for Radezhda. All of Radezhda. You and I, side by side."

Zenya shut her eyes. She could picture every second.

CHAPTER TWENTY-SIX

How can I bear the fury in my own heart? How can I loathe what I once loved? I want to howl it from the highest rooftop! Oh, they left us, they left us!

—Diary of an unnamed disciple

ZEMOLAI CLIMBED through heaven with death in her heart.

The mecha god's forest filled all of her senses. Strange alien fruits, by turns pungent and bitter and sweet, drooped from the posts at irregular intervals. Some were slick, some bristling with quills, some burning hot. The soft posts conformed disconcertingly to her touch, allowing hand-holds and footholds even on those nerve-wracking stretches without knots or plant growth to cling to. Her face came too close to a bright red flower with thick, fleshy petals, and the acid scent of it made her so dizzy, she nearly blacked out.

Galiana made frequent sounds of distress, ascending slowly up the adjacent post. She was climbing in short spurts, crooking the elbow of her bad arm around the post and then hauling herself up a few inches with her good hand.

Zemolai said, "Remember Scholar Pyetka's mirror. Unfocus." Her voice was clear and chiming, stripped of years of airborne battle cries.

Above and ahead of them, the great chrome platform shone with ambient light. They had entered the realm through the dense jungle beneath it, and without wings they had to chart a path across points where the posts touched.

Slowly, carefully, she led the way. Her shoulders and thighs burned with the effort, but it was a distant ache. She felt lighter here, calmer. Pure of purpose in a way she hadn't on Kemyana's rooftop. Even the pressure to hurry was lifted away, though she knew at her core that their time to act was rapidly eroding.

"Unfocus," Galiana breathed.

They wended their way toward the platform, and the only sound in that cavernous expanse was the sound of their bodies rustling the vines. Zemolai didn't have time to fumble with hooks and carabiners, and she was almost relieved to have left Rustaya and their hooked feet behind. She couldn't bear the thought of doing any permanent damage to her surroundings.

So she free-climbed, and her heart crowded her throat every time she reached out from the safety of one post to pull herself onto the next.

Up and over, up and over, until they approached the top of the swaying canopy, and the lip of the platform was nearly within her grasp. None of the posts rested flush against the metal—none but a few flimsy tendrils of growth that would never support her weight. The closest stable point put the platform barely out of arm's length.

"We have to jump," Zemolai said, adding weakly, "Not far."

"Wait, what—"

Zemolai didn't listen to the rest, lest it burst the bubble of confidence she'd been riding this entire way. She flexed her sore thighs once, twice, and then shoved off into open air with her arms outstretched.

She caught the lip and slid, grasping for purchase on the slick metal. Her legs dangled free over the precipice, and for a moment she thought she wouldn't be able to pull herself up—but with precarious, incremental shifts, she pushed up onto her elbows. From there she leveraged the top half of her body onto the platform and, dignity be damned, wiggled up the rest.

Zemolai turned around on hands and knees, breathing hard, flush with success. Galiana was stricken, fixated on the gap between them as though it could be measured in miles rather than feet.

"Start right where I did," Zemolai instructed. "Keep your eyes on me. I'll catch you."

Galiana crept as close as she could without swaying the branch. Her hair had taken on an even more vibrant blue-green cast in the god-light, and her skin glowed from within like varnished wood. She blurred in Zemolai's vision for a moment—twin women suppressing twinned panic—before stabilizing again. Then it was just Galiana, clean and pure and radiantly hopeful and terrified and willing to overcome that terror because she believed in Zemolai's plan.

Because she believed in Zemolai.

Galiana leapt—landed—cried out with the force of the impact and slipped, one elbow on the platform and the other bouncing loose. Her cry reverberated through the crystalline stillness of the world, terrible as a growing tidal wave. Zemolai grabbed her under the arms, landing face to panicked face.

"I've got you," Zemolai said, and her voice washed out the endless echo. The world was still again. The world was calm. "Give me your hand."

Galiana grabbed tightly onto Zemolai's wrist. Zemolai leaned over her body, grabbed her by the toolbelt, and hauled her onto the platform.

They knelt there for a moment. A moment was all they could spare.

Breathlessly, Galiana said, "You look . . ."

"What?" Zemolai was so terrified of what the god-light might reveal that she'd scarcely looked at her own hands. If her face was that of a shadow-haunted skeleton, she didn't want to know.

Galiana shrugged, embarrassed. "Beautiful."

Zemolai turned away, looking across the platform instead. Her heart hitched at the sight, even though it was exactly as it had appeared on her other visits.

The raised dais. The soft bubble of pearly light. The impression of limbs, arranged in artful slumber. In every direction alien treetops stretched to the horizon, unnaturally still and shimmering, the platform like an island on a strange sea.

Excitement and dread overtook her in equal measures as they approached. Their steps on the chrome platform were discordant scratches against perfect silence, and the mecha god loomed ever larger, waiting for them. Zemolai had never dared creep closer than twenty or thirty feet.

Vodaya had always stood protectively at her side.

Fifteen feet away. Ten. The god slumbered within her protective bubble, a hint of body behind a pearly fog. The strange optics of the god's realm bent more sharply here, blurring the edges of the dais. Blink, and the god was a frail wisp buried deep in her bed. Blink again, and the god was dense, swollen, her limbs crowded snugly against the curvature of her casket. But she breathed. Undeniably, she breathed.

Zemolai choked back tears. She wanted to fall to her knees and beg forgiveness. She wanted to list every ill thought, every slighted duty, every long night questioning her resolve—as though the mecha god couldn't pluck that information from her with the single touch of a finger. As though she hadn't already seen every second of it during Zemolai's judgment, and found her wanting.

"Where is it?" Galiana whispered. She squinted, pained and overwhelmed and clearly struggling to remain calm in the presence of a sleeping god. It was one of the Five stretched out before them. It didn't matter which one.

"There's an item embedded in the base," Zemolai said quietly. "It glows red when Vodaya is speaking to the god."

Galiana paused. "Okay," she said. "I had hoped you were going on more than that, but okay. Which one?"

They were close enough now to see the elaborate design of gems and metals and stones encrusted around the bottom of the dais. Smooth or faceted or spiked, some in simple shapes, and others carved into dizzying swirls, and some forming symbols that could be art or could be writing or could be something else altogether. The vivid colors were shocking against all the pearl and chrome.

Zemolai circled the dais slowly, inching into strange, dense air that was neither warm nor chilling, and she scrutinized the items near the mecha god's feet. There were ruby comets and granite trees and copper fruit—and in between all of that natural imagery, where the foot of the dais curved around to the other side: a dense iron fist.

"There," Zemolai said. "The fist."

It had to be right. It was Vodaya's favorite emblem, her signature, reproduced all the way down to the buttons on her vest, and it didn't fit with the rest.

"Are you sure?" Galiana asked nervously. "You have to be sure. I don't know what would happen if—"

"I'm sure," Zemolai said.

She felt it before she saw it: a rustle in the canopy, sound where there hadn't been a breath of sound. They weren't alone.

Zemolai's heart sank. They'd come so far.

"Hide," she said urgently. "Destroy it. She's coming."

Galiana cursed—jarring in that purified voice—and ran. She dropped behind the dais, out of sight, just as the foliage birthed forth a Winged warrior with glowing skin and silver hair and fury raised before her like an axe.

"Once-Winged Zemolai," said Mecha Vodaya. "If you have a shred of decency left, you'll stop where you are."

Vodaya landed lightly on the edge of the platform. She had not bothered to draw a weapon. She didn't need to. She *was* the weapon, the mecha god's Voice, forged like a blade. When she spoke, her power shook the sky.

But beneath it all, she was a person. A well-seasoned warrior, a cunning strategist, a powerful leader, but still a human being, afraid of losing everything.

Zemolai was about to die.

She stiffened her back, stilled her face, begged pleaded *howled* for dignity, praying that if the mecha god cared even a sliver, she might grant her this one request. She said, "You aren't my commander anymore, Vodaya. You made sure of that."

Vodaya clucked her tongue, advancing slowly with steps like ringing anvils. "Don't blame me for your shortcomings. It doesn't suit you."

"What did you say to her?" Zemolai asked. "When you lashed me to the god-tree, what did you tell the mecha god?"

"I told her what I always tell her. To judge the penitent by their actions." Vodaya cocked her head, quizzical and pitying. "Is that why you've come all this way? To ask for judgment again? Dear, sweet, traitorous Zemolai, if you are entertaining the delusion that your judgment was somehow compromised, you are going to be *sorely* disappointed."

She continued to advance. Zemolai stood her ground, heart hammering, ears pricked for the slightest hint of Galiana at work, craving the assurance that she was completing her task and dreading the moment Vodaya realized they were not alone.

Vodaya held out her hand. "Come with me."

"No."

"You don't belong here," Vodaya said coolly.

Zemolai took a shaky breath. "Neither do you."

Vodaya darted forward without warning, a blur of silver on chrome, and slapped Zemolai in the face. The sting was sharper here, eye-watering. Zemolai tried to push her away, but Vodaya grabbed her by the upper arms, and the woman's grip was steel. She jerked Zemolai forward an inch, and Zemolai jerked back.

"You failed us," Vodaya said.

"I did what was right."

"You betrayed her command."

"I escaped yours!"

Decades of bitterness swelled between them, and they fought within sight of the sleeping god. Zemolai took another blow to the face and one to the gut. It was a desperate boxing match, reminiscent of her days of being beaten to the floor of the training ring. Zemolai had never won a match against Vodaya. She wasn't going to win this one, either.

She only had to hold her attention until Galiana destroyed the power source.

An odd shadow slid over them. It was the portal wandering overhead, returned along its unpredictable rotation. Zemolai glanced only briefly, afraid to give Vodaya the slightest advantage, but that single look knocked the breath out of her.

The portal was still open, shockingly dark and dull against the white sky. Bodies jostled against one another behind it, a disorienting slice of Radezhda peering into the god's realm. And there, at the edge of the shimmering oval: Timyan and Rustaya, shackled together, very much alive and watching with guarded courage.

It was a mirror, like the one used by Scholar Pyetka, except these were

Pava faces frowning through the surface. Timyan and Rustaya had been captured, but—Zemolai thrilled with unexpected hope—they had convinced their captors to look up.

There were witnesses now.

Zemolai hooked a hand into the straps of Vodaya's vest, holding on tightly even though it left her side exposed. Vodaya struck her on the training port, grinding metal against old scar tissue, and Zemolai gasped—but she didn't let go. She staggered back, drawing Vodaya away from the dais.

Every second Vodaya failed to shake Zemolai loose only infuriated her more. "You're worthless!" she shouted. "Every second I spent on you was a mistake."

They were the same old recriminations, tried and true. But instead of shrinking, Zemolai felt herself expanding. Her anger was a living thing, a beast that had been gnawing through its ropes one thread at a time, finally breaking loose. She couldn't hold it back. She didn't want to.

"You're a liar," Zemolai said. "You stole your power. What really happened to Mecha Petrogon that day? What did you do to him?"

Zemolai was covered in an armory's worth of projectiles, but she didn't dare let go long enough to arm herself. All of her preparations had been for nothing. The thought that she could storm heaven with a handful of earthly defenses had been a joke.

She grabbed the only weapon she could reach: a short knife at Vodaya's waist. Zemolai drew back, but she barely had the leverage to strike. Vodaya caught her easily by the wrist, grinding Zemolai's bones, and they struggled for control of the knife, hand over hand on the hilt.

"Give up," Vodaya growled. She pressed forward—pushing Zemolai toward the edge of the platform.

The knife scraped across Vodaya's forearm. Zemolai tried harder, angling for her breastbone. Vodaya's eyes locked on hers, but behind the shine of silver they were human, they were pained. They were the wounded eyes of Zemolai's mentor, a woman who had devoted her entire life to justice, only to be betrayed by her closest disciple.

"Why are you doing this to me?" she breathed.

Zemolai faltered. It was wrong, she *knew* it was wrong—but it wasn't, was it? Not to Vodaya. It had always been impossible to win her compassion, to beg her sympathy, because Vodaya's distress was real. She was genuinely hurt when others didn't bend to her will.

Zemolai faltered, and in that bare second of succumbing to old habit, Vodaya had her. The knife twisted in Zemolai's grip, cracking her wrist—

And the blade slid into her belly.

Zemolai's legs went weak. She heard a gasp, which was strange, because Vodaya's expression hadn't changed. And then she was falling. She didn't feel any pain, not yet, but she was falling all the same. She lashed out convulsively and took hold of Vodaya's vest, dragging the woman with her.

Zemolai hit the platform hard. The sky was blotted out by Vodaya's wings. Only one thin edge of the portal was visible behind them.

She had to believe there were still people watching.

"Let go of me," Vodaya ordered. "It's over."

"You've been deceiving the mecha god for decades," Zemolai said haltingly. "Concealing your intentions. Ruling Radezhda with your own fist." Vodaya's knee crushed her thigh. Vodaya's hand was still on the hilt of the blade. Zemolai tightened her grip, clutching her in a macabre embrace.

"You're a fool," Vodaya said. "We've *always* ruled with our own fists." Her heart glowed red in her chest, brighter and brighter, bloody and mesmerizing—but it wasn't her true, heart and it never had been.

"I know about the signal blocker," Zemolai said hoarsely, and now there was pain, oh there was pain. Her body wept, and its tears were thick and red. "What does your heart really look like? What have I been following?"

Vodaya tried to rear back, but she was caught tightly. Her last shred of calm shattered. "Do you think Petrogon wore an open heart?" she shouted. "Do you think Vitaly before him wore an open heart? The gods are *sleeping*, Zemolai. They rouse now and then, they brush their fingers through the world and devastate all they touch—and then they *retreat*, they leave us alone, they don't care what happens next!"

Zemolai fought off a wave of dizziness. "That's what he told you, isn't it?" she said. "The day of the bombing, when he nearly died in the council square." The day that everything had changed between them.

And Vodaya, still furious after all these years, hissed, "*Yes.* He told me the Voices were lying. He told me to seek out Faiyan Sanador, because he needed a successor he could trust to take the mantle. But then he *survived*. He survived, and he wanted me to continue taking the mecha god's orders as though I didn't know they came from *him*." Her glower intensified. "For generations, she's been ignored, a pact made between the warriors and the engineers, but only at the highest level—the Voice could pick a successor, and the lead creator would place a trusted engineer in their midst, and no one else must know. But it's over now. Creator Talley died without passing it on, and Sanador worked for me till the end."

"But why?" Zemolai pleaded. "Why continue to deceive her?" A thought struck her and, fearfully, she added, "Were the scholars right? Are the gods truly gods?"

Vodaya's lip curled. "Do you want the truth of it? Do you want to know what I've concluded, after all my years of coming here, all my years of serving at her feet? Because I did try, Zemolai. I did ask her guidance, at the start." She leaned in close, her breath hot, her eyes hotter, and she said, "There is no answer."

Vodaya barked a laugh at the look on Zemolai's face. She repeated, "The answer is I don't know! I'll never know! The mecha god doesn't speak, she doesn't stir except to show her fist, and in all my years of begging at her feet, she has not given me a *single answer*. Maybe the scholars *were* right. Maybe the gods are merely giants. Fickle and selfish, sleeping until they can return to their home across the stars. Or maybe they really are the spirits of our earth, all-knowing and wise. Who can say! All I know is that we did our very best to live up to them, our *very best*, but they didn't love us back, and they went to sleep."

She shook Zemolai by the arms. "They *abandoned* us. Is that what you want to hear? They don't care, Zemolai. Gods or not, they don't care. You have no *idea* what I went through when I found out about Petrogon's little trick. But he was right, in the end. We only have ourselves, so let the strongest will prevail."

For a long, painful moment, Zemolai couldn't breathe. She could see it now, the terrible spiral that followed the shattering of Vodaya's faith. A secret she clutched tightly for decades, growing ever angrier, seeking ever more control. And how far back had it gone? Vodaya's trust broken by Petrogon. Petrogon's broken by Vitaly. A cycle ever turning, a betrayal that stretched all the way to the first Voice who saw her god turn its back.

But as much as Zemolai wished it, she couldn't pin all of Vodaya's failures to that single cause. Vodaya had been a harsh master beforehand, quick to abandon trainees who disappointed her, and her actions afterward had not been inevitable. They'd been a choice.

Zemolai had had her answer all along, and it wasn't Vodaya's grim self-reliance, or the scholars' perpetual search for context, or even the common mythology of a benevolent Five, though all of those provided comfort in their own way. It was something Niklaus had said, though she hadn't been willing to listen at the time.

"Faith isn't believing in gods," Zemolai said. "It's believing in their wisdom."

Vodaya laughed, incredulous. "A child's answer!" she exclaimed. "Clever-sounding and meaningless."

"It doesn't matter who's right." Zemolai's breathing hitched. "We can argue ourselves to death, and we'll never know what they are. It's the path you choose that matters. It's how you live your life. It's what you do along the way."

Vodaya tore at Zemolai's hands. "You're delirious," she said curtly. "Because you're dying."

"Just the path," Zemolai insisted, and maybe she was delirious, and probably she was dying, but nothing had ever been so clear. "The path itself, and whether the path is good. You chose your path, Vodaya, and it's *rotten*, it's rotted you out—"

Vodaya hit her, again and again. Zemolai laughed, and then she cried, but it wasn't fear, and it wasn't the pain. She cried because she wanted to go back and shake her young self by the shoulders and take that girl under her wing and tell her: we do what's right because it's right, because it helps the most people live their lives the way they want to live them. We protect the vulnerable and we use our strength to shield the weak, and if they don't care, we carry on anyway, because that's our path.

The mecha god had judged her correctly, and that was a pain that would never heal. But Zemolai's sin hadn't been the one time she said *no*.

It had been all the times she said yes.

The more Zemolai cried, the more Vodaya raged. Tears had always made things worse. "I wasn't going to kill you," Vodaya insisted. "You've done this to yourself."

And then metal clattered against metal, and there was nothing Zemolai could do to mask the noise. Vodaya froze, twisting to look, and Zemolai knew they were lost.

Galiana's frightened face appeared around the side of the dais. She snatched up the chisel she'd dropped.

"What is this?" Vodaya demanded.

Zemolai grabbed Vodaya's vest, holding on desperately as Vodaya rained down blows. "What is she doing?" Vodaya demanded. She struck Zemolai in the face again. Stars burst in Zemolai's vision, and fresh blood slicked from her nose.

Galiana worked frantically at the dais, in full view now, crouched on her knees. She wedged her chisel tightly against the iron fist and beat at it with a hammer, no longer trying to quietly work it free. The sound rang out like a scream. Galiana cried out, dropping the chisel again from her broken hand, but the iron fist had shifted. It was coming loose.

Zemolai's hands lost the last of their strength. Everything pulsed red and black, and chimes rang continuously in her ears. She felt Vodaya move away, and she tried to roll over, to grasp for her, but she was stopped by the agony in her gut. The knife came loose, slippery in her hands, and Zemolai turned her head, dizzy and fading, hoping against hope that the deed was done, that she'd bought enough time.

That she'd see it end.

Galiana knelt at the mecha god's feet, finally prying the iron fist loose from the dais. It was nearly a foot wide, and it was glowing red, pulsing in time with the device over Vodaya's breastbone. Galiana abandoned the hammer and lifted the fist with both hands. She smashed it against the chrome platform.

The fist glowed brighter, but it didn't break.

Vodaya flew toward her in a blur. Galiana smashed the fist down again and again, sobbing with every use of her broken hand. The impacts reverberated through the platform, violent in the rarified air. The red light reflected ghoulishly on Galiana's face, her panic etched deep as the lines on a festival mask.

Vodaya closed the distance in seconds. Galiana raised the fist high over her head and brought it down as hard as she could. There was an unholy crack—the casing gave way—and then Vodaya grabbed Galiana by the front of her shirt and lifted her into the air.

The fist fell open on the platform. Light sputtered from the exposed core, but it was sporadic, ebbing.

There were two more half-hearted pulses, and then it went dead.

Vodaya's signal blocker blinked out, leaving a void of darkness behind her vest. "What did you do?" she raged. "You stupid girl, *what did you do?*"

She hauled Galiana away from the dais. Galiana kicked and shouted, but she couldn't twist free of Vodaya's grip. The portal still hovered in silent witness overhead, crowded with perturbed faces, but Vodaya wasn't taking Galiana to the portal. She was dragging her to the edge of the platform.

"Zemolai!" Galiana screamed.

But Zemolai couldn't help her. She couldn't even help herself. If the portal itself had come to a stop inches from her body, she wouldn't have been able to pull herself through. She pressed weak hands to her stomach, trembling to hold back the mess.

She took a shaky breath and whispered, "I'm sorry, Galya."

And then the mecha god woke.

The sweet, crisp air turned oily and acrid, like overheated machinery, and the pearly bubble surrounding the god began to ripple and steam. It coalesced as a dense fog, ominous and concealing. The god's limbs rustled within; the barest impression of movement.

All this time, Zemolai had been viewing the god's realm with the half-unfocused vision necessary to parse optical trickery. As the mecha god rose to a sitting position, however, even that proved worthless. The world brightened to razor-sharp edges. The light bent around her fog-shrouded body, reflecting and refracting in dizzying contradictions.

Staring at her was like staring into a wind tunnel. Zemolai was desperate to look upon that visage just *once* before her death, but her eyes burned and watered. She could only squint to the side and try to catch something in her peripheral vision.

The mecha god rose and swelled to impossible size, shifting and sliding and clicking upward. She sat on the dais—except that was impossible, she couldn't possibly have fit on it before, the dais was only fifteen feet long, and she was at least double that. Her size changed every time Zemolai blinked; now an ordinary woman, now a towering monster. The fog stretched and snapped and gathered around her. It poured out around her legs, pooling silky and elastic across the chrome—

And the mecha god slid her feet to the floor.

She did not rise entirely. She didn't need to stand. All she had to do was extend one hand through that pearly enclosure, the wisps of fog trailing from her wrist and forearm like ephemeral wires. The mecha god reached across the platform, to where Zemolai lay prostrate and shaking. Her hand blotted out the light but cast no shadow.

Zemolai's body was cooling. She could feel the impending chill in her bones as her time trickled away into the sticky pool beneath her side.

She braced herself for the divine touch, hoping only that it would be brief, that the pain would not be too much, that the mecha god would show her mercy through swift death.

The great hand settled over her body like a blanket—like a grown woman cupping her hand over a newborn kitten—and this time her touch was not the burning, bone-clattering vibration it had been when Zemolai was strapped to the god-tree.

It was warm. It was nurturing. It was a gentle caress, encompassing and comforting, the lightest of pats against Zemolai's back like a master absentmindedly assuring its loyal pet: *Good job, well done, thank you dear.*

Her presence lifted away, leaving Zemolai devastated in her absence, a puddle of a person, and the mecha god's hand skimmed onward, to the figures struggling at the edge of the platform.

To Vodaya holding Galiana over the precipice.

Galiana screamed at the sight of the hand coming for them, at the sight of the mecha god simultaneously seated on her dais and stretching bodily across the platform. Galiana struggled to hold on to Vodaya's wrists, but she was entirely at the woman's mercy, flailing over the canopy of pale, fruiting trees, living by the grace of Vodaya's fists balled in her shirt.

Vodaya let go.

It was almost an afterthought, the way the mecha god's hand tilted to catch Galiana. Her knuckles brushed the nearest trees and set off a cacophony of tinkling collisions like a storm of wind chimes, rising and rising, the volume unbearable. She tipped Galiana back onto the platform, benignly uninterested in one of the creator god's people.

Galiana bounced and tumbled across the uneven surface. She landed on her hands and knees and scrambled toward Zemolai, casting wide-eyed looks over her shoulder.

"Oh, god, Zemolai!" She was barely audible over the rising chimes of the trees.

Zemolai wavered on the edge of consciousness. She hardly noticed Galiana ripping off her outer shirt and wadding it into a ball, hardly noticed her pressing the cloth to the wound in her belly. Zemolai struggled to stay awake, but only because she had to see this through.

Vodaya saw her fate coming. She pressed a hand to her chest, where her signal blocker remained lifeless and dark. She flew upward, jerky with fear, angling toward the portal and the slim possibility of escape.

She was swift, but not swift enough.

The mecha god plucked Vodaya from the air with casual precision and held her like a captured bird. The god's hand pulsed with light, translucent and then opaque again, revealing and concealing Vodaya's trapped body in little bursts. No longer did the Voice's heart beat with crystalline beauty, bloody and pure. She was a shadow skeleton, hollow and bird-boned, and where her heart resided, the god-light vanished into a bottomless pit.

It was bitter validation. The foulest of medicines. Zemolai was right, and a part of her still wished she hadn't been. Vodaya's body shook, and Zemolai's back ached at the memory of that burning, righteous grasp.

Zemolai cried out for her—not for the woman she'd been, but for the woman Zemolai had so desperately longed for her to be.

Vodaya never made a sound. For a brief, horrible moment, she stared at Zemolai with furious outrage, refusing to acknowledge her guilt to the end—and then her back arched, and her head snapped back, and she went limp in the hot, squealing grip of the god.

The mecha god opened her hand. Vodaya fluttered out and over the side of the platform, slow as molasses in the dense air. The trees sang like bells with her descent, the sounds growing fainter and fainter.

She was gone.

The mecha god eased back toward the dais, her feet drawn up, her arm snug against her belly. She pulled up the pearly fog like a warm blanket, shrinking in size and presence until she was stretched once more in peaceful repose.

And Galiana waved at the portal, still reflecting the horrified faces of their audience in tower Kemyana, and she screamed, "Help! Help! I can't lift her alone!"

And Zemolai whispered, "It's over. Oh, god, it's over." She blinked, sluggish. She wanted to sleep.

Galiana's face hovered close to hers. She was still god-lit, beautiful, weeping diamonds. A little saint framed by glowing, blue-green hair. "It's *not* over," she said. "Listen to me! It's not over. There is too much work to do, and if you leave us alone to do it all ourselves, I will never forgive you, Zemolai! Can you hear me? Keep your eyes open. Keep them on me. We're going home."

INTERLUDE

WHEN I SAY the gods do not love us, I mean they do not love us in the way we wish. They believe they do; they have said they do; but we operate in a relationship so terribly unbalanced, it is more akin to master and pet than parent and child. Now and then we catch their attention. The rest of the time, we are an afterthought.

Here is the truth: they love themselves, and they warm to those who reflect them best. The scholar god values knowledge for the sake of knowledge; the creator god values invention for the sake of invention; and so on, and so on, we know these chants by heart.

They shine their light upon those who share their ideals and turn away from those who don't. The turning away is not malice (take comfort in this), but neither is the light a sign of love. It is wonderful, to bask in that light. It is addictive. A person may do anything to feel it once again. But it is not love.

It is a smile at a mirror's reflection.

And when we accept this truth—this truth, that the gods do not love us in the way we wish—then we must face another truth: it is our choice to follow or not, and always has been. It means the threat that hovers over our every action (*do not put a step wrong, or they will not love us anymore*) is, in the end, an illusion. We are struggling to hold on to something we never possessed to begin with.

I ask again: what is Radezhda? What is our purpose? What is the story of this city, if it is not the story of our gods? Who are we, if we need not strive to be like them?

We could follow their teachings anyway, picking and choosing as they suit us, because we value what we are being taught. At least then it is an honest decision, not made under duress. Or we could pick another life entirely.

It is terrible, in its way, terrifying, to be responsible for the course of one's life, with no higher authority to blame. But there is a freedom in it, as well.

The freedom to choose what comes next.

EPILOGUE

Every step forward is a choice, and every choice is made in the shadow of choices we've made before. You are every person you have ever been, continual and simultaneous, an iterative being composed of a million decisions, large and small. The question is not whether you can shed the past, but at what point you begin to control your future.

— Saint Lemain, *An Essay on the Nature of the Self*

Two years after the battle for tower Kemyana, Zenya returned to the biting cold of the surgeon's hall and the owl-eyed magnifying glass of a surgeon. She was seventeen. Not the youngest graduate (that record still belonged to Vodaya), but respectably young.

For nearly four hours, she bit down on her mouth guard and let the tears flow. Her back was a solid sheet of fire, one incision indistinguishable from the next. The pain was so all-encompassing that it became background noise. A state of being. Zenya stared hard into the distance and let her thoughts wander, determined to focus on anything other than the here and now. Periodically the surgeon would prod or tug or cut somewhere new and spark a startling agony, pulling Zenya out of her trance and beginning the whole process over again.

She thought about flight. About the wind through her hair, about hurtling toward the ground and then catching herself, about rising, about soaring. She thought about the hand of the mecha god emerging languorously over the god-tree and the white light bathing her place of rest. She imagined an orderly city. A city at peace.

And then, when Zenya was so deep into her state of drunken euphoria that she could no longer ignore the pain, the surgeon knelt in front of her face, loosened the bite guard, and said, "Very good job, little Pava."

She cried then, big ugly tears of relief and happiness. Somewhere along the way it turned into grief, and she no longer knew what she was crying for, only that it seemed to come from a bottomless pit.

Zenya had back ports. They were thick, heavy things. Eventually, she was told, she would hardly notice them, but that reality felt inconceivably far away. The wide cylinders held her back open, raw and hot where metal met flesh and bone. The slightest movement sent achy shivers through her body despite copious painkillers.

But it was worth it. Even now, there was an engineer in a laboratory off the Pava training compound crafting wings to her specifications. After a few weeks of recovery time, she would begin to test the connection. She would shoulder her own wings and learn to flex and maneuver them, giving the engineer one last chance to tweak the design.

And then: Ruk Head Mountain. First flight.

Zenya spent that night in a recovery room, a sheet draped loosely over her back. She was one cot among many, though only three other cots were burdened by the freshly ported. She was dizzy, overwhelmed by the after-effects of physical trauma and ineffective drugs, unable to get any real rest because it hurt to breathe.

Vodaya sat in a low chair at her side, wingless, stroking her hair and speaking quietly of days to come. Mecha Vodaya, the Voice of their god, with a silver port at the back of her neck to prove it.

She was the only visitor that Zenya had received. After the battle at Kemyana, her old five-unit had looked at her with new respect, her allegiances clear and her actions in the sky rousingly bold. The memory would stay with her a long time: Romil laughing in delight, Lijo and Dolynne clapping her on the back. But in moving ahead, she had left them behind. They were still in port training, and she was in the surgeon's hall.

When Zenya began her tour on the border, she would not be flying out with tight-knit heartmates who had seen her through all the years of

319

her youth. She would be starting over among strangers, filling in gaps here and there among people with relationships of their own.

There was only one constant in her life, and she was sitting right here.

Vodaya said, "You're ready."

And Zenya said, "Yes."

Two weeks after climbing into the heavens above tower Kemyana, Zemolai was still recovering in a surgeon's hall. Those initial days after the confrontation were a blur to her, another sequence of pain and confusion rivaling her near-death by withdrawal when she was cast down by the mecha god and awoke in a cage.

This time, at least, she had the comfort of a bed.

There was a new scar on her abdomen, ragged and angry-red next to her old training port. The surgeon had predicted her death, but Zemolai had always been full of surprises. It was only a shame that recovery took so much longer without the old drugs. She could walk now—slowly, carefully, taking pains not to lift anything heavier than a book. But she was infection-free and confident that time would knit her flesh.

She had not planned this far ahead, to the work of surviving.

Rustaya was resting in the bed beside hers, their abdominal scar a mirror to her own. Their legs (the regular set, not the climbing gear) were tucked neatly between the head of the bed and a side table stacked with sweets—gifts to both of them, which they had been haggling over with good-natured ruthlessness.

Galiana and Timyan sat on chairs between the beds, a daily visit that often stretched for hours as they delivered news, and reminisced, and spoke in hushed voices of the uncertain future. Galiana's broken fingers were splinted and mending and waving around at high speed whenever she grew excited, which was often. The surgeon's hall stretched far in both directions, but the four of them were contained in an intimate bubble of air.

"The Council of Five is going to meet," Timyan whispered, grinning giddily. "I don't know when or under what conditions. I have to imagine they'll want serious security in place. But it's really going to happen."

Rustaya snorted, giving Zemolai a sidelong look. "Still hard to believe your batshit plan worked."

"Nothing's changed yet," Zemolai murmured, but her heart wasn't in the protest. She knew too well how far the city had fallen into paranoia and disrepair, and how hard it would be to re-create old structures and norms. She could only imagine the chaos currently taking place in every sect and every cell of the resistance, as they settled on representatives, priorities, strategies for the coming meeting, preparations if it were a terrible ruse to get the greatest troublemakers in one place . . .

The Radezhda of her childhood was gone. Whatever came next would be new, untested, and born of much sorrow. But that did not need to be said now, when their joy was so bright.

Zemolai felt the strange circle of her life closing in again, as she convalesced in a surgeon's hall on the cusp of great change. She felt more than ever like the girl she'd once been, wounded and desperate for things to get better, the first moment folding upon the second, as though they had always been happening side by side.

She only prayed her eyes were open this time.

Bed-bound and forced to rest, Zemolai had spent several long nights reflecting on the recursive progression of her life, but there was still a piece missing. She longed to close this painful sequence, and there was only one way she could see clear to do it.

Galiana, ever watchful, spotted the broody look on Zemolai's face and asked, "What is it?" Timyan and Rustaya immediately looked to her as well, expectant, and Zemolai could not help but feel a pang at their regard. She did not deserve it, though she hoped one day she might.

She told them what she had in mind, the trek she wanted to make as soon as she was capable of it. She would not be rash, she promised, only lying a little. (They did not need to know how grueling it would be; it would only make them fret.)

Galiana fretted anyway. "Are you sure you're ready for this?"

And Zemolai said, "I will be."

Ruk Head Mountain. The lumbering giant protecting Radezhda's eastern border. The home of mountain bears and monstrous birds and snapping lizards and all the many flowering plants that fed the surgeon's apothecary.

And there, jutting out shortly before the peak: Vitalia's Cliff. The well-worn launching point for all of Radezhda's Winged warriors. The starting location of the ceremonial first flight.

You fail or you soar.

It was a cold night, full of crisp winds and whispering grasses. Zenya appreciated the chill. It was a balm on her hot flesh and overtaxed muscles. She carried a flaming torch, which she transferred hand to hand, fearful of developing an uneven cramp in one shoulder. The torch illuminated a path worn smooth by the passage of many feet, penned in on either side by craggy wilderness eager to reclaim its territory.

Months had passed since her surgery. The surgeons had pronounced the site free of infection. Of course, they warned, it might take some time to grow accustomed to the ache within.

Her wings were glorious and copper, exactly as she had dreamed. But she had never imagined them so heavy or the burden so painful. Every step up the side of the mountain drew from her a ragged breath. Her lungs burned in the cold air. Her thighs. Her back. She passed another climber at the next switchback. Pava Kitros leaned against a boulder on the side of the path, wheezing beneath the weight of her wings. Her torch hung precariously from one hand. She didn't even look up at the sound of Zenya's steps.

As Zenya climbed, she thought about all those who had fallen in the final battle, struck by bombs or debris. So many lives snuffed out in the middle of their training, before they could ever reach the sky. There were fallen Winged as well, each one afforded a hero's funeral. The warriors who'd given their lives in defense of their god's own home. The warriors that Zenya and the rest of her laboring peers were so eager—and terrified—to replace.

Her feet were bleeding in her boots. Her face was cold and chapped. She passed her torch to the other hand and kept climbing.

Ruk Head Mountain. The home of snakes and sorrows, ambitions and defeats.

Zemolai climbed in the dark. She carried no torch, no water, nothing but the clothing on her back. Even unburdened, it was a slow journey. She didn't have the strength of her youth. Her wound was still healing, five weeks so far and nowhere near finished.

Every step tugged at her scar and the tender flesh beneath, but it wasn't only physical weakness that slowed her down. It was the weight of memory. Of responsibility. The Council of Five had reconvened at last, a tentative but necessary step toward reconciliation. The representatives had left the meeting with cautious optimism.

But there were no magic fixes. There would be no divine hand from the heavens—from any of the heavens—that could cleverly erase the past two decades. Trust might be restored between the sects one day, but for now it was a distant dream, an aspiration held together by hope alone. Until then, there would be negotiations. Security precautions. Hard-fought treaties and weighted votes, with the earth god's people as mediators.

Zemolai paused by a large boulder. She pressed her fingertips to its surface, still warm from the day's sunshine. It was another marker, another step on the path.

She thought about all those who had fallen to her hand over the years, directly or indirectly, the victims of her twin desires for accomplishment and revenge. She didn't know most of their names. She couldn't even remember their faces. Chae Savro was the last of them, though not by her choice. Or perhaps she should count the Tooth once known as Winged Vedelsen. Or Mecha Vodaya.

The mountain hummed and sighed with nocturnal life, but she was the only human climbing its face tonight. She'd briefly considered carrying a torch, as a practical defense against errant ursines or snakes, but the idea was rejected almost as quickly as it occurred.

Zemolai didn't fear anything on this mountain.

At times, Zenya thought she would have to rest, to lean against a tree or boulder and shift the weight of her wings. But she knew that if she stopped on this path, she would be unable to start again.

She remembered the day, age eight, when she had leaped from the Ario-Zavet bridge. Her wood and paper wings had been light on her back. Niklaus had been waiting for her down below. Everything had felt possible.

Nothing is ever truly lost, Scholar Pyetka told her, five years later. *You are every person you have ever been.*

She did not think she believed the first part anymore, but she desperately hoped the latter were true. It meant she had always been headed for this moment, this climb, these wings upon her back.

So she fought through the pain, the way she always fought through the pain. When encouragement failed, she berated herself. She hadn't come this far to fail now.

If she didn't reach the cliff by dawn, this had all been for nothing. Her family had died for nothing. They would go unremembered, unrevenged. If she didn't reach the cliff by dawn, she might as well pull off her wings and throw herself from the heights.

It was her own voice urging her forward, but it was Vodaya's too. Zenya's burden grew heavier with every step, but her resolve was steely. She would not stop, not unless her heart stopped first.

Zemolai ascended into thinner air, but instead of weighing heavier, her load lightened with every step.

One week earlier, she had finally tracked down the essay Scholar Pyetka had been so eager for her to read in her youth. She had stood before the archivist sheepishly, ready to be cast from the room, but he only marked her name down and filled her request. *Every step forward is a choice*, Saint Lemain had written, *and every choice is made in the shadow of choices we've made before.*

She sat there in silence until the reading room closed and handed the essay back without a word.

Now she rounded another bend in the path, and she knew by the slope of it that she was near her goal. The ground was scruffier here, less often traveled. The path doubled back on itself with each rise, a snake that couldn't move left without first moving right, that couldn't move forward without first moving back. She had believed for so long that her life was inevitable. She had thought her decisions mapped a path forward from which she could not deviate, when in reality they had only reflected the path behind her, which she could have left at any time.

The strands of her life had always been woven inconveniently. She was the scholar who wanted to fly, the warrior with too many questions.

Now she was something in between. They all were. Radezhda was filled with fighters stripped of the fight. Engineers and workers and scholars who had spent their lives resisting rulers who no longer ruled. Mecha warriors without a war (and, oh, there was an old guard who would never be persuaded, who would go down in flames; but there was no place for them in the god-light anymore without Vodaya holding it at bay).

There were young people of every sect, wondering what they would have chosen for themselves if their parents hadn't chosen for them.

Galiana was waiting for her down there, as were Timyan and Rustaya. They hadn't reached a consensus yet about how to use their talents. They had spent so long resisting, they'd barely had time to imagine the world after they won.

And Zemolai would forever carry the melted lumps of metal in her back that once powered her wings. That was painful, but that was just. The future didn't exist without the past, and Zemolai had inhabited this body far too long to begrudge any of its scars.

She kept climbing.

She'd made it. She was there. She'd made it. She was *there*.

Zenya staggered to a halt on the little plateau, hardly daring to believe she was in the right place. The mountain itself continued on for a few dozen yards above her, but it was a steep hike to the top. Vitalia's Cliff was the real heart of the climb, a ten-by-fifteen-foot stretch of cleared earth. At one end, a shallow stone basin of water nestled against the rise to the peak. At the other end, a sheer, unprotected drop into nothingness.

She extinguished her torch in the basin with a satisfying hiss of steam. It wasn't the first torch there, but it wasn't joining many. She couldn't help feeling the sting of disappointment at failing to arrive first.

Zenya stood at the edge of the cliff and looked out. The sun was ready to rise, announcing itself with the barest hint of purple on the distant horizon. She'd cut it closer than she liked, but she was here, and there was only one thing left to do.

Radezhda stretched before her, dizzyingly beautiful. From here she could only see its peaks and valleys, its bridges and towers. She couldn't see any of the damage done by the war, not yet. That would come into focus when she made her final approach, but for now it was only her sleeping city, resting before the new day.

Zenya leaned into the breeze. She settled her thoughts, her body, her breathing, her nerves. She focused all of her attention on the not-so-distant terminus of her ordeal.

Tower Kemyana stood guard at the edge of the city. Between the tower and the mountain stretched nothing but wild, uncultivated land. It didn't bear wondering how many pairs of wings marked the open graves of failed fliers below. All that mattered was the tower itself, and the flickering lights of the lanterns placed all around the rooftop, guidance and welcome all in one.

Vodaya was waiting for her there. Her new life was waiting, spiraling out in front of her with breathtaking promise. Zenya only had to reach out and take it.

It was the same plateau, the same tamped earth, the same stone basin, the same view. Zemolai sat with her back to the mountainside, one arm propped on the edge of the basin, stretching out her legs and letting the breeze dry the sweat from her face.

The city twinkled below. It was the same Radezhda she had viewed from this mountain so many years ago, but it wasn't, not at all. It was older. It had seen things it never should have seen. Its scars ran deep, but it was a survivor.

She waited for the sun to rise, something she had never seen from the mountaintop. The sky went purple before it went pink, crawling languorously from one end of the world to the other like a stretching cat. She'd feared that in the light of day, with all its pits and stains cast in bright relief, that Radezhda would not be as beautiful as she remembered.

And it wasn't. But after some consideration, Zemolai decided she liked it better this way. Her age gave her character.

Zemolai reached into her vest and pulled out a small bundle of papers tied with twine. They were brittle and beginning to yellow, their edges nibbled and torn. Her brother's letters had been sealed for decades, but they didn't have to hold up much longer.

She read them one by one. She was in no hurry. The final letter was longest, and not at all what she'd expected when she refused to read it the first time. She lingered on it for a while, indecisive. So much violence had been wrought to suppress what was, in the end, one person coming to grips with the same insecurity that plagued them all.

After some hesitation, she tucked Vikenzy's paper into her vest. She folded the rest of the letters again and tidied the stack. She arranged a ring of stones at her feet, and within its confines she built a small fire with twigs and brush and a match saved for the occasion.

She placed the letters on the pyre and watched them turn to ash.

Then Zemolai brushed the dust from her pants and walked to the cliff's edge. She shut her eyes and leaned out, into the breeze. It was so easy to imagine the drops and climbs, the rush of air over her face, the freedom of flight. There were bad nights ahead of her, desperate nights, nights when the weight of all she had done would sit on her chest like the hand of a god, and she would pine for this cliff once more.

She would never not be the person who took the wrong road, and that would haunt her—but she had a new path to follow when she woke up.

Zemolai stayed until the sun warmed her through, and then she walked back down.

Zenya braced herself. Set her legs. Felt the energy build in her muscles, nerves, wires, wings—

And jumped.

AFTERWORD

A**T ITS HEART**, this is a book about disillusionment. It is about shaping one's life and worldview around one's idols, and then losing all faith in them. How do you come back when you've spent years hurtling down the wrong road? When you've doubled, tripled, quadrupled-down rather than admit the person you love isn't who you thought they were? *Just leave them* is easier said than done when leaving means leaving your whole world behind with them; when you fear the backlash more than the everyday; when you've racked up regrets of your own and feel like you deserve whatever comes your way.

Poor Zenya. She fell victim to one of the classic blunders: *irrational escalation of commitment.*

When I started this book, I only knew that I wanted to write a story in two timelines, about a woman who loses everything in service to a charismatic leader and then has to find her way out again. The world grew from that concept, spawning a claustrophobic setting in which my main character could not get any outside perspective while she was in thrall. We never leave the city, which is both geographically isolated and isolationist in policy; we barely leave her home, the most zealous and isolated neighborhood within that city. If I had made it through another dozen drafts, we might not have even have left the tower!

I quickly found that this seemingly narrow story had the markings of fascism—fear of nebulous external and internal threats, strongman leadership, insecure people seeking a sense of purpose and having their preexisting biases weaponized accordingly. The illusion only stands if the outside world is kept at bay, whether that's told on the scale of the individual (a controlling authority figure snipping away one's former relationships) or on the scale of the institutional (closed borders, doctored history, militant patriotism and faith and paternalism all chucked in a blender and set on high).

I was thinking about what it takes to choose a new path when you've spent your whole life walking someone else's. Sometimes it means an ugly rock bottom, and a lifetime wishing you'd made a choice before the choice was made for you. Sometimes it means facing the shame of your past and accepting that you may never be forgiven, but atoning anyway. (Why yes, I *did* watch a great deal of *Xena: Warrior Princess* as a kid.)

I wound up with an entire city abandoned by its gods; an entire city in denial and blaming themselves for their own abandonment, descending into a frenzy of self-policing in an effort to recapture that perception of love, re-traumatizing one another over and over. And I had Zemolai, deeply wounded by a leader she loved like a mother, who was in turn betrayed by the leader that *she* idolized, in a chain of worship > crisis leading back to that first abandonment by the gods. If I've done it right, people can read whatever relationship they want into it: emotionally abusive partners, controlling parents, toxic religious sects, the nation-state. If I haven't done it right . . . er, sorry I suppose. I hope the fights were fun.

It was not the scenes of abuse that were hardest for me to write—it was the honeymoon phase beforehand. One of the core pains of an abusive situation (whether it's coming from a family member, a partner, a mentor, a leader, a friend, or someone who occupies too many of these roles at once) is the memory of good times. Those memories haunt you. They convince you: *you've had it before; you can have it again, if only you behave.* You know your loved ones intimately. You know their sad backstories, their insecurities, why they act the way they do; and so you feel responsible for setting them off when you crunch one of the eggshells that are, inexplicably, strewn everywhere you want to walk.

You find yourself speaking in second person because it's easier than speaking in first.

I've had to learn the hard way that some people only love you when you belong to them. The moment you show an inkling of being your own person, the mask drops. But remembering the good times, when they were showering you with affection as you obliviously climbed on top of that pedestal? It can make a monster of you, as you scrabble not to fall off.

I asked: what would we do to keep the affection of a god? And the answer was: anything, anything.

But I also found a light on the other side.

I hope you found something resonant in this story. (I also kinda hope you didn't.) I hope that if you ever find yourself hurtling toward rock bottom, caught in a maelstrom so bewildering you can't even remember how it started, that you remember this instead: it's never too late.

Samantha Mills
2024, San Diego

ACKNOWLEDGMENTS

I finished the first draft of this book in 2017 while pregnant with my second child, chasing my toddling first child, working opposite shifts with my husband so we could hand said toddler back and forth and save enough money to escape our haunted house (I'm kidding) before it sank into a pit *Poltergeist*-style (I'm mostly kidding). I wrote a second draft, I set it aside, I gave birth, I wrote another draft, I set it aside, I learned how to write short stories, I edited an entirely different book and started querying that one instead, I wrote another draft, I set it aside, I tried to write a new book but flamed out in a fit of pandemic stress, I tried to write a *different* new book but flamed out in a fit of continued pandemic stress, I wrote several more drafts, I sent it to my agent, I experienced a family tragedy that derailed my writing entirely for a year, and then at long last I returned to the book, finished the book, sold the book. And here we are. An overnight success!

To my agent, Lisa Rodgers: thank you for always seeing what I'm trying to do and helping me clarify the ways in which I can make each book more the thing it wants to be. The last few years have been a rollercoaster. The next few better level out, I swear to god.

Additional thanks to everyone else at JABberwocky who has chipped in their help and expertise on this and other projects—Joshua Bilmes, Susan Velazquez Colmant, Christina Zobel, I appreciate you!

To everyone at Team Tachyon: thank you for getting behind this book! Jaymee Goh, you've got a keen eye for small details and an encouraging editorial style that had me looking forward to my notes. Jacob Weisman,

Rick Klaw, Kasey Lansdale, Elizabeth Story, Liz Colter, and anyone else whose name I didn't manage to snag in time: you all rock.

Thank you to Kate Heartfield for introducing me to a writing community that I only vaguely realized existed before my first pro short-story sale. Your warmth and encouragement really set the bar high, and if I have one goal, it's simply to pay it forward. Thank you to Aimee Ogden and Lisbeth Campbell for reading one of my many middle drafts. Your comments helped me trim this thing into shape! And thank you to the rest of the Codex Writers' Group for all the advice, the support, the camaraderie, the endless COVID commiserations—you made me feel less alone during the most isolated years of my life.

To the Bitches of Book Club, aka the Angriest Girls, aka the Judge Club, aka whatever other permutations I've forgotten over the last twelve years: you've made me a better reader, better person, and better friend. You're all gorgeous, brilliant, and cool, and our group chat kept me sane when everything else was burning down around my ears. SEE YOU AT THE CABIN.

To my children: Mommy wrote a book! You're right, it would be cooler if it had illustrations. Thank you for making me laugh when things were grim, keeping me grounded when everything was up in the air, for being perfectly yourselves at all times. You're pretty cool kids.

To the rest of my family: I love you, even when you're making me tear my hair out. I'll always be two of six.

And to Randy: my best friend for twenty-three years, my partner for fifteen, my confidante, cheerleader, and first reader, my shoulder to cry on, my good-morning hug and good-night kiss, the reason I learned to write a love letter—thank you for everything. Your infectious enthusiasm has pushed me to all new heights of frenziedly embracing hobbies for several months at a time before forgetting all about them and running after the next shiny thing. I used to think the only constant in my life was writing, but it's you.

SAMANTHA MILLS has published a dozen short stories since 2018. In 2023, she received the Nebula, Locus, and Theodore Sturgeon Memorial Awards for her short story "Rabbit Test." Mills has also been nominated for the Pushcart Prize, has appeared on the British Science Fiction Award long list multiple times, and was included in *The New Voices of Science Fiction* from Tachyon Publications. Her fiction has been published in *Uncanny Magazine*, *Beneath Ceaseless Skies*, *Strange Horizons*, *Escape Pod*, and others.

A graduate of the University of Santa Cruz with a B.A. in Pre- and Early Modern Literature, Mills also received a Master's in Information and Library Science from San José State University. In the other half of her life, she is a trained archivist specializing in primary documents, with a particular focus on helping local historical societies and research libraries preserve and manage their collections.

Mills grew up in Southern California, where she still lives with her family and cats. When she isn't working, writing, or taking care of children, she's watching B movies, binding books, and crocheting stuffed animals. You can find more, including social media handles and a full list of published work, at www.samtasticbooks.com.